Also by Leslie Hayertz

Down to the Soul
a novel

———

You Can't Pick Your Ghosts
stories for middle grade readers

———

The Subwhative? The Subjunctive in Spanish:
A Step-by-Step Workbook & Guide

The Lady Photographer's Sister

A Novel

Leslie Hayertz

Sassy
Crow

BOOKS

Oregon, United States
SassyCrow@gmail.com
SassyCrow.com

A publication of Sassy Crow Books
Oregon, United States
SassyCrowBooks@gmail.com
www.SassyCrow.com

For information contact: SassyCrowBooks@gmail.com

ISBN: 978-0-9997718-5-3

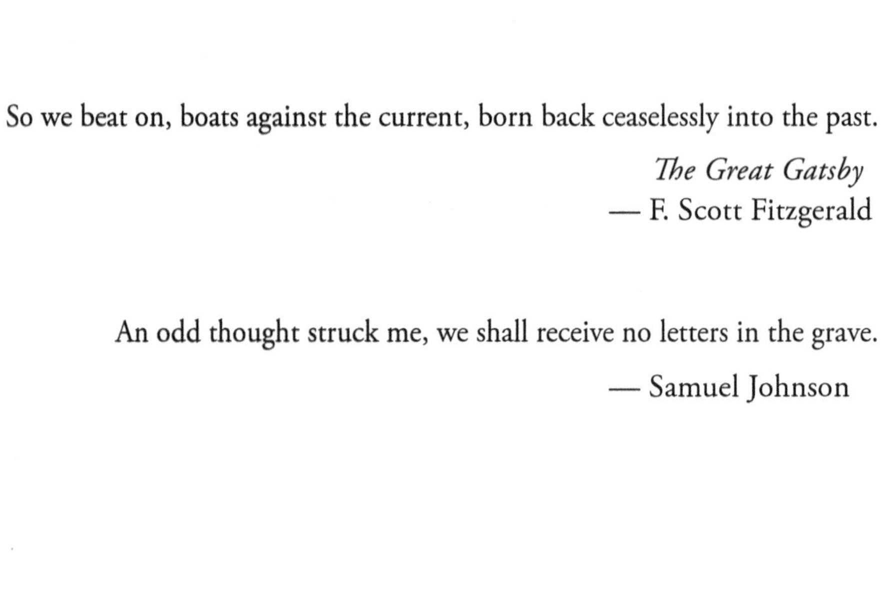

So we beat on, boats against the current, born back ceaselessly into the past.

The Great Gatsby
— F. Scott Fitzgerald

An odd thought struck me, we shall receive no letters in the grave.

— Samuel Johnson

Contents

Map

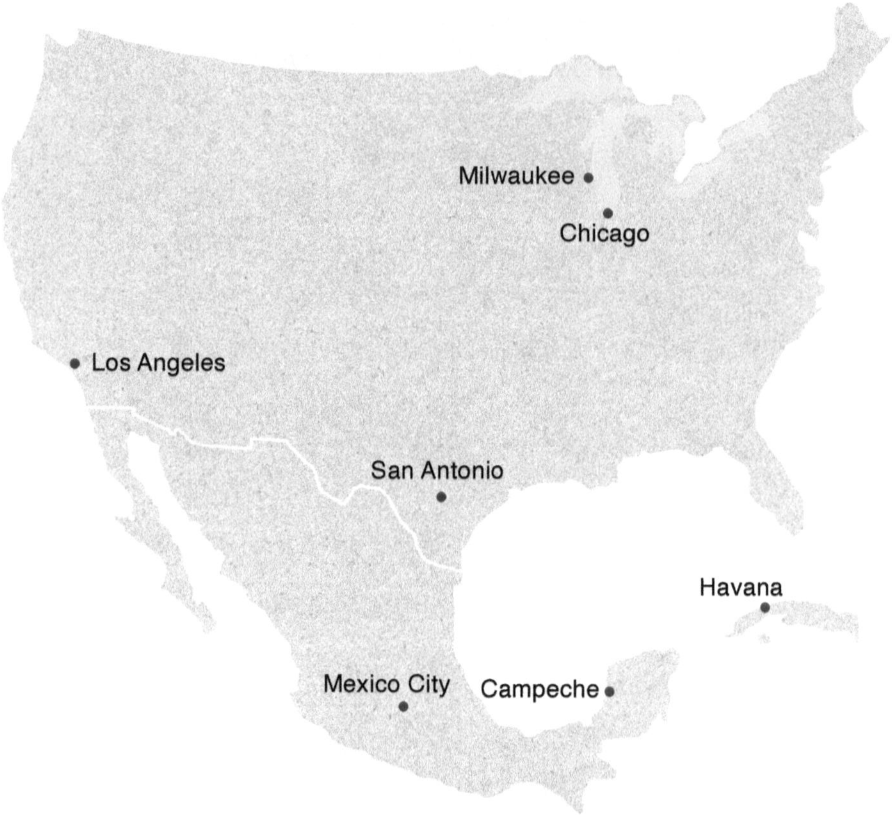
Milwaukee
Chicago
Los Angeles
San Antonio
Havana
Mexico City
Campeche

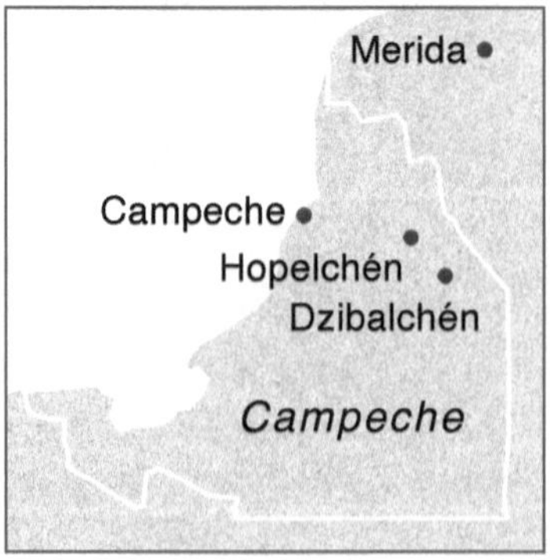
Merida
Campeche
Hopelchén
Dzibalchén
Campeche

Families

Lulu & Ruby

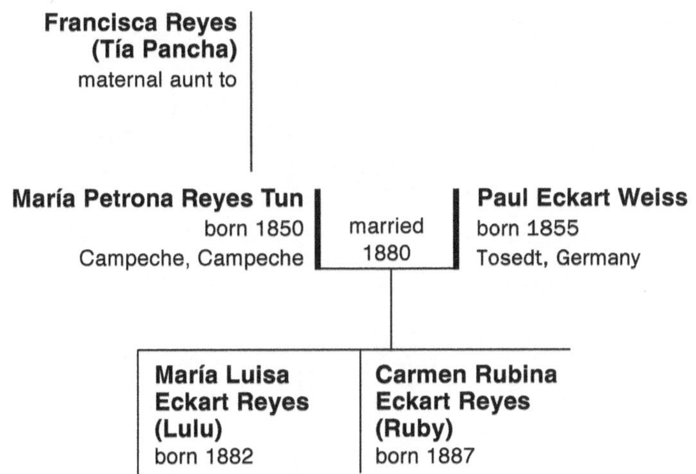

Soli & Mechi

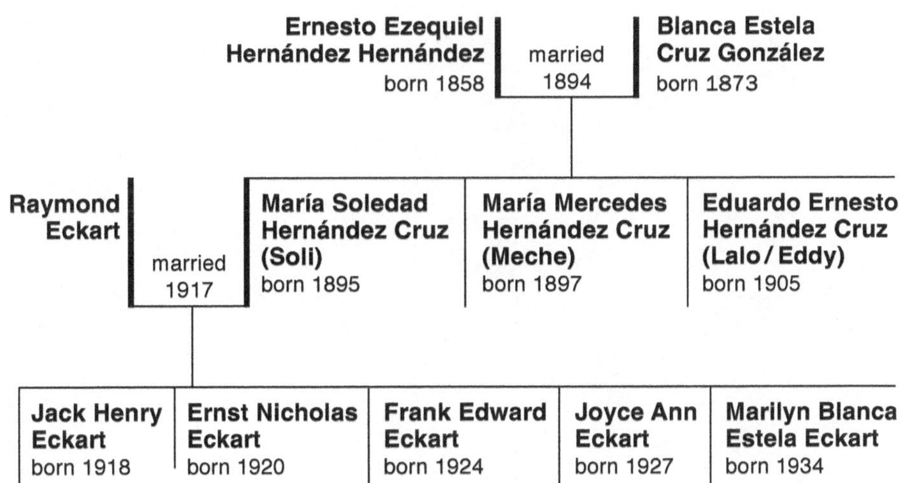

The Lady
Photographer's
Sister

1 9 5 3 ...

M

Meche *squinted* into the glare—like all the streets in Campeche City, Calle Ocho lay awash in sunlight and iron heat. Her head pounded and she dreaded leaving the studio. She half wished for a pair of sunglasses, those things actresses wore—cat-eye frames with rhinestones on the points. Not that she felt in the least bit glamorous, but she wouldn't mind something to hide behind.

A man coming towards her stepped off the high narrow sidewalk, and a woman pulled her child to her, hugging the wall of the building to let her pass—deference one received for being of a certain age, or for the black armband. Muttered greetings. No eye contact.

Arriving at the doorway of the long-distance telephone office—her task to call her sister in the United States—Meche paused and took a deep breath before going inside.

Coming in off the street, it seemed dark inside, and cool—thanks to the thick walls and high ceilings—but it reeked of institutional cleanser, dried sweat and aftershave.

A man brushed by her going out the door—a blur of white shirt.

As soon as her eyes adjusted to the dim fluorescent lights dangling from on high, she saw that every booth was filled and there was a line of people waiting. A woman, her arm linked with an older woman in black —probably her mother—met Meche's eyes and quickly glanced away. She leaned in to whisper something to her companion. The older woman's eyes widened and she stared at Meche with open curiosity.

Meche turned and bolted.

She couldn't face it—not the people, not the wait, not the publicness of the place. Maybe she could send a letter instead—far less expensive, but somehow disrespectful, not only to her sister, Soli, but to Ruby. Besides, mail service to the U.S. could take weeks. Sometimes letters didn't arrive at all. It was probably all that snow up there, not to mention floods and tornados, and all those cities and people. That was Meche's theory, anyway, but Ruby had always scoffed at it.

"Please, Mechecita, the United States is not the root of all evil." She'd hold up a hand to stem Meche's objections. "I really don't think the Mexican Postal Service is deserving of your patriotic fervor. Isn't it possible that the mail is so slow because of what happens in Mexico, that maybe, at least some of the time, it's our postmen who lose the letters and packages?"

Meche, feeling twice her 57 years, trudged on to the telegraph office. Even the simplest chores seemed overwhelming, but there was nothing easy about this one. Her low heels pounded the narrow sidewalk, and her large handbag swung on the crook of her arm—her skin under its strap felt sticky with sweat.

Once inside—again sheltered from the sun and under fluorescent lights—she stared at the blank space on the telegram form.

How many times had she already had to say it aloud? How many times silently to herself? And now write it, too? Well, better that than shouting it over a bad telephone connection with half of Campeche listening. She picked up the stubby pencil and scribbled:

> *Soli*
> *Ruby died Monday. Heart Failure.*

She closed her eyes to hold back tears, and took several ragged breaths before continuing:

> *My soul is broken.*
> *Meche*

Ruby's voice spoke in her mind, telling her she must remember not to let her guard down, even now. Meche scratched out the last line. After a moment she added another after it:

> *Soli*
> *Ruby died Sunday. Heart Failure.*
> ~~*My soul is broken.*~~
> *Please inform Lulu.*
> *Meche*

Leaving the telegraph office, Meche retraced her steps to their photography studio. Without Ruby, it was just walls and hollow space. Like Meche herself.

She slowed her pace. She dreaded facing the emptiness she would find in the studio, dreaded the sun setting and the shadows softly consuming the living quarters upstairs, the moment when she would turn on the lights and face the stark absence of Ruby.

Meche had prided herself on keeping the studio running smoothly for Ruby. She'd been a talented photographer, but was hopeless with customers. Small, dark and intense—she preferred observation to conversation, and darkroom images to live people. Meche could not claim a sunny disposition, but at least she knew to say "Good morning, sir," and "Thank you, ma'am," and to pick up the phone when it rang.

Ruby had been even worse at recordkeeping. She couldn't read her own scrawl, so the name of a client and appointment time would turn into a cypher, and columns of numbers—the ones, tens and hundreds— would get hopelessly scrambled. Meche would tease her about it, and Ruby would give her a blank look, because running the business was Meche's job, and she was welcome to it. Wasn't that how Meche had wormed her way into Ruby's life in the first place? Meche's work at the studio would always be secondary to the photography, for truly, what was Fotografía Eckart without Ruby?

Meche let herself into the studio and locked the door behind her. She felt shaky—every part of her body ached, as if someone had punched and punched and punched her.

She pressed her lips together and her chin jutted forward. How dare Ruby die on her like this?

And die alone!

Meche should have been with her. But how was she to know there was a problem when Ruby kept her own counsel on every goddamn thing.

Quiet, assured, and downright secretive, that was Ruby.

Damn her!

But it had been something else in Ruby, an underlying bitterness, new and out of character, that had truly troubled Meche. Yes, Ruby had been cranky, but it was that other something that had caused Meche to leave for the rancho days earlier than planned—leaving Ruby to die alone.

Now, in hindsight, she tried to tell herself that Ruby's bad mood must have been because she wasn't feeling well.

Meche laid her hand against the wall at the foot of the stair and looked up.

But what if Ruby had had a presentiment? What if she'd been afraid? What if she'd cursed Meche for not being there? What if, facing death, she'd regretted their life together?

What if Ruby had stopped loving her?

Her heart constricted so hard she wondered if this was what a heart attack felt like.

The next day there was a knock on the door downstairs. Meche didn't answer it, thinking it was a customer too intent on his own concerns to notice the black satin ribbon over the lintel. When the knock came again, she trudged to the window to see who it was, opening the closed wooden shutter a few inches. Below stood a man in a delivery uniform, and she saw her neighbor Don Arcadio come out of his shop next door to gossip with him. They both looked up towards the window at the same time. She stepped back, but supposed she had to go down.

Making her way to the reception and the door to the street, she wondered again what she should do about the studio. Hire a photographer? Rent out the downstairs? Or sell the whole shebang and move to the rancho for good.

For good?

She unlocked the door. The man handed her a telegram and she gave him a few centavos.

She read:

DEAREST MECHE STOP
FLYING TO DF FRI STOP
HOPE TO ARRIVE CAMPECHE BY BUS MON STOP
MY HEART IS WITH YOU STOP
SOLI

It was as if her big sister had intuited the line she'd crossed out in her telegram—My soul is broken. To Meche's great surprise, a sense of relief washed over her.

F*ive AM.*

Barreling through the dark in the family car. At least that's how it seemed to Soli, like she was rushing headlong into the unknown. Her chest felt hollowed out and achey.

Meche's telegram had set off a whirlwind of planning, calling, arranging (all the kinds of things Soli did best), but now everything was out of her hands, which was not a state of affairs she was at ease with. Raymond simmering next to her only made things worse.

Still, she sat on the bench seat smack dab next to him, which after 37 years of marriage was still her custom. Today his tall, stout body felt rigid next to hers, which made her feel very alone, made her snuggling up against him seem a charade. But after 37 years, she couldn't very well scoot over. Not now.

Without having to ask him, Raymond had taken the morning off work to drive her to the airport in Chicago. Flying seemed the best option. Raymond didn't want her traveling for a week on her own on trains. She didn't like the idea either, plus she wanted to be with Meche as soon as possible.

She'd never been on a plane before. Just thinking about it made her stomach do a flip. And the cost!

Soli had called Raymond at work when the telegram arrived. They spoke for only a few moments, and that evening over dinner, she laid out the details that had taken the rest of the day to gather. Her making a trip like this was almost unimaginable, and she was unsure what his reaction to her plans would be. Of course she'd told him on the phone that she needed to go to Campeche, but he may have thought that by the time he got home, she would have thought better of it. She knew he would never say, "You can't go," or plead loneliness to get her to abandon the idea. Nor would he accuse her of neglecting her responsibilities to the family here at home. All of that would be very un-Raymond-like.

What he said was, "It's a long time for you to be away."

She agreed.

He did not throw the cost in her face, although he did shake his head in apparent disbelief when she cited the figures. Nor did he rail against the impropriety or detail the dangers of a woman traveling on her own.

He simply said, "I sure don't like the idea of you traveling alone."

She said nothing to that.

Whenever they were at odds, Raymond became tight-lipped, and Soli knew he expected her to take the hint and come to her senses. Instead Soli would react by filling in the silence with her opinions and arguments. The more she jabbered to make things right, the quieter he would become. She knew this about him and about herself, but it didn't change a thing about the way they quarreled. So Soli's silence now was uncharacteristic, and Raymond took her hand resting on the table. Soli felt a tenderness for her husband, almost a nostalgia, as though already missing him.

After a few moments, Soli gave his hand a squeeze, and said, "Te quiero, viejo."

"I do know viejo means old man," he said.

She smiled at him. "And you also know it's an endearment."

She got up to clear the table.

"Some endearment," he grumbled.

She turned at the doorway to the kitchen, their two plates in one hand, a serving bowl in the other.

"You know, I'm not going because I want to, but because I have to."

When she came back for more dishes, Raymond had gone into the living room to read the paper.

Later that night when Raymond joined Soli in bed, she put aside her notepad with her to-do lists and turned off the light on her side of the bed. Soli's mind circled through time schedules and arrangements as it spiraled down towards sleep.

In the dark Raymond said, "I don't get why you think you have to go all that way. It's only Ruby. She's wasn't even your real aunt."

The comment took her by surprise and snatched her from sleep.

"I'm not going because of Ruby," she said, bringing her hands from under the covers. "I'm going because of my sister. She needs me. I can feel it."

He sat up with a groan. Was he groaning because of her or because of his aging body? He turned on the lamp on his side of the bed and the mattress rocked a bit as he slid his feet into his leather slippers. Soli ran her hands over the white chenille bedspread next to her body, smoothing it, trying not to feel irritated with him. She listened as he lumbered down the hall to the bathroom. He hadn't said anything earlier, but she knew he was thinking that she shouldn't condone such things.

But her sister was heartsick. That was all that mattered to Soli.

She was prepared to make the trip no matter what, and that made her feel queasy, like standing on a cliff and looking over the edge. The concern, the unease about how Raymond would take it had been there all day, but the phone calls and calculations and schedules had pushed aside the fact that this trip might very well cause one of those rifts in a marriage that mended poorly, or not at all.

But, she had no choice. She listened for the toilet to flush.

It would not be the first breach. There was the time Raymond had forced their young son Ernie to fight another boy, and Ernie had come home bloodied. She still seethed anytime she remembered it.

And there was the time Raymond moved his infirm father in to live with them, and it had fallen to her to take care of the disagreeable old man.

When Raymond slid back into bed, she'd already rolled on her side, facing away from him.

Of course, Lulu and Soli's brother, Eddy, had lived with them when she and Raymond were first married, crammed into that little rental house, and barely scraping by. There had been no more discussion of that than of her father-in-law moving in. Family was family.

Might Meche come live with them now?

Another cliff edge, and a pretty high one. Still, Soli's mind raced with the possibilities. She could clean out the boys' old bedroom, put up new wallpaper, something cheerful with flowers. Meche would finally meet all her lovely nieces and nephews and great-nieces and great-nephews. An extra place at Easter dinner! April 5. Oh dear, would she be home in time? She'd hate to miss the Easter egg hunt for the grandchildren. If not, then a family get-together when she got back… Presents, especially for the little ones… Meche's introduction to the family… Soli fell asleep making lists.

Raymond said nothing the next day. He informed Soli that he would be taking her to the airport, and then he clammed up again.

Now they were driving towards Chicago.

The airplane ticket had taken a huge chunk out of their savings. She told herself that that was what savings were for. Still, she felt guilty. Raymond always lingered over magazine ads for cars, and he visited the showrooms every fall to look over the new models. But he only looked, and steadfastly socked away money in the bank. The family car taking them to the airport? A '41 Nash 600, bought used after the war.

A drop hit the windshield. Another. Raymond turned on the windshield wiper. Big drops splatted on the window, snow pretending to be rain. He laid a hand on Soli's leg. His hand was stiff, as if he'd never laid it on her leg before, but after his coolness of the past two days, she appreciated the gesture, and laid her hand on his. She felt a sudden pang for Meche. All alone now. She took a deep breath.

"Nervous?" he said.

She gave a rueful laugh. Nervous? Where to begin?

She'd never traveled alone before. She would be changing planes and spending nights alone in hotel rooms. And other than when she was in the hospital having babies, she and Raymond had never been apart for more than a day or two. She tried to cozy up to him now, thinking how much she would miss him, but despite his hand still on her knee, his body remained ramrod-straight next to her.

And she'd have to take a taxi from the airport to a hotel, and then the next day another to the bus station. The travel agent couldn't find anything out about the bus. Soli hoped it ran daily and that there would be a seat available and frequent bathroom stops. It was about 700 miles from Mexico City to Campeche. It might well take two days.

Although the kids were all grown, she felt she was deserting them, as if they and the grandkids couldn't very well get along without her. She certainly was abandoning Raymond and Marilyn. Marilyn was the youngest, still in college and living at home. She wished Marilyn could have come with her, but there was the cost, plus she was too busy with school and her job, which is why Soli didn't want to burden her with running the house.

There hadn't been much time to prepare, but Soli had put some meals in the freezer, showed an inattentive Raymond how to heat them up in the oven for when Marilyn was at work, and alerted the older kids to be forthcoming with dinner invitations. She'd even bought a few of those new TV dinners. Needs must. And Betty, one of her daughters-in-law, was going to come help with cleaning and laundry.

The car heater blew hot air onto Soli's nylon-covered legs. It made a constant whooshing sound. The windshield wipers thumped and squeaked in two-step time. Raymond squeezed her knee.

"You'll be fine," he said.

And she knew then that he was telling her that they would be fine, too. The marriage might be left with a hitch in its gait, but only time would tell.

She was glad, but she could not instantly warm to him any more than he could to her. She reminded herself that, justified or not, she'd instigated the discord, so she had no right be prickly. She made an effort.

"But what about you and Marilyn?"

He glanced in the rearview mirror and didn't answer. If it weren't so dark, she knew she would see him clenching and unclenching his jaw. She gripped his hand.

"Don't worry about us," he said.

"But worry is what I do best."

Meche had once written to her about that. She didn't understand why Soli had been so hell-bent on having one kid after another (there were only the five), when judging from her letters, all Soli did was fuss and stew over them in a constant misery of worry.

Raymond nudged her shoulder with his. "If you're going to do this, you might as well enjoy yourself." He frowned then, his face barely illuminated by the lights of the dashboard. "We haven't taken a real vacation in years."

"I don't expect it'll be much of a vacation, and it certainly won't be one without you."

"You know I can't go with you," he said.

His face in the reflected light of the dashboard was an impassive mask, which meant he was worried or feeling bad. She opted to respond to the latter because she was in no position to reassure him. She barely had her own worries in check.

"It's probably just as well," she said. "As I remember it, the studio's rather small. Best not to overwhelm Meche right now with company, especially a brother-in-law she's never met."

"Hmph," he grumbled. The windshield wipers swiped back and forth several times. "The time was never right."

"I know, viejo." she said.

"Four thousand miles is a long ways."

Yes, but she knew that was only part of it.

"She never came here either," she said, thinking bitterly that Meche had no family to tie her down.

She immediately chastised herself. Her little sister had had the photo studio to run for Aunt Ruby, and of course with a Mexican peso worth less than a U.S. dime, the cost of the trip would have been exorbitant for her.

Still.

She thought of Meche all those years ago, standing on that dock, only thirteen years old. She could still feel the panic of not being able to reach her, of leaving her behind. And the anger. At Meche. At Ruby.

Truth be told, she was still mad.

"How nice for you to make a visit home," the travel agent had said when she'd gone in to pick up her tickets. "Especially now. Seems like spring will never get here. It must be traveling standby." He chuckled at his joke, but Soli didn't get it.

A visit home? She seldom thought of Mexico as home anymore. Not that Milwaukee was either. She supposed home for her now was an abstract America, one without McCarthyism (Raymond would not agree with her on that) and with a better climate. She hadn't particularly liked the weather in Texas, but maybe someplace else that used to be Mexico. California was said to have a marvelous climate. She'd seen the pictures of attractive people in convertibles, traveling on wide boulevards lined with palm trees, and of families playing in ocean waves. That was her idealized United States.

If Meche came back with her, she'd have a thing or two to say to Soli's children about the U.S. grabbing a third of Mexico's territory: California, New Mexico, Arizona, Texas, Colorado, Utah and bit of some other state. Wyoming? Meche would gladly tell them things that weren't in their history books. Soli herself bristled when she heard the "Marines' Hymn". It might be a catchy tune, but their gloating about invading the "Halls of Montezuma" and seizing Mexico City was galling! It was not to be sung or played in her house, which her children, depending on the child, found either cute, dumb, unpatriotic, endearing or weird.

A nice visit home! The travel agent hadn't known what he was talking about. If it weren't for Meche, Soli wasn't sure she'd ever go back. Her Mexico had been a country plunging into revolution, and her Campeche was the one of her childhood, both long gone.

And what she understood now as an adult, with the benefit of distance and experience, had tainted even her innocent memories.

When Soli was growing up, she and her family were the only people for miles around who spoke Spanish as their first language, who knew how to read and write. Everyone else spoke Mayan and only a handful could sign their name. She'd never asked how her grandfather had acquired the land for the rancho, although even as a girl she must have realized that it had not been uninhabited, because everyone knew the Maya had been there forever.

She'd explained to her kids that her family's rancho hadn't been anything like those Texan cattle ranches they saw in Western movies. In her region, rancho really just meant a good-sized farm, bigger than a tiny holding where a family eked out a living, and bigger yet than a sitio or a ranchería, but nothing anywhere near as extensive as an hacienda.

She would tell little stories of growing up on the rancho, stories that could have taken place on any farm pretty much anywhere, and that's all they knew. Because how could she explain, for example, that she'd found it quite natural that even as a child, Indians both in town and on the rancho had deferred to her as if she were the Queen of Sheba?

For heaven's sake, her grandfather had had peons. Not many. And her father, only a couple. Baalam Kab wasn't one of the grand haciendas with hundreds of indebted workers. Some haciendas owned whole villages! Still, it was something she'd never admitted to her children.

She could just hear her son Frank, indignant, "Debt peonage is the same as slavery!" He, the most political of her children, was inordinately proud that Wisconsin had entered The Union as a free state, as if he personally had signed whatever it was that they signed for such things. And she imagined her other son Ernie, the sensitive one, exclaiming, "You named me after a slave owner?" And with a bitter taste in her mouth, she would have said, "No, Ernst, I named you after my father."

It was not a discussion she wanted to have with them. It was a different world that they could never understand, and she didn't want them to be ashamed of their family, or of her.

The road ahead glistened in the headlights. She touched her hat, small and brimless with a touch of netting, pinned securely in place. No, she was not going to Mexico on vacation. And she was not going on a visit home. She was going because, whether Meche admitted it or not, she needed her.

And that's what Soli was most nervous about, seeing Meche again after more than 40 years.

M

eche paced as she waited for the bus—breathing in the smell of sun-baked concrete, the smoke of her cigarette and diesel fumes.

If it weren't for Soli's maddeningly regular letters—written once a fortnight!—Meche might go months at a time without thinking of her. At least not when she was in Campeche City. It was a different story at the house at Baalam Kab. She and Soli had been girls together there—memories were tucked in every corner—and lately Meche had been spending a lot of time at the rancho.

A bus with a destination sign for Merida backed away from the concrete platform, and Meche dropped her cigarette and ground it under the thick heel of her work boot.

There were two kinds of letters in her life. Business letters were filed at the studio. Personal letters—almost all from Soli and written on diaphanously thin paper that weighed less than the stamps—Meche tied with a satin ribbon by year and deposited in a hatbox that she'd taken to keeping at the rancho. For years she did this almost furtively, in case it was a sore point for Ruby, given that her own sister seldom wrote. Instead, once or twice a year Lulu called—an incredible extravagance— and always at an inconvenient time.

The bus was two and a half hours late. Meche lit another cigarette.

Since the day before, an anxiousness had started to fill her, like a drip slowly filling a stoppered sink. And since that morning, she'd been overtaken by a physical longing that became a high-pitched whine in her body. She vibrated with it. It felt like the only thing holding her up.

The bus pulled up, finally, and Meche threw her cigarette down. Her heart beat faster. She felt it lift her and make her taller. She scanned the line of passengers getting off the bus. She saw a lady who was alone and past middle age. She looked a bit like a gringa—sensible black shoes, American-looking clothes and an over-sized straw bag. Soli? The woman was compact and squared of figure—as girls both she and Soli had been considered tall, both slender. As she strained to decide if this really was her sister, the hum in her body became almost unbearable.

The bus driver helped the lady down the final step to the ground.

My God, Soli!

Meche's and Soli's eyes met. Soli's were filled with maternal love—after all, she'd had plenty of practice: raising Lalo, then five children of her own, and grandchildren arriving with alarming regularity. Out of habit, even after all these years, Meche bridled at that maternalism, but just for a smidgeon of a second, because she felt so cold-stone alone. Goddammit, let Soli mother her.

Then not knowing how, they were in each other's arms.

"I am so tired of being cooped up on that bus," Soli said as Meche put her suitcase in the back of an old Ford workhorse of a pickup. "Couldn't we stay here in town for a day or two?"

Ever since she'd boarded the flight to Mexico City, Soli had been swaddled in Spanish for the first time since she'd left San Antonio, Texas, in 1925. It was like putting on an old familiar silken shawl, one whose luxurious feel and perfumed scent she'd forgotten. And speaking to Meche, simple statements like this, "en uno o dos días," made her feel strange, young, old, out-of-time, herself.

After the planes and taxis and bus, she longed to be out in the open, walk along the malecón, smell the salt air and watch the sun set in the ocean. She was also curious to see the photo studio again.

"I can't bear another minute here," Meche said. "For a week now I've been taking care of business—death business. Let's go to the rancho, Soli. Let's go home."

Soli sighed and nodded.

As they left the city, Meche shifted into third gear. The truck smelled of leather, battery acid and overripe fruit. Still, Soli's spirits lifted with the acceleration. The feeling, however, was short-lived, for the road soon became rough and Meche had to slow down. With no steering wheel to hang onto, Soli bounced about in the cab. The windows were rolled down and the wind and humidity worked at her hair, trying to undo the braid she wore pinned up in a bun.

"It's even more out of the way than I remember," Soli said, shouting to be heard over the truck's engine.

Meche stiffened—her sister had deserted their country, and Meche could only see that as disloyalty, so she'd better not be criticizing anything now. Maybe Soli had thought she had no choice in leaving, but she could have come back. And she never had.

"Remember the trip to Campeche City from the rancho in that horse cart?" Soli said. "It took days, didn't it?"

Meche nodded.

At 13, it had been horrible for Meche to be torn from her home—dramatic, tragic, the end of the world. Now she was 57, and Ruby had been snatched from her. Not dramatic, not even tragic, just the end of the world—quiet, gnawing, bitter. She'd finally recouped the rancho, but Ruby had been her real home. She understood that now.

They fell silent, each with her own thoughts. Each dealing with the heat, dust, smoke from burning fields, potholes and ruts. Neither up to the effort of talking over the engine noise and even less over the span of years between them.

Soli's thoughts might be wandering about in her past, but this was Meche's present—and her future, such as it was.

Meche always felt lighter when she aimed the truck out of the city, even now. Although lighter than what? Lead, perhaps. She might not be able to see past tomorrow, but farm work—driven by the demands of the next harvest, and the next, and the next—never stopped. She went over it in her mind. It was March—there was corn to pick and store, beans and castor-oil plants to harvest. It was time to start burning cornfields. Cut the sugarcane and deliver it to the mill at Hacienda San Isidro. She'd been looking into Baalam Kab processing its own sugar, making its own piloncillo—hard cones of dark-brown sugar. It would mean getting a small gasoline-run press, building the oven, purchasing a couple small vats and the molds. The question was, would the investment pay off? And would they have enough hands? Meanwhile, there were orange trees to graft, tiger-nut sedge to plant, garlic to dig, braid and hang up. It was too soon to harvest honey, but she needed the hives seen to. Check that the workers had finished cutting wood to make charcoal. Decide which ramón saplings to transplant and see that the mature trees were pruned…

Soli studied the profile of the middle-aged lady next to her. Meche looked exhausted, but Soli saw the same determination there that she remembered from childhood, the same stubbornness in the focus of the eyes and set of the brow. Was there anything else left of the girl, of her kid sister? This lady's figure was well-padded. She wore wide-legged slacks (the only woman Soli had seen in trousers during the entire trip), a man's work boots and a long-sleeved white blouse with a black armband. A broad-brimmed, finely woven jipijapa hat lay between them on the bench seat. She wore a silver and black-onyx necklace, a ruby ring on her left hand and gold hoops in her ears. Her hair was short and permed, and the flatness of the brown color made Soli think it must be dyed. Soli herself wore a sleeveless, cotton summer dress, and thought she might take her girdle off the first stop they made. Who was there out here to care?

The image from long ago that haunted Soli came back to her once again. From the deck of the steamer that would take them to Veracruz, where they would embark on a ship for the United States, she'd looked down into the crowd on the dock and seen Meche there. Defiant, standing straight and thin as a stalk of sugarcane, in a new white dress, a powder-blue bow in her hair. Their eyes met, and despite the distance, it was as if they were inches apart, face to face, locked together.

It was the last time Soli had seen her.

Until now.

A wave of sadness and anger washed over her. But this trip wasn't about her. It was about Meche. And Meche shouldn't be alone right now.

Meche was not unaware of Soli sitting next to her. It was just that now that the initial reunion had been achieved, this person next to her was a stranger. As far as Meche was concerned, the enforced silence was not a bad thing. From the corner of her eye she saw the familiar profile —so much like their mother's. She noted the soft pillow beneath Soli's chin. The old-fashioned hairdo, brown strands mixed in with the grey. The powder and rouge on her cheek. And lipstick—she never thought she would see Soli with lipstick.

She didn't want to rehash the past—their past. As for the future, she couldn't see one. There was just this black pit of a now. And it was her black pit. Not Soli's.

Still, there was an undeniable familiarity with her, an undeniable comfort.

They stopped in a village and bought two bottles of coke from a lean man in a little store the size of a closet. The air smelled of smoke from the burning of fields, and the sky was hazy. A pig snorted in a pen next to a small house near the store, otherwise it was quiet.

Soli pulled a brownie camera from her large straw purse and asked the man to take their picture.

Meche groaned, "Not you, too."

Cameras were one thing about her life with Ruby that she was not going to miss. Soli looked pained.

"I'm sorry. My son bought it for me for the trip."

The shopkeeper eyed the camera with keen curiosity, but refused to take it from Soli.

"Please, señor," she said, "I'd like a picture of my sister and me."

The man grinned and shook his head.

Meche spoke a few words to the man in Mayan, and he started nodding. Meche and Soli posed in front of the pickup, holding up their soda bottles. Then Meche took a picture of Soli with the storekeeper.

Soli was glad they had to finish their drinks and return the bottles before they could continue, glad of the reprieve from the road and the noise.

They leaned against the pickup. Meche was looking at her strangely.

Soli raised her eyebrows. "What?"

"What was it like flying?"

Soli thought, 40 years and this is her first question to me?

"I've always wanted to fly," Meche continued. "I used to think I'd like to be a pilot."

"I'm not sure you aren't, the way we sailed over those potholes."

"I idolized Amelia Earhart."

"Really?"

Meche nodded. "I loved it when she appeared in a newsreel."

Soli shrugged. She'd never given the aviatrix much thought. In fact when she disappeared, Soli was a bit surprised at the uproar. The woman had spent her life risking it setting flying records. What did people expect?

"Mostly," Soli said, "I was scared. Speeding down the runway, that big heavy plane shaking and roaring, I didn't see how it could possibly get off the ground. And so noisy! Between the plane and your pickup, I'm nearly deaf. Although decades of babies crying in my ear hasn't..." her voice trailed off, "helped any." She looked down at her soft drink and took a long sip from the straw. Perhaps Meche's childlessness was a sadness.

"It's alright, Soli. You can have the babies. I never wanted any."

Soli reached out to squeeze Meche's shoulder, but Meche pulled away. It was a reflex—she did not mean it as a rejection, but did not excuse herself. Instead, she looked at Soli with irritation.

"That's it? It was noisy?"

"Well, after we'd been flying a while, I couldn't keep the terror up. It was too amazing, looking down on the fields and rivers, looking down on the clouds, the sunset from up there."

Meche nodded, and Soli felt she'd acquitted herself. Meche held out her hand for Soli's bottle and returned both to the storekeeper.

"The road is better, isn't it? Than before." Soli said.

"It's not paved, but it helps that some of it's compacted, like here."

Since they'd left the city, they'd passed many a cornfield. Soli had no trouble recognizing corn, she planted several rows of it in her garden in Wisconsin. But the track into and out of the village had been cut through fields of sugarcane. Such a pretty green, such a non-Wisconsin kind of green. Meche pointed out other plants: the pointy henequen plants for rope, the palo de tinte trees used for dye, the caoba trees for mahogany.

"Every plant has a use," Meche said. There's no Mayan word for weed."

"I know," Soli said, although way back then, she'd paid little attention to the crops. Plants she required were brought to the service patio, and she and Susana de los Ángeles would do what was necessary to turn them into food and medicine and other things the household needed.

"Wide enough for a truck now," Soli ventured. "The road, it's wider."

"Well, for a pickup at least. But nothing like the highways I see in the movies—Mexican or American."

"Still the hinterland."

"Yup," Meche said, and for the first time Soli saw her smile.

"Look there!" Soli called to Meche over the rumble of the motor.

She pointed out the window at an abandoned chapel that stood atop a small rise. The facade of the building, bare of plaster or paint, was pitted and stained.

Meche nodded. Without being asked, she pulled over and killed the engine.

Sudden silence, stillness.

For Soli the quiet was a balm, but she noticed how Meche's face, set in concentration while driving, now drooped as if she'd been wired into the ignition of the old Ford.

Soli climbed out of the truck, her legs a bit unsteady, the vibrations echoing in her bones. The western horizon was marbled with clouds aglow from the setting sun, and with the sun low in the sky, it felt a bit cooler. She walked to the base of the knoll, which most likely had been a

Mayan pyramid. Weeds and brush obscured the steps leading up to the church.

Meche came to stand next to her. She pressed her hands into the small of her back and stretched.

"I think I remember this place," Soli said, her eyes fixed on the desolation.

What she remembered was a a tidy, ochre-colored chapel that glowed on its pedestal above the flat landscape. Now the roof had collapsed and an upper corner looked as if a bite had been taken out of it. The large arched doorway gaped, the doors missing. Grass and small trees grew along the top of the walls.

"What happened to it?" she asked in wonder.

A ribbon of bats flew overhead, darkening the sky.

"Artillery fire," Meche said, as if the answer were obvious.

"What?"

Meche tilted her head. "1915."

"A battle? Here?"

Meche saw a flash of irritation cross her sister's face, but did not understand why.

Back then, Soli had been isolated in San Antonio, Texas. Meche had almost never answered her letters, and when she did, she never mentioned the war. Soli had gleaned news from newspapers, American and Mexican, but the far-off state of Campeche never figured in their columns. Emigrants and refugees shared war news received in letters from home, and newcomers were bombarded with questions, but she never met anyone else from her state. Most of the news concerned the Capital and the many battles across the North, but also the fighting of the Zapatistas in Morelos. Of course, Pancho Villa's victory at The Battle of Zacatecas was covered. And there was no shortage of stories about rebel incursions into Texas, or the U.S. occupation of Vera Cruz.

"I thought Campeche was untouched by the Revolution," Soli said.

The corner of Meche's mouth tightened. "The war lasted ten years, Soli."

"I know that," Soli snapped.

"Right here, this battle, some 500 died."

Soli was aghast and closed her mouth tight.

In Texas, the air had buzzed with rumors of spies and gunrunning. She'd been surrounded by exiles of every faction: followers of the deposed dictator Díaz, of his nephew Félix (whose later revolt had failed), of the assassinated president Madero, as well as of his assassin, Huerta, and of the Flores-Magón brothers, who fomented various uprisings. There were activists of every political stripe: reactionaries, convencionistas, federalists, anarchists, liberals, zapatistas, socialists, colorados, syndicalists, marxists, constitutionalists...

A lady in Soli's neighborhood used to travel 150 miles to Laredo on the border, where she and other volunteer members of La Cruz Blanca would cross over to work as nurses when there was a battle. Soli had toyed with the idea of going with her, but she had Lalo to think of, and she worked six days a week. Instead she joined a mutual aid society that helped the multitude of refugees straggling into the city.

Somehow she'd thought that in Texas, with the war just across the border, she'd been closer to the fighting than her sister in distant, peaceful Campeche. She saw now that that had been a selfish delusion. It had served to keep her concern for Meche's safety at bay and which, most nights, let her sleep.

"They even dropped bombs from airplanes," Meche said. "A new innovation, that was. Our old neighbors, the Casillas, were in the ranks of the dead, father and son, fighting on the side of the landowners. And on the side of the carrancistas, Paco Pacheco. Remember him? He would visit sometimes at the farm," Meche reminded her. "He had a crush on you."

Soli blanched. Why had Meche never told her? Paco, long dead? And the Casillas, too? She bowed her head and closed her eyes. She said a prayer and crossed herself. When she looked up, Meche was studying her.

"Soli," she said, "no one was untouched by the Revolution."

Soli wanted to say she knew that, but honestly, did she?

She trailed Meche back to the pickup. There Meche's high horse abandoned her. Her shoulder's sagged, she drew in a ragged breath and turned to face Soli.

"Are you all right?" Soli asked.

"Would you drive?"

"I'm sorry. I never learned."

Soli looked down the straight, flat road and considered offering to try, but Meche sighed and climbed behind the wheel. Soli got in and saw Meche's face firm up as she maneuvered the gear stick and pedals and turned the key.

They passed a thatch palm, a skinny dog lying by the side of the road, a broad branching pich tree, a cornfield smoking from a burn, a withered old woman in a white huipil dress bent under a load of firewood. Soli had always preferred the view ahead to the one over her shoulder, but here she was, with the past lying in ambush in every sight and smell.

As they bumped over potholes, dusk fading to night much more quickly here than what she was used to in the north, she thought of her children, so far away.

People said children moved you forward, linked you to the future. She shook her head at the thought. In reality children twisted linear time into a pretzel, spun it into a dust devil. When the kids were little she existed in a never-ending present, a whirl of attention and exhaustion. She couldn't see five minutes ahead of herself. And yet, at the same time, every childish moment awoke buried memories and she relived her childhood on a plane parallel with theirs. Their dog was shaggy, while hers had been hairless, but seeing the shock in their eyes at the touch of the dog's tongue on their cheek made her hand go to her face in sympathetic surprise. Watching as Raymond reached down and enveloped their son's tiny hand in his, she could feel the stretch in her arm as she'd reached up to her father, could smell him next to her. Hair oil and starch, with a whiff of leather and horse. Then, seeing her daughter arch an eyebrow like her grandmother, time would telescope away from her in a lash of vertigo.

She felt something like that now, trapped in an old Ford pickup of a time machine. She'd expected to stay in Campeche City, a place she'd never considered home, not lumbering backwards to a destination that for her was one of loss and sadness.

It was dark now. Meche drove more slowly, the beams from the headlights bouncing along the road. Soli felt lost and disoriented. She peered out along the pencils of light, but they revealed only a straight dirt road hemmed in on both sides by impenetrable walls of vegetation. Everything outside their reach was blackness. Her arm ached from bracing herself against the door.

They must be getting close to home, that is, to what had been her home.

What might she find? All these years the house had stood pristine in a seldom-visited corner of her mind. But now, considering the destroyed chapel from earlier, she steeled herself. The house could be a similar ruin —charred remains, or gutted, the roof collapsed. Or it might be remodeled past recognition, or replaced with something entirely new, something modern and practical.

They turned onto an even narrower road, and the truck slowed to a crawl. The hair on Soli's neck bristled. In the high beams she glimpsed the familiar iron arch over the road and the wooden sign that dangled from it on chain links, its looping letters burned into the wood: Rancho Baalam Kab.

Home.

They passed through the arch and the weight in her chest gave way to a fluttering of foolish butterflies. She strained to see what the headlights might reveal, and there it was. The painfully plain facade of their one-story house. No wrought iron grill work, no cornices, no windows to create the semblance of a welcoming face. So little had changed, it took her breath away.

The truck came to a halt.

Meche cut the engine and headlights, and Soli found herself in sudden, muted blackness. Looking up through the dirty windshield, she saw, despite the dust and bugs, a sky seeded with more stars than the accumulation of all the stars she'd seen in the last forty years.

Meche switched on her flashlight and Soli remembered to breathe.

In the beam of light, she saw the old concrete steps that rose up along the wall to the door, no railing, then or now. Breathing in the evening breeze that felt and smelled like an old friend, Soli drew her fingers along the stucco wall as she followed Meche up the steps. Crossing the threshold, she stalled, overcome with a kind of déjà vu, a sense of knowing a place from one's dreams, a place that doesn't really exist.

Meche switched on an overhead light in the parlor on their left, and Soli saw that the old place was indeed the same. Except the furniture and carpets were tired and threadbare, the tiles chipped and cracked, the walls spotted and dingy. Her butterflies folded their wings and dropped into her stomach. The whole house oozed with a shabbiness acquired over decades.

Of course, Soli thought. Of course Meche would neglect the house, she who'd never overseen the sweeping or scouring or tidying of it, who'd run from it each day as from a prison. This would just be where Meche slept, where she ate, where she pored over reports and ledgers. She would use the house like an old battered kitchen utensil. If a tin sifter sifts, what matter a dent or two or the green paint worn off the wooden knob?

As her eyes surveyed and judged, she took in the smell of the house. Of course the scent of her father, her mother, of herself, Meche and Lalo as children had dissipated long ago, but she recognized the smell arising from the bones of the house, from the furniture and the quality of the air. She also detected traces of soap and polish. Nothing rundown about the smell of soap and polish.

She went to the modest interior courtyard with its covered corridors. At the back was the dining room, and beyond that, the kitchen. It all lay in darkness, but she heard the kitchen door swing open, the sound as familiar as the song of a mourning dove. She saw a shaft of light, and, oh, the odors that then drifted across to her: venison, beans, tortillas and chicken lime soup!

Even in the dark, the narrow road straight and flat, Meche had known exactly where they were on the route home. Miles before reaching its property lines, she'd felt the little buzz of anticipation in her chest that meant she was approaching Rancho Baalam Kab. But the fatigue that had been tracking her since Ruby's death, stalking her like a jaguar, had finally pounced—she was exhausted.

Now inside next to Soli, Meche saw the house through her eyes—the shoddiness and disrepair. But what did it matter? She brushed past Soli and turned a light on in the arcade around the interior patio.

She called out, "Hello. We're home."

A shuffling noise came from the direction of the kitchen and Soli saw a wizened old woman hobble along the corridor towards them. She wore a long, full skirt that might have once been black or brown or even green, a white blouse embroidered with a simple geometric pattern in red, leather sandals, and a dark-blue rebozo twined around her skinny arms. All of it remarkable only because none of it was in the Mayan style. The old lady stopped short when she saw that Meche had someone with her, which Soli guessed was not a common occurrence.

"Buenas tardes," Meche said. "I've brought a guest."

Guest! This was no longer her home, true enough, but, guest? She felt a pang of something. Regret, anger, both?

The old woman doddered forward. Stopping in front of Soli, she peered up at her. Soli thought her eyesight must be very poor.

"Señorita Soli?" the old lady croaked, and her head swiveled in Meche's direction.

She looked as if she'd like to chase her employer down and slap her on the hand as she would a child. As, Soli realized, her mouth dropping open, this housekeeper had indeed done when Meche was a little girl.

"Susana de los Ángeles?" Soli said, gaping at her. She looked over her head at Meche. "Meche, you never..."

Soli stopped herself. When they were alone she could ask why Meche hadn't told her that Susana de los Ángeles was not only alive, but still at the rancho. Seeing no gleam of mischief in Meche's eye, she realized it simply had never occurred to her to mention it.

Susana de los Ángeles took Soli's hand in hers and her chin slid towards her. She smiled benignly, proudly, at her. "Welcome, niña. Welcome home. Are you hungry?"

Soli teared up. She nodded.

Susana de los Ángeles patted her hand.

"I'll help you," Soli said.

Susana agreed and led the way to the kitchen.

"Why can't I eat in the kitchen like normal?" Meche groused, as Susana de los Ángeles shooed her into the dining room.

"Because, Doña Meche, this is not a normal day."

"Just because Soli..."

"Not just that," the old lady said, nodding at the black band on the arm of Meche's blouse.

Following Meche out of the kitchen, Soli carried the soup tureen, of Czechoslovakian porcelain, white with little pink roses. It matched the two scalloped, gold-rimmed place settings used for special occasions that she'd dusted off and laid on the lace tablecloth along with the silverware and crystal goblets. Relics from her past. Remembering how her mother had treasured them, wedding gifts all, she kept wanting to stroke them.

Meche, a little frown on her face, watched Soli ladle soup for the both of them.

Soli lowered her head and murmured a prayer. Saying grace was a habit she'd picked up from Raymond's family. She crossed herself and then, smiling, looked up first at Meche and then at the bowl in front of her. Taking a spoonful of the soup, she tilted her head, closed her eyes and sighed.

"I make this soup once, maybe twice a year," she said. "You wouldn't believe what I have to pay for the limes, if I can find them. And they still don't taste anything like this."

"I don't know why she made all this food," Meche complained. She leaned back in her chair. "We usually eat simply."

"I'm glad to hear that, that you're not working her to death."

"If I am, and I'm not," one corner of Meche's mouth became a knot, "it's none of your business."

Soli looked at her a bit quizzically, warily.

Meche was surprised by how thin-skinned she felt around her big sister. And after she'd come all this way. To see her. But damn it, Soli should never have left their home in the first place, or her, so easily.

Were Ruby here, Meche thought, she would point out that technically it had been Meche who'd run away from Soli. Meche grumbled inwardly—Ruby, reasonable even in death.

"*But I chose Campeche—*Meche argued back in her head—*I chose my country. And I chose you, Ruby. Soli just did as she was told. She just tagged after Lulu.*"

Even now, from death, Ruby was not going to let the discussion drop.

"*She's certainly ruffled your fur the wrong way.*"

True enough.

"*She never liked you, you know,*" Meche countered.

"*That's because she thinks I stole you from her.*"

"*She thinks you perverted me.*"

In her mind's eye, Meche saw Ruby's quick shrug of the shoulders.

"*She loves you, though. Sisters do.*"

Meche rested her elbows on the table and dropped her head in her hands. She wanted Ruby to stop talking. Soli was saying something to her, too. Meche refused to meet her eyes. She wanted everyone to shut up—conversation, eating, both seemed gargantuan tasks.

"I think I'd better go to bed," Meche said.

"Of course," Soli said, her voice thick with concern. "I wasn't thinking. We should have eaten something light in the kitchen as you wanted, something quick and easy so you could get some rest."

"You don't have to take care of me, you know," Meche said, "I've been taking care of myself for some time now."

And, Meche thought, of the studio, Baalam Kab, Susana de los Ángeles and the other workers. And, of course, Ruby, although in the end, she'd botched that. She felt awash in guilt and resentment.

Seeing Meche look at her from under heavy lids in a landslide of a face, Soli reached out and touched her hand. "We all need taking care of now and again."

Meche straightened up a bit in her chair. "You must be tired, too."

Soli nodded. She was, in fact, worn out from all the travel and also raw with the emotions of the day. Her mind turned to Susana de los Ángeles. She should help her put the food away and clean up.

"Did you know," Meche said, as if reading her thoughts, "Susana is only nine years older than you?"

Soli set down her glass and looked at Meche in surprise. "How can that be? She took care of us when we were little."

Meche shook her head. "When you're a kid, everyone seems old."

Soli lowered her voice. "She looks eighty or ninety now."

"You know how it is—workers tend to age quickly, and not gracefully. Or maybe it's different up there in Meel-wow-kay-ay. Meel-wow-kay-ay, Wisconseen."

Soli felt there was an accusation there, in the awkward pronunciation of her city, but she didn't know what it would be, and was too tired to ask.

Two rooms lay on either side of the arcaded courtyard. Apparently Meche now occupied their father's old room. Soli was to stay in the bedroom opposite that she and Meche had shared as girls.

At the sound of chairs scraping only minutes after sending the soup tureen to the table, Susana de los Ángeles stuck her head into the dining room. Meche was already out of the room.

"Forgive us, Susana de los Ángeles. We're going to bed," Soli said. "You've prepared a wonderful meal, and we haven't done it justice."

"*Señora*, please, sit and have some coffee while I make up the bed and get your room ready. Doña Meche didn't tell me you were coming."

Soli had noticed when they came in that there was a telephone in the entryway, and Meche had clearly called ahead because Susana de los Ángeles had known of Ruby's death and had made an elaborate dinner. Soli wondered why Meche hadn't also informed her that Soli would be with her.

"She's got a lot on her mind," Soli said aloud in explanation.

"I'll have your old room ready in no time."

"Don't bother. I know how to make a bed."

In fact, it had been Susana de los Ángeles who had taught her according to the standards learned from Soli's mother.

Susana de los Ángeles insisted, and they made the bed together. Then Soli unpacked her suitcase and stood awkwardly by as the old woman fussed about the room, lighting lanterns, supplying the basin stand with towels and water, opening the windows for some air, placing a jug of drinking water on the night table, pulling the chamber pot just into view.

As Susana de los Ángeles paused at the door before leaving, she and Soli looked at each other. The last time they stood like this, Soli was a teenager and Susana de los Ángeles was in her twenties.

"Goodnight, Susana de los Ángeles. And thank you."

"Señora, do you have children?"

It suddenly struck Soli that the old woman was as much in the dark about her life as Soli was about hers.

"Five. Three boys and two girls. Plus eleven grandchildren and counting."

"In the United States?"

Soli nodded. "And you?"

She shook her head no, and shrugged.

"I have pictures. I'll show you tomorrow."

Susana de los Ángeles smiled. "Buenas noches, niña. Que duermes con los angelitos." She softly closed the door behind her.

It was the dry season, so although there was no need to worry about mosquitos, Soli ran the mosquito net through her fingers, remembering the texture. It was a bit dusty, but seemed in good repair. Mosquitos were a problem in Milwaukee, too, but they had screen doors, screened windows and even a screened porch, which had the extra benefit of keeping out flies. Of course the mosquitos didn't carry malaria in Wisconsin, or yellow fever, as they had in Texas. She remembered her young children cocooned in the white netting. That was in one of their first rented houses in San Antonio. She'd found the sight comforting, and had taken pleasure in nestling with Raymond under their own tent, despite the heat of it.

At Baalam Kab, in addition to the phone and the propane stovetop in the kitchen, her sister had invested in an electric generator, and in each room a single bare bulb dangled from the ceiling. Earlier, Soli had heard the gas motor chugging away in a shed off the service patio when she visited the outhouse. Susana de los Ángeles had lit the kerosene lanterns in her room because she would be turning the generator off when she retired to her room behind the house.

Soli hadn't given much thought before to why the servants' rooms were built separate, but now she realized it had to do with the Caste War. The Maya of the Yucatán Peninsula, of which Campeche was a part, had risen up against the whites and mestizos in 1847, and the bloodshed continued into Soli's childhood, so it was likely a precaution to not have potential enemies, your servants, sleeping under the same roof. It was possibly also a factor in her mother's bringing Susana de los Ángeles from Campeche City, an Indian of Aztec ancestry rather than Mayan.

Soli slipped on the pale-blue summer nightie she'd packed. She sat at the vanity and slathered on Pond's cold cream to remove her makeup.

The lightbulb went out.

The abrupt change jolted Soli, but after a moment, as her eyes adjusted and the room relaxed into memory, she was glad of it, because aglow in the lamplight was how she most fondly remembered her and Meche's bedroom.

She finished cleaning her face and turned her thoughts to the present. What now, she asked herself. She'd expected to be busy helping at the apartment over the photography studio: cooking, cleaning, serving visitors, writing letters, whatever Meche needed. Then come evening, they could catch up, just the two of them. She would even encourage Meche to talk about Ruby, if she really wanted to.

Heavens, she didn't expect or want gratitude, and she knew people grieved in different ways, but it seemed she was making Meche even more miserable than she already was.

It had never occurred to her, not seriously anyway, that she might not be welcome. She brushed out her single braid and, calling to mind their meeting at the bus station and how right it felt to be in each other's arms, told herself she was being silly.

She re-braided her hair into two plaits as she'd done every night since she could remember, including sitting at this very vanity. Only, back then she was a child with chestnut-brown hair. She'd sit at the vanity and Meche would be on their bed, the two of them brushing and braiding, chattering or bickering. Now Soli was a mostly-grey-haired granny who ignored her daughter Marilyn's urgings to cut her hair and get a do more up to date, while Meche, alone in a separate room, wore her hair short. Permed and dyed too.

Outside, a rabble of insects sawed and chirped and buzzed, and although the lanterns gave off a warm, gentle light, they also cast looming shadows. Soli felt out of time and out of place, both hollowed out and pressed in by sadness. At the washstand she brushed her teeth, her hand aching from arthritis, and put on more face cream.

She climbed into bed, feeling stiff from the long ride in the pickup. The sheets smelled stale, of linen cabinet. She missed her own bed. She longed to talk to Raymond and Marilyn, and her arms ached for the grandkids, whom she saw many times a week. She was tempted to go home straightaway, but she'd come all this way (and spent all that money), and she did want to be with Meche. She blew out the lamps, closed her eyes and drifted to sleep.

Sometime after midnight a raucous noise startled her awake.

A rooster!

The beastly things. She'd forgotten how much she disliked them. Why was it said they heralded the dawn? In her memory they crowed throughout the night.

It was her rule: if she couldn't sleep, she got up and did something useful. So she hauled herself out of bed, lit a lamp and, not so usefully, wandered about the room. She straightened the crucifix over the bed. She thought about Meche in their parents' room. Had she changed bedrooms because that had been her father's room and now she was in charge, or because it was east-facing and this one, west. Towards the end of their last dry season together on the rancho, Meche had harped on and on about it, some Mayan mumbo jumbo about the west being the way of night creatures and death, whereas the east was the direction of good food and life.

Soli opened the lower compartment of the night table, and there was the miniature coffer she'd treasured as a child. She opened it. Empty. In the center drawer she found a little bowl in the shape of a jaguar head that, as a girl, Meche had prized. The jaguar's fangs were bared, and Soli always thought it creepy, as well as tacky. When they'd left Baalam Kab all those years ago, Meche had taken it with her to Campeche City. Well, it was back home now. A pair of tarnished silver earrings nestled in it.

She poked about in the wardrobe, mostly empty except for the clothes from her suitcase. She'd noticed the old-fashioned hatbox on the upper shelf earlier. It was large and round with faded pink and grey stripes. Hats in fashion now were bits of felt with some netting, but this was from a different time when ladies' hats boasted broad brims and were topped with feathers and fake fruit and flowers that would put Carmen Miranda to shame. Soli pulled the box down. It was heavier than she expected and something inside shifted. She laid it on the bed and lifted the lid.

Packets of letters filled the box to the brim, each packet tied with a ribbon. She recognized them at once. They were her letters, the ones she'd written in tiny script on the thinnest of paper and addressed to: Srta. María Mercedes Hernández Cruz, c/o Fotografía Eckart. She hugged one of the packets to her chest. She'd taken great comfort writing these accounts of her life.

They were bundled by year. At random, she pulled out a letter from 1924. She'd written in pencil and it was very faint. She got her reading glasses from her purse and held the letter near the lamp. After reading it, she read one from another packet. And then another. She kept reading. First steps and lost teeth, a miscarriage, funerals for pets, the deaths of her in-laws, a change of house, world wars, blizzards, graduations, her lovely grandchildren... These letters held her life.

And in a way, Meche had witnessed it. In a way, Meche must love her. Tears wet Soli's face.

After putting the box away, she got back in bed, but her mind turned to food. She'd only had the chicken and lime soup at dinner, and thinking of the limes she recalled the rancho's other fruits, none of which were known in Wisconsin: juicy papayas, creamy custard apples, rosy mangos, prickly guanábanas and seedy, fluorescent-pink pitahayas. With a hankering for fresh fruit (she couldn't remember the last time she'd eaten pineapple that didn't come out of a tin), she tiptoed into the hall with a candle. She felt like a girl again, creeping along the walkway to sneak into the kitchen. Loud snores drifted from Meche's room across the small interior courtyard. At least, sleeping alone in her old room, she didn't have to listen to that all night.

To her delight, she found a cluster of huayas on the counter, round and walnut-sized. She bit into the green fruits to break the skin, popping the coral-colored balls of flesh into a bowl. She squeezed a lime over them, sprinkled them with salt, and ate them with a spoon by candlelight, spitting the seeds back into the bowl.

Her mouth was tingling bitter-sweet when she passed Meche's room. This time, instead of snoring, Soli heard something else. Was Meche muttering in her sleep, crying? She detoured to her sister's room. At the door she could hear Meche's distress more clearly. She knocked. Meche did not answer, but the whimpering and cries continued. Apparently she was asleep and not able to wake up. Soli cracked the door and looked in.

"Meche?" she called softly.

Meche lay on the bed in a tangle of sheets, and her face glistened in the candlelight with sweat and tears. To Soli's dismay, she was nude, her sister's body that of a stranger, a stranger on the eve of old age. Soli went to her side, calling to her and shaking her.

Slowly, Soli saw Meche's eyes come into focus and meet her own. Then, clenching them closed, Meche clung to Soli and sobbed.

Soli's heart broke for her sister all over again. And all over again, she forgave her everything. She murmured to her. She patted her shoulder and stroked her head. When the spasms slowed, Soli eased Meche down and covered her with a sheet. Then she lay next to her and put her arms around her, with Meche's head on her breast.

Soli cooed to her and smoothed Meche's sweat-dampened hair away from her face. She thought back to how she'd comforted Meche in the months after their mother died. But later on Meche had not let Soli console her about anything. Or was it that Soli had been too hard-pressed with her own problems to try?

When Meche's breathing slowed and thickened, Soli disentangled herself and tucked her in.

Back in her bedroom, Soli lay awake worrying. The notion of her sister moving to Wisconsin seemed preposterous now, but how would Meche live here on her own? What was her life like in the city, and what was the situation with the photo studio?

It was mid morning when Soli woke to a darkened room. She'd slept through Susana de los Ángeles's coming in and out to close the interior shutters to the morning sun, replenish the water pitcher, and empty the basin on the washstand, as well as the chamber pot.

Soli put on her new dress, a blue-white-and-pink polyester floral-print. She was curious as to what the day and the rancho would hold, and whether she might coax Meche into talking about her nightmare. Or was it better not to speak of it? She strolled into the kitchen. The aromas brought back a flood of memories.

And there was Susana de los Ángeles, wrangling a banana leaf almost as tall as she was and toasting it over the flame of the stovetop. Soli wondered if it was for pibil. Her mouth watered at the memory of the slow-roasted pork. Through the door she saw a young Mayan woman in the service patio kneeling before the old stone metate and putting all her weight on the cylindrical grinding stone, working grains of corn into masa. So the banana leaves might be for tamales. She hoped so.

Susana de los Ángeles was very subdued when she turned to greet her. She nodded to an invoice from a vet on the kitchen table. Soli looked at it, puzzled, but picking it up, she saw the note written on the back.

> *Dear Soli,*
>
> *I want you to leave. I know you mean well and you've come a long way, but this reunion—I can't cope with it, not on top of Ruby's death.*
>
> *Vicente Maldonado, the farm manager from Chun-Ek, the next hacienda over, is driving into Mérida today. You can make any necessary connections for your return trip from there. He'll pick you up at 11:30.*
>
> *Please understand, Soli. I can't take another goodbye.*
>
> *Yours,*
>
> *Meche*

Soli dropped into a chair, gripping the note.

Susana de los Ángeles looked away and addressed herself to the banana frond. She circled her index finger and thumb around the top of the stem and in five pulls ripped the stem through her fingers, leaving the leaf gathered like green cloth in her hand. She spread the leaf on the counter, rubbed a cloth over it and then folded it into a neat eight-inch square. That done, she shuffled close and put a basket packed with lunch on the table. Hesitantly she patted Señora Soli on the shoulder, and Soli leaned against the old lady's side.

It was several moments before either spoke.

"Where is she?"

Susana de los Ángeles raised a shoulder and swooped her hand upward, palm out, meaning, Out there—God knows where.

Soli's chest heaved with a deep sigh.

"They say Mérida is very beautiful," Susana de los Ángeles murmured.

Soli's spine straightened. The hurt drained from her and anger surged into the vacuum. She got up and paced. Coming to a halt, she asked herself how many times she had paced like this in this kitchen, frantic because Meche had taken off in a huff. Only Soli wasn't frantic, not this time.

"Ingrata maldita malcriada," Soli muttered, exasperated that she had never learned to swear properly in Spanish. Or in English. She stopped and glared at Susana de los Ángeles, "It's one thing, Susana de los Ángeles, for a twelve-year-old to run away, with no thought to the effect she has on others. It's quite another for a grown woman of fifty-seven!"

"But, niña… Señora, she…"

"She's a spoiled brat, and I'm not going to wait around stewing. And I'm not going to do her the favor of disappearing."

"Señora, with all due respect," the older woman murmured, "Doña Meche is many things, but not spoiled."

"What?"

How could Susana de los Ángeles defend her when Meche had plagued both of them with her fits of temper and running away?

"You have to get your own way to be spoiled, and your father, may he rest in peace," the old woman crossed herself, "never let that girl have her way."

Soli was perplexed. Was that true?

"But…" Soli started to protest.

Susana de los Ángeles shook her head solemnly.

There was a knock on the door.

"That will be Don Vicente, señora," Susana de los Ángeles said.

Soli raised her eyes to the ceiling and sighed in exasperation. "Show him in."

Susana de los Ángeles plodded to the front door and led the farm manager into the parlor. Soli came a moment later, and they shook hands. Susana de los Ángeles waited by the doorway. Don Vicente was a mature man, with a touch of grey at the temples. His mostly black hair was slicked back from a widow's peak and he had a tidy mustache. He smelled of competing odors of aftershave, cologne and hair pomade, and although he held a finely woven cowboy hat in his left hand, he was otherwise the picture of a proper businessman: polished shoes, grey slacks and a white guayabera shirt.

What had she been expecting, that he would ride up on horseback, a whip in one hand and a rifle in the other? She gave a shudder with the sudden memory of Don Eusebio, her father's overseer.

"It's a pleasure to meet Doña Mercedes' sister," Don Vicente said. "My condolences on the passing of your aunt."

"Thank you, Señor Maldonado."

Soli offered him refreshment, and after he had declined for the third time, Susana de los Ángeles returned to the kitchen.

"It's kind of you to offer to take me to Mérida," Soli said. "I'm sure you're very busy."

"It's my pleasure, señora. Doña Mercedes knows that I make the trip regularly—hacienda business." Don Vicente held his hat against his belly now with both hands.

"Still, my sister should not have imposed on you," Soli said.

"Not at all. I'll be glad of the company, and she thought you would enjoy seeing the White City."

"I'm sure it's beautiful." Soli beamed at him.

"It's not a bad drive, at least not once we get to the Camino Real. You'll find it much easier than the trip you made from Campeche City. I hear that this is your first visit in many years."

"Yes, it is," Soli said. "I grew up here on Baalam Kab, but we left when I was fifteen."

He was too polite to pry into the date, obviously before his time, but she could see he was making calculations. Before the Revolution, during, after?

"It's a good farm," he said, nodding. "At least it's getting there now that Doña Mercedes has taken it in hand."

"It's comforting to know that my sister has good neighbors."

"Well, señora," Don Vicente said, looking at his wristwatch, "shall we get your luggage in the car?"

"Ay, Señor Maldonado, I'm sorry you came all this way for nothing. I'm sure you have important business waiting for you in the city. But I've decided to stay longer. You see, it's been such a long time since I was last here. Please forgive the inconvenience, and excuse my sister. Doña Mercedes was unaware of my change of plans when she contacted you." She was pleased, and a bit surprised, at how easily she slipped into the expected formality and courtesy. "Please forgive me for delaying you."

"Not at all. I'm at your service. I only regret losing your charming company for the trip."

She called to Susana de los Ángeles to bring the basket she'd packed and walked the farm manager to the hacienda's shiny blue Plymouth Suburban. She pressed the lunch upon him and then took the opportunity to take her Brownie camera from her bag and ask him to take a picture of her and Susana de los Ángeles. Who knew what the rest of the day would bring, if there would be another opportunity? The old woman was embarrassed, but stared stoically into the lens.

Don Vicente handed back the camera. "It's been a pleasure, señora. Give my regards to your sister."

Soli smiled and thought, I'll give her something all right. He got in the car and her smile collapsed like a castle of cards.

Normally the first thing Meche would do the morning after arriving at Baalam Kab would be to take her glass of café con leche into the office at the front of the house. There she would go over the accounts and Don Jacinto's reports.

Don Jacinto would have liked to be a full farm manager, like Don Vicente. But Rancho Baalam Kab was no Hacienda Chun-Ek—a farm manager was a luxury Meche could not afford. Nor was Don Jacinto's education up to the job—his reports were sometimes a puzzle to solve, and she had to do the bulk of the bookkeeping. But he was a capable foreman on the ground. With his sweat-stained cowboy hat, boots dusty or mud-caked, depending on the season, and his beer belly straining the little white buttons of his plaid shirt, he managed the farm work and the workers well enough, but she could only expect so much from him when it came to dealing with buyers, bankers and government officials. If only she had had someone like Don Vicente. It would have taken a lot of strain off her and Ruby's union.

After looking at the books and reports in the office, Meche would then usually consult with Don Jacinto and check on the work of the farm. But nothing was normal today. Early that morning in the kitchen, Meche put aside the café con leche that Susana de los Ángeles handed to her and sat down to scribble on a stray piece of paper. She then walked past the office door and went out and sat in the Ford. Her hand shook as she wrote out a list on the back of an old envelope:

> *corn—harvest / store*
> *check on hives*
> *beans—harv.*
> *braid garlic*
> *cane—harv. / transp. to S. Isidro*
> *plant veg.*
> *burn* milpas
> *graft orange trees*

She stared at the mishmash of tasks, and didn't know where to begin.

Or how. She'd had that wretched nightmare only hours earlier and could not seem to shake it.

She'd dreamt she was standing on a station platform as a train began to slowly depart. White steam billowed about her, like in an old foreign movie. She wasn't sure why she was there, but she knew she wasn't supposed to be on the train. She watched as the car nearest her crept forward. Then, framed by one of the curtained windows, she glimpsed her mother onboard, head bent as if reading. Meche tried to call to her, but could not get her voice to work. The train was picking up speed, so that her mother's car slid out of reach and Meche was looking into the windows of the following car. There was Pedro Mu, whom she'd followed around the rancho when she was a child, his straight black hair severely combed, and next to him his brother-in-law's grandmother, Doña María Inés, her head covered with a shawl. Both looked past her, their black eyes devoid of expression. Before she could even try to call out, the car advanced several windows and she saw her father lean out of one of them.

She knew then that all the passengers aboard were loved ones—loved ones who had abandoned her. She was desperate not to be left behind again.

She ran alongside the train until she reached the end of the platform. As the train pulled out of reach, she saw that the last car had a little balcony, and on it stood Ruby. She looked just as she had in 1910, when Meche first met her. She wore no hat, and her black hair swelled asymmetrically into a bun on top of her head. She had on a long brown skirt and a starched white blouse with a high collar. A box camera hung around her neck, and she was peering down the track via the view finder.

Look at me, Meche tried to scream. But nothing came out. Blinded by tears, she sank to the platform. She became aware of something sharp-edged in her trousers pocket—a photograph, one of Ruby's sepia-toned art shots. In it, steel rails gleamed with a blur of cross ties between them.

She knew Soli had woken her. No doubt she would want Meche to tell her all about it. But besides being painful to recall, the meaning of the dream was transparent, and it was not Meche's habit to air her weaknesses. Letting down her defenses had never been a luxury she could afford.

As soon as Don Vicente's car pulled out of sight, Soli stormed back into the house and into the kitchen. She was famished, and she wasn't going to let Meche deprive her of a meal.

"Susana de los Ángeles, breakfast, please. And have a horse saddled for me."

The old woman raised an eyebrow. They both knew that Soli was a tentative horsewoman at best.

The aromas in the kitchen intensified and very shortly Susana de los Ángeles placed eggs fried crisp in bacon grease in front of Soli, along with beans, papaya, fried banana, tortillas, orange juice and coffee. Soli ate as if she'd spent the last two days digging ditches.

When she finished, she went to look for Nestor Antonio. The boy was responsible for the horse that turned the water wheel, and Susana de los Ángeles said he would have a horse ready and waiting for her. At the well, harnessed to the wheel, a nag of a horse plodded the circular path to fill the concrete cistern, and nearby a boy, barely teenage, sat on a low whitewashed wall in the shade of a fuchsia-colored bougainvillea. He was skinny, had a pronounced cowlick at the crown of his head and wore traditional white cotton clothing. He held the reins of a saddled horse loose in his hand, and when he saw her approach, he jumped off the wall.

The sight of the horse triggered Soli's fear. She'd forgotten how big horses were.

It seemed to eye her with equal suspicion.

"Buenos días, señora," the boy muttered, looking at the ground, but sneaking glances up at her, the patrona's sister from America.

The saddle caught her attention. "This isn't the right saddle," she snapped.

"Perdón, señora?"

Soli had never straddled a horse, and of course she hadn't packed pants because she didn't own any.

"I want mine... I mean, I need a sidesaddle."

Nestor Antonio looked at her and away, a bit panicky. He obviously didn't know what she was demanding.

"For a lady," she said. "A saddle for a lady."

"There are the two saddles, señora," The boy said, obviously rattled.

"Two? Only two?"

She wanted to demand to know the fate of her mother's saddle and the one that she herself had used. And two? There'd been five or six. What about her father's? This wasn't it. And the second sidesaddle that Meche used, that is when they could convince her to not ride bareback? But this boy was a minute-and-a-half old. Not even his father would be old enough to answer her questions.

"The saddles, señora, they are pretty much the same. This one is a little prettier."

"I don't care about pretty."

The horse lifted its tail and plopped stinking dung onto the ground.

"It's a good saddle, señora. It's the one the patrona uses, and I oiled it just yesterday."

Staring at the boy was not going to make her old saddle materialize. She was going to have to make do.

"And Eclipse here is the horse she usually rides."

Soli and the mare eyed each other warily. She was not a beautiful animal. Her best feature was her markings. Almost entirely white, she had brown patches on her unfriendly eyes, a few brown spots on her flank, and a sparse brown tail.

Soli waved the boy aside. (It was surprising how the arrogance of command returned just as easily as that of courtesy to visitors.) She didn't send him away because she might need help, but she ordered him to turn his back while she clumsily mounted the horse. The dress she was wearing had a full skirt, but her slip did not. She hitched the slip up and tugged the skirt of her dress down and over her legs as far as it would go. At least her girdle would keep the leather from rubbing the inside of her thighs raw.

Now if she could just keep from breaking her neck.

Meche parked the pickup at the edge of the forest. The small rise in the far corner of Baalam Kab was home to the rancho's lone stand of timber, the woods continuing on past her property line. She told herself that she'd come here to choose trees for cutting, but instead she wandered idly as when she was a girl. It was the dry season and the ground slippery—thickly littered with fallen leaves. While up in the canopy, dark patches moved from branch to branch: spider monkeys.

In a couple months, after the rains started, the woods would be lush with riotous jade and emerald colors, but not now. Some trees were bare and the foliage of the rest, sparse, with the color of the trunks and branches—grey, white, green, milky brown and peeling red—outshining the dusty and subdued greens of the leaves.

She stopped to inspect a chicozapote tree, running her fingers along the deep cross-slit scars in the grooved bark. The machete cuts created a channel for collecting chicle, the tree's milky latex used to make chewing gum. This tree still had several years of rest ahead of it before it could be harvested again.

Demand for chicle had fallen sharply in the last few years—the U.S. companies had started using synthetics. Fortunately she didn't rely much on the white gold. She might have made that mistake if she'd gotten hold of the rancho earlier, seduced by the promise of big profits. At least while the price of chicle was high, they'd gotten some better roads in the region—a boon now to transporting Baalam Kab's other products to markets. It also made it possible for her to get here from Campeche City in one day instead of two.

Economic ups and downs seemed to be a hallmark of her beloved state. She turned to look at a palo de tinte tree—not what you would call stately, a number of suckers growing together to form the trunk. And yet logwood had dominated Campeche's economy for centuries, producing the red, purple and black dyes that Europe had been prepared to kill for. Because of this unimposing tree, the British buccaneers had skulked along the coast of Campeche, and other Englishmen had colonized British Honduras. Then around the time of Mexico's Revolution, palo de tinte was replaced by chemical dyes. These days she could barely give it away.

She recalled her father often saying that Baalam Kab was too small to indulge in get-rich schemes—a boom is always followed by a bust.

His strategy was to use the Indians' traditional mix of crops and products, but improve on the old techniques by applying scientific methods, and now and then—with careful consideration and on a small scale—introduce a new, profitable crop. The problem, he would rage, was that the Indians were not interested in his scientific methods. He never fully accepted that the Maya had their own science, based on thousands of years of practice and observation. But she had to admit that since she'd been in charge, she herself—when thwarted by tradition—had indulged in more than a few outbursts.

She kicked at the leaves on the ground. What, she wondered, would her father think of Baalam Kab today?

"To hell with him," she shouted up at the monkeys.

They chittered back and the branches overhead rustled.

She made her way to a great-grandfather of a tree, a large ceiba she knew well. She looked up the trunk studded with thorns—they were shaped like a rose's, only each spine measured a couple inches long. The rancho hadn't been doing anything with the pods. She should discuss with Don Jacinto if it made sense to take workers away from other tasks to collect them—remove the kapok fiber for stuffing and the seeds to make oil for soap.

The base of the tree was a swirl of finlike buttress roots, large and smooth. She found a route between them to a spot where she could reach up and touch the trunk. She broke off a thorn, and then eased herself to sitting and, clutching her knees, leaned into the curved wall of root. She heard the lazy buzz of a bee, and somewhere overhead a solitary clock bird made its tock-tock sound.

The real reason she'd come to the forest was to escape from all the probing glances and muttered condolences of Don Jacinto and the workers. She studied the thorn lying in the palm of her hand, then she licked the broken part and stuck it in the center of her forehead—it was supposed to cure headache.

And, of course, she wanted to avoid her damn sister. The instant intimacy and the awkwardness, the forgotten memories and grudges, the lost time and the absent future—all were crisscrosses scoring the length of her body, the scars all oozing sap. Meche ran her hand over the ceiba root and up towards the spiked bark, which she couldn't reach from where she sat. The hollow spaces inside her body gnawed. Every muscle ached, and the absence of Ruby stretched endlessly in every direction—a barren plain, a wasteland with no promise of relief. She fought the urge to find a younger ceiba—one with smaller roots, one whose trunk she could embrace and let the thorns pierce her.

Soli caught sight of the pickup parked at the edge of the woods. The workers were all alert to the boss's Fordcito, so it hadn't taken long to narrow her search.

Looking about to see that no one was watching, she clambered down from the saddle, the horse side-stepping and snorting her contempt of Soli's clumsiness. Soli tied the reins to the door handle of the truck and gave Eclipse a pat on the neck that they both recognized as halfhearted.

Taking a few unsteady land steps toward the trees, she felt a tingle of apprehension and stopped. She'd heard so many stories, been warned so many times. You could easily loose your bearings in the bush and get lost, die of dehydration or snakebite or even jaguar attack, not to mention the more supernatural dangers (which she rejected), like the easily offended aluxo'ob, reminiscent of leprechauns, but without the pot of gold. They could put snakes in your path or cause you to have an accident with your machete.

"Meche!" she called out. "Meche, I know you're in there!"

Nothing.

Soli took a deep breath and gathered her resolve.

Meche leaned against the broad root of the old ceiba tree and closed her eyes.

When Meche was a girl, Doña María Inés, a grandmother in Pedro Mu's family, had taught her that Yaxché was the sacred ceiba tree at the center of the world—the axis of the cosmos. Its holy color was green, the color of power, of new growth, of life itself. The Yaxché bridged the three realms of creation—its roots sank into the nine spiritual worlds below, its canopy reached into the 13 worlds in the heavens, and in between, in our earthly sphere, its trunk united the physical world's dualities: the dry season and the wet, light and dark, male and female, life and death. It was to be respected and revered. That's why this tree—surrounded by others that were relative youngsters—had never been felled, in deference to its cosmic twin, the first tree, the center of the universe.

Meche recalled Chiich's other teachings. "M'ija," she'd said, "each direction has a color and a wind and its own power and significance."

Meche recited these now—as she had as a child to fall asleep—for comfort, yes, but maybe if she could remember them properly, she could also tap into Doña María Inés' wisdom. Everything in the old woman's world had had significance and portent. Everything reflected a cosmic reality. Right now Meche thirsted for that, thirsted for some kind of meaning.

East was Likin. Its color was red—chak. Its wind, Likin-ik, enriched the earth. Its saint was Santo Domingo. Likin was blood and thought, fire and strength, fresh tender foods, and the meat of deer and hares. The victorious jaguar sun rose there from the Underworld of the dead.

West was Chikin. Its color was black—ek. Its wind, Chikin-ik, was cold and unwholesome. Its saint was Saint… Pedro? No, James. Saint James. It was the road to death, drought and all night creatures: owls, bats, tarantulas and scorpions. Chikin was the entrance to the Underworld of the dead where the wounded sun went down to fight for its life.

South was Nohol. Its color was yellow—k'an. Its wind was the hot Hohol-ik. Its saint was Mary Magdalene. Nohol faced the rising sun, and was the haunt of Venus. It was maturity, richness, skin and muscles, seed and sickness. Meche thought suddenly of Soli, and shook her head. Soli did not belong in this litany.

North was Xaman. Its color was white—sac. Its wind was the cool Xaman-ik. Its saint was Saint Gabriel. It was where Uh, the moon, traveled. It was purity, seed, life, bones, semen, the white of the eye. The North. White. Meche turned her face north. She should try to embrace Xaman, she thought, the path of the moon, seed, bones, the white of the eye.

She squeezed her eyes shut against tears. With the heel of one hand she rubbed at them, and with the other hand she gripped the smooth, hard rib of ceiba root.

She remembered that there were three crosses in the body—the one in the forehead should align with the constellation of the Southern Cross. She looked to the horizon and bent her index finger behind her thumb to form a cross. With it she drew another cross on her forehead, knocking her thorn off. She re-licked it and stuck it back on. A second cross was on the chest and should align with Yaxché, the world tree. Meche looked up the trunk of this ceiba and crossed herself again. The third was in the navel, the center of balance, and should align with the earth. She sank her left hand into the leaves on the ground and drew a cross on her navel with the right.

She supposed only a shaman could do the aligning properly. Even so, at the base of the ceiba, contemplating the sacred directions, she felt a blessed calm—or rather, she sensed its existence, apart from her, just out of reach. And feeling it nearby, almost caressing her skin, was like a balm.

Soli entered the woods, stopping every 20 feet or so to call out, "Meche! Where are you?" She called and called, her emotions see-sawing between concern and anger.

No answer came.

"Meche!"

Soli glimpsed a bit of white ahead. Meche's blouse? Worry dropped away, but then she saw that the patch was partially obscured by the broad buttress root of a large ceiba tree. Had she fallen? Had something happened to her?

"Meche?" she called, her voice quavering.

The sliver of white moved and turned into Meche getting to her feet and turning to face Soli.

Soli let out a heavy sigh. She hadn't realized she was holding her breath. She prepared to rail against Meche for scaring her yet again, but as she approached through the trees, seeing how drawn and pale Meche's face looked, she bit her tongue.

"Soli. What are you doing here?" Meche said, weary and defeated.

Soli, facing her, broke into laughter.

Meche frowned. "What are you laughing at?"

"My sister, the unicorn."

Meche glared at her, then her eyes widened and her hand felt for the large thorn she'd stuck to her forehead.

"It's for headache, you know," Meche grumbled.

Soli shook her head, thinking what nonsense. She would offer her aspirin from her purse, but it was back at the house. Instead, with some sarcasm, she said, "Did it work?"

Meche looked at the ceiba thorn on her palm. She smiled sadly and nodded. "What do you want, Soli?"

What did she want? Instead of answering, she said, "I rode Eclipse out here to find you."

Meche raised her eyebrows and waited.

"It's the first time I've been on a horse since I was 15. If you'll remember, I don't much like horses."

"Am I supposed to congratulate you, or what?"

"Yes, you are. I got on that damn horse because I wanted to find you."

Meche's mouth set in a firm line and color came into her face. "Didn't you get my note?"

"Of course I got your note. Why do you think I'm here?"

"I don't know, Soli. I don't really care."

Soli felt as if she'd been punched in the gut. Her mouth fell open in a gasp.

"I'm hanging on here by a thread, Soli, hanging on with both hands. I can't deal with your drama right now."

"My drama?"

"Rushing to my rescue. Planes, buses… I've done just fine without you. Ruby and I did just fine."

"I didn't come here for me."

Meche glared at her. "That's what you think, isn't it? Good old selfless, spineless Soli."

"Meche!"

"I can't…" Meche stopped herself. She closed her eyes a moment and started again. "Soli, you despised Ruby. So how can you console me? How dare you think you can?"

"You ran away from me, Meche. Away from me and to Ruby." Soli's face twisted. "You were a child, and she…"

"I was a child who didn't want to leave her home, who didn't want to live with that vain, pathetic Lulu. I didn't trust her. The woman couldn't take care of a barn cat, and she was going to drag us to a foreign country? And then what?"

"But you abandoned me and Eddy to our fates?" Soli said. "With someone you didn't trust?"

"No, you and Lalo left me. I was and am exactly where I was meant to be."

"And Ruby stood by and let you. What kind of sick…"

"She didn't know I was going to get off that boat. You know that."

"That's what you wrote, eventually. But…"

"She was a lifeline, at that point, nothing more. A grown-up who could take care of herself. So I gambled that maybe she could help me— help me take care of myself. She had a house and a profession. I admired her. Love came later."

"Love!"

"Yes, and I've lost her, Soli. I've lost Ruby."

"Don't you think I know that? That's why I came, so you wouldn't feel you were all alone."

"But I am alone. If you had visited even once before this… If you had even once in your damn letters asked after Ruby, or sent her your your regards."

"I can't talk about this."

"Exactly. And if you can't talk about Ruby, if you can't talk about Ruby and me, what is the point? Why are you even here?"

Soli blinked back tears. "Because you're my sister. And I couldn't stand to think of the pain you must be going through."

"When I saw you get off that bus, I was never so happy to see anyone, Soli, honestly. But you keep stirring up all these memories, emotions I thought I'd forgotten. It feels like you're tearing at me, clawing into me for a foothold. It's all too much, Soli. I don't have the energy for it—it's all I can do to drag myself out of bed in the morning. And in a couple days, after luring me into this quicksand that's us, you'll leave again. And I'll sink for sure."

"Come back with me. You have a big family waiting for you."

Meche looked at Soli in disbelieve, and then she let out a bitter laugh. "Oh, Soli, please. Go home."

Soli sniffed. "This is not how I imagined this."

Meche walked past her towards the edge of the woods. She stopped and looked back. "Come on. You don't want to get lost out here."

Meche led Soli to the edge of the woods. Eclipse saw or sensed Meche and nickered.

"You go back to the house," Meche said. "I'm staying."

That evening Soli and Susana de los Ángeles ate together in the kitchen, and Soli showed her pictures of her children and grandchildren. Outside a blanket of insect noise lay over the otherwise silent night. Meche had not yet returned.

Later, as Soli lay dozing in her childhood bed, the unnatural sounds of the old Ford's engine and the thud of its door jerked her awake. She heard the heavy front door groan open and shut. She held her breath as Meche's boots thudded on the tile on the opposite side of the interior patio, and she breathed out when she heard Meche's door click shut.

Soli woke once in the night, and thought she heard sobbing, but she did not go to check.

When she rose in the morning, Meche had already gone out. On Eclipse, Susana de los Ángeles said.

After breakfast Don Jacinto loaded Soli's suitcase into the back of the old Fordcito. Soli set her other things on the front seat and took both of Susana de los Ángeles' hands. She kissed her on both cheeks.

"Safe journey, niña," the old woman said.

Soli felt a tightness in her chest and a queasiness in her gut, and although her face did not contort nor any cry escape her throat, tears rolled down her face.

"Take care of yourself," she said. "And of my sister."

Susana de los Ángeles nodded.

Soli settled in the front seat of the pickup.

Don Jacinto offered to take the large striped hatbox from her to put in the back. She thanked him, but told him she would hold it in her lap.

1 9 5 2 ...

Lulu looked straight ahead. There was another bed in the room with another person. She didn't want that bed or that person to exist, so she did not look at them.

Her fingers fiddled with the long thin braid that hung over her right shoulder. She preferred to wear her hair in a broad and intricate bun low on the back of her head. She missed the weight of it, the familiar prick of hairpins. But her shoulders would not allow her arms to bend in the necessary way anymore, and who in this hellhole was going to help her? She had to make do with the braid. An aide could manage that much. But Lulu resented having to make do.

She heaved a sigh of self-pity. She'd had such dreadful luck in her life.

She should have gone home to Mexico. Why was it that she hadn't? Well, there was Joe. She was married to him for awhile, and that was all right, but then he died. Why hadn't she gone back to Campeche then? She should be living with Ruby. After all she was Ruby's only sister, her only living relative, if you could call this living. Surely once she was in Campeche, there would be a maid to tend to her. But there was the problem of getting there. She wouldn't, couldn't travel alone.

Eddy! Of course that was the answer. He could accompany her to Mexico. He was always so good to her. Maybe he'd want to stay. After all Campeche was his home too, even if he didn't remember it.

Soli took a deep breath before she knocked on the door. She opened it slowly and saw that Lulu was awake and sitting up in bed. She noted that Lulu looked about the same as during their last visit. Her once pale complexion was pallid and her hollowed cheeks sagged like dewlaps below her soft jawline. Her white hair, now yellowed as parchment, was almost the same blond color as when Soli first met her. Strictly speaking, Lulu was Soli's stepmother, but Soli never thought of her that way.

Raymond followed her into the room, his grey felt fedora in hand.

It was hard for Soli to keep from wrinkling her nose. The smells in the hallway and in the room were sharp and unpleasant. She muttered a greeting to the patient in the next bed and Raymond also nodded to her before they turned their attention to Lulu. Lulu's eyes, a washed-out blue, rested on Soli without expression. It was as if she didn't recognize her.

Lulu asked herself if she knew this person. But the question slid from her mind, because look, there was Raymond. Raymond! Her face lit up. She could feel it, the warmth of the flush, the lifting of the muscles around her eyes and mouth. Such a gentleman, and handsome as always. Back home Lulu's white skin and pretty blushes had often been remarked upon. She expected Raymond noticed, too, the delicate coloring of her complexion.

The other one set a potted plant on her night table. What was she supposed to do with that?

"*Raymond, dear,*" Lulu said in Spanish, "*you've come to visit me in this dreadful place!*" She reached her hands out to him, networks of blue veins with gold rings with stones on her fingers. "*You are so kind.*"

Raymond set his hat on the end of the bed and took Lulu's hands. He leaned in to give her a peck on the cheek. Soli stepped in behind him for her kiss. Lulu stiffened and pulled back.

Soli, never quick to anger, made an exception. Her eyes narrowed and her lips tightened. Raymond placed a hand on her arm.

He whispered to her, "Maybe she doesn't recognize you."

"Of course she recognizes me!"

"Look, she doesn't have her glasses on."

Soli looked at her husband with disbelief. Raymond had always been too patient with Lulu.

"She seems to know you just fine," she said. She turned to Lulu and said, "Lulu, soy yo, Soli. Your stepdaughter. How are you?"

Lulu pursed her lips and thought, of course she knew her. Didn't she?

But stepdaughter? No. Under those white, Sunday gloves were the hands of a servant, Lulu was sure of it. No stepdaughter of hers would have hands like that. Lulu's mother always insisted that a real lady took care of her hands. "*Lotions, gloves, manicures,*" she thought in Spanish.

"What?" Soli said.

Apparently she'd muttered those last words aloud. Lulu offered her cheek to the person.

"And please speak English," Soli said. "You know Raymond doesn't understand Spanish all that well. And the nurse on duty says that you refuse to acknowledge what they say to you."

"You tell 'em, lady," Lulu's roommate called to Soli in a wavering voice. "This is the U.S. of A. and we speak English here. What's that lingo she's talking anyway?"

"Spanish," Soli answered.

"What's she doing talking Spanish?" the old lady said.

Raymond put a finger to his lips. The old lady raised her hands in surrender. She turned over in her bed with her back to them, but the position of her head indicated that she was listening.

"I know English isn't easy for you," Soli said to Lulu, "and I know you don't like speaking it, but..."

"*You must be mistaking me for some one else, madam,*" Lulu said in Spanish, "*I only speak Spanish, and German, of course.*" She tilted her head back. "*My father was German.*"

"I know your father was German, and you know about five words."

Lulu twisted her lips tight and looked away.

"Honey, you're upsetting her," Raymond said.

Lulu wondered what Raymond was doing with this person. She really was quite disagreeable. Perhaps she did know her. Did she? Well, she didn't want to.

Raymond and Soli dragged the two straight-backed chairs in the room to Lulu's bed.

Raymond insisted they speak in Spanish, "Hon', remember she's not well," he said, "and I need the practice." He winked at Lulu.

Lulu beamed back.

"Practice for what?" Soli said.

Twenty minutes later, when they got up to leave, Lulu pulled on Raymond's sleeve.

"Raymond, dear, please call Eddy. He needs to come get me and take me home. He's so busy at the bank, I think he must have forgotten."

Raymond looked at Soli, pained and confused. Soli's brother, Eddy, had never come back from the Pacific.

Soli rolled her eyes and said to him under her breath, "Might as well call Joe while you're at it."

"Don't be silly," Lulu snapped. *"Joe's dead."* She turned back to Raymond. *"But Raymond, dear, do call Eddy, won't you?"*

Campeche | Ruby

Ruby and Meche's apartment above the photography studio was homey, in the sense that over the 24 years that they'd lived there it had molded to their needs like a pair of old shoes—and they to it. They'd never made any improvements and most of the furniture had been left behind by the previous owner, the Widow Canetti, when she moved to Havana to live with her daughter and son-in-law. Ruby had sold the family house and furnishings to purchase the building, but held back the phonograph for Meche. For her part, Meche had brought little to the apartment other than her clothes, her notebooks from the rancho, and a few personal keepsakes from her childhood, like a little ceramic bowl in the shape of a jaguar's head, which now sat on the dresser and in which she kept a couple pairs of earrings.

Now, from the bathroom, Ruby could hear Meche making her morning café con leche in the closet-like kitchen. Carmen would come in later to do housework and make the main meal. It was a bit unusual not to have her live in, but the apartment was very small, and it suited them all.

Ruby tugged at the shoulder of her blouse. White and short-sleeved, with traditional Campeche black embroidery on the squared neck—it was one of several in the wardrobe. Meche didn't much like Ruby's market-bought tops. She referred to them—disdainfully to Ruby and defensively to others—as folkloric. She told Ruby they were bad for business because they raised eyebrows. Their clientele were mostly of the opinion that a lady, that is to say a decent woman, didn't wear such things.

"Decent!"

"You may not care," Meche said, "but I, for one, have become accustomed to eating."

Decent referred to an arcane concoction of race, class, and social expectations, generously laced with morality, which had more to do with race and class and propriety than it did with any notion of right and wrong. Ruby couldn't be bothered with keeping it straight, or pretending to care. She ignored it all as much as possible, which was to say, as much as Meche would put up with.

Ruby's Aunt Pancha, however—may she rest in peace, which seemed highly unlikely—was never one to ignore such things and had had much to say about the tyranny of decency. It hearkened, she would lecture, back to Mexico's colonial race system, a pyramid of some 20 castes. At the top point were perched the descendants of white Spaniards. Below them and spreading wider, came those who were the offspring of a white person and someone of another race. They in turn rested atop the broader group of people who were mixtures of mixtures, say a *mestizo* with a *mulata* or an Indian with a *china* (the combinations were numerous). Finally at the bottom, broad-based and numerous, existed the pure *indios* and *negros*.

And Meche railed at the Americans for their racism!

"The tyranny of decency," her Tía Pancha would cry out. "Tyranny" had been one of her tiresome aunt's favorite words. She couldn't go for more than a minute without exclaiming about the tyranny of one blasted thing or another.

She claimed that decency and correctness were a stranglehold, an insidious scheme designed to keep women in line, to squash any instinct for independence and originality. Only those at the uppermost tip of the racial pyramid held title to it, and they let fear of losing it dominate their lives. Meanwhile, below them, middle-class mestizo women bustled about striving to submit themselves to that very slavery. For the lower classes, try as they might, gentile respectability was out of reach. Their social betters would never recognize them as capable of "decency".

"Lucky you!" Tía Pancha would proclaim to an audience of

proletariat women. "Fortunate to be free to pursue excellence and independence on your own terms!"

Ruby didn't care about any of that. She just wanted to wear her embroidered tops. They formed part of her uniform for the studio—the "folkloric" blouse worn with a more conventional skirt. She had three, all purchased by Meche: a full black one, a brown A-line with two pleats in front, and a pair of dark-green culottes with red and white piping along the hem. They all reached a bit below mid-calf which was longer than the style these days. Meche kept threatening to get them shortened.

She'd started dressing like this—skirt, blouse, flats—about the time she bobbed her hair. It was comfortable, and if she looked eccentric, so what?

Meche also encouraged her to use makeup, but Ruby refused. What a discouraging way to start the day that would be, peering at herself and daubing on paint, as if she were one of the portraits she tinted by hand. The technique she used these days in the studio was similar to how she used to colorize photos before the advent of color film. She'd liked doing that, using brush and water colors to add pastel shades—soft blue, creamy pale yellow, subdued coral pink. She did not, however, like touching up the color photos. She disdained the painterly effect that customers wanted. If she had her way, that is if her customers would buy them, she'd still do portraits in black and white—there was a beauty and clarity to black and white that was lost in color film. Rather contradictorily, black and white revealed subtlety and nuance that color did not.

She looked away from her reflection and splashed water on her face. She seldom indulged in such self-scrutiny. It was a good policy, the avoiding of mirrors. She didn't need anything to remind her that she was shriveling up—shriveling up and accumulating aches and pains. Like going up the stairs from the studio to their living quarters—it used to be just the ache in her right knee, but now she'd pant like an old dog, and there was this pain in her chest.

She didn't tell Meche because she'd want her to go to the doctor. Ruby didn't like doctors, didn't like being poked and prodded.

Her poor Meche, saddled with an old woman.

At least that's what she thought on a good day, that for better or worse, they would go on as they were to the end. But on a bad day, she fretted about the ten years she had on Meche, worried that if Meche ever visited Soli in the north, she'd never come back—even though she knew that Meche hated the United States on principle. And now Meche had that blasted farm. Ruby had never been to Baalam Kab, but she hated it all the same. She didn't understand the hold it had on Meche. It obsessed her, beckoned to her. Like a mistress.

Today was not a good day—not only was she fretting about losing Meche, she was missing her father and Lulu.

Once, as Meche looked at herself in the mirror, she'd told Ruby that she saw traces of her sister, her mother, even her father in her face, and that somehow it made her feel less lonely.

"You're lonely?" Ruby had snapped.

"No, mi vida, of course not. Wrong word. Connected, maybe? Attached to a familiar strand of time?"

Remembering this exchange Ruby glanced at the mirror again. Black hair, black eyes, dark complexion. Yes, her own mother was there, disapproving, horrified at the short hair and bangs, but she saw nothing of her father. Nothing of her sister, Lulu. Ruby had grown up looking into Lulu's blue eyes—Lulu with her pale skin and blond hair. That was what was familiar to Ruby. And she couldn't recall any of that by looking in a mirror.

Ruby was the negative and Lulu the print. Ruby a cenote hidden in a cave, and Lulu, clouds like fluffy kapok. Ruby missed that fizz, Lulu's emotions blooming pink on her skin for all to see—no darkness, no secrets—no secrets because her sister was incapable of keeping them.

The last time Lulu called—six months ago?—something had been a bit off.

"How can you tell?" Meche had said with a curl of her lip.

Well, Lulu would probably be calling again soon. During the holidays—she got sentimental.

Meche sat at the dining-room table, drinking her morning coffee—a tall glass of boiled milk with instant coffee and sugar stirred in. When Ruby walked by her en route to the kitchen, Meche reached out to touch her hand as she passed. Ruby shied away, just a whisker. If Meche noticed, she didn't show it and kept reading her newspaper, forehead furrowed under her short permed hair.

The milk was still warm on the stove. Ruby assembled her own café con leche and sat across from Meche. Meche glanced up at her and smiled.

Ay, Meche.

For Ruby, looking at Meche's face felt like being in her darkroom, like having a camera in her hand—something akin to home. She liked Meche's brown eyes—the color of burnt umber, with flecks of green— and the familiar contours of her face. She was not, Ruby noticed, dressed for work—no belted dress, no heels—and Ruby remembered with a stab of anger that Meche was off again to the rancho.

Would this be the time she did not come back?

"When are you leaving?"

Meche did not to react to Ruby's frigid tone. "After Carolina arrives. I need to fill her in on a few things before I go."

"How long will you be gone?"

"Ruby, I told you all this."

"No, you didn't."

"You mean you weren't listening."

Ruby shrugged. "I don't find your rancho as fascinating as you do."

"Ruby, I've been playing second fiddle to your photography for decades! The rancho…"

"How long?"

Meche looked at her confused.

"How long will you be gone this time?"

"A few days. A week at most."

"I thought you said October was a slow time."

"Relatively. Mostly just checking in. There's some sowing of vegetables—onions, garlic, peas. There are some cows to sell off for butchering. I'd gladly get rid of all of them, but..."

"I don't care about the damn cows. Or the damn garlic. Or..."

"What is wrong with you lately?" Meche sounded exasperated, which irritated Ruby even more. "I'm tired of tiptoeing around you all the time."

"Go to hell!" Ruby said and leaped to her feet.

Well, leaping was the intent, but it was more of a stagger, and in the process she knocked the chair over with a clatter.

"Ruby!"

Ruby flounced out of the room without a backward glance. As soon as she was out of Meche's sight, she leaned against the wall and clutched at the black embroidery at her chest.

1 9 5 1 ...

This *morning* Soli did what she hated in others: she pulled the blankets up over her head and did not stir. Every so often, instead of plowing ahead as usual, she would hit a quagmire that stalled her, her legs sinking deep into the muck, swallowing her up.

Like today.

She pulled her knees up to protect the hollow at her center. Experience had taught her that the aching sadness would pass, but what if this time it didn't? How could she trust a return to normal when she felt she'd rather die than feel this way? Or was it that she'd died years ago and this was, what? Purgatory? Hell?

She heard the toilet flush and her husband's footsteps returning to their bedroom. Feeling his heavy hand on her shoulder, she held her breath, did not move. And so he knew. After a moment the weight lifted, and she heard him close the door quietly behind him. She heard Marilyn calling for her from the bottom of the stairs, and her husband shushing her in a harsh voice that made her cringe further.

She should get up. See what Marilyn needed. Make morning coffee for Raymond. Cook breakfast. Pack his lunch. Go to church. Light a candle for Eddy. She should, but it seemed no more possible than if she'd broken both arms.

She'd had a terrible dream, and in the depths of the night had succumbed to whatever this was (she refused to give "it" a name). It often happened this way, "it" taking her unawares, in her sleep, when she was unable to defend herself, her busyness laid aside. No matter that she was awake now, the despair persisted.

Today was the anniversary of Eddy's death. Eddy who'd been more like a son than a brother. Eddy in all his incarnations: Eduardo Ernesto, Lalo, Lalito: the baby she'd cradled, the clinging little boy, the easygoing teenager, the serious young man, the not-so-young draftee. All gone. And she could not even bring herself to mutter a prayer. Eddy, another iron link added to the already weighty chain of deaths in her life.

She knew she was not alone in her sorrow. Lulu mourned him (she and Eddy had been surprisingly, and annoyingly, close). And so did his nieces and nephews. And Raymond, who'd helped raise him. But they couldn't feel the loss the way she did. They were all a step removed.

She remembered that when she'd learned the news of his death, there was only one person she wanted, only one who might fully understand, only one whose embrace she needed to feel. Meche.

So thinking of Eddy, painful enough in itself, always brought with it that memory, that longing for her sister. The ache to hold her. It was with her now, the old gnawing emptiness. Eddy's death added a fresh sheen of grief to what Raymond termed her "spells," but they had begun decades before, when she'd first come north.

She heard the door open and her heart contracted even tighter. A weight next to her on the bed, a clink of metal on glass.

"Mom…? I brought you a cup of chamomile tea…"

Her daughter's normally welcome voice was like a drill.

"Would you rather have coffee? …It's just that chamomile is what you give us when we're sick. Dad's reading the paper, but I brought you this mystery I checked out from the library. It's a page-turner. You might like it."

Soli knew she should sit up and hug her daughter, but her head was too heavy, the morning light, too painful. And she couldn't face seeing the concern in her eyes.

"…I've got to go. …I'll leave the book and the tea on the nightstand. …Love you." Marilyn's voice trailed off. "Bye."

Soli heard the door click and she burrowed deeper into herself.

The next day Soli spent in misery. On the third day she woke mid-morning, the house quiet as a tomb. Returning from the bathroom, she did not bury herself once more under the covers, but sat up and took a sip from a fresh, but tepid, cup of tea. She opened the mystery left on the nightstand. By evening she was bored with the book and her back was sore from being in bed so long. She cursed Meche for laying her low, and herself for letting her, using the handful of bad words she knew, which struck her as too few and too feeble. She stripped the bed, and when she opened the bedroom door she found that Marilyn had left a dinner tray on a chair. She ate a few bites, took a bath and was just finishing putting fresh sheets on the bed when Raymond came home after a Knights of Columbus meeting.

He said nothing, but went to her. He kissed her on the forehead and held her tight.

She did not recoil.

"Nice to have you back," he said.

She nodded. "I have a request," she said.

He raised his eyebrows, wary.

"I need you to teach me swear words," she said.

He looked at her askance. "You? Salty language?"

"The saltier the better. English. German. Spanish if you know any."

His face was taking on a puzzled, yet stern expression, and she felt a flash of irritation. Before he could deny her, she slipped from him and went to Marilyn's room.

Marilyn, with big pink curlers in her hair, sat hunched over her desk, wearing a robe, pajamas and fuzzy blue slippers. Soli switched off the overhead light, and Marilyn looked up, startled.

"Mom!" Marilyn said.

"Time for bed, mi amor. I'm going to tuck you in."

Marilyn gave her a funny look. "Mom, I'm 17."

"I know how old you are. Bed."

Marilyn dutifully took off her robe and slippers and climbed in.

"I don't know how you can sleep with those things all over your head," Soli said as she turned off the desk light.

She tightened the bedclothes around Marilyn, and Marilyn let out an amused huff. Soli made the sign of the cross on her daughter's forehead and kissed her on the cheek.

Once in the hall her face hardened, and she muttered, "Damn Meche, damn her to hell."

1 9 5 0...

Lulu felt a tingle of excitement as she sidled into the empty kitchen. Soli's household was teeming during the holidays, but for the moment there was no one in this part of the house. Just to be sure, she checked the mudroom. No one was there, and she smiled, feeling smug. Finding the rooms vacant seemed rather an accomplishment.

Turning towards the basement, her attention was drawn to Soli's cookie tins stacked at the end of the counter. She picked a red one with a rosy-cheeked Santa on the lid. Steadying it against her tummy, she pried the lid off. Zimtsternes! Soli had learned the recipe from her German mother-in-law, but Lulu's mother also used to bake something similar for Lulu's father. Lulu bit into one of the cinnamon stars and met the same spicy-sweet taste of her childhood. Mini explosions of pleasure and memory tickled her brain. Brushing crumbs from the shelf of her bosom, she wondered in which tin she would find the shortbread besitos.

Don't get distracted, she told herself. She slipped a couple cookies into the pocket of her cardigan sweater and went to listen at the basement door.

Who might she find down there? Soli, of course, but Soli had gone to the market. Raymond was at work. Several of Soli's older grandchildren were playing Monopoly on the coffee table in the living room, their crowing and groaning and arguing reaching into the kitchen. Upstairs the younger children had been put down for a nap. Soli's daughter Joyce, the pregnant one, and Lulu's own hubby, Joe, were also taking a snooze. And two of Soli's sons, Jack and Ernst, also at work, wouldn't arrive till later.

Meanwhile their wives were talking in hushed tones in the dining room, grown-up talk not meant for young ears. Who was she missing?

Lulu did so enjoy coming to Soli's house for the holidays, although at times the endless hubbub made her miss her little house, her and Joe's. Although, their house really was awfully small, quite modest. Joe insisted it was plenty big for just the two of them, but two or twenty, what did that matter? She wished it were grander.

She'd lived with her stepson, Eddy, up until the time he was drafted. That was in '43. They'd just raised the upper age limit, so even though he was 37, off he went. So handsome in his uniform. The spitting image of his father. She could never understand how they could take Eddy when she depended on him so. She told him to refuse. She'd heard there was a hardship deferment, but he wouldn't listen to her. He should have listened to her.

Lulu had moved back in with Soli because money was tight, and she couldn't bear living alone. So then, when Eddy didn't return, she was left stranded in that particular hell: the bustle of Soli's tribe and the day-in and day-out bedlam of kin. And none of it hers. Not really.

Well, her Joe had rescued her.

But their house really was terribly small.

If only she hadn't lost Ernesto, everything would have been different. So so different. Ernesto was her real husband, her first one. With him, everything would have been better.

"I tried, Ernesto," she thought. "Ruby warned me about taking on another woman's children, but it was my duty, wasn't it? My duty to you. Besides, I thought they would console me. I thought your children would love me.

"Oh, dear heart, I miss you still. I hope you don't mind about Joe." She sighed and took a cookie from her pocket. "And I miss Eddy. And my mother, too. And Ruby. (Of course, Ruby's not dead.)

"I miss Campeche. I even miss San Antonio."

She shook her head. "Life has not been fair to me, Ernesto," she mumbled aloud.

Then she smoothed her fine white hair and turned her attention back to her task: discovering where Soli had hidden her presents. She'd found the grandchildren's in Soli's closet, but not a single one for her.

She tiptoed down the basement steps, eyes shining with anticipation. How she loved American Christmas: presents and mistletoe and Christmas trees and stockings and Santa Claus and candy canes and tinsel and parties and lights and jingle bells and presents. She might be 68, but at that moment she felt like an eight-year-old.

She gave the basement room a cursory glance. The concrete floor radiated damp coldness and the furnace rumbled. Think like Soli, she told herself. The tip of her tongue lay against her upper lip and her brow furrowed in concentration.

She switched on the light in the laundry room and started looking in cupboards, singing under her breath a Christmas song from her childhood:

> *Naranjas y limas,*
> *limas y limones.*
> *Más linda es la Virgen*
> *que todas las flores.*

Aha! Why would there be dry towels in the wringer tub?

She lifted the pile and there underneath nestled a modest treasure trove. She found not only a present from Soli and Raymond and sloppily wrapped packages from Soli's grandchildren (homemade ashtrays and trinkets, no doubt), but an elegantly store-wrapped box. She picked it up and saw that, as she expected, it was from Joe.

Alas, it was too big for a jewelry box. Her other hand went to her ear, to the sapphire earring there, the pair that showed off her blue eyes. Eddy had had such good taste. Joe didn't, more's the pity. She loved surprises, but Joe was not good at those either, at least not agreeable ones, so after a little guidance from her, she could now count on some Chanel No. 5 perfume or bath talc when a gift was due from him. She rattled the box and something thudded inside: bath talc.

And look, a flat package from Ruby! It must be one of her photographs. Lulu slid her finger along part of the seam of the red tissue paper. The tape did not lift and the paper tore, and when she slid the cardboard folder from its wrapping, the corner caught and ripped the thin paper past repair. Oh well. She held the black folder and ran her thumb over the silver embossed logo: Fotografía Eckart, San Francisco de Campeche, Campeche.

Singing "Let it Snow," Marilyn, Soli's 16-year-old daughter, in bobby socks and black-and-white saddle shoes wandered into the kitchen with its green-and-yellow checkerboard linoleum. She saw the open tin of cookies, and crumbs on the floor. One of the little kids? Or…? The basement door was ajar and the lights on. She rolled her eyes and made her way down to the laundry room.

"Grandma Lulu!" she scolded.

Lulu's hands fluttered to her bosom and the black folder fell to the floor.

"Dios mío! You scared the living daylights out of me."

"It's Mom that's going to kill you, not me," Marilyn said. Lulu turned an impish face to her. Marilyn shook her head. "Why do you have to sneak open your presents? You know it drives Mom crazy."

"She doesn't have to know."

"Of course she does. You do such a terrible job of rewrapping them."

Lulu shooed the comment away. "They're my presents, aren't they?"

"Not until they're given to you."

"You sound like your mother," Lulu pouted. "Let's just look at this one, okay?" she said, picking up the folder.

Marilyn had to smile. Grandma Lulu had charmed her since she was little. Maybe because Marilyn was the baby of the family and Lulu was the only one who seemed more childish than herself, the only one who didn't boss her around. Grandma Lulu wheedled, but she didn't boss. Marilyn came to stand next to her, and Lulu pinched her cheek, which Marilyn hated, but would probably miss if Lulu didn't do it.

Lulu opened the cardboard folder slowly and with great drama, making Marilyn giggle.

The photo was a rather old-fashioned, formal portrait in sepia tones with Aunt Meche seated, and Great-Aunt Ruby standing. Only instead of standing beside her, Ruby stood behind with both hands resting on Meche's shoulders. Marilyn thought a second to make sure she had it straight: Meche was her mom's sister and Ruby was Grandma Lulu's sister. The painted backdrop behind them was of a balcony overlooking the ocean. Aunt Meche smiled slightly and Great-aunt Ruby did not.

"I don't think Mom is going to be too happy with this."

"I don't see why not."

"Well…" Marilyn was tempted to explain, but she didn't quite know how to put it in words.

"My, Ruby looks so much like Mother in this picture."

Then Lulu's expression changed. She pouted and pointed at the photo. "What is that blouse Ruby wears? And look at that." She jabbed her finger at the chair, the large pot that held a potted fern, and the rug. "And that, and that. They are all from the house at the rancho." Her voice took on a disapproving tone. "Looks like your Aunt Meche has made herself right at home there."

"But it is her home, isn't it?"

Lulu sniffed.

1 9 4 9 ...

Ruby kissed Meche on the top of her head, or rather on the fluffy curls of her perm, and sat down across from her. Meche kept reading the morning newspaper, her forehead crinkled in concentration.

"If you didn't read the newspaper, you'd be a happier person. Just look at me."

Ruby expected that to get a rise from her—Ruby was hardly known for her cheerful temperament—but Meche only looked up at her distractedly and gave her an unfocused smile. Ruby knew that Meche would be heading to the rancho after breakfast, and she was trying not to be waspish about it.

"And then," she added, rather jauntily, for her, "you wouldn't get wrinkles and you'd never need makeup."

"Already got them, thank you." Meche folded up the newspaper and set it on the table. "I was just thinking about Tía Pancha."

Ruby arched an eyebrow. Mention of her great-aunt soured her carefully framed mood.

"Do you ever wonder what she would think of the world today?" Meche tapped the newspaper. "On the plus side, there's free university in Argentina, thanks to Perón. She'd like that. And constitutionally disbanding the army in Costa Rica. Mao's close to winning the war in China. So many colonies gaining independence…"

Ruby shrugged. Tía Pancha's opinions were not something she'd ever been interested in, even when the woman was alive.

"But what would she think about Russia testing an atomic bomb?" Meche said. "And Israel and that war they just had with the Arab League?

Last month the Allies ended their occupation in Germany, well, West Germany. And now, this week, there's an East Germany!"

Ruby, a sour taste in her mouth, stared over Meche's shoulder at a stain on the wall and listened like a censor, blacking out the names and places in Meche's recitation—what she cared about was her corner of the world and Meche's running off to that blasted Baalam Kab.

The irony was that after Eddy's death it had been Ruby who'd sold Lulu on Meche's proposal for the rancho, resolving what had been an estate quagmire. Meche's father, Ernesto, had his will drawn up in 1910, just before the Revolution. He had thought that tradition and law mandated that he divide his estate equally amongst his children, but his lawyer informed him that the law had in fact changed in 1884—he was now allowed to favor one heir. Unfortunately for Meche, he chose Eddy, his only son, to inherit the largest portion of the rancho. But Eddy had never had any interest in returning to Mexico, much less in running a farm. His will, written in the US, left everything to Lulu, the only mother he'd known. Lulu's conjugal portion, as dictated by Mexican law, complicated things further, and Soli and Meche each had a minor share, as well, although Soli said her only concern was to honor their father's wish that Baalam Kab never be sold or broken up.

If it had ever gone to court, the lawyers on both sides of the border would have had a field day, or rather field years.

Meche had longed to run the farm ever since Ruby had known her. And she'd always complained bitterly about the ineptitude of the lawyer —whom Ruby quite liked—charged with overseeing the rancho's management. Ruby only half listened—after all, their life was in the city. But over the years, Meche became only more determined to take on Baalam Kab.

With Eddy gone, Lulu needed money. So despite Ruby's lack of interest in business matters, she decided it was time to get involved and help Meche, if only to get the notion of running the rancho out of her system. At the same time she would be helping her sister, who was back living with Soli and her husband and complaining of penury—claiming that the pittance she received from the lawyer was almost worthless in the US. More to the point, she proposed coming to live with Ruby in Campeche City. Impossible! The apartment was too small, not to mention that Meche detested Lulu. Nor could they let Lulu find out about her and Meche's consociation.

So Ruby, serving as go-between, sold Lulu on the rent-to-buy plan. Lulu would sign the rancho over to Meche, and in return, Meche would pay Lulu a percentage of the profits as long as Lulu lived, promising that, by getting rid of the lawyer and his fees, and running Baalam Kab properly, she could pay Lulu more than she was now receiving and that the amount would only increase as the rancho prospered. If Meche ended up selling the farm, Lulu would receive a set sum from the sale equivalent to the rancho's estimated worth at the time of transfer, minus all payments Meche had made up to the time of the sale. Meche was not happy about buying her own home from Lulu, but as Ruby reminded her every time she grumbled her way to Western Union to send a another payment, getting Baalam Kab was what mattered.

Ruby had told herself that the rancho would be a good thing for both her and Meche. They both had strong characters and neither was mellowing with age—the farm would get Meche out of her hair for a bit now and then, allowing Ruby to spend more uninterrupted time on her art photography.

But Ruby never imagined Meche would become so consumed, or that she would be gone so much. The litany of chores and mishaps and problems—beehive pests, the cost of processing sugar cane at a mill, fighting some disgusting horse disease called blackleg, the seven classes of hemp and which she should be cultivating—seemed only less endless than Meche's lengthy discussion of them.

Nor had Ruby fully considered the recklessness of the venture when it was only on paper. Over and over again, she expressed her concern for Meche traveling on back roads and being out in the sticks all alone.

"And," Ruby said. "farms are such dangerous places—horses to trample you, bulls to gore you, chemicals, machinery, machetes. And all those Indians. You could be killed in your sleep."

Meche had caressed Ruby's face. "Boxita, the Caste War ended, what, thirty, forty years ago?" She added, "You know, my father told me that my grandmother was terrified every time my grandfather came here to Campeche City. She was sure he was going to be killed by pirates."

Ruby scoffed, "But by then there wouldn't have been pirates for a couple hundred years."

Meche kissed Ruby. "And you don't need to worry about Indian uprisings any more than my grandmother about marauding buccaneers. Anyway, cities are much more dangerous than the countryside. Remember my father."

Now, this morning, Baalam Kab's siren call would once again pull Meche away from her. Ruby's black eyebrows knit together and she shifted her gaze from the stain on the wall to Meche's face.

"And President Alemán," Meche said, referring back to the newspaper. "What would Tía Pancha make of him? He did make a Campechan second in command, but he's too cozy with the United States, don't you think?"

"Leave me out of it, that's what I think," Ruby snapped.

Meche shook her head and closed the newspaper. "Really, Ruby. How can you not care about what's going on in the world?"

Meche was only 52, and on mornings like this, when she was anticipating a trip to Baalam Kab, Ruby saw flashes of the girl Meche had been. It made her feel old. She picked up the newspaper and dropped it on a chair seat.

"You're leaving me again," she said.

Meche's eyes narrowed. "I'm going to the rancho, if that's what you mean."

"Running off to play farmer."

"I'm not playing, Ruby. This is something I've always wanted. Always. You know that."

"You do realize, you're a grown woman. You don't need to prove your father wrong anymore."

Meche opened her mouth, and then snapped it shut. She took a deep breath. "You could come with me. If you would just come once, I know you'd fall in love with it."

Ruby harrumphed.

"Boxita, when are you going to accept Baalam Kab as part of our life?"

"Your life." Ruby felt the pressure of unhappiness inside her, misery bunching up in her chest. She picked up the newspaper again, but dropped it. What was she going to do, pretend to read it?

"You're away so much."

Meche looked away. She took a sip of her coffee, and staring into the glass, she said, "It's taking more time than I expected to get the rancho back in shape."

"Meche, don't lie to me."

"I'm not lying."

"You've always said how demanding a farm is."

"I know. It's just that it's not practical yet to hire a farm manager. I can't expect Don Jacinto to be much more than a supervisor. I've explained that to you."

"And we can afford to pay Carolina to fill in for you at the studio?" Ruby said resentfully.

"Yes. Barely, but yes. Ruby, Baalam Kab will become more profitable. I'm working on making it more profitable. For us."

"The studio hasn't done so badly."

"Ruby, the studio is yours. Besides, we're often scraping by. We could use more income."

Ruby stood abruptly.

"Where are you going?" Meche said.

"I'm not hungry."

"I'll come find you before I leave."

Ruby shrugged and headed for the stairs.

"Ruby!" Meche called after her.

Ruby turned to face her, hurt spreading across her face.

"I hate it when you're like this," Meche said.

"Like what?"

Meche shook her head. "Ay, tontita. Come here." And when Ruby did not move, Meche went to her and put her arms around her. Ruby remained rigid, but only for a breath or two.

As Meche pulled away from the city, she stepped on the clutch and slipped the gearstick into third gear. She felt the familiar surge of exhilaration, not from the old Ford pickup's unimpressive acceleration, but from seeing the city buildings fade from her rearview mirror.

And part of the feeling of lightness came from leaving Ruby behind.

Ruby had been so crabby of late. At the studio she behaved like a jaguar with a ceiba thorn in its paw. And at home she moped about Meche's involvement with the rancho, which wasn't fair, because Meche had worked in the studio for nigh on 40 years, without complaint, to help Ruby and support her work.

But Ruby was right. Meche had been spending more and more time at Baalam Kab—more time, if she were honest with herself, than was absolutely necessary. When Ruby had challenged her about her motives, she'd almost said that the rancho had been her first love, that it was her home. Luckily, she'd stopped herself—it would only have hurt Ruby, and there was no need for that.

Besides, no matter how happy she was to get away and be on the farm, the return trip to Campeche City always seemed interminable because, by then, she was ready to be back home with Ruby. And Meche always brought peace offerings: jam, tamales and empanadas made by Susana de los Ángeles, a braid of garlic, honey, fruits, vegetables, the sticks of fresh sugar cane that Ruby liked to chew.

Meche had two touchstones now: Ruby and Baalam Kab, and she wanted and needed them both.

Ruby would come around. She'd have to.

1 9 3 4 ...

Homesickness was like malaria. It never went away for good, and it would overtake Soli when she least expected it. Like now, as she laid Joyce's old baby clothes out on the bed to sort them, making ready for the new baby, the sadness rose like sap through the trunk of her body until her joints ached with it. She thought back to the rancho, back before her mother died, when they were a proper family and she and Meche were fond playmates.

It didn't help any that they were in the middle of an endless, icy, buried-in-snow winter—their eighth since leaving San Antonio for Wisconsin. It made Campeche seem farther away than ever, and to her children, a fantastical place.

She sighed. On days like these, it made her heart ache that there was so much of her childhood she could not share with her children, things like squeezing honey fresh from the comb, bathing her hands in what felt like the most luxurious lotion. Or the excitement of putting her shoes out on the night of January fifth for the little presents that the Three Kings would bring.

In preparation for their arrival, she and Meche would collect leaves and fruits from a ramón tree for the camels, which somehow seemed both more exotic and more tangible than the Magi. With great care and excitement, they arranged the forage at the edge of the service patio. And they begged Susana de los Ángeles for her three largest bowls so that they could put fresh water out, too. Surely a camel's head was too big to fit in a pail. Their mother told them to stop pestering Susanita, that the big bowls were all needed to prepare the holiday dinner.

The next morning, they would squeal with glee to find presents in their shoes, but then Meche would run to the back of the house, always returning disappointed that the camels had left no dung behind. She claimed she was curious to compare it to horse droppings, but Soli thought Meche felt cheated of proof of the miraculous. For Soli, her little gifts were thrilling enough, and all the evidence she needed.

Now, because her children believed in Santa Claus, she kept all of this to herself, like a dirty secret.

And to think that her children had never tasted a mango or a banana-leaf tamal! They'd never smelled freshly mopped terra-cotta tile in the morning before the heat of the day descended. They'd never fallen asleep to the smell of burning copal resin or the sound of chanting, flutes and drums drifting into their room late at night from some ceremony or other of the workers, the repetitiveness more than the volume making the songs heard across a distance. They'd never seen a coatimundi or a ceiba tree or the adobe walls of her family's home. They'd never heard the croak of a toucan or the rattle of a rattlesnake.

Soli hadn't actually heard a rattler either, but they were a constant fear of her childhood, and one of the reasons she'd stuck close to the house. But Meche had heard the warning rattle and claimed to love the sound, while at the same time narrating how frightening the encounter had been. One of the workers, probably one of the Mu's, had killed the thing with a machete and given Meche the rattle, which she used to tease Soli, chasing her around the house with it. But rattlesnakes were not the only creatures to spark nightmares. Once the sisters had heard a jaguar scream, and even though it was from the safety of their bed, just the memory of it sent chills up Soli's spine.

She and her children even shuddered over different terrors.

The world of Soli's children was all their own, a Wisconsin childhood they shared with their siblings and friends, not with her. What did she know of ice hockey or sleighs pulled by reindeer? She didn't know how to make snowballs or popcorn balls. The memories her children would linger over when they were grown up would be alien to her.

The stairs creaked and Lulu popped her head in.

"Here you are," she said in Spanish.

Soli forced a smile. Lulu always complained that the arrival of the children from school was loud and bothersome, but she always seemed at loose ends the couple hours before they arrived. So here she was.

Lulu came next to her, put her arm around her and gave a squeeze. She and Lulu spoke in Spanish when they were alone, which was a comfort, as was not having to explain anything about home.

Soli held up a tiny hand-knit sweater, pink with a stain on the shoulder. The smell of moth balls clung to it, and Lulu's nose twitched.

"Remember this?" Soli said.

"Looks like something one of the German relatives would make."

"Raymond's mother," Soli confirmed.

Soli's in-laws had followed them to Milwaukee within a year of their move.

Lulu pushed piles aside and sat on the bed with a bounce.

"Remember how sweet Joycie looked in it?" Soli said.

Lulu cocked her head. "It looks old-fashioned."

Soli frowned. "Really? Well, it is about 16 years old. Remember when I was expecting the first time? Mother Eckart made a blue one and this pink one, just in case. Three boys in a row! The poor sweater languished in the closet for years and years. Until Joycie came along." Soli smiled.

Joycie was six now, and Soli missed the heft of an infant in her arms. The memory of holding her babies was keen. It made her breasts ache as if ready to nurse. Losing herself in the sensations of her body, she held her taut, stretched belly and felt how the baby seemed to lean into her arms. Come out and play, she thought.

"Is something wrong?" Lulu asked, alarmed.

Soli met Lulu's blue eyes a bit surprised. She pulled invisible marionette strings to jerk a smile into place and shook her head no. She knew it made Lulu nervous to be alone in the house with her so close to her due date. Lately she would look up and find Lulu watching her with a somewhat martyred look on her face, as if Soli were having a baby purely to cause her distress.

"I suppose," Soli said, to shift the subject a bit, "I should sort through the boys' old things. Just in case. Find some clothes that aren't pink."

"Soli, no more boys, please."

"Not to worry. I think this one's a girl. A little sister for Joycie."

Lulu raised her eyebrows, unimpressed by Soli's prediction.

"I'd like another daughter," Soli mused. "I'd like to name her after my mother."

Lulu's face clouded, as if Soli had slighted her.

Soli often found Lulu easier to read than her own children. So she knew Lulu was thinking, what about me? But Soli, fifteen when Lulu came into her life, had never considered Lulu a mother. Maybe an aunt. Or a cousin. After 24 years together, mostly under the same roof, their relationship was a tangle of layers and events and emotions. That was enough. That was plenty.

"But Soli," Lulu said, "your mother's been dead forever."

Soli flinched a little. Even after all these years, hearing the word "dead" and her mother in the same breath was like a jab in the gut.

Lulu didn't notice. In fact she pouted a little. Soli laid the little pink sweater on the bed and smoothed it with her hand. After a moment, Lulu jabbed at the shoulder of the little sweater.

"What about the stain?" she said.

Soli shrugged. "It will be just as warm."

"Ay, hija, you sound more and more like your in-laws."

Maybe she did, but did Lulu not remember they were in the midst of a great depression? Soli handed Lulu a pile of diapers.

"Here, count these."

Lulu took the stack and set it back on the bed.

"Lulu!"

Lulu smiled impishly and Soli picked up the pile and counted. Some of the cloths were pretty thin and worn. Could she make them do? She started to calculate the minimum yardage of flannel needed to make a more comfortable number, but Lulu interrupted her thoughts.

"We should go home," Lulu said.

"What?"

"Home! Home to Campeche. It's too cold here. Too dreary. I don't like it."

"Lulu! You can't…"

Lulu waved Soli's words away. "Think of the sun. The blue sky. The…"

Soli held up her hand to stop her. "Besides the fact that my home and family are here, you and I don't have enough money to get to Chicago, much less the 2,500-plus miles to Campeche." She plopped the diapers on the bed. "Campeche does have its drawbacks, you know."

Lulu looked affronted.

Soli persisted. "Don't you remember how you used to complain about the sun and the heat?"

"Nonsense. It's the perfect climate."

Soli wondered if she were serious. Sometimes it was hard to tell.

"Ay, hija," Lulu coaxed. "Let's go. You're not happy either. And you're cold, too."

Soli giggled. It was absurd. "I'm due in two weeks."

"Poor baby, having to be wrapped in smelly wool sweaters so it doesn't die of exposure."

"Lulu, really!"

"Your problem, well one of your problems, is that you have no imagination."

"Be sensible."

"No. And you're no fun. You worry all the time."

"Of course I worry. I have four children, and a fifth about to be born." And, she thought, you and Eddy living with us again.

"But Raymond has a job." Lulu said.

"But for how long? You know more than half the workers in Milwaukee have lost their jobs!" Tears slid down Soli's face. She couldn't help it. "What if Raymond's next?"

Lulu stood and gave her a hug. She felt soft and pillowy.

"Don't cry, hija. Raymond tells you not to worry, and he's your husband. Love, honor and obey." Lulu snapped her fingers. "So, don't worry."

Soli groaned.

"Besides, there are those work programs now, aren't there? And the state passed that unemployment insurance scheme, so if worse comes to worse and Raymond…"

"Don't even say it!"

"And," Lulu squeezed Soli's cheek and jiggled it, "you always have me and Eddy."

Soli looked into Lulu's smiling pale-blue eyes and shook her head in disbelief.

"I told you, mi amor," Soli said, "I want to name this baby Blanca Estela for my mother.

"Blanca Estela?" Raymond said in his matter-of-fact way. "That's quite a mouthful."

"No, it's not."

"She won't thank you for it, Soli."

"I don't know why not. It's a pretty name," she said. "Romantic."

Although, she thought, not so pretty the way it came out of Raymond's mouth.

Raymond held up the solid little baby, whose face relaxed into a frown.

"Somehow I don't think this one will be very romantic," he said.

The name was important to Soli. She hadn't pushed for it when Joyce was born. Now she was forty. This baby might well be her last.

"I'm afraid," Raymond continued, "she's going to take after my father's mother. She's the spitting image of Oma Hildeberta."

Soli made a face, like she'd smelled pickled herring, which she loathed (and Raymond loved).

"Don't worry," Raymond laughed. "I'm not suggesting we saddle her with that name. But having Lulu and Eddy as her godparents, isn't that enough of a connection to your family?"

"No, it is not."

"But Soli, this is Wisconsin. Blanca Estela is too…"

"Too what?"

"No one will say it right or spell it right. She won't fit in."

"Why does she need to fit in?"

"I'm just telling you. Once she's in school, she'll hate the name. She'll end up resenting you, you and your mother both."

"Nonsense," she said, but a doubt crept in.

"Let's at least consider some alternatives."

"No," she said. She hated it when he treated her like a recalcitrant child. "You named Jack. You named Frank. And you named Joyce."

"Ah, but Ernst is named for your father."

"My father's name was Ernesto."

"Same thing."

"No it's not."

She took the baby from him. Cradling her, Soli brought her face close and studied the little face. The baby gazed back at Soli with solemn eyes.

"And we didn't name Jack 'Johannes' as my father wanted," Raymond said. "He's still sore about it."

"That's different. We couldn't very well give Jack a German name when the United States was at war with Germany."

On the way to the christening, Soli's oldest, fifteen-year-old Jack, grumbled about the baby's name. He was sitting behind his father and he leaned forward, resting his crossed arms on the back of the front seat.

"Aw, Dad, it's not too late to change your mind. I mean, that name! It's just too long and too foreign. It's embarrassing."

Raymond glanced at Soli, eyebrows raised, but she avoided meeting his eyes and instead stared straight ahead, holding the baby tight.

"The baby's name is your father's and my decision," Soli snapped.

The night before, standing by the crib in the privacy of their bedroom, Soli had agreed to a last-minute compromise: the baby would be called Marilyn Blanca Estela. But in the haste of getting everyone up and dressed and bundled into the car, they hadn't said anything to the children.

"But Ma..."

"That's enough," Raymond growled. "One more word and I'll give you something real to complain about."

"Doesn't a fellow have a right…"

Raymond's hand flung backward, avoiding Joyce sitting in the front seat between him and Soli. The blow glanced off Jack's ear.

"Ow!"

Jack sank back into the seat. Frank smirked, and Ernst looked miserable.

Soli knew she shouldn't let herself be offended by a 15-year-old boy, but she was.

She tried to put aside the resentment she felt, the regret at giving in on the baptismal name. In Mexico this baby would be christened Blanca Estela Eckart Hernández (her family name added after Raymond's), but here her children weren't considered Hernández's. She couldn't even give them her family name.

When they piled out of the car at the church, she called sharply to Jack. He trudged over to her, slouching and sullen. She handed him the baby, and he looked at her questioningly.

"What is my maiden name?" she said.

Jack glanced in his father's direction, but he was busy greeting his parents, who had also just arrived. Ten-year-old Frank came and leaned against Soli.

"Jack?" She looked seriously into his face.

"Hernández?" Jack said, sobering under her gaze.

"What else?"

Jack shrugged.

"Cruz," Soli prompted. "Hernández Cruz. Your grandmother's name was Cruz."

"Yeah," Jack nodded.

"And your grandfather's name?"

He looked mischievous. "Jacob Joh.."

"Your other grandfather, may he rest in peace."

Jack rolled his eyes. "Ernesto Ezequiel Hernández."

"What else?"

"Ernesto Ezequiel Hernández Hernández."

"Bueno."

"It's a dumb name," he grumbled.

Soli narrowed her eyes in response.

"And your grandmother, my mother, may she rest in peace?"

Jack sighed. "Blanca Estela Cruz …I don't remember."

"González," Soli said.

"González," he said, and then added sheepishly, "May she rest in peace."

Soli nodded, and taking advantage of Jack's arms being full, she tousled his hair.

1 9 3 3 ...

Lulu hated afternoons, the hours dripping slowly. Cold-molasses hours, she called them. And it was so cold out. Cold, freezing, icy, chilly. People back home had no idea what those words really meant. She certainly hadn't. So dark, too, the winter sun in a race to set ever earlier. What had she been thinking letting Soli drag her and Eddy away from San Antonio? Would she never again have a pan dulce with her morning café con leche? If she thought about it anymore, she would cry.

She plopped into her light-blue wingback chair and put her feet up on the ottoman. She picked up a magazine that she'd bought at the drugstore: *Photoplay,* with Greta Garbo on the cover. She looked halfheartedly at the pictures.

She supposed she could go visiting. Soli might have a nice tidbit to eat, even though she couldn't get the ingredients to make anything truly delicious, that is, something like in Campeche. But Lulu didn't like taking the bus. It was freezing waiting for it, freezing riding on it, freezing walking to the house—the wind biting at her stockinged ankles and swirling up her skirt. Ice lying in wait to bring her low. Besides, by the time she got there, and settled in for a nice chat, it would be time for school to let out, and there would be the four kids demanding Soli's attention. Of course she liked Soli's kids, but all of them at once was trying. No, going to Soli's wasn't worth the effort.

She could go shopping, but again, there was the cold to fend off. Besides, she didn't like struggling with English. She wanted to speak Spanish. And who did she know who spoke Spanish? Soli.

Oh, to be back in Campeche. Or even San Antonio.

It was Raymond who'd charmed her into coming to Wisconsin with him, Soli and the kids. It wasn't fair. Soli had her handsome husband, while Lulu's husband was dead.

"Muerto, bien muerto!" she said aloud, her face screwed up. She tossed the magazine aside. Dead. Deader than ever.

Here she was in this ugly, foreign city. Alone. Fifty-one years old, Fifty-one! Though she was the only one who knew it. Her age was no one's business but her own.

The radio next to her wasn't working, and the unwelcome quiet made the little bungalow seem even lonelier. And chillier, too. She stared at her wool stockings, smoothed her housedress over her legs. It was a green cotton with cheerful little white, orange and yellow flowers. Not very warm, but she found heavier clothing dispiriting. She did wear the cardigan that Soli had knit for her. It was almost the same blue as the chair upholstery, which seemed in questionable taste on Soli's part. Just because Lulu liked curtains or a sofa or a rug, didn't mean she wanted to wear them!

She tapped her fingers on the arm of her chair.

The radio's insistent silence felt hostile, like it was snubbing her, and she glared at it. She had wanted a highboy model, one that also had a phonograph, but Eddy had brought home this tabletop one. He'd pointed out that it was a Philco, and cathedral style, and some gobbledegook about its inner workings. When the radio died, she suggested they get a new one, but Eddy said it just needed a tube. He promised to take care of it, but he kept forgetting, which was unlike him. He was usually so attentive.

Cooking would warm the house up. It was too early to start on dinner, but maybe she could bake something nice for herself and Eddy. She'd asked him again about getting some household help. She thought they might just afford it, but he was reluctant. Well, that would come in time, as he advanced in his career. Meanwhile, it turned out that cooking was largely a matter of organization, and she could always do that, ever since her days at the photo studio, keeping the books and ordering supplies.

Not that it gave her any satisfaction. Luckily Eddy was not a picky eater, and always so appreciative. And if she had one of her sick headaches, he would fend for himself. He would cook something for her, too, if she was well enough to eat. Yes, a little treat for Eddy and herself, even if her having to make it took away from the enjoyment. She got to her feet.

Soli had made her two aprons as a housewarming gift (she would have preferred a nice vase), and Lulu took one of them from the drawer and put her neck through the loop. Needless to say, style was not Soli's strong suit. The practical garment hung down to her knees, with no ruffles, a bit of rickrack for decoration, and lots of pockets. Lulu was pulling the tin of flour from the cupboard when she heard the front door open. How odd. She peered from the doorway to the kitchen.

It could only be Eddy, and it was.

Her face broke into a smile. "Eddy, cariño! I'm so glad you're home. I've been so bored! It's been a molasses afternoon if ever there was one."

She always spoke to him in Spanish and he always answered her in English. She went to him and offered her cheek for a peck. His face was grave.

"You're home early. Are you sick?"

He returned her peck and plopped on the couch.

"Eddy, what is it?

"I'm sorry, Mamalú. I'm so sorry."

"Ay, hijo!" She sat next to him and took his hand. "Tell me."

He pulled his hand from hers and ran it through his hair.

"I've failed you."

"What are you talking about?"

"You took me on as your son. You didn't know me from Adam, and yet you did that."

"Of course, cariño. You are your father's son, so I loved you even before I met you."

He bit his lip and covered his mouth with his hand.

Looking at his stooped shoulders, she thought, when I married his father I was 28, and here he is, 27, and how world-weary he looks.

Looking at his bent head, the chestnut-brown hair, she recalled the little five-year-old who used to cling to her, when what she needed more than anything was someone strong enough for her to hold on to. He'd intuited that, or had she told him? Because ever since he was a little boy, he'd always promised that when he grew up, he would take care of her.

"The bank closed today." His voice quavered. He drew his hand over his eyes.

"Oh, hijo," she said, a bit relieved, because, after all, a job was just a job.

And yet a cold queasiness in the pit of her stomach took hold. Were they, she and Eddy, to be swept up in this terrible thing they called a depression? Dios mío, did her tribulations never end?

"I'm sorry. I'm so sorry," he said.

"Hijo, look at me. You have no reason to be sorry. It will be fine. There are other banks, no? You're smart, well-mannered, from an excellent family. You'll get another job."

"Banks are closing right and left, Mamalú. I know more people who are out of work than who are working."

"Well, if it takes time…"

Eddy's eyes took on a haunted look. She'd seen that look on the newsreels. She did not expect to see it in her home.

"Stop that. Right now!"

"Stop what?"

"Looking like that. Like some whipped puppy."

"But…"

"Remember who you are. You're not some peon begging for a handful of beans. You are your father's son. You are Eduardo Ernesto Hernández, so act like it."

He sat up a bit straighter.

"I'm relying on you."

He swallowed hard.

"And I'll help, Eddy. We may not have a lot of money, but I can be quite good with budgets and all. Remember, I used to run the photography studio back home. We'll pull through, you'll see. I did not take us out of a revolution to perish in Wisconsin because of some stupid bank."

He took her hands, and she again felt the strength she'd come to rely on.

"I'm not sure you completely understand," he said. "We don't have any money. We may end up losing the house."

"But your savings…"

My savings were in the bank. And yours too. They're gone."

October 23, 1933

Today I am 96.

So, what is my secret for a long life, you may ask; and how do I find myself on this somewhat momentous day?

Well, surprised, for one thing; my family, as a rule, is not long-lived. But then, I never paid much attention to rules. Rules almost always conceal some inequity or other. Perhaps my longevity is due to a contraband bloodline of which I'm unaware. It's not impossible, for my mother had opportunity. My father was a sea-going captain of very modest vessels transporting people and goods a very modest distance. He was really more of a coastal-going captain, Champotón and Mérida being his most common destinations. Like many in our San Román neighborhood, he carried on the family sideline of smuggling that he'd learned at his father's and grandfather's knee (I wonder if my great-nieces, Lulu and Ruby, are aware of that? It's not type of information their mother would pass on). My father's extracurricular profession necessitated many nights away from home, so it's not inconceivable that my mother might have participated in some illicit traffic of her own.

I am 96 years old.

I repeat it not because my bandolier is short a cartridge or two, but to convince myself that it's true.

Am I proud to reach such a venerable age? Not particularly. Not dying is a dubitable accomplishment at best. And looking down at this page, I am chagrined. Can this truly be my hand, age-spotted and claw-like, and this my handwriting? The ink drooling from my pen looks more like Arabic than proper Spanish. And to think I once taught penmanship!

If I were inclined to take pride in being old, so very old, I would be put in my place by the report that this past spring, Li Ching Yuen, the oldest man since the Bible, died in China at the age of 256 years! Not that I believe everything, or anything, for that matter, that I read in the capitalist press (or the Bible), but I do read it, for it's important to know the latest lies they are propounding.

It's a cloudy, rainy day, and I peer at my pages in the dim afternoon light, swathed like a mummy against the cold, which seems to emanate outward from the marrow of my bones rather than seeping in from outside. Because of the chill or because of my age (96 years!), I close my strained eyes and think of Campeche: the air hot and cottony, the light so bright it makes you squint, the sky and sea so blue it saturates the eye and memory forever so that no other color can ever claim to call itself blue with any conviction.

In my mind's eye I see the buildings there painted in cake colors: pastel pink and yellow and green. I wind my way to San Román, my old neighborhood outside the crumbling city wall where the sea-going workers live: sailors, captains and smugglers, sailmakers and rope dealers. I'm heading for my father's house, passed down through three generations (my great-nieces the last of the family to have lived there). I arrive at the coral-colored house with the plain facade, the shuttered windows with iron grillwork and the lovely little interior patio.

Oh, to have the Campeche sun soak into my bones and the humidity wrap me in its soft blanket. Oh, to smell the salt in the air and the aroma of frying fish.

How am I today? Apparently uncharacteristically sentimental.

But I am content. My day started with a telegram from my Lulu, the dear, and a birthday card from her sister, Ruby. Of course, it's really from Meche. A good one, that Meche. She's just what Ruby needed, and just what she got, despite herself. Lulu and Ruby: my Campechanas, I haven't seen them in ages. Ten years, twenty? But I think of them often, and am pleased they still think of me. I remember them as toddlers, almost five decades ago now, the two of them like someone might make salt and pepper shakers: Lulu, pale and pink and chubby with wispy yellow curls, and Ruby, dark and wiry, her deep-brown eyes wide with wonder, and always searching for Lulu's, also wide, but blue and a bit apprehensive.

I have no other blood family, nor do I want any. But, if I did have a daughter, I would want her to be strong in character like Ruby, and soft in spirit like Lulu. My perfect daughter would have both Ruby's depth and Lulu's playfulness, and like Lulu, she would accept love, and accept me. And of course, unlike either of them, my daughter would be politically committed. That's my overly fertile imagination at work, but if not for this feverish imagination, how else could I have been a feminist socialist-anarchist in Mexico in the earliest years of this 20th century, envisioning against all odds a different world for my working-class brethren and for all my sisters?

The girls' telegram and card have place of honor on my desk. I can glance at them as I write. Besides this diary, there's the article I'm working on in support of the boycott of German goods called for by the Israelite Chamber of Industry and Commerce. I must ask Elena to type it for me, and find a place for it in one of the revolutionary papers (I do miss the days when anything I wrote had an instant outlet.).

My hand tires and this scrawl worsens. It's as good as a cipher. I could say that that permits me to write in total freedom, but I have always done that. It's landed me in jail more than once. I think of what our great Ricardo Flores-Magón wrote from prison:

> *"Perhaps when I die, my friends will write, 'Here lies a dreamer,' and my enemies, 'Here lies a madman.' But there will be no one who dares put this inscription: 'Here lies a coward and a traitor to his ideas.'"*

He was near death when he wrote that, as I must be: I am 96, after all. (I have no intention to rival Li Ching Yuen.) Maybe I'll use it for my epitaph. What's a little plagiarism among comrades?

Do not misunderstand. I am not being morbid (at my age, what more proper subject than death?). Nor am I depressed. Quite the contrary.

This evening, my young comrades (Some of my "young" comrades are in their sixties!) will crowd into my dusty little room and bring a cake. They are my family, like-minded revolutionaries bonded not by mutual blood as I am with my Campechanas, but by the blood of the fallen. I look forward to our little party. I'm anxious to hear the latest news, particularly of this new League of Revolutionary Writers and Artists. Fascism must be confronted and fought!

Carlos will play his guitar. There will be singing, and they will ask me to tell my tales of fighting the Porfiriato, of the underground newspapers and going to jail, of the Revolution, and of Ricardo and the other heroes I knew and worked with. I should be glad they listen to me, but I want to be more than a musty history book. I want to do more. I can still lift my pen. As Ricardo said, "Defiance is life. Submission is death."

My revolutionary family holds those words dear. My Lulu doesn't understand them, but she loves me. Ruby understands only too well, but refuses to understand me. Ah, well.

I must write them, my dear Campechanas of my blood, and thank them for their kind wishes. When my hand is stronger. And the article finished. Tomorrow.

1 9 3 1 ...

People at the market
looked at Susana de los Ángeles strangely. Here she'd just asked to do
chores in exchange for food, and in the next breath was asking about
photography studios—perhaps she was a bit mad. A lady who worked at
one of the vegetable stands told her not to bother with a studio—there
was a man in the Plaza de la Independencia who would take her picture
on his wooden pony for a lot less money. It was a fishmonger who told
her what she needed to know—and with a smirk, a lot more that she
wished he hadn't.

That was yesterday. Now she stood under a blazing sun on a street of
two-story buildings. The impassive expression on her face masked raw
nerves and desperation. She hoped, she needed, to find Señorita Meche.
She waited half a block from the studio.

So far she hadn't seen anyone enter or leave.

She stared down at the concrete sidewalk. More precisely at her foot.
The left one, and the sandal on it. At the upper made of narrow leather
strips woven together. So many had come unsewn from the sole that it
cost her to walk. The right sandal was holding together better, but she
saw that a third piece had worked loose. What could she do? Not buy
new ones or pay to get these repaired.

Madre de Dios, don't let me end up shoeless, she pleaded silently.
Please, Virgencita, please. That would be almost as shameful as going
without clothes.

Her head swam. She'd heard things about Señorita Meche, disturbing
things. From the fishmonger, yes, but others, too. Susana de los Ángeles
wanted to have a look at her before deciding to speak to her.

Deciding? Did she have a choice?

Ay, la Meche! Was she, of all people, really Susana de los Ángeles' last hope? Her stomach would churn with embarrassment, but it was so damn empty.

And how was she to even recognize her? Señorita Meche would be thirty-something now—the last time Susana de los Ángeles had seen her, she was a mere girl, thirteen years old.

The door to the studio opened.

She saw a lady step onto the sidewalk. Brown hair, short and wavy. A green linen dress almost to her ankles, a cloche hat, low black heels with ankle straps. She carried a clutch bag in one hand. Susana de los Ángeles squinted. Could this stylish lady be the tomboy who used to gallop up to the patio? Slide off her horse and shout for the boy José María to come tend to it?

Or might this be that other woman? The one people said took the pictures and had the same name as above the door? Eckart, they said. She could read enough to make out the name.

The man who owned the shop where she waited on the sidewalk had pointed it out to her. Bored, he stood in the doorway, resting his hands atop the bulge of his stomach. He lifted a hand from his belly and waved in the direction of the lady who was heading down the street.

"There. That's Señorita Meche, the lady you asked about."

"Gracias, señor," she said, bobbing her head.

"Well?" he said.

She took a deep breath and hobbled down the sidewalk, the sole of her sandal slapping the concrete.

Meche stopped to look at a display of sewing machines—she had zero interest in needlework of any kind, but admired the metalwork and wondered about the mechanism of the treadle.

She'd been anxious to get out of the studio, if only for a moment—it was clear Ruby would not be emerging from her darkroom for some time—so she'd invented an errand to the pharmacy down the street.

Continuing on, Meche heard someone behind her, someone with an odd-sounding, lopsided gait. She glanced back and saw a ragged Indian woman who stopped and lowered her head when Meche looked at her. There was something familiar about her, and Meche walked toward her.

"Susana de los Ángeles?"

Susana de los Ángeles nodded. "Buenos días, Señorita Meche."

"What are you doing here? Why aren't you at the rancho?" Meche felt an irritation. Did no one stay where they were supposed to?

Susana de los Ángeles's eyes flashed, and Meche took a better look at her: the worn-out clothes, the broken sandal, the beaten look of her stance. "You're not at the rancho anymore?"

Susana de los Ángeles shook her head. "I wondered, señorita, if you had a job for me here."

Although Mexico felt smug about escaping the horrors happening in the U.S., their country was far from unscathed by the North's economic collapse.

"Me?" Meche scoffed.

Business at the studio was not good, and if there were any odd jobs to do, Meche was the one who did them. She saw Susana de los Ángeles blanch.

"I'm sorry, we... I don't have a housekeeper. I live very simply above the studio."

"I don't have to be a housekeeper, señorita. Any little job..." she forced herself to say, and even as she tried to put herself forward, she took a step back. She tripped on the sandal and Señorita Meche caught her arm and kept her from toppling.

Meche looked into Susana de los Ángeles' eyes before she darted them away.

Meche remembered those eyes well. They used to narrow when Susana de los Ángeles scolded her, which she did often. One day Meche stood up to her—she was thirteen by then.

"If I choose to track muck into *my* house, Susana de los Ángeles, because it is *my* house, I will."

After that, slaps on the hand and harsh words stopped, but dirty looks and sighs abounded—on both sides.

Meche mostly recalled Susana de los Ángeles bustling in the kitchen alongside Soli and delivering platters of food to the dining room table. Now she looked as if she'd missed more than a few meals. Meche could at least give her a good lunch. Well, maybe not good, but adequate. And she did want to know why she'd looked angry when asked about Baalam Kab.

"Listen," Meche said, "come back to the apartment. We can have a proper talk there."

Susana de los Ángeles remained staring at the sidewalk. Señorita Meche said there was no job. So why enter her den of iniquity? But she'd also said, *I* live simply, not *we*. Maybe Susana de los Ángeles wouldn't have to meet this Eckart woman.

"For heaven's sake, let's get out of this sun," Meche said.

Susana de los Ángeles nodded. "Gracias, señorita."

Meche headed back to the studio, Susana de los Ángeles behind her on the narrow sidewalk, the sound of the broken sandal letting Meche know she was following.

"And I want to hear all about Baalam Kab," she called over her shoulder.

Of course she does, Susana de los Ángeles thought. She's always been in love with that rancho.

When Susana de los Ángeles Azteca left Baalam Kab, she'd decided to give Mexico City a try. After all, she was a descendent of Mexica from there, converts to Catholicism who had arrived in Campeche City with the Spanish conquistadors way back in 1540. Her family was proud of their Aztec heritage, proud of their religion and proud of being a part of colonizing Campeche. When she had to leave the rancho, she thought, why not check out her family's ancestral home?

But Mexico City did not feel like home. It was big, dirty, noisy and cold. It didn't help any that, at the time, the capital was the jewel—a tarnished one in her opinion—being fought over by the various factions of the Revolution. There were times when food was scarce, times when she could not go out in the street for the shooting.

In 1925, she decided to try her luck in California—the land of sun and movie stars and opportunity. When the great depression hit, repatriation drives—to preserve "American jobs for real Americans"—targeted Mexicans and Mexican-Americans. Susana de los Ángeles, caught up in one of the many deportation sweeps, was packed onto a train crammed with deportees. During the trip south she'd befriended a woman who—when the woman wasn't crying—told her in halting Spanish how she was seized along with hundreds of others in a neighborhood park. She told the officers that she'd never been to Mexico even once, that she'd been born right there in California, but they turned a deaf ear.

Since Susana de los Ángeles had no reason to return to Mexico City, she made her way to Campeche City, the city she'd left when she was a little girl. But she'd been away too long. In Mexico City or Los Angeles she could walk up to a factory and get a job, but here, since no one knew her, all doors seemed shut. Señorita Meche was her last, her only, straw to grasp.

As Susana de los Ángeles followed Señorita Meche up the narrow stairs at the photography studio, her eyes searched in every direction for signs of depravity, even as she told herself, a person had to eat—she had to eat.

"Señorita Meche, the stairs need sweeping," she pointed out.

Meche, eyebrows arched, looked back and down at Susana de los Ángeles. First she thought she was criticizing her, then Meche realized from the expression on the woman's face that she was still fishing for a job.

"That's ok," Meche said. "Nobody sees them but me."

Señorita Meche went to the stove in the small kitchen. Susana de los Ángeles saw two cups on the table, and two plates with toast crumbs, two greasy knifes. Señorita Meche turned, a tea kettle in her hand, and saw her staring at the table.

"Nobody sees that either."

Susana de los Ángeles met her eyes, then looked away. She quickly stepped forward to take the kettle from Señorita Meche.

"Let me, señorita," she murmured.

Meche handed the kettle to her and dropped onto one of the two chairs at the table.

"Are you hungry, señorita? I'll make you lunch."

"All right. As you can imagine, I'm a lousy cook. There are some bits and pieces in the ice box. Make enough for two."

Susana de los Ángeles' empty stomach flipped.

"Two, señorita?"

Meche thought about Ruby, busy in her darkroom. She wouldn't want to be interrupted for lunch.

"You are going to eat, too, aren't you?"

Susana de los Ángeles nodded with a tight-lipped smile. A spot of hope splashed inside her chest.

Meche arrived at the lawyer's outer office with Susana de los Ángeles in tow. She bade her sit while she spoke to the licenciado's secretary. The young lady behind the desk responded in the negative to Meche, shaking her head, petulant about appointments and such.

Meche cut her off, "I cannot wait."

She strode to the door of the inner office, rapped twice and opened without waiting for a response. Licenciado Mauricio De la Cruz looked up from his desk, his head resting on one hand as he tapped the end of his fountain pen against his teeth.

"Thank you, Miss Sánchez. I will see Señorita Hernández now," he said loudly, because he could see his secretary seated at her desk, as startled by Meche's trespass as she was irritated.

He rose and came around the desk, smiling paternally. He held a chair for Meche before closing the door. Meche couldn't dislike the man. He was always thoughtful and always seemed pleased to see her. He was also the only friend of her father that she knew. But a lawyer had no business running a farm. And certainly not from an office days away from Baalam Kab.

"Señorita Meche, what can I do for you?"

"Our housekeeper, Susana de los Ángeles Azteca, is sitting out there..."

His eyebrows furrowed.

"Our housekeeper at the rancho," she said.

His eyebrows flew up to say, ah, I see.

"She's just been shipped back from the United States under some bogus repatriation scheme."

His eyebrows were sneaking together again.

"She needs her job back. She belongs at Baalam Kab."

"As I've explained before, I leave such matters in the hands of the mayordomo."

"And that's the problem, licenciado."

Mauricio De la Cruz sighed. This opinion was not news to him. He doubted it was the farm manager per se that she was upset about. The real issue was that Ernesto's daughter had never accepted that her father had left the rancho to her baby brother Eduardo.

Ernesto had consulted De la Cruz about his will. That was in 1910. As a widower, he'd been concerned for some time that the farm wasn't big enough to split up amongst his three children, and now that he'd become betrothed, there was the prospect of more offspring.

Mauricio explained that the law had changed since Ernesto had inherited the farm and no longer required the mandatory designation of all legitimate children as equal heirs. Ernesto was relieved, and Mauricio himself drafted his friend's will, and with the usual formalities.

> *I, Ernesto Ezequiel Hernández Hernández, declare I
> was born at Rancho Baalam Kab in the Municipality of
> Hecelchakán and do there reside.*
>
> *First, I profess my faith in the one Holy Church:
> Catholic, Apostolic and Roman, and in all its mysteries,
> in which I have lived and wish to die.*
>
> *Second, upon my death, I beg my executor to bury my
> body in a modest manner...*

The will named Mauricio executor and assigned him to oversee the farm until Eduardo was of age, and in accord with the law, it directed him to use the earnings from the rancho to provide a pension for his wife and for any underage children.

The last time the lawyer had seen Eduardo, right before he and the others left for the United States, the boy was in short pants, shy and clinging to the nearest skirt, usually his sister Soli's. But Señorita Meche had stayed in Campeche. She had his friend's brown eyes and the same set of the jaw, and he'd watched her grow into a young lady. Now in her thirties, she was a spinster, while the brother was an accountant in the U.S. with apparently no interest in farming or in Mexico.

How the Revolution had scattered the country's sons and daughters! How many more it had put in the ground! One million. Maybe two. Thinking this, a pang of grief tore at his chest, and he shook his head.

Meche took the gesture as a denial.

"That man *is* the problem," she said, incensed. "He's not to be trusted."

"But your father did trust him, señorita, and so do I."

"Hijo de puta!" Meche exclaimed.

Mauricio, appalled, protested, "Señorita Meche!"

She stood and paced. "I didn't mean you, licenciado. You're not a son of a bitch. And not my father either." She hesitated a moment, well maybe her father a bit. "I'm referring to Escalante. He's been robbing us for years, you know."

"I review the books once a year."

"Once a year! And what do you know about a rancho's accounts, what they mean or what they should say? The books he gives you are pure fiction. You allow him an entire year to compose them."

"Really, señorita. Your brother is satisfied with the arrangement."

"My brother! He knows even less than you. Escalante runs Baalam Kab like it's his own little fiefdom. I saw what he was like when I was a girl, and now you've given him carte blanche. If you want to know what's really going on at the rancho, just ask Susana de los Ángeles. She's out there in your waiting room."

"Señorita Meche, you know I would gladly turn this responsibility over to you, but it's not my place, legally or morally, to do so; it was not your father's wish."

She plopped back into the chair in front of the lawyer's desk.

"My father..." She shook her head and sighed. "What can I say, licenciado? You're here to yell at—my father is not. Nor is my brother or Escalante."

Lucky them, Mauricio thought.

"The family has a duty here. Susana de los Ángeles came to Baalam Kab, still a child, to serve our mother, which she did. She was our nursemaid when she still needed one herself, and when my mother died, she helped Soli raise Lalo and run the household. When my stepmother abandoned the farm, she left Susana de los Ángeles behind, and that snake Escalante made her life unbearable."

"Señorita, please. Petty jealousies. Servants trying to expand their bailiwick. These things happen all the time. I see it in my own household. I don't know how my wife deals with it."

"For one thing, your wife is there every day."

"You must remember that Don Eusebio is in charge, and he has to be seen to exert his authority in order to run Baalam Kab efficiently."

"Efficiently? Licenciado, from childhood on I studied my Bible: Espinosa's *Manual for Mayordomos of the Rural Farms of Yucatán*. And my missal: *Manual of Mexican Husbandry*. And nowhere in either of those substantive works is rape listed in the duties of the farm manager."

In the outer office, Susana de los Ángeles stared at the floor—the secretary kept casting snooty looks in her direction, and she didn't want to see them. She heard Señorita Meche's voice now and then soaring in anger. She was torn between cheering her on and slipping outside—and once outside, leaving for good.

Silence followed. Too much silence.

Then the inner door flung open and Susana de los Ángeles

scrambled to her feet. Señorita Meche swept into the waiting room, swallowing a smile.

"Shall we go, Susana de los Ángeles?"

1 9 2 8...

Ruby *trudged homeward* for the midday meal. It was a bit past 1:00, and she paused at a corner while a car chugged by. She squinted up at the sun, which lorded over the sky, a living, iron-fisted despot—Mesoamerica's god under one name or another, one guise or another. It pounced on the crown of Ruby's head and licked the back of her neck with a rough tongue. If only, she mused, she could get this intensity of light in the studio.

But, without sacrificing shadow…

Lost in thought, she continued on, failing to greet people she passed.

The paradox of her profession: darkness illuminates. Photography dancing between light and shadow. The alchemy of the darkroom. The magic of negatives—black turns white, white becomes black.

Bringing to mind the images from that morning's work in the darkroom, she worried them this way and that. Oh, the portraits had turned out fine—that was routine. But her own work… She'd been experimenting with double exposures.

It galled her to drop everything and head home, when what she needed was to tackle the obstacles, work through the frustration. To be in her darkroom—with its red light and trays and timers, the air close with its chemical tang, prints hanging everywhere, clothes-pinned to lines to dry. But in the last year Meche had developed strong opinions about regular meals and Ruby's work schedule. Maybe it was the farmer in her resurfacing—one's life dominated by daily routines and seasonal cycles, up before dawn, early to bed, etc., etc.

Whatever the reason, and presumably for her own good, Ruby was to present herself for lunch and dinner at the house in San Román. Meche also insisted that Ruby forgo the streetcar in favor of getting some exercise and fresh air. Diesel, horse manure, frying fish, hair lotion and sweat—Ruby did not find the air all that fresh. She much preferred the crisp smell of her chemicals.

Again she recalled the morning's disappointing images—they'd been clumsy, inert, lifeless.

She kicked at a small stone in her path.

Maybe the project was simply stillborn, her vision unattainable... But, no, it felt within reach. She just needed more time. Time she didn't have. There were sittings scheduled that afternoon, and if she stayed after closing, Meche would get bent out of shape. The next couple days were also booked. Any unscheduled time would need to be spent developing the studio portraits and printing, retouching and hand-coloring them.

To do her own work, to create and process the images she wanted, she needed uninterrupted time in which to concentrate and experiment. She craved that. But what she got was endless intrusions and disruptions. Oh, for the miracle moment, that focused instant that leached into minutes, hours—the bread and fishes of time.

It was tempting to blame Meche, but Ruby knew that it was Meche who kept the studio afloat and allowed Ruby what little time she had.

But this dropping everything, just to eat...

Ay, Meche, Ruby thought, Meche who was most likely already home —she'd left the studio early to do errands before everything closed for the afternoon. Home and waiting. Hands on hips. Ruby knew her admonishing stance by heart. She half-smiled envisioning it—Meche's head tilted, chin raised, pursed lipsticked lips, the furrowed brow framed by marcel-waved hair, and below eyebrows plucked and penciled, the wrinkle on the bridge of the nose...

The wrinkle! The folds of skin there...

That was it! Extreme closeups. And gum bichromate for more control of the image...

Coming to a corner, she stopped and glanced up. She'd reached the place where the San Román gate used to stand in the city walls. As a little girl she'd loved passing through it, holding on to her father's hand, or her mother's—in towards the novelties of the city, out towards the familiarity of the San Román neighborhood—picturing helmeted soldiers of old patrolling it with swords and muskets, and marauding English pirates wielding cutlasses and flintlocks.

But the gate and the crumbling wall on either side of it—considered an unsightly impediment to the flow of traffic—had since been demolished for the sake of modernity.

Up ahead she could see the single steeple of the Iglesia de San Román —a clock face on each of its four sides.

Oh, how her mother had hated that clock. Always insisting it had no business being on a church—the Church was about eternity. She hadn't approved of the façade either. A mud hen of a church. Graceless. Unbalanced with its single tower on one corner. When Ruby's father would point out that it was simple because it dated back to the mid 1500's and the early years of Campeche City, her mother would argue that that was no excuse, that something should be done to make it presentable—in its present state it was not a worthy home for the holy Black Christ.

The life-sized Cristo Negro, brought from Italy in 1565, was an elegantly gaunt figure—white loincloth, gold halo, arms outstretched— agonizing on a silver cross. That it was the focus of great devotion— miracles, great and small attributed to it from day one—did not particularly impress Ruby. But she thought it a beautiful piece of art, and it made her uneasy when it was trotted out in procession—precariously gliding down the street over the heads of the crowd, then floating over the bay on a platform between two festooned fishing boats, escorted by a flotilla of small boats crammed with worshippers. Of course, now that the Calles government had closed the churches, such public demonstrations of faith were illegal.

The old church itself was indeed plain, a frontier stronghold—Ruby admired its medieval, pre-baroque starkness. Was the tower built to watch for Indian attacks? For the arrival of ships, friendly or pirate? Or was it added later, precisely to hold a clock?

As she proceeded in the direction of the church, her thoughts shifted from her mother to her sister—Lulu had always hated this trek to and from the studio. To protect her fair skin from the sun she always wore long sleeves and high necklines, as well as the obligatory and fashionable wide-brimmed hats of the time. She also grumbled about walking over rough streets and sidewalks in her spool-heeled shoes. But most of all Lulu, like their mother, detested living in San Román, longing instead to live within the city walls—or what was left of them.

But Ruby, like her father, had always loved San Román. Ironically, she might be the one who ended up leaving it.

There was a chance she could buy the building that housed the photography studio—the owner, the Widow Canetti, who occupied the upstairs, was talking about moving to Havana to live with her eldest daughter. It would mean Ruby's selling the family home in San Román to finance the purchase, but what did she and Meche need with a house? They could move into the rooms above the studio.

And if by any chance there was a bit of money left over from the sale, she could buy one of the new Leica 35mm cameras she'd been reading about, a small fortune at around $100 US.

Meche said she didn't care about the house, but she did not relish the idea of being cooped up in the studio night and day—she would miss walking to and from work. But, she pointed out, if they moved to the apartment above the studio with its single full-sized bedroom, they would finally share a room. Meche had always grumbled about their separate bedrooms—separate, in great part, because Ruby valued her privacy, but mostly because of María Asunción.

Moving would mean letting María Asunción go.

Unthinkable. Or was it?

She and Meche did not get on. The housekeeper balked at taking orders from her. And even though María Asunción knew that Meche took care of the finances at both the studio and the house, she was always taking things up with Ruby, no matter how many times Ruby told her it was up to Meche to decide.

Ruby suspected the older woman only stayed with them out of inertia, and perhaps some tattered loyalty to Ruby's mother. And she wondered if María Asunción might not have her suspicions about her and Meche—she'd taken to wearing a martyred look of late.

Maybe María Asunción would welcome the chance to be rid of them.

Of course, there was Lulu. It would be like her to get sentimental about selling the family home. But then, Ruby didn't need her approval. When Lulu married Ernesto—in a pique of noblesse oblige, and of guilt about leaving Ruby to fend for herself at the studio—she'd signed her interest in the house and business over to Ruby, expecting in future to be taken care of by her husband. Oh, how she'd enjoyed playing the grand lady!

Ruby was now approaching the small San Román park and plaza, and the church—a squat Statue of Liberty raising its clock-tower arm, black stains streaking its face. Their house was located a few blocks beyond it.

The streets were empty, everyone already home and at table. Ruby's stomach gave a little growl.

She reached the corner of the park and cut across it. At the far side, nearest the church, a wagon with low sideboards was parked on the street —not an unusual sight, except for its cargo. Instead of stacked crates of chickens or baskets of fruit, it held a single cage: large and iron, maybe six-feet long and four-feet high. And something lay inside it. As she came closer she saw it was a large animal, tawny with spots.

A jaguar!

Of course she'd seen pre-Columbian ceramics and paintings of jaguars and jaguar gods her whole life—Meche kept a little ceramic bowl in the shape of one on her dresser. And there was that pelt Tía Anastasia used as a rug. But she'd never seen a live one.

The sun beat down stronger than ever—on the street, on Ruby, on the caged jaguar.

The animal lay on its side and its tongue, long and pink, lolled. Its larger spots were squarish, defined by dark broken lines like daubs of paint, some filled with orange, a dark dot in the center. Hypnotic. But the fur had no sheen.

Even caged and defeated, half-crazed, she guessed, from captivity, the creature took her breath away. If only she had her camera.

A word came to her lips, unbidden. "Baalam," she whispered.

Its tail flicked once.

Baalam
closes his eyes
his spirit pulls in
deep and still
awaiting darkness
bright, this big pueblo
too bright—hard to see
night lies distant
hunger
thirst
half-eaten deer carcass
out of reach, far away
dragged to ceiba tree
covered with leaves
between two ribs of root
shaded, cool—for his return
return
no return
wagon
bone-wracking, jolting
smell of horses
big grass-eaters
days and days, nights

their fear
in his nostrils
on roof of his mouth
longing to stretch his legs
to pounce
smooth and powerful
bring one down
his fangs—coated with hunger
the need to sink into flesh
pull neck vertebrae apart
the snap

Ruby, like all Campechans, knew Mayan words. Most didn't even always know they weren't Spanish—children pointed to their tuuch, not their belly buttons. And one of Meche's pet names for Ruby was boxita, little dark one—box, dark one, plus the affectionate Spanish ending -ita. But baalam was not a word Ruby had known—she'd learned it from Meche.

She took note now of the horses harnessed to the wagon—fretful, under the miserly shade of a palm tree, their ears flicking forward and back, alert. They did not relish being so close to a predator such as this, even caged.

Where was the owner?

Ruby went nearer. The animal's eyes followed her. Its instincts were not entirely crushed. In a pulse beat, it hefted itself to a crouch. For a moment neither it nor Ruby saw the iron bars. Ruby froze, held in check by the animal's green eyes, both she and the animal calculating distance, speed, chance of success.

Neither jaguar nor prey saw the man crossing towards them from the bar on the far side of the park. He was middle-aged, a thin man with thin hair and a pot belly. He wore a shabby suit, with a gun belt around his waist, partly hidden by his jacket.

"Hey there! Miss!" he barked. "Best stay back!"

He picked up a machete from under the driver's bench, and walked up to the cage. He dragged the blade across the the rungs, making a crass rattling, upsetting the horses who snorted and jigged in place. The jaguar growled and bared his teeth. Ruby leaped back, the spell broken.

The man moved up to the horses' heads and spoke quietly to them.

"See what you've done?" he said to her. "You've upset my horses."

"What do you intend to do with this animal?" Ruby's voice was not much more than a whisper.

"How's that, miss?"

"Señor," her voice came out stronger, "what are you going to do with him?"

"Why, sell him, miss. Take him to the capital. Some zoo or circus should pay top money, don't you think? Not easy catching one of these. Not easy at all. Or cheap. It cost me a goat. And then there's the wagon and all."

"He'll never make it all that way. Not if you don't get him out of the sun, give him some water and food."

"Expert on the care and feeding of cats, are we, miss?"

"It's common sense, señor. You could lose your investment."

"Oh, I won't do that, miss. Plan to charge to see him along the way, too. You just got one good long look for free."

She wanted to demand he take the cat back to the jungle, to set him free.

"You must not be from around here," she said.

He grinned—did he think she was flirting with him. "Why's that?"

"Otherwise, you'd know."

He raised his eyebrows in a question, still smiling.

"That the jaguar gods are sure to curse you."

She didn't know why she'd said it. She was improvising, but she also felt it was true. Maybe the man thought so too, because his smile withered.

Her mind was aflood with stories—from childhood? From Meche?

The Jaguar Hero Twins, Hunahpú and Xbalanqué, playing at the ball court, playing with death, taking on the Lords of Xibalba, the Underworld, and outsmarting them again and again.

The man narrowed his eyes and huffed. "Fine talk for a young Christian lady, miss, and in front of a church, to boot."

"I think you should know, sir, that the Black Christ in the church there is one with Xbalanqué, the black jaguar-star. And together both of them, both the Black Christ and Xbalanqué," she looked into the sky and crossed herself dramatically, before nodding toward the spotted cat in the cage, "both watch out for Hunahpú, the yellow jaguar-sun."

He shifted his weight. "You're crazy."

She took pleasure in his discomfort. Could she possibly scare this loathsome man into releasing the baalam?

"Am I," she said, making her voice low and confidential. "I for one wouldn't want to cross the Black Christ or the Jaguar Twin Gods."

"Like you said, miss, I've got an investment."

"Hmm," she said. She looked at the jaguar. Its gaze made her blood run cold, and she quickly looked away—but her fear of the cat did not make its fate any less cruel. "Think of Job, sir. Better yet, think of Pharaoh—frogs, boils, darkness." She made a show of a shudder.

Now the man crossed himself.

As if on cue, bless her, a lone teenage girl in white Mayan dress, a basket on her head, probably rushing home late from an errand, saw the jaguar in the cage. She stopped short and crossed herself. Then she faced the church and crossed herself again. Ruby was not given to prayer, but she thanked the Virgin for sending the young girl to help. When the girl glanced at the man and Ruby, it was with a mixture of fear and disgust.

Ruby stepped away from him, somewhat theatrically.

"Sir, if I were you, I would ask the Black Christ for forgiveness and take this animal back to where he belongs."

He narrowed his eyes, looked her up and down. The hair on the back of her neck raised.

He slapped the machete several times gently against the side of his leg. "Not likely, missy. Not damn likely."

He reached for her, but she pulled away, escaping his grasp.

The girl, one hand on her basket, ready to hurry away, hesitated, and Ruby rushed to her side. The girl linked her arm in Ruby's, and they ran from the park.

"Bitch," he yelled after her. "What do you take me for?" The sound of the machete clanged again across the iron bars. "To hell with you! Do you hear me? To hell with you!"

When Ruby looked back, the man was crossing the street back to the bar.

Meche's finger tapped the cream-colored cover of the paperback—a red border framed the title: *The Cosmic Race: The Mission of the Ibero-American Race*, by José Vasconcelos. She gave a frustrated sigh and slapped the book down on the sofa. Ruby was not home yet. How could she be expected to concentrate on a groundbreaking essay when she was getting hungrier and crosser by the moment?

Great-Aunt Pancha had sent the book, which purportedly laid out a vision of a new race and a new civilization based in Latin America. Meche wondered if she could get Ruby to read it.

She was well aware that Ruby had no patience for politics, philosophy, or her great-aunt, for that matter, but Vasconcelos had gone to school here in Campeche, and had been the nation's first Secretary of Education, with a budget second only to the military. And now that he'd resigned in opposition to President Calles, there was rumor he would run for president. How could Ruby not be interested?

Meche's stomach growled. If Ruby was still at the studio, Meche would throttle her.

She glared at the sofa's faded pattern of gold flowers and repositioned *The Cosmic Race* to cover a stain on the yellow silk upholstery. She would never understand Campeche City's obsession with French-styled furnishings. Well, if she and Ruby did move above the studio, the ugly Louis-the-something-or-other sofa would definitely not be going with them. She stretched her legs out in front of her and ran her fingertips up the back seams of her ivory-colored cotton stockings. The skirt of her dress covered her knees, plus a bit— she liked the shorter styles these days. María Asunción shot disapproving looks at her hemline, but María Asunción was an old fuddy-duddy who should mind her own business.

Meche heard the creak of the door between the kitchen and dining room. María Asunción was preparing sea bass in mole sauce for the main dish and the aroma of grilled fish wafted into the parlor, making Meche's mouth water.

Really, if Ruby did not walk in that front door in the next five minutes...

Last week she and Ruby had had a big argument over just this, her late arrival home anytime Meche did not walk back from the studio with her.

"Ay, Meche," Ruby had said, "you worry too much. What could happen between the studio and here?"

Meche had stared at her dumbfounded. Where to begin? She opened her mouth to elaborate the list of possible disasters that had been running through her mind as she'd waited for Ruby to turn up.

Ruby interrupted her and circled her arms around Meche's waist. "You always call me boxita, but it's I who should call you that," she said. She reached up and knocked on Meche's temple. "Of the two of us, you are the much darker one."

"I'm not dark. I'm realistic."

"Why have you forgotten how brave you've always been?"

"I'm not. You're the brave one."

"No, you said it before, I'm just oblivious."

Meche went to the telephone table in the entry and called the studio. There was no answer, but that did not mean Ruby was on her way home —she would not pick up if she were in the darkroom.

Meche strode to the kitchen. María Asunción stood at the stove, her back towards the door. The woman's hair, plaited into two thin grey braids, was pinned up in a bun. She was plump, and her worn black housedress pulled tight across her back. A couple inches of hem had come unstitched that she might not discover until next she ironed it. Meche said nothing—if she pointed it out, it would be taken as a criticism.

"I'll have dinner now," Meche said.

María Asunción turned to her. "Oh, has the señorita arrived?"

"No, she has not."

Looking down, Meche noted that María Asunción's huaraches looked new, and her flesh puffed around the stiff leather straps like rising bread dough.

"Ay, Señorita Ruby, she works so hard," María Asunción said, looking at Meche with disapproval. "I'll make her a plate."

María Asunción could make up all the plates she wanted, but Meche wasn't about to carry Ruby's meal back to the studio.

"Suit yourself," Meche said.

Leaving the kitchen, she heard the front door open. Her shoulders unknotted and she smiled in spite of herself. She stuck her head back into the kitchen. "Señorita Ruby's here," she said. Then she called to Ruby, "It's about time!"

But she heard no footsteps on the tile, nor did Ruby come into the dining room—Meche found her in the entryway, slumped with her back against the door.

"Boxita?" Meche said. She placed her hands on Ruby's upper arms. Ruby was shaking. "Ay, mi vida! What's wrong?"

Meche led Ruby into the parlor and sat her in the curve of the sofa arm. She called to María Asunción to bring a glass of xtabentun—Ruby detested the honeyed anise drink, but it was the only alcohol in the house, kept on hand to offer visitors. She noted, with unease, that Ruby accepted the cordial glass from María Asunción without protest.

María Asunción withdrew, but hesitated in the doorway, no doubt dying of curiosity. Once she was gone, Meche pressed Ruby to tell her what the matter was.

Ruby told her about the jaguar and the man and the girl.

"The bastard!" Meche exclaimed. "Did he hurt you? Are you okay?"

"No, I'm not! I feel wretched—leaving that animal in that horrible cage." She covered her eyes with the palm of her hand.

Meche took Ruby's hand from her eyes and stroked it. "But, boxita, if that odious man was able to capture a jaguar, it must have been hanging around a village, it could have been killing livestock, even people. He may actually have done some village a great favor."

Ruby looked at Meche as if she had betrayed her. "How can you say that?"

"Jaguars are very dangerous."

Ruby pulled her hand from Meche's. "You're the last person I'd expect to react like that. What about all your talk about the old ways, the beliefs you supposedly have such respect for?"

"I do, but it's like the Communion wafer."

Ruby twisted her mouth in impatience.

"What I mean is, there's the ritual and then there's the wafer of flour and water. We were taught to believe it really is the body of Christ. Transubstantiation—isn't that what it's called? But if any transformation happens, it happens in the Eucharist, in the ceremony.

"It's the same with a baalam. In the jungle, in the stories and rituals, Baalam is a supernatural being. No doubt about it. And the jaguar gods are momentous—fierce and powerful. Incredibly so. But when a baalam starts raiding farms, he's just an animal. And a very dangerous one."

"Damn it, Meche, we heard one in the jungle. At Uxmal. Remember? You were thrilled."

"Yes, and I had a shotgun next to the bedroll."

Ruby shook her head. "I can't believe you condone caging that animal like that."

"I don't condone it. It just is. Pigs are slaughtered. Fish are netted."

"A jaguar is not food."

"Sweetie. It's just the way things are sometimes. There's nothing to be done."

"I'm not a child," Ruby snapped.

Meche blanched and lowered her head, justly rebuked. Indeed, she had felt like a mother soothing a child. Ruby was older than Meche by ten years, but she was a city girl—shielded from the rough truths of life in the countryside, the life-and-death decisions, the blight, stench and blood.

And yet, Baalam Kab, how Meche missed it!

The name meant Jaguar Bee, queen bee—and bees were some of the many things she missed about the rancho. She was fond of the insects in a way that Ruby could not fathom. Long before the birth of Pedro Mu, her friend and mentor on the rancho, his grandfather had found a hive in a downed tree trunk. He'd cut around it, capped both ends with wooden discs that he'd carved to fit, and brought it home. Its bees were like family pets—she'd gone to say goodbye to them as well as to the Mu family before Lulu had taken her away from the farm.

To think of the life and death of a single hive. All those expendable worker bees, picked off by birds as they work to exhaustion. The hive itself the target of marauding pests—like the implacable xulab ants that in their attack covered a hive so completely it looked black as obsidian, while the bees guarding the door sacrificed themselves one after another in the hopeless defense of the hive. What did Ruby know of any of that? And when a hive was successful and undamaged, the beekeeper came and took his knife to the combs.

But Meche admired Ruby. She owed everything to her. When the others had left on that steamboat, she'd let Meche stay with her, and she'd taught her the ropes of the city, of the business, and so much more.

She reached out to stroke Ruby's hand, but Ruby pulled it away. Meche winced at the rejection. But scrutinizing her face, she saw that Ruby was staring into space, fidgeting with her lower lip, the dark arches of her eyebrows crumpled in distress. Ruby wasn't thinking about her— the caged animal had laid claim to all her attention.

A hatred flared in Meche for the man who was making her Ruby so unhappy.

"Maybe we could buy it," Ruby said.

"With what, mi vida? Your virtue? Mine?"

Ruby groaned and leaned her head back in defeat.

"And how would we transport it back to the jungle? Or do we let it loose in the city?"

Ruby shook her head and looked miserable.

"Ay, boxita, mi vida. I'm so sorry," Meche said, and kissed Ruby's temple.

Ruby recoiled.

Meche felt a pang of hurt, and had to check a rush of anger—not something she was particularly good at. But she did not stomp off. Ruby needed her, whether Ruby knew it or not, whether she wanted to or not. Meche had been romantic and naive all those years ago to think that once she broke through Ruby's stubborn reserve, they would live happily ever after. She had had to accept that storming Ruby's defenses would be the work of a lifetime.

"Ruby," Meche said measuredly. "Dinner is waiting. You'll feel better after you eat."

"I'm not hungry," Ruby said coldly.

Meche reached for Ruby's hand, but Ruby stepped away.

"I'm going to lie down."

Meche opened her mouth to offer to accompany her, but Ruby's glance cut her. Her reproach made Meche feel queasy.

Alone at the dining room table, she picked at the fish on her plate. She told herself that Ruby was just taking her distress out on her. It would pass. It would have to. Without Ruby, what would she do, where would she go? When she called Ruby "mi vida," she meant it—Ruby was her life.

Meche had only seen Ruby this shaken once before—during the Revolution. That time had brought them together. Meche pushed her plate away. Would this time tear them apart?

But to think, a jaguar. Here in San Román.

"Dios mío!" she said aloud, shaking her head.

María Asunción stuck her head out from the kitchen, "You called, señorita?"

Meche snorted and shook her head—the woman was hardly any god of hers.

Instead of retreating, María Asunción came and stood next to her. Meche looked up at the woman. A trickle of sweat paralleled the hairline at her temple. Up close like this, she appeared older than Meche's mental picture of her—the wrinkles on her angular face, deeper; the whites around her brown eyes, yellower; her lips, broader and more drooping. She usually looked daggers at Meche, but her expression now was one of concern and Meche realized, with a flash of gratitude, that she was not alone in trying to take care of Ruby. For the first time she wondered for whom the old woman wore black. And how old was she, anyway?

"I can make up a plate for Señorita Ruby," she said.

"Thank you, María Asunción."

Meche's thoughts returned to the caged animal. She remembered when she was a small child, her mother teaching her that God was always watching her. The double meaning was not lost on her—yes, she should not be afraid because God was looking out for her, but she'd also better behave herself. Somehow, in her mind the ever-vigilant God the Father became forever confused with Baalam lurking in the shadows. After all, both were invisible presences. Powerful. Feared and revered. Jaguar could be just out of sight, day or night—he might be up a tree or in a cave, he might be watching from the jungle, maybe stalking you without your knowing it. He wielded the power of death. But unlike God—who left nebulous miracles behind, mostly in far-away places and far-away times—Jaguar left convincing signs right under your nose: prints in the soft earth, a killed animal, spine-tingling screeches in the night.

Meche had never seen a baalam, not really—she'd never seen God either. Once, as a young girl, there'd been that flash of movement in the trees. While sure it was a jaguar, she'd kept it secret—if she'd told anyone about it, they would have insisted that she'd startled a deer. And she'd also have gotten in trouble for being so far from the house. But had she told Soli? She must have.

She picked up her fork and took a bite of fried banana—it seemed tasteless and the oil lay heavy in her mouth. She pushed the plate away. She went to Ruby's room and gave a gentle tap on the door. There was no answer—Ruby, shutting herself away from her. Again. Only this felt different somehow, and worse.

Meche went to her own room. She undressed. Wearing just her slip, she lay on the bed. But feeling hot, vexed and restless, she got up. The tile felt cool under her bare feet. She picked up the fan that she kept on her nightstand. Ruby had bought it for her three years earlier on their trip to Mérida. Although a souvenir of a wonderful trip, she never took it out of the house—it was too kitschy. So much so that, in a way, it seemed a mock present, which hurt her feelings a bit.

Fanning herself, she thought of the very different fan she kept wrapped in a navy-blue square of velvet in her drawer, an anniversary gift from her father to her mother. Soli had one of their mother's fans, too— she assumed Soli still had it. It was from their mother's wedding ensemble—white silk, with white embroidery, on staves of ivory. Meche's was white silk, too, but with tortoise shell staves and embroidered with silver and gold. A serious gift.

The fan from Ruby was made entirely of wood—she did love the clack it made when snapped open, but it was the color of guacamole. And the flowers painted on it were the kind seen on ceramics that look intricate but are achieved with a few brush strokes. The words "Mérida, The White City" were splayed across the ribs in white.

She fretted about Ruby—this caged jaguar was coming between them.

Needing to act, Meche tossed the fan on the bed, and, opening the door of her wardrobe, reached for the shotgun she kept propped against the back corner behind the clothes. But she changed her mind. Instead she retrieved her father's loaded Colt revolver from the drawer of her nightstand.

She put on her dress, stockings and shoes. The drop-waist dress had no pockets, and the revolver was too large to fit in her small embroidered bag. She looked about the room and grabbed her cloche hat and placed the gun in it. The barrel was a bit long, but she could disguise it if she held it just right. With the Revolution only eight years past, and the Cristero Rebellion looming, there was no shortage of arms about the city, but it seemed best to keep the gun out of sight.

On her way out of the house, she had a thought, and holding the gun and hat by her side, almost behind her back, she went into the kitchen. As she crossed to a cabinet, María Asunción's eyes went straight to the hand Meche was trying to conceal.

"What are you looking for, señorita?" María Asunción asked from where she was eating at the worktable.

The woman's tone shriveled Meche's earlier good will towards her. Having María Asunción around all the time, looking down her nose at her—really, it was like living with a spy!

"That's my business."

She waited for María Asunción to turn back to her plate before getting what she wanted from the cabinet.

Baalam
his spirit pulls in
deep and still
awaiting darkness
bright, this pueblo
too bright
can't see
night lies distant
hunger
thirst

human
small, female
his nose twitched
peculiar smell

not of the forest
tangy

he fixed his eyes on her
she stared back—no fear
not-prey
his legs tensed
his claws readied
his body pulled into a crouch
coiled strength, intent
then—
her body
strong odor
fear
clear, tantalizing
his eyes locked on hers
gauged the tiniest twitch
intrusion—
stench
reek of metal
alcohol, sweat
the man
ear-piercing clang
metal on metal
fear pouring from the grass-eaters
pulling at their ties
wagon lurched
Baalam growled
bared his fangs
his prey—
small female
gone
escaped

man
reek of metal
alcohol, sweat
no scent of fear
crush the windpipe
kill the man
hunger
thirst—blood, moist meat

Baalam fears no animal
steers clear of
long-tusked boars
caution,
not fear
wariness
Baalam fears no animal

man comes near
no scent of fear
stirs up
unwonted sensations—
clatter of rattlesnake,
sudden rush in his blood
and hatred
hatred edging into fear
fear
he's become a thing that fears
prey, not predator
prey

Going out a door, any door, always lifted Meche's spirits—the sense of freedom and escape in that first step. Opening the front door now, her excitement spiked. A jaguar! Would it still be there in the park to see?

Meche slipped into the empty street. It was mostly silent, except for snores rasping from the house next door, and in the next block, the whine of a gramophone. She turned a corner and the neighborhood streets flung open like arms, revealing the park and the Church of San Román. Her stomach did a little flip—excitement, dismay—for there was the wagon, and in its bed, an iron cage.

She did not rush to gape at the jaguar. Although the heat was like sweaty hands heavy on her shoulders, it was something else that held her back. So close now, she feared facing a god and being disappointed. She also feared not being disappointed. What then? What if she felt like Ruby?

She was drawn instead to the two horses, in particular to the reddish-brown bay with black points that eyed her with interest and had a narrow white stripe the length of her face. Meche fought the urge to unhitch her and ride off bareback—she'd not ridden in years, not since their trip to the ruins. The other horse, an undistinguished chestnut with no markings, looked miserable with fear. Meche stroked first one horse's neck and then the other—with one hand, because in the other she held the pistol covered by her hat. Her palm felt slick where it grasped the wooden grip of the gun, and her shoulder and arm complained from its weight. She cooed to the horses and cursed their owner to them in the same loving tones, for they did not look well cared-for. She caressed their noses and gave them the bits of hard brown sugar she'd dropped into her hat in the kitchen. Their stance relaxed.

Meche still had not looked at the cage.

Turning from the horses, she walked hesitantly towards the back of the wagon. It stank of urine, feces and fetid hay. The big cat was lying down. Its body—at least five feet long—took up most of the length of the cage. Its ears were erect—it knew she was there—but it did not turn to look at her. She saw only its back, the intricate spotted pattern of its coat. Even so she felt a silent communication between them.

She was not ready to walk around the cage and look Baalam in the eye.

Meche saw the animal's rib cage concertina as it breathed. She could detect the curved bones as the lungs labored—his captor must be stinting on meat. The man who'd accosted Ruby, if not outright cruel, was unthinking and ignorant. And foolish—a hungry predator was much more dangerous than a sated one. Not to mention mistreating one's merchandise like this…

Baalam as merchandise. She flinched at her own thought.

Ruby came tromping around the corner—with one hand she steadied the lacquered cherrywood camera strapped around her neck and with the other she lugged a canvas case with the tripod and extra film holders. She saw the wagon, and her heart constricted.

If it were she in that cage, she'd rather die.

Someone was standing by the cage, and it wasn't that horrible man.

"Meche!" she called.

> *Baalam pulls his spirit in*
> *deep and still*
> *night lies yet afar*
> *bright, this big pueblo*
> *too bright—hard to see*
> *hunger*
> *thirst*
> *trapped*
> *trapped*
>
> *new woman, metal, fish*
> *hunger*
>
> *senses other female*

small
peculiar smell
not of the forest

too bright
hunger
thirst
lie still
attend
draw back the flesh from his teeth
bring the odors into his mouth
alert
alert

Meche turned and saw Ruby hobbling towards her with her load. She was taken aback for only a moment—of course Ruby would return to the studio for a camera.

They faced each other, each feeling glad of the other as always.

"You came," Ruby said.

"So did you," Meche said.

She searched Ruby's face. It was clear that she'd been hurrying—her black bangs plastered to her forehead, her face dark from heat and exertion. Meche nodded at the Seneca Competitor around her neck, the sun glinting off the camera's brass fittings.

"It will be a wretched picture, you know."

"I know," she said, her face stricken.

She set the canvas bag on the grass, took the tripod out of its case.

"But, to start, if he stays as he is, with his back to us... I want to take a close-up between the bars of the markings of his fur."

"Maybe the newspaper will buy the other pictures."

Ruby glared at Meche. "I will not make money off the misery of this doomed soul."

Meche bit her lip—there would be time to be practical later.

"Of course not. Let me help you."

"Hold this steady while I attach the camera," Ruby said.

Meche reached for the tripod with both hands. Ruby stared at the gun in Meche's hand—the cloche dangled from its barrel for a second before falling to the ground. She looked quizzically at Meche.

Meche shook her head and shrugged.

"He's in a cage, Meche."

"I know."

She couldn't explain. Something had told her to bring it.

Ruby sighed with disgust and attached the camera to the wooden tripod without aid. She stretched the camera's leatherette bellows and framed the shot. She then slid one of the wooden frames holding film into the camera with a clack. The sound alarmed the jaguar. He was up, facing Ruby and Meche, fangs bared, hissing.

Ruby grasped Meche's arm. They both froze with the same thought: he was terrifying, he was magnificent, he was piteous. The horses whinnied and shifted. The bay pawed the ground.

The big cat lay down, surveilling the women with eyes that seemed half dead.

"Meche, I can't bear it," Ruby said.

In an instant Ruby had darted to the rear of the wagon. Meche saw her reach for the cage door.

"Ruby, no! You can't let a wild animal loose in San Román."

Ruby slid the latch. The wagon was on the level, and the heavy door did not move. The cat snarled at her, and Ruby jumped back. The hair rose on the back of Meche's neck and fear gripped her heart.

"Ruby, stop! Please! I warn you, I can't let him hurt you. You or anyone else."

"As long as he's out of this cage, I don't care what happens," she said and placed her hand back on the bolt, her face full of entreaty and horror.

Was Ruby telling her she wanted her to kill the jaguar? Meche felt cold with dread.

"You'll hate me," Meche said.

"No," Ruby said, but her voice trembled and gave no assurance.

"Will you forgive me?"

"If I were in that cage, I'd beg you to… to end it. If I'm ever like that, Meche, in any way…"

Meche's brain screamed that she could never, but she kept her mouth clenched.

"If you don't…" Ruby's voice trailed off, leaving an unspoken threat hanging between them.

Meche understood that no forgiveness lay in that choice. Tears blurred her vision and she wiped her sleeve across her eyes.

"There'll be hell to pay," Meche warned.

Ruby nodded, tears rolling down her face.

"You don't have to be here," Meche said, thinking, I don't want you to see me kill him.

"And it's better if I do it with him in the cage."

"No, Meche, not that. Not in the cage. He has to be free."

Meche gave a shuddering sigh.

"Ruby, listen…"

Ruby's look was defiant, it said try and stop me.

Meche held up a hand in acquiescence, but she was calculating. If Ruby stood by the door, Meche was certain that the jaguar would turn on her. If she ran, he would pursue her. But if she was out of his line of sight, Meche felt sure he would not go out of his way to attack her, but instead would attack one of the horses or race to put distance between himself and captivity.

"Fine," Meche said, "But, listen to me. When you open the door, quick, slide under the wagon. As fast as you can, okay?"

Ruby glanced at the door and the jaguar, and then back at Meche. Her eyes widened. She seemed to understand and nodded.

Meche shifted the gun to wipe her palm on her dress. Ruby reached to open the door, and Meche cocked the revolver.

The wagon rocked a bit, and Meche realized her mistake.

The baalam was on his feet. He shouldered into the bars, growling and snarling. The horses reacted to his sounds and movement. They jiggered and pranced in place, hell-bent on fleeing. The brakes on the wagon were set, but how long would they hold?

Under the wagon would be a very dangerous place for Ruby to be.

Meche shouted and ran to Ruby, yanking her away from the wagon before she had a chance to dive under it. Ruby's hand was on the latch, and when Meche jerked her away, the cage door flung open. The baalam, however, thrown off balance by the pitching of the wagon, did not leap from the cage.

At that moment, the man emerged from the cantina—either his ear was tuned in to the noises of jaguar, wagon and horses or Meche's shouting had roused him. Alarmed at what he saw, he screamed obscenities at Ruby, at the horses, at the jaguar. His hand reached for his gun belt. The commotion grew as other men poured out of the bar to see what was going on.

Just as the horses bolted forward, the jaguar leaped from the back of the wagon.

Meche, standing in front of Ruby, both to protect her and to obscure her view, aimed her father's pistol.

The baalam landed on his feet in the street. He staggered a moment on stiff legs. Then without a glance in Meche's direction, he darted forward, bounding smoothly in the direction of the church of the Black Christ. The baalam's lean body was soaring above the ground in full stretch. Several shots rang out.

The explosion from Meche's pistol shook her, the force and noise a blow to the chest. Ruby cried out from the thunderous shock of it and dropped into a crouch in animal instinct.

Baalam yowled and dropped to the earth. He twitched a few times. Then Meche saw the subtle shift from stillness to death.

She was awash in emotions—her head and gut reeling. She was angry Ruby had made her shoot the baalam, she was sorrowful he was dead, and deeply troubled—killing Baalam must bring bad luck. The very worst. She was glad no one was hurt and proud her bullet hit its mark. She was apprehensive that there would be financial repercussions, maybe legal ones. But most of all, she feared Ruby would turn from her. Forever.

Ruby stared at the downed animal, blood staining the tawny pattern of his fur. She covered her mouth to keep in a second scream. She looked up at Meche, grief-stricken.

That look cut Meche to the quick. She knew she would never forget it.

The shouting from the men grew louder, changing from calls of fright and warning to whoops of triumph. Meche scooped up her cloche hat and slid her revolver into the canvas equipment case. Then she reached for Ruby with trepidation, dreading that Ruby would recoil from her. She did not, and Meche put an arm around her—despite the heat, she was shivering.

A stocky man in business slacks, vest and tie, and wearing a derby, stood in the middle of the street where he'd come running from the cantina. He was someone Meche and Ruby had seen now and then in the neighborhood. His jacket had been left inside and in his hand he held a compact pocket pistol. Beside him Flaco Martínez, the owner of the bar—his stained bar apron covering his torso and skirting most of his legs—held his rifle parallel to the ground.

The man who'd brought the jaguar to San Román was blind with fury. He waved a gun at them and shouted, "You've ruined me!"

A number of Don Flaco's bar customers came up behind the man. They restrained him and wrested the gun from him.

He turned his fury on Ruby. "You. You bitch. This is your doing! You let my jaguar out. You owe me! My horses, wagon. You owe me!"

The man in the business suit said, "Have some respect." He tipped his hat to Ruby and Meche. "Ladies," he said. He turned back to the man struggling against the hold of Don Flaco's patrons. "Señorita Ruby here is a noted lady photographer in our fair city. It's hardly her fault you did not close the cage door well. That's what happened, isn't it? You didn't lock it, and when your horses spooked, it flew open. I wouldn't go accusing this lady. She could have been killed. You'll be lucky if she doesn't call the police on you. In fact if she doesn't, I will. I'll have you thrown in jail for endangering the public safety."

He had an audience now—the shots and uproar had roused people from nearby houses. And with the end of the siesta, other people started filtering into the area.

The man who'd caged the jaguar roared. The men dragged him to a narrow street leading from the park and propelled him down it. He came back at them. They threw him down the street again, this time with punches and kicks and jeers. When they were sure he'd given up, pleased with themselves, they made their way back to look at the downed beast.

"Señorita Ruby, take our picture," the man in the suit said, and the others egged him on. "Like this," he said and put his foot on the body of the jaguar. He displayed his small gun—mostly concealed within his meaty hand—by holding his arm across his vest, which was festooned with a gold watch chain.

"Then me," Don Flaco said.

"Just a moment, gentlemen," Meche said over her shoulder as she moved Ruby away from the scene. She seemed in shock. "Wait in the church, boxita. I can take the pictures." Ruby looked at her, startled. "I can take the kind of pictures they want. I know how the camera works." She quelled Ruby's objections before she made them. "There will be no denying them. When it is done, I will come get you and you can take the photos you need to, the ones only you can."

Meche, as requested, took the picture of the man in the suit— someone had fetched his jacket—and then of Flaco Martínez, without his bar apron, and then of the two of them together. After that the bar customers surrounded the animal. Meche readjusted the camera and slid in another plate, feeling sick to her stomach. It reminded her of the newspaper photos from 1919: the eager, fresh-faced young men surrounding and holding the bullet-ridden corpse of Zapata—not the men who'd fought with him and revered him, but strangers who wanted to be photographed like that with a murdered legend. These men, wanted to be photographed, too, with a god made carrion.

1 9 2 6...

M^a

Mª *Soledad Hernández de Eckart*
San Antonio, Texas, USA

Jan. 24, 1926

Dear Meche,

Snow! Half a foot of it! Oh, how I wish you could see it. Everything is clean and hushed. And cold! The air is so frigid that it tears at one's face like the grit of a dust devil, scalds like the steam from a pot of tamales when you lift the lid.

The boys are beside themselves with the excitement of it all. They come in wet and panting, with cheeks the color of hibiscus, and hungry out of all proportion. I put them in dry clothes and give them hot chocolate. They can barely stop chattering about their adventures long enough to drink it. The neighborhood children mount epic wars with snowballs as ammunition, and with more factions and intrigues than the Revolution. Sometimes it's the Great War, sometimes the Mexicans versus the Texans at the Alamo, sometimes both. It's all a jumble: Carrancistas and Huns and Texas Rangers and Villistas and doughboys and Comanches and I don't know what all.

The next time the boys come in, they will have to stay put, because the only dry things they have left are their pajamas.

I've strung a line in the kitchen and their clothes hang dripping from it, making puddles on the floor.

Snow is such a rare event here, so where did these children learn to make a snowball? Or the snowmen that are popping up in every yard? Maybe one of them learned from a father or mother from further north, or maybe a German parent or grandparent. As it happens, my children are without their German grandparents today, so it's not their doing. No church for us because of the snow, and no after-church meal at my in-laws. I'm thinking this is what "playing hooky" feels like. It's rather delicious. And it affords me the opportunity to sit and write, so you get an extra letter from Texas this month. If only I could press a snowflake, as if it were a flower, and send it along.

When we were girls, I wished that you and I could go to a regular school. Do you remember that horrible tutor we had for awhile? Though I imagine sitting in a schoolroom all day, everyday, would have been torture for you, don't you? Ernie doesn't seem to mind, but it's hard on Jack.

I took little Frankie outside yesterday. The look of wonder on his face! He toddled and then fell flat. As you know, he's been walking for a number of months now, but he's never had to deal with anything like this. My, but he screamed bloody murder. I suppose all he could see down there was white, white, white, and it terrified him. I find it a bit frightening myself. Today he was quite content to watch his big brothers from inside the house.

Sometimes it feels like I watch my whole life through a window, past and present. Sometimes when I'm in the kitchen, I look out through the glass panes and expect to see the orange tree at the edge of the kitchen patio at the rancho, and you dropping from its branches, twigs in your braids. Instead I see a tiny yard, mostly dirt, and a scrawny mesquite tree.

That tree is a nightmare because, of course, the children want to climb it (it must be in the blood), but it's studded, trunk and branches, with three-inch thorns, like a ceiba. And in the summer when it blooms, it's infested with bees.

But snow seems to transform everything, even the ugly little backyard. Last night after the sun had set, the sky glowed grey-white in an eerie way, and the snow on the ground gleamed as well. Snow lined the bare and twisted branches of the hateful mesquite, making it look quite artistic. And the manner in which snow muffles noise is extraordinary. I felt like the house was wrapped in a cocoon, a quite lonely one. But during the day, I am, in my way, as excited about this snow as the boys. Eddy, too! He went sledding today with his friends from high school.

Here I am chattering to you as the boys do to me. I will close now. I think I had best try to iron some of the boys' clothes to dry them. Otherwise I'm afraid they will still be quite clammy in the morning.

Eddie, Lulu and Raymond ask to be remembered to you.

Your loving sister,
Soli

"Lulu," Soli called out, "I'm writing Meche about the snow."

Lulu shuffled into the room, wearing gloves and two sweaters.

"Do you want to add a note for Ruby?"

Lulu paused at the clothesline, leaned down and peered between the legs of Eddy's jeans with a martyred expression.

"My fingers are too frozen to hold a pen."

"Oh Lulu!" Soli said, raising a hand to indicate the steamed-up windows and the beans and chicken soup simmering on the stove. "It's not that cold in here."

Lulu plopped in a chair across from her.

"Well, do you want to dictate something?" Soli said.

Lulu shook her head. She pursed her lips and rubbed her leg.

The day before, she had ventured outside, insisting that Raymond escort her. Soli and Frankie watched from the window. Lulu's reaction, Soli thought, was not unlike little Frankie's. And then Lulu slipped and fell, too. (Lulu could rub her leg all she wanted, but that's not what she'd landed on.) No wailing though. She was too mortified. She did shriek a few exclamations: Válgame Dios, Ay Virgencita, etc., until Raymond rescued her. He lifted her to her feet, brushed her off, said something that made Lulu blush and smile. Once again Soli was grateful Raymond was so tolerant with Lulu, and once again also a bit miffed.

Soli set up the ironing board between two lines of clothes.

Is this what life would be like everyday when they moved to Wisconsin, Soli wondered? A landscape she couldn't recognize? Cold and quiet seeping into her bones? A kitchen full of damp clothes? She hadn't told Lulu yet that they'd come to a decision. She hadn't told anyone. Saying it aloud would make it real.

When the possibility first came up, Lulu declared that she would stay behind. Soli couldn't imagine her carrying out her threat, but if she did, Eddy would probably choose to stay with her. He would choose her and San Antonio (the only home he really remembered). Soli couldn't bear the thought of losing him. She didn't even want to lose Lulu.

She shook Milwaukee out of her head. Getting out the heavy iron, she loaded it with pieces of charcoal.

"Do you have to do that?" Lulu whined.

Soli said nothing.

"You're going to burn the house down one of these days."

"You're welcome to do it yourself," Soli snapped.

Lulu swatted the idea away.

"Ay, hija," Lulu pouted. "How did we end up in this God-forsaken place?"

Soli sighed. "It's not God-forsaken."

Lulu sniffed.

"But I do miss…" Soli started to say.

Lulu perked up, lifted her eyebrows.

Soli did not allow herself to say "home," because this was her home, wasn't it, at least for a month or so more? Anyway, home was Raymond and the children. And, she did not want to say "Campeche," because today it sounded too abstract, a fact of geography, a name on a map and nothing more, a map slipping from her reach.

Soli unscrewed the lid of the kerosene tin to pour a bit on the charcoal.

"Just write a note at the bottom of the letter, Lulu. You'll feel better."

1 9 2 5...

Ruby lay on the ground in the darkness, shoulder to shoulder with Meche. Here they were, at the ruins of Uxmal—staring up at The Milky Way, the stars so numerous they created a white swathe across the sky. And uncomfortably close, a stone's throw away, an equally dense number of insects, frogs and other creatures created a galaxy of noise in the forest. Undaunted by the cottony shawl of stars, the Eta Aquarids lashed the sky—a stroke of luck the meteor shower coinciding with their visit. And they alone in the ruins to view it.

Meche counted the shooting stars in a reverent whisper. She quit at 112.

The sky was stunning, but, Ruby concluded, unphotographable.

The fire crackled. Meche had tethered the horses and two pack mules nearby. One of them snorted. Ruby could smell them—animal odors that Meche loved and Ruby did not. But in the absence of exhaust fumes and the ever-present smell of hot pavement in the city, she smelled the soap on Meche's skin and the fragrance of a plant she did not recognize.

The Pyramid of the Magician, a massive black shape with rounded edges, loomed above the walls of the Nunnery Quadrangle where Meche had chosen to set up camp. The whole place was otherworldly. Spooky. And the sky, unsettling—the vastness of it all.

A slash of fire, brighter than any so far, streaked across the sky, etching itself on their retinas as well as on the heavens.

"Ooh," Meche moaned. "Isn't it breathtaking?!" She squeezed Ruby's hand. "Aren't you glad you let me talk you into this?"

Ruby turned on her side and gazed at Meche, her face just visible in the glow of the dying fire. By "this," Meche meant this trip she'd dreamt up to celebrate their anniversary.

"Yes," Ruby said after a moment, thinking not of the meteors or the discomforts of travel, but of letting Meche talk her into "this," meaning, "them."

For once, she didn't look over her shoulder before she kissed Meche.

Meche fell asleep, and Ruby's mind turned to work. It occurred to her when they were at Chichen Itza, that what she needed was a stereo camera. The photos she'd taken would be good, she was sure—provided she could get the glass plates back to the studio in one piece—but if seen through a stereoscope, they would be remarkable. If only she'd foreseen the grandeur of the ruins. Of course even if she had, there would not have been the money for such a purchase.

A rock was poking her shoulder blade, so she rolled onto her side. Now another jabbed her thigh. Ruby's thoughts darted about like the smaller shooting stars overhead: *maybe she should pack the plates differently ...she dreaded getting back on that damn horse ...what if the best plates got broken? ...what if all of them broke?...she needed to look into film negatives ...it would make this kind of trip into the countryside more feasible ...that would make Meche happy ...there were rattlesnake heads carved in stone everywhere here ...snakes didn't come out at night, did they?...Meche was uncharacteristically chipper on this trip...but the cost of investing in a new camera ...who should she contact about selling postcards?...could Lulu maybe find her an outlet in the United States?*

A scream.

It ripped through the forest and tore through her tangled thoughts. The horses snorted and whinnied and stamped their feet. Ruby grabbed Meche and whispered urgently, "Meche, wake up!"

"It's a jaguar!" Meche said, "Isn't it marvelous? I haven't heard that since I was a child, not since Baalam Kab."

She popped up and went to the horses and mules to calm them, and then tossed more wood on the fire. Ruby was rolling up their bedding when she returned.

"What are you doing?"

"Packing. We can go to that village where we stopped for directions. It isn't far, is it?"

"In the dark, it is."

Meche put her hands on Ruby's shoulders, caressing outwards, then she placed her palms on each side of Ruby's face.

"Not to worry, mi vida. He's much farther away than he sounds. And we're much safer here by the fire than riding horses blindly through the jungle in the dark. Besides, think of all the photos you'll take tomorrow, all the beautiful postcards."

"If we live to wake up."

"We will."

"What about your rifle?"

"Don't worry. It's handy. I got us this far. I'll get us home again."

Ruby acquiesced, and they rolled out the blankets again. Meche placed the machete next to Ruby.

"So you can protect me."

Meche held Ruby tight, but fell asleep quickly, leaving Ruby alone again with her thoughts, her hand resting on the handle of the machete.

There were no more screams. The falling stars continued to drizzle across the Milky Way. Ruby moved slightly so that her face was touching Meche's.

"Yes, you got us this far," Ruby whispered.

S

oli hummed

"It Had to Be You," as she swished soapy water over a dinner plate. Her legs ached and the old terracotta tile beneath her feet was as hard and chill as concrete. But the water was warm, and the butter-colored dishes pleased her. Bought only the year before, they were almost square with the corners cropped as if with pinking shears. Triangular flowers (red, orange, pink, periwinkle and mauve) were painted along the four straight edges, as were strange little black shapes, each like the silhouette of a cigarette poking out the top of a pack. She declared the plates cheerful, modern. They made her smile.

Earlier, Lulu had yet again turned her nose up at the dishes when she'd set the table.

"Ay, hija, why must we use these garish things? Why don't we use the good china like decent people?"

The good china, a wedding gift from Raymond's family, was reserved for special occasions.

"Because, it's a Tuesday," Soli answered. "We can't afford to be decent on Tuesdays."

Lulu had made a scandalized, "Oh!"

Soli stretched to set the last plate in the drainer. If she got any bigger she'd have to stand sideways to wash the dishes.

Eddy bounded into the kitchen.

"I'm off."

"Of course you are," Soli said.

"Mamalú!" he called out. "La bendición!"

Lulu had taught him this, this requiring a blessing before leaving the house. For Soli it bordered on superstition.

"She can't hear you," Soli grumbled. "She's listening to the radio."

The rental house was an odd string of low and narrow rooms, an old adobe cabin that had been added on to several times, and at the other end of the house, in the parlor, the radio blared because it was easier for Lulu to turn it up than to try to get the boys, ages six and four, to be quiet.

"Come here. I'll bless you," Soli said.

"Can you do that?"

She squinted at him. She'd been the one who'd raised him since he was a baby. If anyone had any right to give him a blessing, it was she. Sometimes it rankled, this attachment he'd formed with Lulu, who hadn't come into the picture until he was well out of diapers. But Soli saw the mischievous glint in his eye and realized he was teasing her.

She took a soapy hand and reached to mark his forehead with the sign of the cross, but he ducked, and she chased him out the door.

She'd forgotten to ask where he was going. In her family, a boy almost eighteen years old would not be questioned about his comings and goings, but Raymond's family had different ideas.

She turned back to the sink to scrub the pots. There was no need to check on the children. She could hear Jackie in the next room, bossing about his little brother, Ernie.

And Raymond's voice came booming from their bedroom, belting out a song in German as he spruced up to go out. His singing society rehearsed two Tuesday evenings a month.

In response, Lulu turned up the volume of the radio even louder.

The kitchen squared away, Soli hung her apron on the back of the door and turned out the light. Raymond emerged from their bedroom freshly shaven and ready to leave. They came together over the children, who wrestled on a braided rag rug.

She shouted over his shoulder, "Lulu, turn the radio down! …Lulu!"

"What?"

"Turn the radio down!" She turned her attention to the children.

"Say goodnight to Daddy. He's going to go sing."

"I want to go, too," Ernie said. "I sing good, don't I, Mama?"

"Yes, mi amor, but Daddy's choir is all men. You'll have to grow up before you can go with him."

"Off to bed now," Raymond ordered.

Humming the song "What'll I Do?," Soli sharpened her pencil with a paring knife. She readied her letter paper on the dining room table and began to write her baby sister. She reported that the boys were over the flu. Eddy was on the high-school basketball team. She was still expecting and big as a barn, hoping for a daughter this time.

She hesitated. Just the thought of putting the next item of business in writing, in her own hand, in a letter to Meche, made her feel like she'd swallowed a big stone, black and cold.

She forced her pencil onward, "*We might be moving to another state.*"

Since Prohibition, she explained (feeling the need to justify the scheme), the brewery where Raymond worked had become very unstable. The business, which now made soft drinks, had changed hands three times in five years, and rumor had it that it was on the auction block again. As it happened, Raymond had a cousin who worked in a former brewery in Wisconsin State, which was about as far north as you could get, right up next to Canada, and Raymond had a job there if he wanted it. Even though he worked in the supply and shipping department and not on the floor, Raymond said he missed the beer business, missed the smell of hops. Right now his cousin's plant made ice cream, which to Raymond's mind was worse than soft drinks, but there was a movement in Wisconsin to make it legal in that state to brew beer with a low alcohol level of 2.75%.

"*The climate is said to be dreadfully cold,*" she wrote, "*but how cold can it be if they're making ice cream?*"

Soli laid down her pencil. She chewed her lip. Raymond assured her they would do nothing rash, that they would consider it carefully, but clearly he was convinced that it would be a wise move for their future.

If he was holding back, it was because of her.

The Mexican Revolution had ended five years earlier, and yet a visit to Campeche still seemed impossible. And now they were to move even farther away?

Raymond had warned her that Milwaukee would be completely different from Texas, that there would be no Mexican bakeries or grocery stores, no one speaking Spanish. She felt an overwhelming sense of impending loss. She feared she would not be able to adapt, that she would feel adrift and alone and homesick for the rest of her life.

To close her letter she wrote:

> *If you see Great-Aunt Pancha, tell her that women can vote here in Texas and that a lady politician, Ma Ferguson, took office this year as governor of Texas. I'd love to hear what Tía Pancha has to say about that! One of Ma Ferguson's campaign slogans was, "a bonnet and not a hood," because she's against the Ku Klux Klan. I think even Raymond voted for her because of that (the Klan is terribly anti-Catholic) but he won't tell me if he did or not.*
>
> *Dear little sister, I wish I could put your hand on my belly so you could feel how strong your little niece (I hope) kicks. I wish you knew the boys. They're lovely and you could teach them so much. Ay, Mechecita. How I wish I were there, or that you were here.*
>
> *All my love,*
> *Soli*

Meche came around the high mahogany counter to escort Mrs. García and her daughter to the door. The pudgy little girl wore a frothy organdy confirmation dress—her tummy straining the white cloth. The mother carried the girl's rosary, candle and prayer book nestled in a shopping basket, with the lace veil wrapped in tissue lying on top. Taking the child by the hand as they went out the door, the mother admonished her to take care in the street and to not—if she knew what was good for her—get her dress dirty.

Meche made a note about the Garcías in the appointment book and plopped it on top of the ledger. Day after day clients dribbled in and dribbled out—first communions, christenings, weddings.

Meche's eyes landed on the two seldom-used chairs across from her—like the counter, they were from the time of Ruby's father. Upholstered in a murky damask, they squatted against the opposite wall on the brown-and-white floor tiles. Normally the chairs were all but invisible to her, but that morning when she and Ruby had opened up, Ruby had run a hand over the top of the back of one of them as if she'd never seen it before. Sitting and bouncing a little, a puff of dust rose from it.

"Meche," she said, "we should have these recovered. Something more aesthetic. Green- and white-striped silk, maybe. Can we afford it?"

"I doubt it," Meche said, surprised. Green and white stripes? Silk? Where did Ruby get these ideas? Besides, her interest in decor usually confined itself to backdrops and props for the portraits.

Now, the reception once again empty, Meche fingered the spindle of invoices next to the account books—the next client was not expected for some time. She checked the little desk clock behind the counter and wound it. She drummed her fingers. Finally, with some resolve, she opened one of the little drawers and took out a bottle of sepia ink, an eye dropper, a rag and a scrap of paper marked with blots and dribbles and capital M's. After refilling her fountain pen and testing it on the torn scrap, she positioned the two sheets of writing paper that she'd purchased the day before. When had she last written Soli? Probably when Soli's baby was born. Or Christmas. Which had come first?

Soli's letters were always a litany of domestic minutia—the only things that ever changed were the names of the childhood illnesses and the identity of who took what first step. Meche, on the other hand, saw no point in writing something boring. Why waste paper on the steady, or steady-ish, stream of clients, the ordering of supplies and paying of bills? Why write if she had nothing of interest to say, or nothing Soli would want to hear?

The metal nib of her pen scraped across the paper.

Estudio de Fotografía Eckart, Calle 12
San Francisco de Campeche, Campeche
Los Estados Unidos Mexicanos

Tuesday, June 9, 1925

Dear Soli,
I trust this letter finds you, your husband and children
enjoying good health. Even though I have not had the good
fortune to set eyes on Jack, Ernst and...

What was that baby's name again? Rifling through a pile of papers, she pulled out Soli's last letter.

Despite the vagaries of the international post, one of Soli's letters arrived about every two weeks. Although Meche did not consciously keep track, the unvarying rhythm of her correspondence meant that if a letter was delayed or lost, Meche sensed its absence, and worry would gnaw at the back of her mind until it or the next letter arrived. Then Meche would feel a little lift in her spirit. Sometimes. Other times the arrival of yet another letter felt like a nagging reminder, a bill for which she did not have the money to pay.

Meche glanced through the pages looking for mention of the baby. Soli wrote in pencil on impossibly thin paper and in a tiny script that felt like a cipher to read. There it was. Frank. What an ugly name.

> *...Jack, Ernst and Frank, it's easy to picture you taking care of a growing family, but it's very hard to think of little Lalo...*

She stopped and crossed out "Lalo". When he'd started school in far-off Texas, they switched to calling him Eddy. But really, why? "Lalo" was a perfectly good nickname for "Eduardo." She decided to keep "Lalo". Her baby brother—the little five-year-old of her memory, always whining and clinging to Soli's skirts—would always be "Lalo" to her.

> *...to think of little ~~Lalo~~ Lalito as all grown up, or mostly so. Give him a hug for me.*

The required salutations out of the way, she half smiled at the page and continued.

> *I write with news! Our daily routine at the studio cracked wide open last month. Ruby and I took a little trip...*

Her smile faded and she lifted her pen, glancing up at the door that led to the studio. Her brow furrowed thinking how unhappy Ruby would be about how she was going to end this sentence. But what did it matter when Soli was over a thousand miles away?

> *...to celebrate our tenth anniversary.*

Meche imagined Soli in a large living room with a brick fireplace, like she'd seen in magazines, and the children playing on a thick rug in front of a fire. Soli, seated in a wing-backed armchair, would read the letter aloud to the loathsome Lulu, "*...to celebrate our tenth anniversary.*"

"What does she mean?" Lulu would demand, "What anniversary?"

"I don't know, dear. Let me finish."

Meche hesitated—maybe she should cross out about their anniversary and add "Aunt" before Ruby's name as was expected. Because, what if Lulu confronted Ruby—sent a nasty letter or wire?

No. Lulu would never say anything—for Lulu, if she didn't like something, it simply did not exist.

And Soli? Would Soli not know what she meant? Or would she just tell herself that she did not?

Pinpricks of irritation needled Meche's face. Not once, in any of Soli's letters, did she ever ask after Ruby or send her regards. Meche took a deep breath. She would not be cross—she'd started the damn letter and she was going to finish it.

> *We visited Mérida and the archeological sites of Uxmal and Chichen Itzá.*
>
> *Ruby didn't care much for the horseback riding part of the trip and even less for the camping parts (she's such a city girl), but was happy as a brood hen taking photographs. Freed from the tedium of the studio, she was able to be as artistic and noncommercial as she liked. (Still, we do hope to have some postcards made, which is how we justified the trip.)*
>
> *At Chichen Itzá she took pictures of American archeologists excavating the Temple of Warriors and Mexican archeologists working on the pyramid and the great ball court. The scale of the work they're doing is astounding. It really must have been the grandest city ever.*

I can't express how deeply I relished being in the countryside again. It brought back so many memories of Baalam Kab. I've been so enamored with life in Campeche City, I hadn't realized how much I miss the country. It was like coming out of a cave into sunlight.

Do you know that in all this time I've never once been back to the rancho, but I dream of it often. Do you, Soli? Don't you miss it? Living anywhere else is like living with a single lung, don't you think?

Chichen Itzá, as I said, is magnificent, and although farther from Mérida than Uxmal, was fairly easy to get to, what with all the people coming and going because of the excavation work. But Uxmal was magical.

We rode over a rough, overgrown trail (with Ruby complaining every step of the way). Then we caught sight of the pyramid. It rises above the trees like a mountain, a pale, crumbly mountain. And even with the encroaching vegetation (bushes were growing all over it, and only the very top was completely clear), you could see that, instead of sharp edges and angles like the pyramid at Chichen Itzá, its edges were rounded, making it more "organic" (Ruby's word) and more mountain-like. Not that I've ever seen a real mountain.

We found a large quadrangle between the ruins of four ornately carved buildings, each quite tall and very long. I'd say each side of the plaza would measure well over 200 feet. It must have been incredibly impressive and elegant in its time (1,000 years ago, according to the archeologists at Chichen Itzá). We cleared some brush away from a small section of one of the buildings and camped against its wall.

The site in moonlight, in the night shadow of the pyramid, well, just the memory of it makes the back of my

*neck tingle. If only Ruby could take a picture of that, Uxmal
in moonlight (not the back of my neck).*

Meche smiled. Ruby had already taken pictures of the back of
Meche's neck, and more.

There is something sacred at Uxmal, truly sacred.

She closed her eyes and recalled the light of dawn drenching the top
of the pyramid with gold. Since the trip, she'd been given to
daydreaming. She longed to be on horseback again, riding through the
brush, far from the city. When she opened her eyes, she stared at the
sheet of paper in front of her without seeing it.

She rested her chin in her hand. The memories of that night, she
decided, were hers. Hers and Ruby's. She didn't want to share any more
of it. She crossed out the last line.

~~There is something sacred at Uxmal, truly sacred.~~
*When we get the postcards made, I'll send you some. And I
imagine Ruby will make some prints to send to Lulu.*

It had been a wonderful trip.

If the postcards were a financial success, then maybe she'd be able to
pry Ruby away from the studio more often. Maybe she could even talk
her into a trip to the rancho.

Meche put the cap on her pen. She drifted to the studio doorway and
leaned against it. Ruby was setting up for the next sitting.

"I'm writing to Soli," she said.

Ruby stood, her hand on the large camera, staring at the little
platform where the next subject would pose. Meche smiled, thinking, if
only Ruby could take a picture of herself like this.

"That old plaster urn is going to have to go," Ruby said.

"Anything you want to say in the letter?"

"Peacock feathers."

"What?"

"In a vase. Where do you think we could lay our hands on some peacock feathers?"

1 9 2 4 ...

$\mathbf{S}$*oli set the bowl* of scrambled eggs and the bowl of beans on the table. It felt like a kind of dance as she turned this way and that with her expectant bulge. Her apron, hanging loosely from her neck over her maternity smock, swayed with the movement. She went back to the kitchen for the orange juice and coffee. She was no longer a girl, slight and lithesome. Underneath the shapeless clothes, designed for modesty, not style, this, her third baby, was tightly packed in her abdomen, and her muscles, toned.

"No pan dulce?" Lulu pouted as she sat down, eyeing the plate of toast.

Soli didn't answer. They no longer lived down the street from La Sirena Bakery, and Lulu knew there were only sweet buns on the mornings when Eddy was up in time to make the trek. That did not often happen on a school day.

Soli placed one hand on Raymond's shoulder as she poured black coffee in his cup, and he set his newspaper aside. Jackie, age six and wearing his school uniform, tucked his napkin in his shirt collar, and Ernie, two years younger, climbed onto his chair and squirmed there.

"Eddy, breakfast!" she called. "Lulu, the milk for the coffee is on the stove," she said as she poured a bit of steaming coffee in glasses for Lulu, herself and Eddy.

Lulu sighed and rose. Soli knew from photos that Lulu's figure had been matronly from a young age, and during their time in San Antonio she had only become plumper and softer, moving slower than one might expect for her 42 years.

"I want some coffee, too," four-year-old Ernie piped up.

"No," Raymond said. "It will stunt your growth."

"Eddy says he grew up drinking café con leche, and it didn't stunt his growth," Jackie said.

Raymond grew taller in his seat, and Jackie and Ernie both shrank in theirs.

"Just think what a giant Eddy would be if he'd drunk his milk straight," Soli said as Eddy dragged into the room.

Jackie pointed at him and laughed too loud. "His head would touch the ceiling!"

Eddy flicked his older nephew's head with his finger. The little boy ducked too late and cried out.

Soli surveyed the table as she sat. All was fine, if you overlooked the incomplete set of cracked and chipped dishes.

Ernie rapped a tattoo on his bowl with his fork. Tap, tap, tap, tap.

"Stop that," Soli said.

"I want a real plate," Ernie whined.

Ernie had to eat from a bowl, not because he was the youngest, but because there weren't enough plates left to go around.

"Shh," Soli said. "Papa's going to say grace."

After breakfast Ernie, to prove his prowess, charged into the kitchen with his bowl and dashed back for Joey's plate. As he passed Eddy, Eddy placed his plate on top of the one the little boy was carrying. Ernie teetered a little.

In the kitchen doorway, Soli said, "Oh my, Ernie. Let me…"

But Ernie cried out, "No, I can do it!" and pulled the dishes away from his mother's reach.

They slipped from his grasp, crashed to the kitchen floor, shattering on the tile.

Soli's heart sank. Oh no! she thought.

Raymond poked his head in the kitchen to see what the noise was about. There stood Soli with her hands on her cheeks as Ernie gaped at the floor. Raymond grabbed the boy by the arm and popped him three times on his bottom.

"Schwachkopf," he growled.

Ernie wailed.

"Stop that crying!" Raymond shouted, and went to grab the boy again.

Soli, furious, stepped between them. "You'll be late for work," she said. As Raymond left the room, she followed him a few steps and hissed, "It was only a plate."

"Two. But that's not the point. He was careless and unthinking."

"He was trying to help."

Why did Raymond have to create problems with the children where there were none, and then leave her to deal with the aftermath? Seething, she returned to the kitchen, debating whether to fold her youngest in her arms or hand him a broom as Raymond would prefer. Ernie looked up at her with his little, miserable, tear-streaked face and she took him in her arms.

In the following days, Jackie (reduced to eating from a bowl again, "like a baby,") took his displeasure out on his little brother.

When Ernie complained that it wasn't his fault and that his older brother was being mean to him, Raymond asked him, "Did you or did you not break the plates?"

"It was a axdident," Ernie said.

"There are no accidents. Only carelessness," his father said.

"Schwachkopf," Jackie said under his breath.

"Jackie! Apologize to your brother," Soli said while glaring at Raymond.

Eddy, a growing teenage boy, was also reduced to a bowl. After the soup, he started with a heaping serving of potatoes. When he finished off the potatoes, Soli cut pieces of meat to fit in the bowl. (It would have been easier for her to use a bowl and give him a plate, but Raymond said that was not proper. It was the place of the children to make do, not the parents.) After the meat, Eddy ate a bowl of vegetables. Then another bowl of potatoes, sometimes two, holding a series of tortillas or slices of bread in his hand all the while.

Raymond agreed it was ludicrous. The next Saturday they would go downtown and shop for dishes. He only worked a half day on Saturdays, so they would go after lunch. Lulu agreed to take care of the children.

But Saturday came and Lulu found an excuse not to babysit, closeting herself in her bedroom with a sick headache. Soli told herself it was for the best, that they really shouldn't spend the money. Still, she was disappointed, surprisingly so, and she slammed about the kitchen.

"Sis, I'll watch the little monsters for you," Eddy offered.

"Ay, mi amor, you are a treasure." She smiled and kissed him on the cheek, too fast for him to duck.

Soli got dressed to go out. It would almost be like a date, although she was still irritated with Raymond about Ernie. He was always so hard on the boys, and complained that she was too soft. And soon there would be a third child (well, fourth if you counted Eddy, which she did), so there would be even more occasions to disagree.

She was adjusting her cloche hat over her pinned-up braid when Raymond walked into their bedroom. He was rubbing his hands together, a big smile on his face. She couldn't help but smile back.

"What are you so happy about?" she said as she pulled on her gloves.

"Going out with my best girl," he said. "Ready?"

She jollied herself. It was a good thing for them to spend some time together, just the two of them, even if it was at the Five and Dime.

It turned out Raymond didn't want to go to Woolworths. He insisted they start at Frost Bros. Department Store. Soli objected. She didn't like going to stores she couldn't afford. But Raymond said Frost's would have the greatest selection, and he liked to see the big picture.

He ushered her into the elegant store.

"This way we can see what's out there," he said, "what we like and don't like, and so narrow down what we're looking for."

Soli knew what they were looking for. Sturdy, inexpensive, white crockery. She looked past the dishes Raymond pointed out. She didn't want to fall in love with something out of reach.

"Come on, honey. Don't be like that. Take a look, a real look. How about these?"

She was exasperated. Lulu would have loved them. They made their wedding set look shabby. Did her husband not have any idea how much something like that would cost?

"Not china, Raymond," she said. "It's too fancy. We need something for everyday."

Leaving Frost Bros., her waddle couldn't keep up with Raymond's stride, and they got back on the streetcar to go to the stores on Commerce Street. Joske's was still too expensive, as was Wolf & Marx across the street.

"Maybe," she said, feeling disheartened, "we shouldn't spend the money at all, what with the problems at the brewery, and the baby coming, and..."

"Wisconsin?"

Soli nodded.

"We can't hold our breath forever."

"I suppose not," though she wasn't sure of that.

Well, she told herself, they could buy three cheap plates at the Five and Dime and call it good.

He seemed to read her mind. "Or we could just go to the feed store and buy a trough for Eddy."

She laughed, and nudging him, said, "All right. Let's keep shopping. But not here."

In the next store Soli checked the price tags and relaxed a little bit.

"How about these?" Raymond said.

It was a set with pronounced scalloping around the edges of the plates and the cups were completely fluted, inside and out. And it was all mint green.

"Ay, no! " she said. "That color is so unappetizing. And all those green waves! It makes me seasick."

"That's probably," he countered, lowering his voice, "because you're expecting, don't you think?"

"No, I do not."

She turned away. She was about to say that what was called for was plain white, but there they were. The ones. She took off a glove and ran a finger over the edge of the display plate.

"These," she said.

A bit loud, don't you think?" Raymond said.

She shook her head no.

"But the plates aren't round."

Her face lit up. "I know." She had no idea why that delighted her, but it did.

Raymond raised his hands in defeat.

"Oh," she checked herself, "they must be very expensive."

A salesclerk approached. "No, ma'am, not at all. So happens they're on closeout, marked way down."

"Because nobody in their right mind would buy them otherwise," Raymond grumbled.

The clerk ignored Raymond's comment and pointed out other selling points to Soli.

Raymond paid for the dishes and arranged for delivery.

He set his hat on his head, and Soli practically skipped out of the store on his arm. His body seemed to yield to hers, all attentive and protective. If they hadn't been in public, she felt he would have kissed her on the top of the head.

"Now we can go to Woolworths," he announced.

"What for?"

"For coffee and donuts at their lunch counter, to celebrate your dishes."

Later that afternoon, to Soli's delight, a uniformed employee driving a department store van delivered a crate and used a crowbar to open it for her. When she unwrapped the dishes, Lulu feigned horror.

"Dios mío! Raymond let you buy these?"

Soli lied, a bit, smiled and said, "He insisted."

1919...

Soli sat at the kitchen table, writing a letter to Meche. The dented teakettle sighed at her back.

"Lulu, would you get the kettle before it whistles? It'll wake the baby."

"Ay, God forbid!" Lulu said, and Soli heard the bottom of the tin kettle scrape across the wrought-iron grate of the stovetop.

In handwriting that was cramped, but legible, Soli was extolling Baby Jack, her first-born, now six months old. She was besotted and wanted Meche to understand this fiercest and most tender of loves.

If you could see him, and hold him, you'd feel the same, too.

She touched the tip of her pencil to her tongue and thought about how to continue. There were things she wanted to ask, like what did Zapata's assassination mean? Would his followers give up the fight now? Would it bring an end to the Revolution? At least in Morelos? Or would it add fuel to the fire of violence? Soli hesitated because in Meche's infrequent letters, she never mentioned the war. Soli told herself it was because Campeche was so out-of-the-way that it remained untouched by the Revolution. She had no information to the contrary. Campeche never appeared in the newspapers.

Maybe Meche was silent about the war because she was divided in mind and heart. From the start, she'd been vocal in her support of Madero (now five-years dead) and his plans to oust foreign business interests and establish a modern democracy. Of course, just hearing Madero's name drove Lulu to distraction, which had only encouraged Meche in her opinions. But the prospect of agrarian reform had to make

Meche uneasy. The family had no political clout in any camp, and were now absentee landowners. Might they not end up losing Baalam Kab?

Soli rubbed her eraser across a line, and then over the resultant smudge. It wore right through the paper. She whispered a mild curse. Behind her, Lulu was clattering dishes as she made a pot of tea. When it came to writing to Meche, Lulu was another tricky topic. It was only natural for Soli to want to write about her. With Raymond at work and Eddy at school all day, Lulu was her sole adult companion. But since Meche could not abide Lulu, Soli censored her out of her letters.

Lulu set her cup of chamomile tea on the kitchen table and plopped down across from Soli with a sigh. Soli smiled at her. There was something comforting about Lulu, with her blond hair braided and pinned, strands feathering about her full, ivory-white face; her ample bosom; the scent of her rose-scented toilet water; her pale eyes that often had a twinkle to them. Lulu still put on black when she went out, but around the house she wore pastel colors, like the pink blouse she wore today, things that must have been packed at the bottom of her trunk. It suggested that Lulu had all along had the capacity to foresee a different kind of future for herself, an ability that Soli had never glimpsed in her. And still didn't. Perhaps she simply hadn't wanted to part with the colors she was so fond of.

Something else Soli would like to write to Meche about was Texas. After all, it was where she lived. But Meche was averse to all things American. Soli wondered if it was solely about politics, or if maybe Meche blamed the United States for swallowing up her and Eddy. Soli felt that way sometimes, lost in the vast otherness that was Texas.

She immediately rebuked herself for the thought. She wasn't lost, not in any sense of the word. Raymond, and now baby Jack, were her all.

As she watched Lulu stir sugar into her tea, it occurred to Soli that Lulu had been folded into a life that was not of her own making. Was that true of Meche as well, living not on the rancho but in the city, and under the dubious influence of Aunt Ruby?

Lulu, a lace handkerchief to her temple, was babbling away, her chatter a froth of words on the shore of Soli's consciousness. Something about plenitude. The word caught Soli's attention, the way Lulu drew out the syllables of the word as if Soli were deaf or dense.

"Ple-ni-tud, hija."

The last word, "daughter," was just a turn of phrase. Lulu was Soli's senior by only 13 years, and rather than a stepmother, Soli sometimes felt she'd been traded a hapless older sister for her wayward younger one. Looking up from her letter, she saw Lulu's blue eyes swimming with nostalgia. She was talking about Mexico again, and Soli felt equal parts pity and exasperation. But what she was saying was true, Campeche did possess a heaping, pungent, ear-tingling and eye-dazzling plenitude.

"Texas has its own abundances," Soli countered.

"Not abundance, hija, excess: of dust, of refugees, of guns."

Soli nodded. Sometimes she wondered if they might not be living more closely to the Revolution here in San Antonio than Meche was back home in Campeche. Pancho Villa's wife lived in a neighborhood across the river from them, and President Madero's widow resided here, too, on the same street as supporters of Huerta, her husband's assassin. Key players in the Revolution regularly came in and out of San Antonio: generals and politicians and spies in search of refuge, arms, alliances and information. Their intrigues were reported on in the newspapers or whispered about in the neighborhood. While unlikely that any of them would ever set foot in Soli and Lulu's Campeche, they seemed right at home in San Antonio's ice cream parlors and hotel lobbies.

"And gringo soldiers everywhere," Lulu added. "How dare a decent lady go out?"

Lulu was being overly dramatic again. Despite all the military forts in and around San Antonio, Soli and Lulu had never run into any soldiers. Who they did always happen upon were refugees, whose plight tore at Soli's heart. The Revolution had been going on now for nine years. Soli worried that if it didn't end soon, Eddy, almost 14, would end up getting drawn into it.

The evening before during dinner, Raymond had talked about

moving away from the border. Presumably it was to comfort Lulu who worried about the war reaching them in Texas.

Although Raymond spoke only in English to Soli (except in bed where he murmured things in German that she had no words for in either English or Spanish!), with Lulu he used a hodgepodge of Spanish and English, contorting words in both languages to the point of gibberish. Lulu, however, seemed to follow whatever he said with delight, but she refused to answer in anything but Spanish, sometimes requiring Soli or Eddy to translate for her, so that Soli was not sure how much English Lulu had actually picked up in the seven years they'd been in Texas.

Lulu protested the idea of relocating, and Raymond teased her about moving north, maybe all the way to Milwaukee, where he had cousins on his mother's side.

"They say the air is so cold, it cuts like a knife," he said, "that in winter great chunks of ice float in Lake Michigan, and that the snow mounds up so high, the trolleys can't run."

"Qué, qué?" Lulu asked.

 Soli translated and Lulu got all flustered.

"But, Mamalú," Eddy said in Spanish, patting Lulu's hand, "there'd be no rinches up north."

"Oh, I'm not worried about Texas Rangers," Lulu said.

Soli bit her tongue. Hundreds and hundreds, maybe thousands of Mexicans and Tejanos, that is Texans of Mexican descent, had died at the hands of the rinches. If she and Eddy were fair and blond like Lulu, she might not worry either.

"And, hijo, who knows what horrors they have up there," Lulu said. "Clearly the weather, for one."

"You never know, Lulu," Raymond said. "You might like it. It's a land of opportunity, and it's supposed to be beautiful. They make lots of ice cream there." He winked at her. "They invented the ice cream sundae."

Lulu's eyebrows raised in interest, but then she shook her head.

"Ay, Raymondcito. I could never live up north. I could never learn English," she insisted.

"You wouldn't have to speak English up north," Raymond bantered. "You could speak German. Lots of Germans up there. You'd get on famously."

Lulu's father, of course, was German, but she didn't seem to know more than a word or two. At least she never spoke it to Raymond or his German-speaking parents, and Soli had noticed that Raymond didn't add any German words into the mix when he addressed her.

"The United States is at war with Germany!" Lulu exclaimed in a way that Soli suspected was pure acting. "Having escaped the war at home, you want them to shoot me for a German spy in Milwaukee?"

Soli stiffened. Had Lulu so easily forgotten the hostility and violence Germans had faced here in Texas? She still worried every time Raymond left the house.

"The war's over," Raymond smiled. He was patient with Lulu. "You know how you always say how much you miss the ocean? Well, they say Lake Michigan is so big, it's like an ocean, waves and everything."

Lulu sniffed. "The Gulf of Mexico is a proper ocean: no ice."

Raymond laughed, and Lulu smiled coyly, as if making him laugh had been her intent all along, when it was clear to Soli that she spoke quite seriously.

Recalling the conversation now was unsettling. Soli didn't want to move further north either. The turmoil along the border was real: raids and masses of refugees and lynchings and political arrests. But the idea of putting even more distance between her and home, made her feel sick.

What outlandish turns of events had occurred to land her here in San Antonio with Lulu and Eddy, for her to find Raymond, and be blessed with baby Jackie! Circumstances had torn two sets of sisters apart and then cobbled them together in a new pairing, separated by a border and so much more.

Lulu stopped chattering to take a sip of tea. Soli looked down at her letter and the hole in the paper that her words had fallen through. There was so much she wanted to say but couldn't.

R*uby poured the developing* solution into the glass tray. She'd thought long and hard about what she was doing—the technique was new, but what really concerned her was the subject matter. As a single lady in business, her respectability hung by a thread, and yet she'd agreed to take pictures of prostitutes for their identity booklets.

She knew one of her competitors had turned the job down with disdain, and she suspected the other had as well.

What would happen to her portrait business when her association with public women became known? Because of course it would—this was Campeche, after all, which might look like a city, but at heart was a village. The queasiness in her stomach told her that accepting the assignment had been a mistake.

Ruby swished the paper in the developing solution with a pair of tongs. Spectral images began to appear.

How thick the paper was. Stiff and glossy. So different, she thought, from the letter Meche had gotten that day from Soli in Texas—paper thin as tissue. Ghost paper, with a ghost missive. Soli had added a greeting at the bottom from Lulu, but it was not in Lulu's voice—not even an echo of it.

Ruby's compact body felt as solid as ever, and the gloom of the darkroom brimmed with potential as usual, but everything in the outer world seemed just a bit nebulous, unfocused. Unfocused—not a good word for a photographer, she thought wryly.

It was just like Lulu to direct Soli to write her hello—too lazy to write it herself. But then again, Ruby herself had not written in ages. She was busy. Business was definitely slow—the money trickling in—but that afforded her time for her own photography. Besides, she wasn't any good at writing. Their mother had placed great value on elegant handwriting as a mark of a well-bred lady. But the letters slipped about both in Ruby's head and on the page, and her ink-splotched penmanship was, as she'd been told often enough, atrocious.

Lulu was equally critical, but for different reasons. "Why should I get stuck with the bookwork just because you can't be bothered to write a legible line?"

Ruby recalled the account books with the columns of Lulu's neat, spidery numbers, and wondered where she had put Lulu's last letter. She'd like to read it again, hear her sister's voice encoded in that familiar script. And yet it was only Soli's letter that had brought her sister to mind. Perhaps Ruby was as unfeeling and selfish as Lulu had often accused, for without the letter, how long would it have been before she remembered to think about Lulu?

But the letter had arrived, and now it was as if Lulu stood just outside the darkroom door, waiting—the pillowy contour of her torso, the scent of rose water, lavender soap and tangy sweat, the way she said *mi amor* in that way that sounded like an accusation rather than an endearment.

Lulu had gone—eight years ago now—and Meche—no more than a slip of a thing back then—had wedged herself into Ruby's life. From the start the girl had been eager to learn everything about the studio, but Ruby drew the line. She was not to touch the camera equipment, and under no circumstance was she allowed into the darkroom. What Ruby needed was someone to keep the books, make appointments, order supplies, deal with clients—she needed a replacement for Lulu.

"But I want to learn to be a lady photographer like you," the girl said. Ruby snorted.

"Besides, just think, if you get sick or break your arm, then what?"

"Then I'll starve, and you can go back to where you belong," Ruby said.

Since then, Meche had more than filled the vacuum left by Lulu. She and Ruby each ruled their own domain as Ruby had delineated them—

just as her father had before her, relegating Lulu to the reception desk while letting Ruby into the darkroom and under the large studio camera's black focusing cloth.

Her father's decree had made sense. Lulu had no passion for photography, no patience for the mechanics and chemistry of it. She detested the darkroom—she found the odd red-tinged darkness claustrophobic and the chemicals gave her a headache. Whereas Ruby always entered the darkroom with anticipation. For her, entering it was like wrapping herself in a silk dressing robe—or what she imagined that would be like—and the pungent chemicals were as welcome as the aroma of baking bread, the tingle of ripe mango and the scent of her father's hair oil, all rolled into one delicious smell.

An unwelcome thought intruded. Meche had been more excited than usual at the arrival of Soli's letter. Ruby knew she was bored. Meche was only twenty-two and full of verve. Her brown eyes flashed at any hint of novelty. Her muscles were taut and ready, but there was nothing in the studio to exercise them. More than once, she'd found Meche up on a chair on some invented cleaning job, several times foxtrotting to her own humming, and earlier that day she'd come across her walking about the reception area balancing the ledger books on her head.

What if, for the adventure of it, Meche decided to join Soli in the North? Ruby's stomach clenched at the thought. Those first years Ruby had wished her gone, but now she did not know what she would do without her—or how she could run the studio alone. Irritation wrinkled her brow.

She brought her attention back to the developing tray. She needed to count and keep track of the inversions in the development solution. Each sepia-toned face materialized in the liquid, losing its unearthly aspect. Each woman stared back at her with a bleak gaze—each mouth caught the moment before a frown. Except for the second from the last. That one had taken exception to a lady photographer—Ruby didn't understand why—and anger glinted there well before she snapped the shot.

The women were all young or youngish, hair pulled back in proper coiffures, every one in a modest high-necked dress. As far as she could see, there was nothing to mark them as prostitutes, except for these photos that would be glued into their newly issued identity booklets. Trapped there—like moths pinned to a board. Ruby grimaced at the thought.

The room in the city hall they'd allotted her was bare and dusty. Every tap of Ruby's foot on the floor tiles, every scrape of the tripod echoed. Is that what her photos were? Echoes? Echoes of these women as they clutched at dignity, stared her down, one openly angry?

She fastened the last photo with a clothespin to hang on a cord next to the others to dry, and came out of the darkroom to look for Meche. She found her, elbows on the counter, leaning forward in animated conversation. Ruby turned to see who she was talking to so happily.

Tía Pancha!

Ruby groaned inwardly. Her great-aunt perched on one of the armchairs—next to her on the floor a leather satchel and a case that converted into her portable writing desk. The woman must be close to eighty now, or was she even older? Despite looking slightly more shrunken, her posture was erect and she radiated energy. At least, Ruby told herself, she would serve as a distraction for Meche, who for some reason liked the pontificating old bat.

Ruby and Aunt Pancha kissed each other on the cheek in greeting.

"What have you done this time, Tía?" Ruby asked.

"So much, I can't wait to tell you, but nothing illegal for the moment, if that's what you mean."

"It is," Ruby confirmed. "To what do we owe this visit?"

"Can't I visit my dear nieces?"

"Of course, Tía!" Meche said. "It's always a pleasure to see you."

It irked Ruby that her aunt had won Meche over and appropriated as her own.

"What about whatever cause you're consumed with at the moment? Won't you be missed?"

"Ruby, don't be so rude," Meche said.

"As it happens, I'm on my way back from some meetings in Mérida."

"Feminist meetings!" Meche added with enthusiasm. "Why don't we have anything like that here in Campeche?"

"Tía, please don't tell me you're here for rabble-rousing," Ruby said. "Business is bad enough as it is."

"No, my dear. I just wanted to spend a couple days with you before returning to Mexico City. So, business is bad?"

Meche laid out their financial woes, in too much detail, Ruby thought, and then explained the job Ruby had just finished printing.

"At least that will be somewhat regular income," Meche said.

Ruby stared at the floor and shook her head. "I'm not going to take those pictures anymore," she said, the decision made as it came out of her mouth.

When she looked up, she saw that they were both studying her.

"But, hija, if you need the money…" Tía Pancha said.

"It makes me feel dirty. Not the women, but the documenting of them. They need to be left alone. Left to their own devices, such as they are. Certainly not be put in a booklet," she said, spitting out the last word.

"I'd say it's a public service to make sure they're not sick, and in the long run it will protect them, too," Tía Pancha said.

"That's a surprising attitude for you to take," Ruby said.

"I'm thinking of the public health. Our country has a lot of work to do in that area."

"Then make their customers have a booklet," Ruby shot back. "Why do the women need to be… to be catalogued?"

"But, boxita," Meche said. "Isn't it better that you take the pictures? I'm sure you're at least civil to them—well, as civil as you are to anyone. I doubt the same can be said of the doctors and bureaucrats they deal with. Really, you're helping them."

"No, I'm getting paid," Ruby said accusingly. She moved to the counter. "I feel like I'm betraying them, Meche, and debasing my art in the bargain."

Meche placed her hand on Ruby's.

"Well, we don't have to decide anything this minute," Tía Pancha said. "We can talk about it over dinner."

"Tía, this doesn't concern you," Ruby said.

"But, hija, I'm here, and I want to help if I can."

"No, you're here for some nefarious purpose of your own."

"Ruby!" Meche exclaimed.

"You don't know her like I do," Ruby said. "The way business is, her political activities could put the studio under quicker than this city job or anything else."

"Hija, the dictatorship is long gone, and the Revolution is all but over."

"It's never over."

"Ah, hija, spoken like a true revolutionary. But things are different now."

"Ah, sí? Then, Tía, what are you going to do the rest of your life?"

1 9 1 7 ...

It was the first Sunday in June and Soli, Eddy by her side, paused before entering the nave of the church.

Soli had come to the conclusion that wedding dresses were white so that at least one thing about getting married would be simple. They were a deceit, a dustcover thrown over an old divan to hide the threadbare brocade from view, but also a conceit, a blank movie screen on which the audience's myriad emotions were projected. She loved Raymond and wanted to marry him, but long gone was that moment of bliss when he had proposed, and long gone the following weeks of floating with happiness.

Raymond's uncle, Emil, had offered to stand in for her father, a suggestion heartily approved by her future in-laws, as well as by the priest, but Soli declined. She wanted Eddy to give her away. He was only 12, but he was her flesh and blood.

Rising to the occasion, Eddy had checked his boyishness at the church door and donned an unaccustomed solemnity. His slicked-back hair showed the tracks of the teeth of his comb, and he was wearing his first pair of long pants. He might not be someone to lean on, but she was touched by his determination to play the man of the family.

That did not mean that he'd not shown signs of stage fright. He hadn't eaten a thing that morning, and on the way to the church in Uncle Emil's new Briggs Detroiter touring car, Lulu had held Eddy's hand to keep him from chewing his nails. When the other hand slid to his mouth, Lulu had slapped at it, and grabbed it, too, imprisoning both hands. Soli had noticed that since she and Raymond had set the date,

Eddy had attached himself more firmly than ever to Lulu. In the car he slumped against her and tried to lay his head on her shoulder, but Lulu told him to sit up; she wasn't about to have her dress stained with hair oil.

Now at the entrance of the church, Eddy looked up at Soli and proffered his arm by sticking out his elbow. She rested her hand on his forearm, and he turned his gaze to the carpeted pathway ahead of them. She noticed bittersweetly that in his seriousness, he frowned a little, just like their father, whom he barely remembered.

Her father had not died recently (it had been seven years), but today she missed him as she had not for some time, and her eyes welled with tears. She missed her mother, too, but she'd been gone so very long, she was but a sweet shadow in Soli's heart.

Of course Meche was absent, too. But that had been Meche's choice, and Soli felt a flash of anger that left an acrid taste in her mouth. She let out an aggrieved sigh so deep that Eddy glanced up at her. His eyes had always been like their father's, the same shape, the same brown color of toasted pecans. She gave him a reassuring smile. He was a dear boy, but, Soli thought with a pang, it should have been her father by her side.

But then if her father were living, she wouldn't be in Texas, would she? And she would never have met Raymond. She'd never been given to philosophizing, but she wanted to believe, in fact did believe, that this marriage was not the result of a random twist of fate, but of a destiny fulfilled.

Soli suddenly wondered about the day her father married Lulu. What had been going through his mind and in his heart that day? Whom had he been missing? Had he thought about Soli's mother? About Soli, Meche and Eddy?

It seemed that no smile, no tear, no act or emotion of any kind was uncomplicated in a wedding. Thank the Virgin for the simplicity of white cloth. Soli's unadorned dress was high-necked and long-sleeved. The pegged skirt was fuller at the hips than at the hemline and ended, to her mother-in-law's disapproval, quite stylishly several inches above her white-stockinged ankles.

For something borrowed, she wore Lulu's white high-heeled shoes from her own wedding, unearthed from her trunk. The heels, shaped like squared-off hourglasses, were still fashionable, and except for a dark stain on the sole, they were as good as new, even if they were a bit wide, a bit short and the long pointy toes pinched. She would rather not have used them for they reminded her of that wedding she'd not attended, and of never seeing her father again, but her practicality won out in the end.

Soli shifted her weight but the pain in her feet remained. Eddy placed his hand on top of hers, as they had practiced, but his nervous fingertips fiddled with the lace of her veil where it hung over her arm. Raymond's mother had provided the veil from her own wedding gown, an offer made in such a way that it could not be refused, but she agreed to let Soli attach the lace to a new headdress that was broader and more modern. The veil almost touched the floor, and it made her rather plain dress appear more elegant than it was, for which she was grateful. But the lace draped her in the complications of Raymond's family. It brought even more history to the occasion, when Soli already felt burdened and saddened by her own past.

As if family issues were not enough, the greater world bore down on them as well. When they'd set the date, they hadn't bargained on war being declared against Germany. The Revolution still raged in Mexico, and now this.

Ugly things were being said about Germans and German-Americans, and some days Raymond declared he would enlist to prove his family's loyalty. With their wedding in the works, she had convinced him not to, but the newspapers reported that a draft law would be passed within a week. One way or another, would Raymond be taken from her? How soon would conscription go into effect? This month? This summer? Or did they have a year? Would her beautiful young husband perish on some battleground in France? Would she end up like Lulu, the two of them, arms linked forever, co-widows in black.

Her lips moved silently as she called on the Virgin's protection. Then she squeezed Eddy's arm, the signal for them to start down the aisle.

He startled. Where had his thoughts taken him? She hoped somewhere more pleasant and innocent than her own.

The long nave stretched ahead of them. At its end, a Gothic arch framed the altar, and in between, large creamy-white columns supported the airy yellow-and-gold vaulted ceiling. Light danced through the stained-glass windows set high in the walls, and everything gloomy flew from her mind. Only Raymond and the distance between them remained. She trembled with emotion and anticipation. The holy sacrament with Raymond at the altar was what truly mattered. The wedding mass would be in Latin, and so, familiar; but the priest spoke German, and they would take their marriage vows in that language.

She forced herself, and Eddy, to go slowly, to take stately, dignified steps, passing pew after pew. When she reached Raymond and they joined hands, she felt she'd traveled a very long way, and was finally home.

Two weeks later, Soli's in-laws hosted a birthday celebration for Uncle Emil. The house was already crowded when a new guest arrived. *Mutter* Eckart took the new-arrival's derby and, beaming, ushered him into the parlor, which he entered as onto a stage, greeting people left and right. He was a large man in his late fifties, boisterous, suit jacket open and vest straining at its buttons. His arrival immediately increased the humidity in the already sticky room. Men who were seated stood, and several women did as well. Soli seemed to be the only one who did not know him; he'd not been at the wedding. Uncle Emil thanked him for coming to his birthday party, and the man, Herr Keck, slapped him on the back.

Herr Keck noticed Soli and made a show of stopping in front of her. He enclosed her right hand in his two moist ones.

"*Why you must be that little Mexican bride everyone's talking about,*" he bellowed, somehow getting English, Spanish and German all in the same sentence.

Soli got the gist, but she wasn't sure if he were insulting, patronizing or maybe even complimenting her, so she nodded tentatively.

"María Soledad Hernández Cruz, sir," she said, introducing herself. "It's a pleasure to meet you." She looked to Mutter Eckart to step in and finish the introduction, but what she saw was her mother-in-law, mute and pale. Soli startled when the man, still holding on to her hand, guffawed.

"Excuse us, Herr Keck," Mutter Eckart muttered and yanked Soli towards the kitchen. "Get Raymond," she stage-whispered to her husband as she passed him.

In the steamy kitchen, with her fingers digging into Soli's arm, her mother-in-law scolded her in thickly accented English, "That is not your name."

Soli pulled away and rubbed her arm.

"You are Mrs. Raymond Eckart. Eckart!"

Soli knew that American women changed their last name to their husband's, but she wasn't American. And that was not how it was done in Mexico. Her name was Hernández Cruz: Hernández was her father's family, and Cruz, her mother's. She loved and respected them too much to toss their names away like discarded potato peels.

Besides, their names were all she had left of them.

She opened her mouth to protest, but Mutter Eckart raised her hand to silence her.

"You insult my son," her mother-in-law hissed. "You insult our family. And in front of everyone! In front Herr Keck!"

Her father-in-law appeared with Raymond.

"Straighten her out," he said, giving Raymond a shove and returning to the party.

Raymond's mother explained to him in German what had happened. Soli expected him to calm his mother down, but his face grew pinched. Struggling to keep anger out of his voice, he informed Soli, that they were in the United States and she was to use his last name.

"Well, yes," she said, puzzled at his reaction. "In Mexico, too. Sometimes. De Eckart. María Soledad Hernández Cruz ...de Eckart."

"Not Hernández Cruz, Soli."

She felt cornered. The cast-iron stove was stoked to keep food warm, the table and counters were crowded with bowls and platters, and Mutter Eckart stood behind Raymond, mumbling in German in a singsong punctuated by tsk-tsks. Soli backed away from them, and felt the cool porcelain of the sink at her back.

"But it's my name."

Mutter Eckart stopped in mid-tsk, noticing that she still had Herr Keck's hat in her hand. She looked around for someplace safe to put it, and with a huff took it and herself from the room, squeezing by Lulu who was coming in.

"What's going on?" Lulu wanted to know, pausing to wrinkle her nose with distaste at the aromas in the room.

Raymond and Soli did not turn to her. Their eyes were locked on each other. Lulu shrugged and returned to the party.

During their engagement Raymond had promised that, as soon as the Revolution ended, they would go to Campeche to visit her sister and the rancho. He had to be honest, he couldn't see them moving to Mexico. How would he support them? And he had his parents to think of. But they would find a way to make regular trips there. As soon as they set the date for the wedding, the subject had slid to the back burner.

Raymond took two steps toward her now. He loomed over her, his face red.

"It's my name," Soli repeated, her voice unsteady.

"Just Eckart," he said. "Mrs. Raymond Eckart."

She saw in Raymond's angry face and heard in his icy voice what she had refused to fully acknowledge before: the door to Mexico was no longer ajar. By marrying him, she had closed it. Forever.

She turned away from Raymond and faced the sink. It was not the first time they'd argued, but it was the first time she'd felt afraid.

"But it's not fair," Soli said, her lip quivering.

"It's the law."

She felt like someone was reaming a lemon in her stomach. She fled the kitchen and locked herself in the bathroom. To calm herself she repeated over and over a prayer, "Mother of Mercy…poor, banished children of Eve…our exile…"

Once she'd stopped shaking, she looked in the mirror and chided herself. She was not a child, nor a romantic, nor an idiot. Just because she had chosen to focus on the lovely things about her marriage, did not mean she had not known the other side of her situation. Of course when they were courting, Raymond told her what she wanted to hear. There was no one to blame but herself. Besides, she reminded herself, she did love Raymond. Just not at this moment. And home with him was never going to be just the two of them nestled in some idyllic, indeterminate place of her imagining. It was always going to be his family. And Texas. And the United States.

She admonished herself: let no man, or woman, or anything else put asunder what God has joined.

When she came out of the bathroom, she walked up to Raymond and put her hand on his arm. He looked down at her, into her eyes, wary. His eyes did not smile at her. He might have been a stranger.

"I don't feel very well," she said. "I'd like to go home."

He nodded, and they said their goodbyes.

Raymond didn't speak much for a couple days. It was his way. And then everything was fine again.

Except she no longer had her last names.

1 9 1 4 ...

Campeche | Ruby & Meche

Meche, unusually chatty, bounced along next to Ruby. It seemed to take great effort for her to keep from skipping. Like walking with a balloon, Ruby thought. They passed a neighbor, who greeted them politely, but Ruby saw his eyes slide over the girl's lush, young body. This happened ever more frequently—it made Ruby feel sick.

During the last year the girl had blossomed. It was a trite phrase, but Ruby could think of no other way to describe it. She exuded freshness and health and vitality—as if roses were blooming beneath her skin, as if she were a fruit at the perfect point to pick. Compared to her, Ruby, at 26, felt old. Had she ever passed through a stage like that? She very much doubted it.

Although the girl's body had matured, she was puppy-like in her comportment, flinging her voluptuous body about, unaware of its effect on others. Meche had entered Ruby's life three years before, and Ruby supposed a proper guardian would, from day one, have been relentless in reining her in. Ruby remembered that she had been about that age when her own mother's scolding had taken a rather overwrought turn. Ruby was not of the opinion that her mother's nagging had produced any benefits—it was one of the reasons she'd never fully shouldered her duties as guardian. She'd put the girl up, and she'd put up with her at home and in the studio, and even that had been more than she'd ever been prepared to do.

The girl, that's how Ruby always thought of Meche, ever since she'd arrived, gawky and headstrong. Now she was less than a month from turning seventeen, and somewhere along the line, she'd become the point around which Ruby's life—no, she corrected herself—around which the studio pivoted.

The girl nattered away next to her.

Ruby was taking her to an appointment with Doña Olimpia, the dressmaker Ruby's family had always employed, and the girl was excited —eager to dress like a young lady, with skirts long and narrow. No corset though. She'd pronounced them passé.

"There's really no need to be strung up like a side of beef, Tía. Or to be so hot. You should get rid of yours. It must be terribly stifling. How do you bear it?"

It occurred to Ruby that her own mother would have chided the girl for speaking of such things in public, but Ruby could not be bothered to care about such niceties. Besides, the girl had been so moody of late, so prickly, Ruby was rather enjoying her lightheartedness.

When they arrived at the dressmaker's little house, the small parlor given over to her trade, Doña Olimpia fretted that since they had not yet purchased a corset, it would be difficult to get accurate measurements. As Meche repeated her vision for a foundation-free society, Doña Olimpia pursed her lips. Ruby felt sorry for her. It must be a tricky business being a dressmaker—she saw her customers in their underwear, drew tape measures tight around their busts and yet had to maintain a respectful decorum and not presume any familiarity. She had to instill the confidence of the confessional and never, never offend. Nonetheless, Doña Olimpia was clearly taken aback by the girl's brazen opinions and tried, to no avail, to convince Meche of the absolute necessity of a corset to achieve the proper, respectable, ladylike silhouette.

Ruby listened with a rueful smile. As if anyone had ever convinced the girl of anything! Doña Olimpia shot her looks pleading for support.

"Señora," Meche pronounced, "in a couple of years not even you will be wearing a corset."

The poor woman was so shocked, she seemed on the verge of refusing the work, but she and Ruby both knew she could not afford to stand on principle. Did Meche really not understand that she was jeopardizing the woman's hard-won and fragile respectability? Meche's proposed impropriety in dress was almost akin to having prostitutes as clients, and no respectable woman would knowingly share a dressmaker with a woman of ill repute.

"Señorita Ruby, please!" Doña Olimpia pleaded.

"Maybe times are changing," Ruby said apologetically.

Doña Olimpia raised her hands, palms out, in surrender, then clasped them together below her steel-supported bosom.

Meche unbuttoned her blouse to undress so that Doña Olimpia could take her measurements. Ruby felt herself flush and turned to examine a framed print on the wall of the Virgin of Carmen. It was just the kind of art she despised—piously sentimental. And yet she kept her eyes glued on it—the Madonna, barefoot but crowned, dressed in brown and yellow as always, and holding the Christ child in pink. If Ruby could just make her face mirror the Virgin's blank serenity. But the more she tried, the tighter her fists clenched.

Ruby sat in the parlor studying a catalog of photographic equipment while Meche listened to the gramophone. It was Sunday afternoon, and they had the house to themselves—María Asunción had left for her half-day off after serving the afternoon meal.

Ruby looked up from the page—Meche got up every couple minutes to change the music cylinder and crank the machine. Ruby noticed she did so on tiptoe, apparently taking care with her white stockings—she'd slipped off the cream-colored dress shoes she'd worn to mass earlier.

Having set a strident paso doble march to play, she dropped back onto the sofa in a recline. Ruby didn't care much for the machine or the music, purchased by her father years ago—her mind was busy enough without the musical accompaniment of drums and trumpets. She glanced across at Meche. How fresh and crisp her sky-blue skirt looked against the tired yellow and gold silk of the sofa—the new clothes suited her.

Ruby had detected a shift in Meche after their first visit to Doña

Olimpia, followed by a complete transformation after the second fitting. Meche in her smart, grown-up clothes was suddenly and completely a young lady—no more flouncing about. She was self-possessed and happily self-conscious in a way Ruby had never been and was not now. Somehow their old way of being together—that is to say, Ruby ignoring the girl as much as was practical—no longer worked.

Over the years Ruby had not always noticed the girl growing up. It was María Asunción who would point out that the girl's dresses strained at the buttons, the sleeves hitting well above the wrist. And no, María Asunción assured her, not bothering to hide her exasperation, she had not shrunk the clothes when she washed them. And did Señorita Ruby not see the girl was limping because her shoes pinched?

It had been only some six months earlier, sitting across from Meche at the dining room table, that Ruby noticed that the girl had come to resemble her father—fine-looking, like Ernesto, only without his stuffiness, without the rigidity of his posture and expression. The girl had also begun to exude an appeal that Ruby found unsettling. She would have thought it was she who had changed rather than the girl, if it weren't for the way she saw others react to her. The men were the most obvious, but she sometimes noticed the disapproving glances of ladies, their over-solicitous courtesy. Yes, the girl had changed, but something had shifted deep within Ruby as well, like a knot worked and prodded at until it slips free.

Ruby had started having dreams about photographing Meche—she would lead her to the chaise longue in the studio, situated in front of a painted backdrop of the sea, and direct her how to recline. Then Ruby would scurry back and forth between the camera and the chaise, trying to get the pose just right, lifting Meche's chin a bit, repositioning her hands, loosening her hair and arranging it over her shoulder. In some dreams Meche glowed with a dazzling nimbus, and Ruby was frustrated to tears that she and the camera could not capture it, the dreams turning into fretful nightmares.

While waking, Ruby's desire to gaze at the girl, to reach out and touch her, had become worrisome, embarrassing, painful. She thought about sending her away, but the thought of that was even more distressing. Ruby told herself it was a phase that would pass, a phase they would both grow out of. She coped by spending even more hours locked away in her darkroom. When she did emerge, she found herself tip-toeing around the new Meche.

Now, this Sunday afternoon, the girl assumed a languid posture on the yellow divan, but Ruby could see that her fingers drummed and her white-stockinged toes flexed out of rhythm with the tinny, but pronounced, martial beat of the music emanating from the gramophone's brass horn.

As if feeling Ruby's scrutiny, Meche met her eyes. Ruby felt caught in the act and dropped her eyes to the catalog. She flipped a page.

"Ruby," Meche said, her voice a bit tremulous.

Except within earshot of clients, Meche had recently stopped using "tía" when addressing her. The first few times she'd said her name, bare and untitled, it was with hesitation—perhaps waiting for Ruby to reprimand her for her lack of respect. But Ruby didn't mind at all. In fact, she liked it. Who else was there to call her by her name, with no "señorita" hanging from it, and with, well, intimacy? Only Lulu, three years now in Texas. And Aunt Pancha, whom she hadn't seen in almost as long—thank God.

Sometimes Ruby imagined herself and Meche, decades from now, running the studio together—two old women. But that, she always reminded herself, would not happen, because one day in the next few years, Meche would fall in love and leave to get married. Or, at any time she might decide to join her sister and brother in San Antonio —the three siblings reunited, together with Lulu, far from Campeche, but safe from the war. And speaking English, she supposed—hard to imagine Lulu going about her business speaking English, Lulu in a foreign city. All of them up north, and Ruby here, alone, with only the company of her cameras—permanently and forever Señorita Ruby. She felt a cold and heavy weight in her chest.

Ruby would miss Meche when she'd gone. And not just at the studio. Even before the girl's recent metamorphosis, Ruby had come to appreciate Meche's high spirits. Her determination. Her brown eyes stark and bright against her lighter-brown skin.

"Ruby, are you listening? It will be my birthday soon."

"I'm well aware," Ruby murmured as her mind leaped, batting and grabbing at conclusions. This, she thought, is when she tells me a young man will come courting, this is when she tells me she's written Lulu for a steamship ticket to the United States.

"I... I really want to go to Baalam Kab, Ruby. I do so miss it."

It took Ruby a second to realize she was talking about the rancho.

"And I want you to go with me. I want to show you the pozo and the house, the orange tree in the patio, the fields and the beehives and the woods, and the big ceiba tree there. I want you to meet Pedro Mu, and Doña María Inés. I want you to see where I grew up. I want you to love it like I do."

Ruby was surprised—so much nostalgia in such a young girl.

"Honestly, it's the only thing I want for my birthday."

"You mean besides the clothes?"

"But they don't count, do they? I already have them."

Ruby flipped another page.

"Don't you think, for your sister's sake," Meche wheedled, "that it's time someone in the family checked on the rancho?"

Ruby squinted at her, and Meche reddened—they both knew Meche didn't give a fig about Lulu. As for the rancho, Ruby had absolutely no interest in visiting it—for Lulu or any other reason. She had vague and unpleasant memories of an outing or two to the countryside when she was a little girl. She hadn't been out of the city since, which suited her just fine.

"It would take, what, a week?" Ruby hedged.

"Well, travel time might take two or three days each way, so I thought once we got there, we could spend a couple weeks. But," she offered, "we could go for a week instead."

"Ay, Meche, the studio can't be closed for that long."

Meche went to the gramophone and turned it off so she could be persuasive without any competition from the music.

"But, Ruby…"

"I'm sorry," Ruby said, cutting her short. She set aside the catalog. "How about a new cylinder for the gramophone instead?"

Meche jutted out her chin. "I'll go on my own then."

Ruby set down the catalog and sighed. "That's not safe even in the best of times, and it's hardly the best of times."

The year before, to seize power, General Victoriano Huerta had assassinated President Madero and his vice president. In response, the Revolution had recommenced—its original military leaders, those still loyal to its ideals, joining forces to oust the usurper.

"I'm not a child," Meche said. "In five days I'll be seventeen. Were you a girl at seventeen?"

The question startled Ruby, and she was silent a moment thinking back. "Yes, I believe I was."

"Well," Meche pouted, "you still had a mother and a father." She pulled in her lip. She went to Ruby's chair, knelt and took her hand. "I don't, but I do have you," she said, her eyes moist and filled with unbearable tenderness.

Ruby's hand tingled and she pulled it away. She picked up the catalog again. "A paltry thing, I agree."

"I didn't say that. I would never say that."

"I'll do for now, until you start your own life, with some young man or other."

"This is my life," she said, offended. "I'll never leave you."

Never leave her? This was the girl who Lulu complained was always running away to the fields, who had run away from her own sister and brother, who just a couple months ago had run away from the studio in a fit of pique, disappearing for an entire afternoon, driving Ruby to pacing, to wondering whether to call the police.

Don't believe her, Ruby told herself. Meche may believe she won't leave, but you dare not be so credulous.

"Ruby, I love you."

No. Ruby did not want to feel the glimmer of excitement that she felt, the flutter in her stomach.

"I can't take the time away from the studio," Ruby said. "And it's not safe to be traipsing about the countryside. If not a cylinder, how about a new hat? Something fashionable. Or lace gloves?

"Ruby," she pleaded.

Ruby opened the catalog, but out of the corner of her eye she could see the girl's intense regard, her eyes the same brown as her hair, as her fine eyebrows. Her soft skin, her lips a lovely shade, the color of guava.

"I think you should call me tía," she said.

The girl's face blurred with misery. Or was Ruby seeing it through the haze of tears welling in her own eyes?

Meche rushed from the room, her stockinged feet silent on the tile.

Ruby knew Meche probably felt like she'd been kicked in the stomach, because Ruby felt just the same.

Would Meche make good her threat to run away to the rancho? Would Ruby go to Meche's room in the morning and find it empty? Well, Ruby told herself, the girl would leave eventually. Maybe sooner would be better than later. But going to the rancho would be terribly dangerous, and Ruby remembered how she'd felt the last time Meche had taken off. She couldn't imagine going through that again.

Ruby, the catalog open on her lap, listened for the slam of the front door, or maybe just a click.

Meche's good shoes lay near the sofa. She would need to use a button hook to put on her everyday canvas-topped boots, but she could do that pretty quickly. So, was she packing a suitcase? Waiting for dark? Or for the morning?

She picked up Meche's shoes and examined them—strapped, pointy-toed, with French heels, the leather soles barely scratched. She should take them to Meche's room and apologize. But apologize for what? For making the only reasonable decision she could regarding a trip to the rancho? For insisting on the title of respect that was her due?

She went to the narrow settee by the front door, set the shoes on her lap, and hoped that when Meche came to the door to leave, she would know the right thing to say.

The sun set, the entryway darkened, the room cooled. And still she sat. Then she apparently dozed, because a noise startled her awake. She heard movement within, and saw a glimmer of light from the dining room. And then Meche was standing before her.

She stared at Meche's backlit shape, unable to make out the expression on her face. Ruby feared what her own face revealed: exhaustion, bewilderment, fear.

"Are you hungry?" Meche said.

Ruby nodded.

"I've heated up the leftovers from earlier."

Meche waited a moment, but Ruby gave no sign of moving.

"Tía, what are you doing here?"

"Don't call me tía, Meche," Ruby said. "Please don't."

Ruby directed the young man, "Stand there. Lift your chin. Look at the camera. That's it, but turn your face slightly to the left."

It was far from the first portrait she'd taken of a soldier. This one wore a drab military tunic with brass buttons and a stand-up collar. She'd convinced him to take off his kepi—the brim obscured his eyes. He now held the cap at attention on his knee. She didn't bother asking him to remove his hip holster.

"That's it. Now don't move," she said.

At least his chest was not criss-crossed with a cartridge belt. Nor had he brought a rifle. They almost always did, all holding the gun in the same way—grasping the barrel as if holding a scepter. She strode to the camera on its tripod.

"I'm used to taking orders," he said with a wry smile, "but not from a woman."

She almost smiled, feeling big-sisterly toward him—he was so young. Not much more than twenty, if that. Even so, he was not one of the boys getting his picture taken before heading off to war—he'd been fighting for three years already.

"My first battle, up north, my rifle was older than me," he'd said.

She was intrigued by him. The men of her class—middle, aspiring to upper—wallowed in excessive courtesy and, in her opinion, false gallantry. He displayed none of that, and despite his dark skin—much darker than her own—he showed none of the excessive deference to her as a middle-class mestiza that many indios here in the city did.

Three years, and so far he'd survived. The photograph was for his wife —he hadn't been home in 18 months. Was his wife safe, she wondered? It wasn't something she felt she could ask—too personal, too fraught.

"Where's home?" she asked instead.

Small talk was something Ruby only performed in the studio. Her father had taught her it was important in order to distract the subject and put them at ease.

"It's not just good business, kleines Indianerlein," he would say, "It is in the service of producing a finer picture."

In the end she'd learned to ask inane questions without the least interest in the answers, but in this case, she actually did want to know where he was from.

"In the north. Nowhere you would know, señorita."

"My sister's up north. San Antonio," she said.

She saw his expression harden.

"I've been as far as the Río Bravo," he said. "I've watered my horse in it. They said the other side was the United States. Myself, I never had an interest in crossing over."

She'd gotten drawn into the amiable chitchat, and it now pulled away like a receding wave, sizzling over the sand.

She pulled the black cloth over her head. She was accustomed to people viewing her with disapproval, but his censure was directed at Lulu. She knew that many people despised the refugees for running away. She supposed soldiers might feel even more strongly about it. Her sister had indeed run away—she was terrified of the war. Wasn't everyone?

"She's a widow," Ruby said in way of excuse, her voice muffled under the cloth, "and our parents are deceased. She went there to be with cousins of our father."

She pulled her head out and considered him and the pose.

"There are many widows these days," he said.

"What brings you to Campeche?" she asked to change the subject.

"I came with my captain. He's from here," his voice tightened. "He has business."

"Oh? Might I know him?"

"Why would you?"

Campeche may look like a city, to you, she thought, but it's really just an overgrown village.

"I've been to Mexico City," he said proudly, seeming to pick up on what she was thinking, that before the war he'd been a peasant who'd never seen pavement, or even cobblestone. "This place, it's not so big," he said scornfully.

She came and stood in front of him, peering at him. She wondered if she could capture the unfamiliar metallic sheen of his skin tone. And then there were his eyes—they were a surprising golden green.

"I've been to other cities, too." He shifted in his seat. "With my captain. He goes nowhere without me."

"He must trust you."

"I have keen eyes."

She reached out to straighten his collar, but his glare, a warning, stopped her.

She adjusted a light and slid back under the black cloth.

"Now," she said, "look at the camera and don't move until I stop counting." She said this sternly, because most people were prone to fidgeting.

He assumed a stern, martial pose, and the air in the studio changed. He possessed a stillness that was uncanny. An image flashed in her mind of him hiding in the underbrush, lying in wait for hours on end. Her heart raced.

She told herself she was being silly. He could not see her—his green-gold eyes, a predator's eyes, were aimed not at her, but at the camera. He was, in fact, her prey—she would capture him with her camera, trap him on a glass plate.

And yet, holding the flash lamp aloft, she counted to herself, and her voice quaked when she told him it was done.

He stood, stretched, put on the cap that shaded those eyes. He joined her at the door where she held back the velvet curtain that separated the studio from the reception. She intended to escort him to the front door because Meche, out on an errand, was not there to do it.

He looked about the studio with some disdain and then at her. All sisterly feeling drained from her. She'd seen the look before. Scorn and bravado—she ran a business and handled technical equipment he did not understand, both of which were unnatural for a woman. His eyes were those of any man in Campeche, not jaguar eyes at all.

"I can have these ready Wednesday," she said more curtly than she intended.

"That is good, señorita. My captain and I, we leave the next day."

Why did he not go? He fingered the velvet of the curtain near her hand where she held it back for him. Her arm started to ache with the weight of the cloth, but if she dropped it he might think she wanted him to stay. A shiver ran up her spine and lifted the hair on the back of her neck. They were almost eye to eye—he was only an inch or two taller than she. She felt his rising contempt for her—a bourgeois city woman with a sister hiding in the United States, both untouched by the war that he was living, that his wife was probably living. She realized her earlier curiosity had been shallow and naive. She looked away. She could know nothing of his life before the Revolution or of what had driven him to become a soldier. Even less could she fathom his years of fighting. Years of being shot at. Of killing.

"You know, I didn't expect a lady photographer."

Well, she thought, for her part, she hadn't expected a killer—a sanctioned killer to be sure, but a killer just the same.

"You can pick the photographs up anytime after 4:00," she said, making herself look at him.

His lids drooped a bit, a corner of his mouth tugged upward. "Señorita, would you consider delivering the photos to me?"

She looked aside. "No."

"No?" The tone of his voice teetered between challenge and humor.

"I have appointments for sittings all day."

"And in the evening?" His eyes showed hunger—her body meat. His leer took her in, neck to foot and back to her bosom, where it remained.

"Good day, Mr. Ramírez."

His hand on the curtain pounced on her own. She jumped and then went very still.

"Lieutenant," he said.

"Lieutenant."

She tried to pull her hand away, but he held it fast on the curtain, crushing it so that she could not let loose of the wad of fabric in her fist. Pain—and a mixture of anger and fear and humiliation—made her eyes brim with tears. She tried to think, calculate. One hand was free. Scratch him, slap him, punch him, grab for his pistol? She could not imagine any of that turning out well. Maybe Meche would return soon. No! Not that. She wanted Meche far away from him.

He took a step closer. She closed her eyes. She felt the heat from his body, his breath on her face. She waited. The pain in her hand, the ache in her arm, his smokey smell, his breath. She opened her eyes. He was so close his face was out of focus, but she saw him grin, showing stained teeth. He removed his hand from hers and ambled into the reception. At the door he turned and gave her an ironic salute.

As soon as he was out the door, she rushed to lock it. She was shaking from the bones out.

Meche paid the electric bill, the last of her errands. As she stepped from the cool office, the midday air wrapped her in its hot, gummy embrace. She looked up and saw the clouds thickening, building towards the daily afternoon downpour. On the rancho it would be time for sowing corn, beans, sugarcane, tobacco…

The old grandmother in Pedro Mu's family, Doña María Inés, had taught her that the Maya believe that a person has several souls. That seemed sensible to Meche, because she felt one of her souls was at Baalam Kab and one was caught here in Campeche City. And sometimes she felt as if a piece of her had also gone with Soli and Lalo to Texas. She shuddered at the thought, detesting the place without ever having seen it.

Meche dawdled along the high, narrow sidewalk, the tedium of the work awaiting her back at the studio slowing her pace. But then, she thought about Ruby waiting for her—she would be waiting, wouldn't she, anticipating her return? She sped up.

Meche had admired Ruby from the moment she met her. Unlike Lulu, her nitwit sister, Ruby was independent, unpretentious and devoted to her art. Meche considered it the worst of luck that, of the two sisters, she'd gotten stuck with Lulu for a stepmother. What had her father been thinking?

Lulu had made a big show of being maternal, but she was neither nurturing nor protective, and not the least bit fond of any of them. Ruby, on the other hand, had no interest in appearing motherly, which was perfectly fine with Meche—there were other things she wanted, and needed, from Ruby.

Granted, Ruby was not easy to live with—she was indeed self-sufficient, curt to a fault, and obsessed with photography. And stubborn. Meche accepted all of that, but now that she'd turned 17, she longed for Ruby to accept her as an equal, which she clearly did not. Meche was starting to fear she never would.

She was nearing the studio now, and she ached to put her arms around Ruby, to unpin and unbraid her hair, to touch her face, to touch every part of her. Thinking about her this way made Meche's body tingle, and she quickened her step. She glanced nervously at other people on the street—how could these thoughts she pictured so clearly not be visible to everyone who looked at her?

Meche was convinced that Ruby loved her in the same way, and yet she insisted on keeping her at arm's length. If Meche did not break through that hard shell of Ruby's soon…

Why didn't Ruby see that she needed Meche as much as Meche needed her? She feared that without her, Ruby would end up alone, viewed by others as evermore eccentric and, having alienated all her clients, living as a pauper. She would be considered, at best, a crusty old woman, and, at worst, mad. The thought of such a future for her Ruby broke her heart.

Meche arrived at Fotografía Eckart, her thoughts all a muddle, her heart filled with hope for some miraculous breakthrough on Ruby's part, but also with dread of further rejection. How long could she go on like this?

To her surprise, she found the studio locked—Ruby never closed during business hours. Meche rapped on the door. No answer. She could see nothing through the window. She pounded again and called Ruby's name. What could be wrong? People on the street turned to watch.

Finally the door opened a crack, and Meche pushed through. Ruby, holding tight to the door, pushed it shut hurriedly behind her and locked it again. She was pale. Her eyebrows and mouth parallel straight lines. Her dark eyes, darting, full of alarm. Meche had never seen her like this.

The ache to be comforted, to feel Meche's arms around her propelled Ruby towards her, but as soon as she felt Meche's hands on her back, she recoiled. She felt soiled, and the sensation of transferring Lieutenant Ramírez's touch to Meche was repugnant. She pulled away.

Ruby was flooded with love for the girl, and fear. How was she to keep her safe? How could she shelter her from… everything—this place, these times?

How many governors had headed up Campeche since the start of the Revolution? Ten? Twelve? She'd stopped keeping track—one mustached politician seemed much like the next. But this current one, Mucel, was not a politician—he was a military officer. And he'd arrived with troops. Until then, she'd lulled herself into thinking of the war as taking place somewhere else. Campeche City might be the center of the universe for its self-satisfied denizens, but for rest of the country, it was no more than a fly speck—Ruby had been counting on Campeche's fly-speck status to keep them out of the active fighting.

Heat and cold roiled within her. Today she'd been smacked in the face with her complete vulnerability. And Meche's. If Ruby could not defend herself against one lone soldier, how could she protect Meche? What might happen when the next troops marched into the city, either to back up the next change of governor or to attack the one already here?

She must send Meche to join Lulu in Texas. It was the only answer, the only thing Ruby could do for her.

Meche, still holding her arms out to her, was looking at her oddly.

"Ruby, Look at me," Meche cooed, as if Ruby were a spooked horse. "You're trembling. What's happened?"

Meche tried again to put her arms around her. Ruby yearned to sink into her embrace, into the illusion of well-being, but she felt ashamed, and frightened of giving way.

"Don't touch me!" she warned.

She was shaken by what had just happened with the lieutenant, overwhelmed by the thought of Meche being exposed to ugliness and humiliation. She feared for her if she stayed in Campeche, but oh, the desolation if she left! She could not look Meche in the eye, could not bear her solicitude, could not pull herself together, not here, not with Meche staring at her. She tore at the lock on the door.

"Where are you going?" Meche asked.

Ruby shook her head.

"Let me come with you."

"No," Ruby said. "And lock the door after me."

She listened for the click behind her. Then, although the lieutenant would be long gone by now, back to his precious captain, Ruby scanned the street. The coast clear, she set out. She walked quickly, but without direction, the clouds and humidity dense, her memory swinging between the lieutenant's grip on her hand and the electric touch of Meche's hands on her back.

Head down, she walked and walked, concrete and cobblestone scrolling under her feet. And then wood. She looked up and saw the flag of Mexico atop a flagpole—green, white, red, the eagle's wings spread wide. She'd happened on the port. She looked about her, exertion and heat jumbling her thoughts.

The dock beckoned.

Sea gulls lifting from the dock.

Pelicans flapping by.

The Union Jack. On a cargo ship, whipping in the wind.

A woman lifting her arms to steady the basket on her head.

A boy running on the beach, wearing a white sailor suit, tethered to a yellow kite.

The kite floating above.

A little girl all in white raising an arm to wave to a man boarding a boat.

Three years ago she'd turned and seen Meche standing here next to her. A kid in a white dress, a blue bow in her hair. Here.

Ruby left the dock, tears blurred her vision.

She remembered her mother's hands lifting to put on an earring, to wind her hair into a topknot.

Her father raising his hand to conduct a symphony on the gramophone, to pull the black velvet camera hood over his head.

Grief ached in her throat.

Alone.

She trudged on—a low, worthless burro bearing a terrible burden.

It started to rain. The daily afternoon deluge.

Her skirt clung to her legs, drenched and heavy.

Alone.

She came upon a church. It was San Román. Her San Román.

Voices raised in song, drifting from inside the church, floated into the sky.

Lift.

She stumbled into the church. Its black Christ.

Lift me, Lord.

How could he raise anyone, nailed there to his silver cross?

She sank onto the back pew.

The Dolorosa lifting her eyes to the cross, aiming her sorrow at heaven.

Lift me, mi Señora.

The Assumption of Mary—her body rising to heaven, borne upward by angels.

Lift me. Lift my leaden heart, please.

Smoke. From the lighting of candles, from the priest's incense, rising to the ceiling. Smoke in the crystal chandeliers. Smoke trapped against the curve of white ceiling and dark vigas.

Lift me. Somebody. Please.

María Asunción clanged around the kitchen as she cleaned up after the meal, and Meche paced, her stomach in a knot. When Ruby had not returned to the studio, Meche had gone home as usual for the 2:00 afternoon meal, hoping to find Ruby there. She did not.

The kitchen fell quiet, and Meche peeked in—empty. María Asunción must be taking her afternoon siesta. She could hear the rain on the roof—it had started much earlier today than usual. She tried to believe that was why Ruby hadn't come home, that she was keeping out of the rain.

Then she heard a click and a scrape—the front door. She dashed to it. Ruby slumped in the open doorway, the roar from the rain rushing in.

"Ruby," Meche exclaimed, "I've been frantic with worry."

Ruby stared at her, bewildered, as if not understanding why Meche was there. Her clothes were limp with sweat and rain. She looked hollowed out. Was she in shock? Ruby's enlarged pupils made her dark eyes all the darker, and she was even paler than she'd been earlier at the studio. She teetered a bit, and Meche put her arm around her waist.

Ruby let her, but fussed, "Why aren't you at the studio? Why didn't you keep the door locked?"

"It's almost 3:30. I waited for you and then I came home for dinner. I've been waiting for you here."

"3:30?"

Meche guided Ruby to her room. She took off Ruby's drenched blouse and skirt, steadying her with a hand on her arm. Her skin was so cold. Meche sat her on the bed and put a shawl around her. She removed Ruby's shoes and stockings, laid her down and pulled the coverlet over her. Her breathing was off—she'd seen injured workers in shock like this. She tried to remember what you were supposed to do.

Ruby grasped Meche's hand and pulled her to sit on the bed. Meche thrilled—Ruby had reached out to her! She sat and pulled the coverlet up to Ruby's chin. Then lay next to Ruby, her arm around her. Ruby made no sound, and her body did not shake, but tears rolled down her face.

"Ay, boxita, mi vida," Meche murmured. She always thought of Ruby as her boxita, her dear dark one, but she'd never said it aloud. She wasn't even sure Ruby knew enough Maya to understand it.

"Don't go." Ruby sputtered. "Don't go to Texas."

Meche shushed her. "I'm not going anywhere."

"I don't want you to go."

"Shhhh." Meche kissed her forehead.

"I'm selfish. Worthless. But I can't let you go."

"I don't want to go anywhere. I want to be with you."

"I can't protect you."

She was shivering again, and Meche held her more tightly.

"Ay, mi vida, I don't need your protection. I'm a country girl—you have no idea how tough we are. And I have a machete and a rifle and a revolver."

"Where? Why?"

"In my room. The machete is under my bed. The rifle is in the wardrobe and my father's pistol is in the nightstand drawer. Boxita, I can take care of myself and you, too."

Ruby closed her eyes and shook her head. Meche stroked her hair and she grew still.

"Let me take care of you, Ruby. I love you so much."

Ruby burrowed her head against Meche's shoulder. Meche tilted Ruby's chin upward. Ruby let her, and Meche kissed her.

Warmth and love flooded through Meche's body, and tears now rolled down her face as well.

Finally, Meche thought, everything would be all right.

1 9 1 3...

Soli returned with a hammer she'd borrowed from the neighbors and, to her surprise, found Lulu writing a letter at the kitchen table. Lulu was a poor correspondent. She preferred sending the occasional telegram, even though each time Soli warned her that a telegram signaled bad news and might alarm Aunt Ruby. But Lulu seemed to like the drama of it, both the sending and, probably, imagining its receipt. Now, as she penned an actual letter, presumably to her sister, one moment hunched over her paper and the next correcting her posture, Soli saw Lulu alternately smile and frown to herself.

Soli went into the parlor to leave her to it. Letter writing (creating a rapport out of nothing across the ether) was no small task. It required faith. It required its own space, and space was one of the many things they were short of.

It was Soli's day off, and normally she would be looking forward to writing her own letter to Meche, but it would have to wait till later. They'd just moved in the evening before after Soli got off work, and the house was in disarray.

She considered the stack of folded bedding at one end of the settee that was to double as Lalo's bed, and moved it for the time being into the narrow bedroom that she and Lulu were sharing. She stared at the trunks she'd unpacked the night before. Where to store them? Well, she would deal with that later. Meanwhile she would start on the boxes, some piled on the floor of the cramped kitchen and a few more here in the tiny parlor.

Opening the top box of photographs labeled fragile, she unwrapped the top one. It was her father and Lulu's ornately framed wedding portrait. Her father sat ramrod straight and looked solemn, and a bit proud. She touched his face, frozen in time, and detected no hint of prescience in his expression. She looked heavenwards but her gaze was blocked by the low ceiling. If only he could see her, and be pleased. But no, she worked in a hotel kitchen far from home and had not kept the family together. I'm doing the best I can, she told him silently. She rubbed out the smudge she'd left on the glass with the corner of her apron and set the picture on the small side table.

Next came the wedding photograph of her father and mother in an even more elaborate bronze frame, all scrolls and leaves and curlicues. Soli smiled at the bride in the picture, who was looking not at the camera but at an unseen horizon, and who, in some way, was her mother even then. Soli hugged it to her breast. She knew Lulu would not abide displaying the picture in the parlor, so she took it to the bedroom and put it out of sight in her drawer of the dresser the three of them would be sharing. One day, God willing, Lalo would have a room of his own, and the portrait would have place of honor, maybe on his nightstand.

She unwrapped some more frames, tissue and newspaper piling up on the parlor floor. She propped a portrait of Lulu as a baby on the dresser top, and another of Lulu and her sister as young girls with their parents, the mother small and dark, her hair coiled tightly on either side of a stark center part, and the father tall, thin and pale with a light-colored handlebar mustache.

The remaining photographs, all in cardboard folders that carried the embossed name of Fotografía Eckart, were the work of Aunt Ruby. Lulu, in one of her rare letters to her sister, and waxing nostalgic, had remarked that only in leaving Campeche had she come to fully appreciate the city, that if she were back there now, she would see all with fresh eyes. But, banished as she was, all she had was memory. Ruby had apparently taken it as a challenge to create portraits of home for her, unconventional ones, to be sure. Another package of photographs had arrived just the week before.

Soli might resent Lulu's sister, but she could not fail to recognize how striking and evocative her photographs were. More importantly, they were a tangible connection to Meche and to home. She lined the folders up on the battered settee. So far Soli had only acquired two simple frames, one bought at a secondhand store and the other a hand-me-down from the cousins. That morning she'd sent Lalo to the hardware store for a couple of nails to hang the two frames and a handful of thumbtacks for the others. Lulu did not approve of tacking the photos up as if they were bullfight posters or soap ads, but Soli did not think it right for them to languish in a box under the bed for want of proper frames.

In one photograph, the door to a church framed three humble women working inside. They wore white huipil dresses and covered their heads with narrow, dark-colored rebozos. One of the three wore the ends of her shawl criss-crossed over her chest like a bandolier, the second had hers slung over her back with a lump of baby inside, and the third had wrapped hers round and round her old, frail shoulders. It was Holy Week and the women were maneuvering thick, three-foot-tall sheaves of rosemary, standing them up like so many match sticks crammed upright in a jar. The three were packing them tightly into the space in front of a chapel altar. One could see that when they finished, the bundles would reach all the way to the nave. It seemed to Soli that she could almost smell the thick, pungent aroma, as if the fragrance had imprinted itself on the negative along with the image. Rosemary for remembrance. And Soli did remember. She hammered a nail in the center of the wall and hung it.

One by one Soli circled it with others. A broom-maker with an enormous bouquet of his wares (Ruby had hand-tinted the handles green). An old lady in the market surrounded by her wares, baskets heaped with guavas. Chubby-cheeked, black-eyed children sitting in a row on a rough wooden bench, dangling bare feet, a necklace of toes. Coffins stacked high on the sidewalk outside the door of a coffin-maker.

According to Meche (she'd finally answered one of Soli's letters), at the start of the Revolution, a very different type of photograph had bolstered Aunt Ruby's business: men wanted pictures taken of themselves in their military uniforms before they went to war. Sometimes they posed with their wives, mostly they posed with their rifles. Apparently they wanted these photographs out of a sense of pride, of history in the making. And this new-fangled photography added piquancy to their patriotism.

"'Graven images of grave men, of grave fodder,'" Meche quoted Ruby, "'but it paid the bills.'"

It surprised Soli that Meche quoted Aunt Ruby thus, without comment. Meche had never been cynical like that. She'd had political ideals and cheered President Madero. Of course, that was, in part, to spite Lulu, who detested the maderistas. But Meche sincerely applauded Madero for ousting Porfirio Díaz. Since none of the four sisters had ever known any other leader (the old dictator had come to power in 1877, long before any of them were born), it had been hard to conceive of a Mexico without him, but now they had a freely elected president. And yet, even though Díaz was in Paris, in exile for over a year now, the fighting continued. There'd been that uprising in the north and Zapata still fought in Morelos.

Both those areas were distant from Campeche, and the studio now had few soldiers for clients. Meche, sixteen, reported that many of the subjects of the war portraits had been boys about her age, some clad in sandals instead of boots, and wearing the rough, white clothes of a laborer. Most posed with a rifle by his side or slung over his shoulder, but a few prepared to go to war with only a machete. And women, women of every caste, were photographed as well, with guns and belts of bullets and wearing men's hats.

"Lady soldiers! It's unnatural." Lulu exclaimed, scandalized.

Meche had written that sometimes she'd been tempted to join the fight, which frightened Soli because she knew her sister capable of such recklessness. She and Meche both knew how to shoot, but Soli couldn't imagine taking up arms in a war. When she felt guilty about living in safety away from the fighting, she considered joining the Cruz Blanca here in Texas, volunteers who nursed the wounded on both sides of the border. But she didn't have the courage. Besides, she needed her job, and there was Lalo to think about.

She missed Meche terribly. She missed home. No matter what Meche thought, it had not been her choice to come to Texas. But was it her choice to stay? There was the question of Lalo. She wasn't his guardian, Lulu was. If she went back, she'd have to leave him behind, and then what would happen to him? Or for that matter, to Lulu?

But how long were they to stay here in the north? According to Cousin Carl, the war in Mexico wasn't the half of it. "Wobblies, anarchists, revolutionaries everywhere," he said. In which case, were they safer here than at home?

Soli followed the news. She was aware of the broad spectrum of political groups one could join in San Antonio, but she wasn't interested in political philosophy. She just wanted people to have enough to eat, and to stop shooting each other.

Standing back from her display of photos, she drank in Aunt Ruby's images and tried to put the war out of her mind. Lulu wandered into the parlor, and, shoulder to shoulder, they looked at the wall in silence. Soli, longing for home, missing her sister and admiring Aunt Ruby's talent, found it comforting to be with Lulu in this moment, knowing she must share the same feelings.

Lulu smelled the slight tang of sweat coming from Soli standing next to her, and she flexed her hand, cramped from writing to Tía Pancha. Mindful of her mother's lessons when she was a child, Lulu always took care with her handwriting, above all when writing to her great-aunt, who'd been a schoolteacher and had taught penmanship. She could imagine Tía Pancha's commentary on this gallery of photos Soli had put up: praise for Ruby and ideological gibberish on the subject matter. Dear Tía Pancha: brooms, churches, fruit, it didn't matter; she saw politics in everything!

But what Lulu saw on the wall brought to mind memories of the studio. Ruby nattering on with their father about exposures and solutions and whatnot. The nasty smell of the darkroom. Her sister in her leather apron. Her small hands with their ragged nails and rough skin, clipping photos to a line to dry. The deadly dull bookwork. Texas was no bed of roses (as Lulu told anyone who would listen), but how glad she was to be free of the studio.

Next to her, Soli sighed. "¡Qué lindo México!"

"Hmm," Lulu answered. She knew Soli considered it thoughtful of Ruby to send these photos of home, but Lulu knew that in reality her letter about missing Mexico had just given Ruby an excuse to do exactly what she wanted: take pictures that no one would buy.

They were, nonetheless, a vivid reminder of home, stirring Lulu to think about the family house of her childhood with its cool, thick walls. Outside had swirled a riot of color and heat, of flora and fauna, of scent and sound and humanity in every shape and stage, all of which Ruby's photos captured. But Lulu's memory stubbornly kept her away from all that, kept her inside, in her mother's proper household, under her father's critical eye. It had not been an experience of plenty. Her father and mother seemed to begrudge each other even the time of day, the air between them stringy as the old hen eaten for Sunday dinner. If they agreed on anything, it was that waste was not a venial sin but a mortal one. Ever parsimonious, they eschewed any extravagance, be it with lantern oil, meat, sweets, hair ribbons or words of praise.

And now here she was in Texas. Alone, and pinching pennies again. It wasn't fair.

"Have you finished your letter?" Soli asked.

Lulu huffed, "With all that tapping and pounding you were doing?"

She knew Soli would like to put her to work unpacking, but Lulu couldn't face that. It would mean accepting that they were to live in this shabby little house.

"And for heaven's sake, Soli, do take down the photograph of the coffins!"

February 2, 1913

Sra. María Luisa Eckart Reyes, viuda de Hernández
San Antonio, Texas, USA

Dear Tía Pancha,

I hope this letter finds you well, and out of jail, for a change!

You would be proud of me, for there is a newspaper here in Spanish, and (can you believe it?) I read it religiously! But the news from home is so discouraging. What is going on with this Zapata person? I thought that with Mr. Madero being elected president, however detestable, that we could make plans to return home, but the cousins here keep telling me to wait, that things are too unstable. I tell them that Zapata is in Morelos, a long way from Campeche. It is, isn't it?

Apparently Mr. Madero is very unpopular with the Americans, and now they've sent troops to the border to keep the Revolution from spilling into their country. After all I've been through, it would be just my luck to be shot in Texas by a Mexican revolutionary.

What do you think, Auntie? Do send me a telegram as soon as you think it is safe to return.

Americans here lump all Mexicans together. They make no distinction whatsoever between those whose families have been here since the United States was a glimmer in Jorge Washington's eye and refugees who arrive with absolutely nothing to their name except maybe a pot to cook in and a rag of a blanket. And what about we exiles who are cultured and have the wherewithal to live decently? It makes no difference. We're all the same to them.

Not that it is easy to make ends meet. I simply can't rely on income from the rancho. Licenciado De la Cruz says that the political situation is affecting production on one hand, and market prices and transportation of goods on the other. (Personally, I suspect the foreman is pocketing more than his salary. Such a disagreeable man.) And then, if and when the licenciado does wire money, the exchange rate for pesos is abysmal! Father's cousin Carl has arranged for a job for me in a music store, playing sheet music on the piano for prospective customers. It's hardly what Mother had in mind for me when she insisted I learn to play! It pays a pittance, and I arrive home in the evening absolutely exhausted. Cousin Carl also helped Soli get work in the kitchen of a hotel. Her father would not be pleased, but what can we do?

All in all, Soli and Lalo seem to have accustomed themselves to life here. I certainly can't say that I have. I can't imagine ever feeling at home here. It's just not "right." Soli has joined a Tejana ladies' organization that, among other things, helps the refugees ("Tejano" is the term they use here for Texans of Mexican descent). Lalo, only seven, is in school and speaking English and German like a little parrot.

Soli still mopes about Meche staying behind, which is tiresome. As for me, Auntie, I say good riddance! She was a brat and I do not miss her. We have just rented a house, and so will no longer be living with Cousin Carl. It's dreadfully small, and if Meche were here, it would be quite unbearable. Whereas I'm sure she and Ruby get on famously. And now that Ruby is no longer alone, there is no reason for me to feel guilty about leaving her. I remember you once saying that wallowing in guilt is a waste of time. I agree. I've never had a talent for it.

So here I am in San Antonio. It's larger than I expected; the downtown district is extensive, the streets broad, with automobiles racing around everywhere, and the buildings, three-, four-, up to eight-stories tall! Commercial Street has electric lights arching over it. It makes dear Campeche seem like a quaint village, and I wonder how it compares to Mexico City. I have to admit that the city is not unattractive. There are some lovely churches, and the main plaza is perhaps even prettier than ours in Campeche.

Of late, one of Cousin Carl's grandsons, Raymond, has been very kind to us. He is two years Soli's junior, and I believe he is quite smitten with her. On Sunday afternoons his father lends him his Model T, and he takes us for a drive in the countryside, or to one park or plaza or another to see the sights. I don't much care for rides in the country, but of the parks, I am most fond of Electric Park, which has all types of amusements, including what's called a ferris wheel, which is in fact a wheel, an enormous one with seats suspended from it. Maybe there is one in Mexico City? It turns slowly and you go around and around. When you are on top, you can see the whole city. Soli and I prefer it to the roller coaster, which is a little cart that runs on a miniature railroad track on a towering scaffolding, like you're racing over invisible mountains. Raymond swears that it is safe and takes Lalo on it, while Soli and I watch from terra firma. Lalo finds it quite thrilling.

Tía, I can't get used to the fact that there is no ocean here! I never paid it much mind back home, but now I miss it so much! It permeates everything, doesn't it? The food, the air, the color of the sky, the flow of commerce through the city! Simply everything. And I'd never realized. How do you do without it in the capital?

I used to walk the malecón at sunset with my dear Ernesto, may he rest in peace. Living so far inland, he always enjoyed the sea while he was in the city. He said he loved the salt-flavored breeze. What I liked was going to the ice cream parlor on the way home. I loved the strawberry parfaits, I find myself thinking about those days all the time. About Ernesto, of course, and about the salt air. And the ice cream.

Of course, there is ice cream here, and a river. But a river is not the same as the ocean, is it? Instead of nestling alongside the city, it seems to chop things up. People say it floods. How can that be? It seems such a tame thing. Oh, I know we have floods in Campeche, too, but we have a proper rainy season. It's to be expected. Here in Texas, instead of a wet and a dry season, there's a hot and a cold one. And it seems to rain willy-nilly, anytime of year, but not very much at a time. Not compared to home, and so the sidewalks look strange, as they are barely raised above the street.

The prospect of a flood frightens me! You know about the terrible dreams I have. Well, now I have a whole new set of nightmares. Soli pooh-poohs me, says we would know of any danger ahead of time. But if that's so, then why do people die in these floods? Raymond agrees with her (although he would agree with her if she said monkeys fly), and promises that if there is any peril, however slight, he will come for us in his father's automobile. In which case, I say, we can be swept away by the flood waters in style. He laughs at me. I dare say he finds me amusing.

Unpleasant surprises never cease here. I leave Mexico to get away from the war, but everywhere you turn in San Antonio, you bump into a revolutionary or a reactionary. Listen to me! I've even started to pick up the lingo. And, it turns out you are famous, and not just with the police! I had no idea anyone read those articles of yours, much less that they would find their way all the way to Texas! You've given me some social cachet, Tía. I'll have to write Ruby about it.

Part of what is not "right" here is, annoyingly, Ruby's absence. Soli is no substitute. When I look at her, she is not the mirror of our mother as Ruby is. And although Soli does get exasperated with me, as Ruby does, it's not the same. I get no little lift in discomfiting her as I do with our Ruby.

Well, I will close now, with assurances of our well-being.

Your loving niece,
Lulu

1 9 1 1 ...

As they left the rancho, Meche faced forward in the wagon and gripped Soli's hand hard—so hard that Soli unlaced their fingers with a moan. Soli leaned her head into her sister's, linked her arm tightly through Meche's and squeezed.

The two sisters, along with their little brother and Lulu, traveled the narrow dirt tracks of the backcountry, impassable if it hadn't been the dry season. There were two drivers—one for the wagon and one for the two-wheeled cart hauling their baggage. They were accompanied by the foreman on horseback—Don Eusebio.

Meche despised the man, with his twitchy little black mustache and bowed-legged swagger. She hated how he bullied the workers. And he treated her like a snot-nosed kid. Lulu was obviously cowed by him and accepted everything he told her. Well, Meche certainly didn't trust him. At night—the trip took three-days—she made a point of sleeping right next to Soli with her father's Colt revolver under her pillow. Soli knew about the gun but didn't say anything.

They were headed for the town of Hecelchakán on the Camino Real. It was also the terminus of the railway line from Campeche City. From there they would set out on the final leg of their journey.

They arrived at Hecelchakán in the afternoon, and all but Lulu waited on the street while she sent a couple of telegrams. Meche was excited at the prospect of traveling on a train, but they did not board it as planned. Don Eusebio broke the news to the drivers, who grumbled because their families were expecting them home and also because they found the idea of the city daunting. Lulu had gotten it into her head that revolutionaries—taking a page from labor violence in the United States and Europe—would be targeting railroads for sabotage. She was sure there would be explosions and derailments at any moment. So, they spent the night in a second-rate pensión, and the next day continued along the Camino Real towards Campeche City.

Their father's lawyer friend surprised them by meeting them on the outskirts of the capital. With his clerk in tow, he took charge, helping them out of the wagon and giving orders to the cart drivers. Lulu was fawningly grateful, and Meche, too, was glad—Don Mauricio stepping in like that threw Don Eusebio off balance. The foreman, who'd gotten used to running things, clearly did not like being put back in his place.

While Don Mauricio took him across the road to speak privately, Lulu and Soli bought juice at a roadside stand set in front of a wall of brilliant purple bougainvillea. Next to its blooms, the vendor's white clothing and the little pyramids of colorful fruit, Soli and Lulu looked like a couple of mud hens.

The family was in the first year of mourning, and decency dictated that Lulu wear full-blown widow weeds—black traveling suit and black, broad-rimmed hat trimmed with a black veil. Little Lalo, barely five years old, was exempted from such strictures, but both sisters wore wide black bands on their straw hats, and Soli had dyed her and Meche's clothing to appropriate colors. Meche wore a muted mauve dress with grey stockings, and Soli, a grey blouse, black stockings and a black skirt —just below mid-calf.

Soli had been managing the household at Baalam Kab for several years now, and she'd taken to wearing her skirts long—not quite as long as an adult, but longer than usual for her age. Lulu kept urging her to hem them, "They almost cover your ankle!"

But Soli put her off. She was struggling to keep the household running properly, and Meche supposed she felt she needed every extra inch of fabric to bolster her position, for although Lulu had not taken over any of her sister's duties, she interfered and undermined Soli's authority at every turn.

With the trip to Campeche in the offing, Lulu put her foot down. "You must shorten your skirts, Soli! I don't want you to look absurd."

Luckily, Lulu didn't seem to care what Meche wore. Her dresses—all loose-waisted and hitting just below the knee—were those of a girl much younger than 14. Other girls her age would be begging for more mature clothing, but Meche didn't want a skirt biting at her waist and all that extra cloth getting in her way.

Meche glanced over at her sister and the juice stand. Soli was smoothing her skirt down again, almost tugging at it—a nervous tic of late. Lalo was squatting on the ground next to her, peering raptly at a bug. Meche stood apart, watching Don Mauricio and Don Eusebio as they spoke earnestly on the other side of the road—Soli had stopped her from following them, to which Don Mauricio had given her a kindly nod. But Meche wondered if she might slip across while Lulu and Soli were distracted—her view was hindered by passing horses, buggies and wagons, and she could not hear what the men were saying. But she saw Don Eusebio take various postures, starting with patronizing and condescending, then sliding into wheedling.

She supposed that matters touching on the farm went well enough for him, because what did Don Mauricio know about anything? But judging from Don Eusebio's expression when the lawyer turned from him—a storm cloud of a face if ever there was one—something clearly had gone awry for the foreman.

"Don Eusebio will be returning to Baalam Kab posthaste," Don Mauricio announced to Lulu. "I hope that will not inconvenience you. I'm sure you agree that the rancho needs his attention."

"Of course, Don Mauricio," Lulu gushed. "Whatever you think best. I'm very grateful for your attentions."

"My pleasure, señora," he said with a slight bow, while looking quizzically out of the corner of his eye at Meche, who was giggling.

Don Eusebio had alluded several times during the trip to big plans he had for his visit to the city. Meche was delighted that his sure-to-be-sordid schemes had been thwarted.

Glowering, the foreman strode to where he had his horse tied to one of the carts. Once in the saddle, he grimly tipped his hat to Soli and Lulu, and spurred his horse for a big exit. Meche rolled her eyes—it was all show. She knew he was in no hurry to get back to the rancho. Besides, it wouldn't do for him to leave the wagon, carts and their drivers behind. Next to her she felt as much as heard Soli heave a sigh of relief— they were rid of him.

Don Mauricio's clerk stayed behind to tend to matters with the carts and luggage, while the licenciado escorted his friend's widow and children into town in his carriage. Lulu grew uncharacteristically sober as they travelled towards the center of town. But Meche, who'd been prepared to loathe the city, gaped at the sights, besotted. A breeze brought the scent of salt air to her already twitching nose—there was as much to smell and hear as there was to see! An excited Lalito leaned out the carriage window. Soli held on to the loose belt on his pale-blue sailor suit to keep him from tumbling onto the street. The three of them marveled at an odd-shaped carriage being pulled along tracks by a pair of mules—a streetcar, Don Mauricio informed them.

"Where are all those people going?" Lalo shouted. "Where?"

"Lalo," Lulu scolded. She snapped her fan shut and tapped him on the bottom with it. "Stop acting like a little monkey! Sit down like a gentleman and be still."

She gave Don Mauricio an apologetic smile. She reopened the fan with a flick of the wrist. From behind it she hissed at Soli, "Make him behave, won't you?"

"Look!" Meche said. "An automobile!"

"Oh my!" Soli said. "Lalo, look there."

The horseless carriage looked so strange rolling along all on its own. Meche wondered if Doña María Inés back at the rancho, who'd schooled her in traditional Mayan ways, would think it monstrous or comical. Lalo recoiled from the window to cling to Soli. Then he buried his head in her lap and covered his ears. Soli cupped the back of his head and patted his back.

"It does make a racket!" Soli said, wrinkling her nose. "Smelly, too."

Meche liked the smell—oil, gas fumes, hot metal. And she recognized the sound. Although far less thunderous, the automobile's clacking rumble reminded her of the roar of the sugar mill at Hacienda San Isidro. Two years before, when Meche had been 12, she'd hounded her father to let her ride with him when he took their cane to the hacienda to be processed. She'd longed to see the mill, how it cut up and shredded the cane, extracted the juice, and then how the juice was processed into sugar. With its steaming vats, its wheels and belts and spikes, the mill had not disappointed. But she had embarrassed her father—her fascination was unseemly, she'd been far too forward, too intent, asked too many questions... She pushed the memory away, but not before images flashed in her mind—her father striding from the house at the hacienda with Don Pedro, herself in the parlor being rather rude to his boring children, her father on his horse, raking her over the coals and then galloping away, not looking back to see if she followed.

She felt her heart twinge at the sudden recall. Then remembering he was gone forever, the pang became an ache. Looking out the window she thought, this was where he had come so often, this was what he saw. Well, now she was here, and there would be things about her he wouldn't know either, and never would. Then she was struck by a flash of anger. How could her father have deserted them and Baalam Kab? How could he have left them alone with the horrid Lulu?

The carriage stopped on a city street and Don Mauricio helped Lulu down. Then he assisted Soli, who in turn lifted Lalo and set him on the sidewalk. Meche scrambled out behind him before Don Mauricio could extend his hand to her. Although Lulu had gone on and on about how wonderful it would be to be home, she looked drawn, and her eyes darted here and there. As for Soli and Lalo, they looked as dazed as Meche felt. Carriages rumbled by, laborers in white cotton pants and shirts made their way along the high, narrow sidewalks, as did servant girls with shawls over their heads, and businessmen in suits and derbies. Soli held tight to Lalo while Lulu and the lawyer exchanged pleasantries.

Then Lulu turned and made a beeline to a nearby shop door. Soli hurried to follow, dragging Lalo. Meche stopped at the door to stare at a passing automobile. Soli reached out and yanked her inside, begging her to stay close.

Inside the shop, an acrid-sweet odor pricked at Meche's nostrils.

"Ruby!" Lulu called, now aglow with expectation.

A woman, small and dark, with quick eyes, rushed from the back of the shop, wiping her hands on a piece of red cloth. She wore a long leather apron like a blacksmith might wear. She cried out with glee and hugged Lulu.

Meche and Soli exchanged glances. This was Lulu's sister? They would never have guessed. Besides the difference in height and coloring, Lulu—matronly and rounded—looked old enough to be Ruby's mother —while her sister seemed wiry and full of energy.

"Why didn't you go to the house?" Lulu's sister said.

"I couldn't wait to see you."

"Just as well. María Asunción quit shortly after you left, and I haven't had the time, or money, to hire someone else."

"And the studio? You're still here alone?"

"How could I replace you?"

Ruby looked past Lulu a moment and her dark, sharp eyes met Meche's. Meche took a quick intake of breath.

It was not the homecoming Lulu had anticipated. The house was dark, dank, and she heard the telltale skittering of mice. There was a clear track between the kitchen, bathroom and Ruby's bed, but elsewhere the accumulation of dust seemed that of years rather than the eight months she'd been gone.

"Oh, Ruby!" Lulu exclaimed, although Ruby was still at the studio.

"We're supposed to stay in this dump?" Meche said.

Soli looked about, evaluating, while Lalo clung to her skirt.

Leaving the children at the house to await the delivery of their baggage, Lulu went straight to find their former housekeeper and inform her that she had to come back to work for them. When María Asunción balked, Lulu appealed to her loyalty, reminding María Asunción that she had worked for her family forever, ever since Lulu was a little girl.

"Your parents were good people, may they rest in peace," the older woman said, crossing herself. "But Señorita Lulu... Excuse me, I mean, Señora." She pursed her lips and stared at the ground. "Your sister! She forgets to leave money for groceries. I prepare a nice lunch and she doesn't show up to eat. She complains I'm wasting money and says she doesn't need full meals, just some panuchos or scrambled eggs. She forgets to pay me and I have to ask her for my wages. Two, three times." María Asunción shook her head. "No, Señora Lulu. I won't come back."

"Oh, dear María Asunción! I'm so sorry she's been difficult, but my sister has always been in her own little world. You know that. She doesn't mean to be disrespectful."

María Asunción gave a nod, doubtful.

"Well, I'm here now, and I certainly appreciate you. Indeed, truly, I need you," Lulu wheedled. "I have my three stepchildren with me. The poor things." She tilted her head and pouted. "They need a well-ordered house. And your cooking! I've missed it so much. On the trip here I was bragging to the children about all your specialties and how much they would enjoy them. And what do I find? Cockroaches in the kitchen and the cupboards all but bare!"

A few days later María Asunción came out of the kitchen of the Eckart house in San Román to answer a knock at the door. It was a little serving girl of eight or nine, wearing a white huipil, worn-out sandals that were too big for her and a serious expression. She handed the housekeeper an envelope.

"For the Eckart ladies," she muttered.

"Gracias, niña," the housekeeper said, and the child ran off.

María Asunción looked up and down the street. No sign yet of her niece and Señorita Soli. Her Carmencita was helping her get the house back in order—up and running as it should, properly, como Dios manda

—and the señorita was pitching in, too. The two girls were at the market now, getting some things she needed for the next meal. Little by little María Asunción was getting the kitchen restocked—she had a houseful to cook for now. Children in the house after all these years! She judged Señorita Soli a good egg. The second girl, Meche, well, she was at an awkward age, and, of course, she'd been through a lot, but still… Now, the little boy, he was a cutie. And such a sweet tooth!

As for Señora Lulu, it was sad seeing her in black, the poor thing, and she looked a bit peaky. Of course she'd always been pale, but now the pink tones were missing, and the black of her widow's weeds didn't help any. Well, María Asunción would soon put some color back in her cheeks and some meat on her bones.

The letter on the table by the front door caught Ruby's eye when she came in—the sharp-edged lavender rectangle on the round mahogany table top, the laid finish of the paper against the smooth, polished wood. It was from her mother's old friend, Sra. Anastasia Carrillo Rivas, viuda de Álvarez. She'd gotten wind of Lulu's return and was inviting them all to tea on Sunday. It ended with:

> *And Ruby, my dear, don't you dare use work as an excuse*
> *not to come. Sunday is a day of rest. If your dear mother were*
> *here, you know that she would beseech you thus. Remember:*
> *family and friends are more important than commerce.*

Ruby rolled her eyes. The idea of her mother "beseeching" anyone was absurd. "Decreeing" would be more like it. And it was easy for Tía Anastasia to ignore "commerce"—she had a wealthy son to pay the bills. But Ruby recognized that she had to go—she could only be so unsociable before people judged her unforgivably odd—it was a line she dare not cross for it could seriously hurt business. Fortunately for her, lady photographer/shopkeepers were not in great demand in polite society for parties of any ilk.

She found Lulu and the others in the little interior patio. She broke the news to Lulu, who was delighted.

"How kind of her," Lulu said, and turned to Soli. "Tía Anastasia was my mother's dear friend, and she has the best cook!" Lulu caught herself and looked about to see if María Asunción was listening. She lowered her voice. "Wait till you taste her cookies. She makes suspiros that are absolutely scrumptious. Ruby, remember her sweet-potato and coconut empanadas?"

The word "cookie" caught Lalo's attention and he leaped up from the little fountain where he was floating leaves he'd plucked from the potted plants. He ran to Soli and pulled on her arm.

"Can we go, Soli? Can we?"

"Stop pulling on me like that. We do not pay social visits because there are treats."

Meche snorted. "I do."

Ruby looked approvingly at the girl. Lalo laughed and capered about Soli.

"And so does everyone else," Meche continued. "That's why everyone always serves refreshments."

"Cookies!" Lalo sang out.

"No, refreshments are served because hospitality demands it," Soli said. "We pay visits to share companionship with family and friends."

"We've never even heard of this Anastasia person." Meche countered.

"She's a dear friend of our stepmother's family. That should be reason enough."

Lalo jumped in place. "Cookies! Cookies! Cookies!"

Lulu sighed and flapped her fan.

"Eduardo Ernesto," Soli snapped, "stop that this instant. That is no way for a gentleman to behave."

He slumped back to the fountain.

"Eduardo, excuse yourself," Soli insisted.

Ruby remembered floating flowers in the fountain when she was Lalo's age, and—to her mother's dismay—testing to see what other kinds of things would float and which would sink.

"Let him be," Ruby said.

"Yeah, Soli," Meche chimed in. "Let the kid breathe once in a while."

Soli glared at her sister. "Excuse me," she said, stiffly, and crossed to the bedroom she shared with Meche and Lalo.

Soli could spit, she was so frustrated. She looked up at the bedroom's dark vigas and white ceiling plaster, not unlike the house at the rancho. But it wasn't her house, and certainly not her home. Without Baalam Kab, how could she hope to hold the family together? With no waterwheel to check on, no Pedro Mu to pester, no beehives to monitor, what was there to ground Meche and keep her close? Where might she wander off to in this city? What dangers might she run into? Because she would wander off. Oh, speak plainly, she scolded herself. Meche didn't drift away. She ran.

Their stepmother was no help. More often than not, when something had to be faced, Lulu hid away with a sick headache. And to think that Soli's father had said his marriage to Lulu would lift responsibilities off her young shoulders!

Now on top of everything else, she had to deal with Lulu's strange family. Lulu's sister, so peculiar and intense. And undermining her with Lalo! What right did she have to do that? Soli blinked back hot, angry tears.

Ruby tapped at the door—even she could see that Soli was in a tough spot and that she'd butted in where she shouldn't have. She stepped inside without waiting for Soli to respond.

The bedroom was crowded with a folding cot for Lalo, a large trunk and several suitcases. Some of the younger girl's clothes were tossed on the bed—stockings, a dress, a nightgown, a hair bow like a big dead butterfly, as broad as the girl's face was long. A few of the boy's toys were scattered on the floor—tin soldiers and cast-iron animals. With her toe, Ruby shoved a little pig out of the way—surprisingly heavy, most of its pink paint worn off. She picked up a small, but weighty horse. She liked the heft of it in her hand. She would have preferred these animals when she was a child to the dolls her mother insisted on giving her and Lulu. Neither she nor Lulu had been keen on playing at cradling and feeding their baby dolls, but Lulu had treasured her grown-up doll, with its porcelain face and soft blond curls. She'd spent hours dressing and undressing it. Ruby hated it because she could never get Lulu to put it aside and do something more interesting.

Ruby crossed to the interior shutters that were still open to the day's heat. The sun sifting through the lace curtains made intricate patterns on her skin. She closed the wooden panels and the room fell into shadow. She turned to Soli.

At 16 years of age, Soli was a spring bloom, pretty enough, but her spine was stiff and her expression stern, like her father's, her eyes sad.

"Look, I'm sorry," Ruby said. "I didn't mean to interfere."

She set the cast-iron horse upright on the trunk. It tipped over, and she righted it.

"Eduardo can be difficult," Soli said cooly. "I apologize for his behavior."

"He's just a kid, and acting like one," she said, trying to reassure the girl.

Soli drew herself up. "He's not just any kid, and it's my duty to see he becomes a gentleman."

"Isn't that Lulu's job now?"

Soli, taken aback, looked incredulous.

Ruby grimaced. "No, I suppose not."

Several tears escaped Soli's control, and she quickly dabbed them away. She started to apologize, but Ruby raised her hand, palm out and shook her head.

"I was very close to my father," Ruby said. "I miss him every day."

Tears welled in the girl's eyes again. Ruby turned to leave.

"Oh," Ruby said. "You might bring the boy to the studio. I have a wooden pony that I sometimes sit kids on to photograph. He'd probably like playing with it."

Noise at the front of the house drew their attention. Apparently someone was at the door. *Now what?* Ruby wondered as she left the bedroom. Her steps slowed when she saw Lulu with her arm around someone, and pulling that someone, an older woman, inside. Blast! It was Tía Pancha. In her green dress and red and white woven shawl, she gave the impression of a plump flag of the Republic.

"My word, it's hot as blazes!" she said. Strands of white hair lay plastered to her damp temples and she wiped her face with a handkerchief. "In the capital I long for our Campeche sun, but now that I'm here…!"

"Poor Auntie, we'll get you something cool to drink," Lulu said and called out for María Asunción.

"But first, come meet my children. Soli, where are you?" Lulu called. "Come meet my favorite aunt.

"Tía, this little gentleman is Eduardo Ernesto, we call him Lalo."

Lalo clung to Lulu and hid his face in her skirt. Ruby noticed that instead of being annoyed, Lulu looked pleased and placed her hand on his shoulder.

Soli came dutifully out of her room and stood behind Ruby.

"Lalo, give Aunt Pancha your hand."

"Nonsense," Aunt Pancha said. "Come give me a hug."

Lalo didn't budge, and the old woman opened her arms to her nieces.

"My dear girls, let's have a hug of solidarity, the three of us! The dictator's days are numbered! I may have seen the inside of a jail for the last time!"

Jail! Soli let out a little gasp and Ruby turned to see the girl's hand fly to her mouth.

Tía Pancha smiled at Soli. "Don't worry, my child, it was all for a very good cause."

Lalo gaped at Tía Pancha. "Ladies don't go to jail! Only bad guys go to jail!" he said, curiosity beating out his shyness, and his voice gaining volume. "Are you a bad guy? What is it like to be in jail?"

Lulu's mouth dropped, but when Aunt Pancha laughed with delight, Lulu joined in. Aunt Pancha reached out to tousle the boy's hair.

"The food is terrible!" Tía Pancha widened her eyes theatrically and raised her eyebrows. "And the rats!"

Soli swept forward. Glancing disapprovingly at Aunt Pancha, she scolded Lalo, "Don't be impertinent, Lalo, and lower your voice! Go play in the bedroom and let the adults talk."

"Meche's not an adult!" he complained.

"Darling," Lulu cooed.

Soli glanced at Ruby, who did not meet her eyes.

"Go!" Soli said, "or there'll be no visit or cookies for you."

He sulked towards his room, but Ruby saw him veer off and hide behind the fountain.

Ruby stepped forward and kissed her great-aunt's cheek, but she addressed Soli, "Try not to mind our aunt, hard as that may be."

"Tía, this is María Soledad, Ernesto's oldest daughter," Lulu said. "Soli's been like a mother to Lalo and Meche. Ernesto's fondest wish was for me to relieve her of such a heavy burden, so she could enjoy her youth."

"Yes, so you wrote me," Aunt Pancha said. "Pleased to meet you, Soli."

They kissed on the cheek, and Soli dropped back.

"And this is Meche," Lulu's voice tightened.

"I didn't know there was a jailbird in the family," Meche said. "Are you the only one or are there more?"

Aunt Pancha's eyes flashed, and Ruby couldn't help but snort.

Lulu's face turned ugly. "You evil child," she sputtered, and in reflex, her hand shot up to strike.

Meche stuck out her chin and glared, daring her to hit her.

Aunt Pancha, teacher voice engaged, ordered, "Lulu, lower that hand this instant! Corporal punishment is a barbaric expression of a morally corrupt patriarchy."

Lulu looked at her hand as if she'd never seen it before and, chagrined, did as she was told.

A moment earlier Soli had stood gaping at her sister. Now she moved forward and gave Meche a pinch.

"Ow!"

Soli dropped a tiny curtsy to Tía Pancha. "Señora, please excuse my younger sister."

Meche protested, "Why? It's no secret she was in jail. She's the one who brought it up."

Aunt Pancha looked amused now. "Meche is right. There is nothing to be excused. I wear my prison terms as badges of honor. But child, none of that curtseying nonsense. We are all sisters in the Revolution."

Soli was speechless. She tried to pull Meche close, but Meche wriggled free, rubbing her arm where Soli had pinched her.

"Aunt Pancha, what are you doing here?" Ruby said.

"Hija! With city after city falling to Madero, Díaz is running scared! The old son of a…"

"Aunt Pancha, please! The children," Lulu said.

Tía Pancha nodded. "Goat, then. The old goat will soon be history."

"Yes, But what are you doing here?" Ruby repeated.

"I want to be home when it happens, to celebrate with my family."

"You haven't lived here for over 40 years."

"It's still her home, Ruby," Lulu said, laughing.

"Wouldn't celebrating in Mexico City with your co-conspirators be more satisfying?"

Meche's and Soli's eyes grew wide.

"Ruby!" Lulu said. "Don't be so rude." She linked arms with Tía Pancha. "Don't listen to her, Auntie. We're delighted you're here."

"Lulu, she's up to something," Ruby said.

"Ruby!' Lulu admonished.

"It's not a good time. We have a houseful of children!"

"Have you forgotten that I was a teacher for over 40 years?" Aunt Pancha said.

"But you're not here as a teacher, are you?"

"No, I'm here as your great-aunt, who was born in this house."

"Well, we're full up. There's no room."

Ruby lost the battle. That night Lalo was crammed into bed with his older sisters. And the wobbly cot he'd been sleeping in was moved into the adults' bedroom for Ruby—she being the youngest and smallest of the three women. She slept little—between Lulu and Tía Pancha's snoring and fear of toppling over if she moved, Ruby lay awake most of the night.

The next afternoon Ruby trod arm in arm with Lulu as they headed to Doña Anastasia's for tea. Tea! What a tedious activity, and it didn't help any that Lulu had forbidden her to bring her box camera. Its absence gave Ruby a recurring jolt—the sense that she'd forgotten something crucial.

Ruby had missed Lulu these past eight months that her sister had been at the rancho, but now, with the house full of people, she felt hemmed in. Lulu kept promising to help at the studio but somehow never found the time. And yet she expected Ruby to keep regular hours, sit down for long meals, go to tea, for heaven's sake!

Ruby glanced at Lulu—her face was pink, and sweat beaded on her forehead. The temperature was not overly high, but the sun shone brightly in a cloudless blue sky, and the black cloth of Lulu's parasol and clothing soaked up the heat terribly. Ruby wore a white cotton tea dress, and her bare arm attested to the temperature of Lulu's long black sleeve. They walked slowly, with the three children trailing behind—the girls in grey dresses and black stockings, the little boy in a white linen sailor suit. Their little group, Ruby observed, was a study in black and white.

Lalo alternately jigged about—impatient with their slow progress—or, maddeningly, refused to budge as he examined some bug or other on the ground. Ruby was sympathetic with the kid, spoiled brat that he was. How did Lulu put up with it all?

Lulu gave Ruby's arm a squeeze and complained that the heat was making her feel quite ill. Ruby gave her arm a perfunctory pat and reminded her that the Widow Álvarez's house was not far. But Lulu stopped and swayed a bit. Ruby tightened her grip. Lulu steadied, but Ruby saw that her sister had turned pale as milk. Ruby reached down to where Lalo was squatting. Pinching his ear, she lifted him to his feet and he yowled, a satisfying sound to her way of thinking.

The color drained from Soli's face. She removed the little boy from Ruby's grasp and put a protective arm around him.

"We need to get where we're going," Ruby said.

Lalo screwed up his face—sign of a tantrum in the brewing. Lulu sighed and pressed a scented handkerchief to her brow. She leaned down and looked into the little boy's face. Lalo reacted to her attention as if a lamp had shone on his face.

"Do you remember where we are going?" she whispered.

Lalo shook his head, one hand cradling his ear.

"We're going to visit my Auntie Anastasia. And you, little man, are keeping us from her delicious cookies."

Lalo dropped his hand from his ear and took Lulu's hand. He was already holding Soli's, and he now pulled on them both to lead the way.

In the next block when Lalo started to lag, Meche chanted, "Coo-kies. Coo-kies."

Lalo grabbed onto Meche, and she and Lalo marched the rest of the way.

At the widow Álvarez's door, Soli adjusted the little boy's diminutive black armband and smoothed the skirt of her dress. A little serving girl, closer in age to Lalo than to Meche, let them into the house, which was dark and cool.

In the sitting room, Doña Anastasia stood to greet them. She and Ruby and Lulu kissed on the cheek. The older woman fussed over Lulu, and asked after her shoulder. Ruby saw that Lulu colored prettily under Doña Anastasia's attentions, telling her that she was quite healed. And although not asked, she made excuses for Aunt Pancha, who'd stayed home. Then Lulu proudly presented the children, who behaved appropriately, and Doña Anastasia looked pleased.

"Lulu, my dear, I always knew that, in time, you would find your calling. And it seems you have, as stepmother to these poor dears. I never believed for a moment that that grubby shop was your destiny. Now if we could just pry Ruby loose from it.

"I don't wish to be pried loose, Auntie. I'm quite at home in my grubby studio."

Ruby recalled that years ago there'd been a jaguar rug in this room—she'd never asked what happened to it, and each time she was dragged here for a visit, she was glad it was still gone. Meanwhile, as the Widow Álvarez and Lulu chit-chatted, a cake, a tea service and lemonade for the children were brought in. Ruby's knee bounced under the skirt of her dress.

"Really, Ruby, you act like a caged lion," Doña Anastasia said, picking up a silver cake knife and slicing into the torte.

The little serving girl delivered the china plates to the guests in order of age.

Lalo looked at his plate and whined, "I don't want cake!"

"What is that dreadful noise, little boy?" Doña Anastasia said.

"Mamalú said there'd be cookies! Macaroons and marzipan and meringues and pumpkin-seed brittle."

Lulu looked mortified. "I was merely telling the child how accomplished your cook is, Auntie." She turned to the little boy. "Lalo, I did not promise you cookies. Now eat this lovely orange cream cake, and don't drop any crumbs."

Lalo stood up in a pique and the plate of cake balanced on his little knees plopped onto the floor, cake-side down. Lulu and Soli jumped to their feet.

"Lalo, look what you've done!" Lulu said. "You shall be punished."

Lalo slapped at her legs. "I don't like cake. I want a cookie. I want two cookies!"

"Lalo! Stop that!" Lulu screeched.

"Good heavens," Doña Anastasia muttered.

"Soli, do something," Lulu implored.

Soli stood and took Lalo by the hand to lead him from the room. When he balked, she swooped him up and carried him out, his screaming becoming muffled as they disappeared into the back of the house. When it was quiet, Doña Anastasia let out an exaggerated sigh.

"Sit down, Lulu, dear," she said stiffly.

There was an uncomfortable silence as everyone eyed the cake smashed on the tile floor. Doña Anastasia rocked in her cane rocking chair, Lulu and Ruby perched on hard-backed chairs, and Meche looked restive on the wicker settee, her legs jiggling as she stared alternately at the doorway and the ceiling.

The cook entered with a broom and dustpan. She wore a white, square-necked blouse with black embroidery and a long apron over her full-length skirt. The serving girl followed her, lugging a pail of water.

"Excuse me, ma'am," the cook said. "The señorita said there'd been an upset."

Doña Anastasia waggled her finger at the cake and plate on the floor. The cook swept up the mess, and the girl squatted down to hold the dustpan for her. Then the girl dropped to her knees and mopped the spot on the tiles with a cloth.

"Dry that thoroughly now," Doña Anastasia said. "I won't have my guests slipping."

Meche went over to the girl and spoke to her in Mayan, and the girl answered, causing Doña Anastasia's eyebrows to lift.

Turning to the widow, Meche curtsied. "With your permission, señora, Rosita is going to take me to my brother and sister."

Doña Anastasia waved her off, and Meche left.

After a few uneasy moments, the widow broached the silence. "So Lulu, my dear, what are your plans?"

"I haven't decided, Auntie."

"But surely, the times being what they are, you won't be returning to that hacienda of yours?"

Lulu sipped her tea and did not correct the widow's use of the word hacienda, so Ruby did.

"It's just a rancho, Tía. Isn't that right, Lulu? Nothing as grand as an hacienda."

Lulu sniffed, and Doña Anastasia ignored Ruby's comment.

"Wouldn't it be wiser, my dear, to establish yourself and the children here in the city? Near Ruby and myself?"

"Perhaps, Tía, but the memories...." Lulu snapped open her fan.

Soli, Meche and Lalo appeared at the door, and Ruby made use of the interruption.

"I really must go to the studio," she said.

"But, Ruby. It's Sunday!" Doña Anastasia shook her head disapprovingly. "What kind of example are you setting for the children?"

"I don't know, Auntie, but they're not my children."

"Can I come with you, Tía Ruby?" Meche asked. "Please?"

Her eyes gleamed, but Ruby couldn't tell if it was with true interest or at the prospect of escape.

"I can help," she wheedled. "Please, I'd really like to."

Ruby and Meche caught a mule-pulled streetcar in front of San Román Church. While the girl chattered away next to her, Ruby, silent, looked out at the street—her sister not intending to stay in Campeche was news to her. Or was it Lulu just being overly dramatic, playing for Tía Anastasia's sympathy?

"I thought I would die when we left our rancho," Meche said, "but I like the city. I like it a lot. I could live here."

"I don't think that's your stepmother's plan," Ruby said.

Thunder settled on Meche's brow, and Ruby thought that if she were Lulu—having to deal with this girl, and the little boy, too—she'd get sick headaches too.

"After the Revolution is over," the girl said, "I'm going back to run the rancho. I know how. I have notebooks full of what to do. Not the medicinal stuff. I'm not interested in that—that was Mamá's job, and then Soli's. Except I do know some of the veterinary treatments."

"What if the rancho isn't there at the end of the war?" Ruby said. The comment came out a bit harsh, but the girl only looked more determined. "What I mean is that it's hard to make plans while there's a war on."

"Whether the Revolution fails or succeeds, Mexico will need

agriculturists who know what they're doing. Soli doesn't care and Lalo is too little, but I'll be ready. I'm ready now. I can take my father's place. If he were alive, he wouldn't let me, but he's not and Baalam Kab belongs to all three of us."

"What about Lulu?"

The girl snorted. "Oh, her. She hates the rancho!"

"But you like Campeche City."

The girl started to glow and lift. She was like a balloon someone had just infused with hot air.

"I love it," she said.

At the studio, Meche drank everything in. She fingered the velvet drapes and struck a pose in front of the backdrop Ruby had last used. She stuck her head under the black cloth of the camera, and in the darkroom inhaled the smell of the chemicals with a smile. Although amused by the girl's enthusiasm, Ruby needed her out of the way. She took her back to reception and pointed to the counter.

"You want to help? See if you can do something about the papers back there."

"What if I mess something up?"

"There's nothing you could do that would make it worse."

The girl deflated a bit, but went behind to the desk, and Ruby returned to the back.

Hours later, Ruby hung up her leather apron. In reception she found the desk arrayed with neat piles of papers, and the girl—her head lying amongst them—asleep.

When they arrived home, they found Soli helping María Asunción in the kitchen. Lalo was drawing at the table.

Meche leaned over Lalo to look at his picture.

"You smell funny," he said, wrinkling his nose.

"That's chemicals. Stop-bath chemicals. Isn't that right, Ruby?"

"Aunt Ruby," Soli corrected.

"And just the best photographer you've ever seen." Meche said.

Soli sniffed at Meche's hair. "Uf, you do smell strange."

Lulu had drifted to the kitchen doorway. "I'd like to say you get used to it, but you don't."

One afternoon, Lulu, along with everyone else, sought out a quiet spot after dinner for the siesta hour. Soli was lulling Lalo to sleep in their bedroom, Meche was scribbling in a new notebook at the dining room table, and Aunt Pancha was reading a newspaper in the parlor, which left the bed free for Ruby. She was lying flat with her clothes on and her lace-up boots off, snoring lightly. Almost a purring sound, Lulu thought, but she did not find it charming. She didn't like cats. There was something reptilian about the eyes and the way they watched you, like they would steal your soul.

She removed her black clothes: shoes, stockings, blouse and skirt. Black, black and more black. She missed her pastels, especially pinks and peaches. She glowed in those colors, and they always raised her spirits, but she was doomed to total black for at least another three months. She moaned at the prospect. During the following year she might get away with grays, maybe even a mauve. She might be able to trim those twelve months back to six, if she were away from Campeche, if she were someplace where every detail of her life was not common currency.

She took off her corset and left on her chemise slip (black and black again). She poured water from the pitcher into the basin on the washstand and washed with a bar of English soap scented with lavender she'd bought at the pharmacy. (No more of that harsh homemade soap they made at the rancho!) The fragrance alone made her feel cooler and fresher.

She carefully slipped on her boudoir cap over her pompadour. She didn't want to have to redo her hair, which, unlike Ruby's, was fine and hard to get to fan nicely into a topknot. Stepping over Aunt Pancha's leather grip, she skirted her own trunk and the cot to lie down on the bed next to her sister. They had always shared a bed, up until the day of Lulu's marriage. And her first week back in Campeche City, Lulu had relished the comfort of Ruby's proximity. But as the weeks passed, the ease and reassurance drained away, and now the old familiarity chafed. She persuaded herself that, despite the disturbing nighttime noises in the countryside, she missed the loneliness of her bed at the rancho.

Lulu turned on her side with her back to her sister so that the smell of Ruby's feet, the fish and garlic on her breath and the slightly stale scent of her clothes did not assault her as strongly. Lulu longed for a bit of sleep, and it was irksome that, as she fidgeted (her thoughts scurrying like beetles in every direction), her sister lay next to her as still as one of her photographs.

Lulu had come home to Campeche to rest and be taken care of, but the children were out of sorts, Ruby was pressing her to take up her old duties at the studio and Tía had chided her, gently, for shoving too much of the care of the children onto Soli. But Lulu had never forced anything onto Soli. If anyone was taking advantage, it was María Asunción, who always had Soli helping her in the kitchen.

Earlier over dinner, Aunt Pancha and Meche had once again gloried in the details of the latest battle in the north, and Lulu had again reproached them. It was unsuitable conversation for the dinner table.

"You can't stick your head in the sand, my dear," Aunt Pancha had countered.

But that was exactly what Lulu had come home to do! She wanted to feel safe, like she used to, like she feared she never would again. Heavens, whenever she went to the center of town, her heart pounded and she broke into a cold sweat.

Of course she knew fighting was breaking out all over the country. She was at her wits end with worry about it, and certainly didn't need to know every horrible detail. It was a revolution for heaven's sake! Revolution meant disorder and violence and ruin, didn't it? Men getting shot, dying. Women, too. She knew that for a fact. And yet everyone, even Tía Pancha, told her not to worry so. But how could she not? The Revolution might come to Campeche at any moment. And when it did, it would consume everything and everyone. It was too horrible to contemplate. And yet she did little else. It's what she did now as she bit the side of her thumb and listened with increasing irritation to the rumbling of Ruby's breathing next to her. She poked her with her elbow.

Ruby murmured, "Is it time already?"

"You were snoring."

Ruby stretched and yawned.

"I'm so tired," Lulu grumbled, "and you just sleep away like it's the easiest thing in the world."

Ruby pushed herself to sitting. "Well, I'm awake now." She placed her stockinged feet on the floor.

"What are you doing?"

"Getting up."

"But you've got another hour before you go back to the studio."

"If I go back to sleep, you're just going to wake me up again, aren't you?" Ruby said.

"If you snore. But you don't have to leave."

"You mean I can stay here and watch you sleep? Listen to you snore?"

"I don't snore. And I can't sleep anyway," Lulu said.

"So you want me to stay and watch you not sleep?"

"Oh, Ruby! Can't you be nice to me?"

Ruby, padding to the wash basin, bumped into the cot. "Blast! How much longer do we have to put up with the plague that is Aunt Pancha?"

Lulu ignored her outburst. "It's not easy for me, you know," she said to Ruby's back. "I'm responsible for Ernesto's children."

"What's that have to do with me," Ruby said, "other than the fact that they've invaded our house?"

"You're my sister. You oughtn't to make things harder for me than they already are."

"How in the world am I making things harder for you?"

"You undermine me in front of the children."

"I do no such thing," Ruby said, tossing down the hand towel. "I treat you as I've always treated you."

"Exactly, and that undermines my authority."

"Lulu!"

"You're still patronizing me, making fun of me, contradicting me all the time, as if nothing has changed. But it has, and those children are listening. You're their aunt now."

"I didn't ask for that."

"Neither did I." She flung her arm across her eyes.

"Yes, you did, Lulu. When you married Ernesto."

Lulu lowered her hand and glared at Ruby with frustration.

"Look," Ruby said, "You show up with three kids in tow. Three strangers. Maybe if you'd started me off with your own baby, I could see you differently than before, see you as a new mother, get used to the idea…"

Lulu blanched. Did Ruby really not realize that she had dreamt of arriving home with an infant in her arms?

"But as it is, you seem the same as always," Ruby concluded.

Lulu gave a shudder. "Well, I'm not."

Ruby came back to the bed and sat down. She gave Lulu's leg a pat.

"Maybe I shouldn't have said that about a baby."

Lulu agreed.

"But you never really wanted one, did you?"

Lulu shrugged. "Ernesto and I talked about it. I expected to."

"He did leave you with a family."

"Which you warned me about. And you were right. You have no idea how right you were. Though the main problem is Meche," Lulu said. "She's such a pill, Ruby. So disrespectful."

"She's what, 13, 14? It's her job."

"But she hates me."

"Yes, she takes her work seriously."

"But why? What have I ever done to her? If it hadn't been for me, who knows what would have happened to her? She might be in some dreadful orphanage where they beat her and made her scrub floors." She could not keep the gleam out of her eye at the thought.

"I hope you haven't told her that."

Lulu shrugged sheepishly.

"Oh, Lulu."

"Well, it's not fair. You, she adores. She hangs on your every word, your every movement."

"Nonsense."

"Whereas I simply walk into a room and she rolls her eyes and stomps out. It's such a strain on the nerves."

"Give her time, Lulu. It's not been long since she lost her father."

"You think I don't know that?" Lulu cried. "What about me? I've lost my husband. My husband! Much, much more painful than losing a father!"

"Truly?"

"Yes!" she said, then conceded, "Well, losing Papá was hard for you, wasn't it? Harder than for me."

Ruby was silent a moment, then nodded. "Mourning Mamá was different, more… contained. Intense, and then it was over, for the most part. But Papá, sometimes the sadness still ambushes me when I least expect it, and I find myself walking down the street with tears pouring down my face."

"That's how I feel about Ernesto."

"Really?"

"Yes, really!"

She waited for Ruby to say something, to acknowledge her sadness and frustration. But she said nothing. It made her feel so very alone. If her own sister didn't understand…. Her tears flowed, and she gave a shuddering sob.

Then she recalled something Tía Pancha once said: "Ruby loves us, but she doesn't think she needs us. She keeps her own council. I wager she has long discussions in her head. You can tell because her forehead wrinkles and she looks past you and doesn't respond when you address her. That's when she says things out of the blue. I wager it's all part of a conversation she's having with herself."

Lulu had never noticed any of that until Tía Pancha explained it to her. Lulu glanced at Ruby now. Her brow was indeed furrowed.

Ruby patted Lulu's shoulder and said, "I can't remember doing either."

Lulu sniffled. She shook her head and smiled a little. Her life was a misery, but God bless Tía Pancha.

Ruby squirmed in her chair, embarrassed by the way her sister cooed to her lawyer. And in front of everybody!

Don Mauricio seemed to share her discomfort. Lulu had managed to detain him in their parlor for over an hour now—the poor man would start to reach for the pocket watch in his vest, and then stop himself, tugging down on the garment instead. Ruby wasn't sure if Lulu was too busy being charming to notice his desire to leave, or if it was some kind of game to see how long she could hold him in sway. Lulu had always been the boy-crazy one—maybe she was just desperate for male company. Ruby didn't care why she was doing it. She just wanted it to end.

And now Lulu was pressing more hibiscus tea on the poor man. He refused and she insisted again, the usual waltz of politeness, the back and forth that tried Ruby's patience at the best of times.

No sooner had the lawyer uttered the first word of a mandatory third refusal than Ruby abruptly rose and offered to accompany him to the door. She ignored the irritated look Lulu threw her way—she'd had enough of Lulu's coquetry and intended to forestall her glomming onto Don Mauricio's arm.

Ruby regarded Don Mauricio closely as they walked to the door. Judging by the sharp edges of his very short sideburns, the razor-clean back of his neck and the aroma of bay rum, she concluded that he'd paid a visit to his barber that day. His very dark brown chevron of a mustache was equally tidy, and she recalled watching her father in the mirror as he trimmed his much larger and bushier blond mustache—the tiny scissors, the tin of wax used to make the tips smile—secrets of male conceit. And the wink he sent her via the glass.

She'd always liked Don Mauricio, certainly more than she did Ernesto, but she felt small and unkempt next to him. It was not his intent, she was sure. He was ever courteous, ever solicitous of what he would deem the fairer, weaker sex. Look how patient he was with Lulu! No, the problem was that he played his role so much better than Ruby played hers—the glowing patina of his gallantry versus the ill-applied veneer of her femininity.

At the door she handed Don Mauricio his bowler.

He thanked her and lowered his voice. "Miss Ruby, I've advised your sister as best I can, but she keeps changing her mind. I'm not sure what more I can do."

"I know, Licenciado, you've been most kind."

What Don Mauricio did not understand was that Lulu was basking in his attentions—the more effort he made to guide her towards a decision, the more elusive she was likely to become.

"I do appreciate how difficult this must be for her," he said.

Ruby wondered if he did. In Ernesto, Don Mauricio had lost a friend and favored client, but her sister had lost her beloved. That was if Ernesto had indeed been her beloved. Sometimes Ruby suspected marrying him was just a way for Lulu to escape from her and the studio.

Resolved, she strode back into the parlor—Lulu must stop imposing on the licenciado. When she entered, Meche jumped up and tossed aside the embroidery hoop that Soli had foisted onto her. Lalo, released from sitting like a gentleman, was playing on the floor. And Tía Pancha was trying, without success, to interest Soli in a political tract she was reading. But no Lulu.

"Where is she?" Ruby demanded.

Lalo held up a small carved wooden jaguar for Ruby to see.

"Look Tía Ruby. This was Mamalú's when she little!"

Ruby's eyes zeroed in on the rough tawny shape in the little boy's hand.

"She gave him to me, and I'm going to call him Buttons!"

Ruby snatched the toy from him.

"It wasn't Lulu's," she snarled.

Lalo's eyes grew wide, shock staving off tears.

Then the little jaguar was, in turn, ripped from Ruby's hand. She spun around to face the culprit—Tía Pancha.

"Carmen Rubina Eckart Reyes, what in the world do you think you're doing?" her great-aunt said in a voice sternly reminiscent of Ruby's mother, although just the litany of her names was enough to make Ruby shrink.

Tía Pancha plopped the little animal back into Lalo's still-outstretched hand. He clasped it to his chest.

"Poor little Buttons," he whispered to it.

"It's mine." Ruby told her aunt matter-of-factly.

"And how old are we?" she said in her teacher's voice. "Have we not learned to share yet?"

Rebuked, Ruby turned away from Tía Pancha.

"Where's Lulu?" she repeated.

"She went to her room with a sick headache," Soli said, looking at Ruby bemused.

The expression on Soli's face made Ruby feel downright foolish—a grown woman stealing a little boy's toy!

"Thank you," she said and hurried from the room.

Meche followed her. "Aunt Ruby," she called.

Ruby wheeled around. "What?" she snapped.

Meche blinked at her tone, but took her hand. "Please, please Don't let Lulu sell the farm."

"I don't know that she's going to," Ruby said.

"It would be so stupid!"

Ruby pulled her hand away, "I don't have anything to do with it."

"But it's not fair!"

Soli came to Meche's side. They each put an arm around the other's waist.

"If you could talk to her…" Soli said.

"Leave me out of it," Ruby said, grabbing hold of both knobs of the French doors. "It's none of my business."

Ruby entered the dim bedroom—the shutters were closed.

"Lulu?"

Lulu groaned. "Oh, my head. Please. The light. Close the door."

Ruby closed the door, but for privacy.

"I want to talk to you about Don Mauricio."

"Not now," Lulu pleaded.

"You do know that he's married, don't you?"

"Of course I do."

"You're flirting with him."

"Nonsense. Just a little friendly banter."

Ruby sighed noisily.

"He's most kind, isn't he?" Lulu said.

"Yes, and you've abused his kindness and patience long enough."

"I don't know what you mean."

"You, simpering and fawning over the poor man until he doesn't know which way to look."

"How can you say such a thing. I'm a widow in mourning."

"Lulu!" Ruby groaned.

"What? I *am* a widow." Lulu clutched a cloth to her forehead and sniffled. "And I *am* in mourning."

Even in the darkened room, Ruby could see that Lulu's face was drawn with pain. She backed down.

"Of course you are. I'm sorry."

Ruby sat on the bed and stroked Lulu's arm. Lulu leaned into her and sniffled a bit more.

"Lulu, did you love Ernesto? Really?"

"How can you ask that? He was my husband! Of course I loved him."

"What I mean is, were you in love with him?"

"There's no difference, is there?"

"I don't know. I imagine there is."

"Please, Ruby, my head hurts terribly." She handed the cloth to Ruby.

"Fine. But you really must stop importuning Don Mauricio."

Ruby picked her way around Lulu's trunk and the cot to reach the washstand. She poured water from the pitcher over the cloth and wrung it out.

"And if you absolutely must consult with him, go to his office.

Especially if it's about selling the rancho. Can't you see how much it upsets the girls? Probably affects the boy, too."

Ruby came back to the bed. She sat and placed the damp cloth over Lulu's eyes.

"Better?"

Lulu nodded, and they were quiet for several moments.

Then Ruby sighed. "Lulu, you must make up your mind what you will do."

Lulu whimpered, "Oh, Ruby, I don't think I can! I have to do my best to honor Ernesto, do what's best for his children. But what is that? What should I do? And what about me? It's so hard to make a decision."

"Of course," Ruby answered. "But, please, don't contact poor Don Mauricio until you are completely decided."

"You seem more concerned about the licenciado than you are with me," Lulu pouted.

Ruby kissed her on the cheek. How to advise her? For everyone's peace of mind, the situation would be best resolved without delay, but it was all such a muddle, and if Ruby couldn't get her mind to sort through it all, how could she expect Lulu to, who was so frightened and sad?

Her thoughts were interrupted by an uproar in the patio—the reprimand of Soli's voice, the sass of Meche and howls rising from Lalo's powerful throat.

"Ruby, dear, can't you quiet them. My head hurts so."

"Lulu, they're your children."

Lulu groaned and sniffled again.

A letter arrived for Lulu.

Pancha looked up from the article she was writing to see her great-niece swish past, half hiding an envelope by her side. Lulu could easily have concealed it from her completely, so Pancha knew that she wanted her to see. Since childhood, Lulu had delighted in secrets. For her they were like little gifts, toys, trinkets, and she itched to show them off.

Pancha had secrets, too, but hers were like a derringer secreted in a lady's beaded clutch or a grenade hidden in a carpet bag. If they fell into the wrong hands, they could have lethal consequences. But in truth, her weapon of choice was this, her portable desk.

She'd set the mahogany box on a round marble-topped table crammed in one corner of the interior patio. Inside the desk were a little drawer and various compartments for storing a fountain pen, a bottle of ink, blotting paper, stationery, and envelopes. The lid, lined with nut-brown leather, when opened (when cocked, she liked to think), provided an excellent slanted writing surface. At this moment, a scathing denouncement flowed from the scratching of her pen: *Down with the dictator's henchmen and sycophants! Down with the despot Díaz!* (She liked the alliteration of that.) She would end the article with an incendiary call to arms.

She called to Lulu, "What do you have there, hija?"

Having seen the sly smile playing about Lulu's lips, Pancha asked the question partly out of curiosity and partly to tease. She'd seen that same smile since Lulu was a child. It could slip into a pout or break into a grin of pure sunshine. Her great-niece really was rather transparent. At times, Pancha thought, to the point of being simple.

"Nothing, Auntie," Lulu said, avoiding her eyes. "Don't let me interrupt you," she said and rushed to her bedroom.

What was she up to, Pancha wondered. She considered herself blessed with superior skills of observation, not to mention a fine imagination (an essential quality if one was to be a feminist and political visionary in this country of theirs). She'd noted that Lulu's letter was thick and well-traveled, with many stamps.

Might Lulu have a lover?

Pancha considered the question with interest. It wasn't implausible, and if true, she could only applaud Lulu for breaking free of social convention. Although she was wearing black…

All those bourgeois rules of mourning were no more than a ploy, and a blatant one at that, to control women. Rigid and formularized, they dictated every particular of a widow's clothing and behavior, whereas a man wore a black armband for a few months, was mostly free to do as he pleased and encouraged to go out and find a new wife. But not the widow! God forbid she enjoy her newfound freedom. No, she must be hidden behind a veil and encased in black, head-to-toe, for at least a year, if not forever, and is not permitted to attend a concert or even a family birthday party. The husband might be dead and buried, but mourning strictures extended and even tightened the constraints of marriage, which itself was clearly a capitalist invention created to oppress women. Women's bodies were, after all, the primary, most basic means of production, and marriage, like debt peonage, was a barely disguised form of slavery. She should make some notes. It could make a good article. Although once the Revolution was over and the old order fell, she expected such antiquated customs to die a natural death.

As for Lulu taking a lover…

For Pancha, believing in free love was a logical extension of her political convictions. In fact, she'd intuited its importance early on and had practiced it even before she knew it was a social philosophy. But a lover was, perhaps, not the answer for Lulu.

But what about a suitor? Her great-niece was clearly not doing well on her own. Pancha had hoped that after Lulu had had some time to recover from the shock of Ernesto's death she would dredge up the strength to create a new life for herself. But there was no sign of that in the offing. Attaching herself to a man, while a reactionary solution, might very well make her niece happy. And Pancha did want Lulu to be happy.

Pancha sighed and took up her pen to finish her article. She intended to mail it to Amparo, a contact in Patzcuaro, before the post office closed for the afternoon. Amparo would forward it to her cousin Lupe, a member of the textile union in Mexico City, who would hand deliver it to El Futuro, their revolutionary newspaper. Since Lupe was not a known leader in the union, perhaps she could mail it directly to her with a false return name and address on the envelope. Pancha furrowed her brow. Sometimes it was a fine line between caution and paranoia.

Lulu presided at the head of the table. An expanse of white linen edged with crochet lace made by her mother stretched between her and the others. She'd decked the table with the family silver, crystal and porcelain, and yet no one commented on the elegance of the table. No one seemed to notice. She ladled portions of the seafood soup from a china tureen into shallow, gold-rimmed bowls, sulking a bit, but by the time there was a plate of soup in front of each person, she'd regained her sparkle.

"I wonder if we'll miss seafood?" she murmured with a mysterious little smile.

Soli glanced at Meche.

"What do you mean?" Soli said with trepidation.

"Oh, nothing," Lulu said.

With each course she dropped more hints and observed the people around the table carefully, while, of course, hiding her scrutiny of them. Soli, always so careful, spilt some papaya water on the tablecloth and rushed to the kitchen for a damp cloth, and then during the main course, she dropped her knife with a clatter on the china plate. Later Lulu saw her wince and her hand fly to her cheek. She must have bitten herself, and Lulu was pleased that her intimations were having some effect. Across from Soli, Meche seemed to be growing more sullen and her glower darker. Ruby was mostly lost in her own thoughts, but next to her, Tía Pancha eyed her with raised eyebrows. Lulu responded with a charming smile. She could hardly wait to break her news.

Finally Tía Pancha said to her, "The table is set rather elaborately today, my dear. What's the occasion?"

"Occasion?" Lulu said, feigning surprise.

"Yes, Lulu," Tía Pancha said. "Spill the beans. You know you want to."

"Well, I was going to wait until after dessert..."

Everyone's eyes were on her now, and she felt herself blush with pleasure. She was so anxious to tell all.

"I received a letter today from Cousin Carl," she said.

"Cousin Carl?" Ruby mused.

"Yes. Father's cousin. In Texas." Lulu prompted.

"Why would you get a letter from him?"

"He wrote after Ernesto passed away, to send his condolences. We've been corresponding since, and the good news is that he's invited us to their home in San Antonio."

"For a visit? Now?" Ruby said. "It's so far."

"He's concerned about our safety, and he wants me and the children to come to the United States until the war is over. You, too, Ruby."

Ruby gave a harsh laugh, which Lulu ignored.

"So today, when I went to the post office for you, Tía, I sent a telegram accepting his offer."

Soli stared open-mouthed.

"What about Baalam Kab?" Meche demanded in a raised voice.

"Oh that." Lulu waved the question away. "Don Eusebio will keep things running and report to Don Mauricio."

Meche slumped with relief, but only for a moment, because Lulu continued.

"Don Mauricio says that the midst of a Revolution is not the time to sell the rancho, at least not for anything near what it's worth.

"Children," she beamed, "isn't it exciting? We're moving to San Antonio, Texas!"

Soli had observed her stepmother with trepidation all afternoon. It had been obvious that she was up to something. There were all the pains she'd taken setting the table, usually Soli's task, and then her impish demeanor throughout the meal. But Texas?! Soli felt sick to her stomach. In the wake of Lulu's big announcement, a bolt out of the blue if ever there was one, Soli stared at her, trying to read the intent there. Her stepmother glowed. Her blue eyes twinkled. Was she pulling their leg? Lulu was often playful when in a good mood.

Soli reached for Meche's hand under the table, but Meche shook her off, pushing out of her chair.

"No!" Meche cried out.

Meche let herself be shushed by Tía Pancha and Tía Ruby, but refused to sit down. She paced the room like a caged cat. Soli worried that she might pick up a plate, a crystal glass, a silver knife, and fling it at their stepmother. From the look on Lulu's face and the way her eyes kept darting in Meche's direction, Soli suspected it was of concern to Lulu, as well. But Meche returned to stand behind her own chair, gripping the carved-wood back, as Tía Pancha told Lulu that moving everyone to Texas was perhaps ill-considered, and Tía Ruby declared the plan outright ludicrous.

Everyone's opposition flustered Lulu. She stood, complaining, "Why are you all ruining my surprise like this?"

Lalo added to the ruckus. Up till then he'd been listening, wide-eyed, trying to make sense of what he was hearing. When Lulu stood up, he ran to her and tugged on her skirt.

"Mamalú! What's a texas?"

Lulu, focused as she was on her aunt and sister, paid no attention to him.

Tía Pancha said, "It's a big decision, hija, one that must be taken calmly."

Lalo's voice got louder and louder, edging toward hysteria, "What's a texas? Mamalú!"

She pulled Lalo's hands from her skirt, and Lalo wailed.

"You both think I'm stupid," Lulu said over the din of the little boy's cries, her eyes brimming with tears. "Well, I'm not! And I'm not going to wait around like of big black blob of a bullseye to be... to be..."

Her sniffling turned into sobbing, and she rushed from the dining room to shut herself away in the bedroom.

Meche, her face as dark with anger as Lulu's was pale with her martyrdom, went to Lalo, but Lalo pulled away from her and ran to Soli on the far side of the table.

Soli pushed her chair away from the table and pulled Lalo into her lap. She caressed the back of his head, the fine soft hair the same color brown as the wooden arms of the chair. She felt his little rib cage heave, his hot tears on her neck.

"Ya, ya, mi amor. Don't cry," she murmured. "Everything is fine." Poor motherless boy, she thought. Then she found herself weeping, too.

She'd been trying to keep her little family (Meche, Lalo and herself) intact, since they'd come to the city, since Lulu entered their lives, since their father died, since her mother died, since, really, almost before she could remember. When they'd come to the city, she'd worried about her brother and sister adjusting to the change, especially Meche, but her sister seemed surprisingly content. As for Lalo, although some of his more childish behavior had returned, he didn't act that all differently from at the rancho. It was she who was the one truly struggling, floundering, really. She felt unmoored. She missed her house, her kitchen. She missed Susana de los Ángeles and their routines together. Here, she was always looking for something, a paring knife or the baking powder, always turning in circles, or bumping into María Asunción. She was, just now, in the last few days, feeling like she was starting to find her footing, making a place for herself amongst all these new people: María Asunción and her niece, Carmencita, Tía Ruby, Tía Pancha, even Don Mauricio and Doña Anastasia.

And now? Texas?

It was later that afternoon, after the siesta, with Lulu still closeted in her room, that Soli realized that Meche had slipped out of the house with no one noticing. Fighting down panic, Soli went to the tías to tell them. She caught Ruby at the door as she was about to head back to the studio.

"But Lulu says the girl's always running off," Tía Ruby said. "She always comes back, right?"

"At home, yes, but…" Soli didn't know what to say. She feared this time her leaving was no mere sulk.

"Really, Ruby," Aunt Pancha said, joining them. "Can't you see the girl is worried about her sister?" Tía Pancha turned to Soli, "Where do you think she would go?"

Soli had no idea. She didn't know the city at all, and she didn't think Meche did either.

There was no telephone at the house, but Aunt Pancha made Ruby promise that she would call Don Mauricio as soon as she got to the studio. Perhaps he could send his household servants to help look for Meche.

"And I'll accompany Ruby to the studio," Tía Pancha said. "Then I'll take a look around the Plaza de Independencia. I know that's where I would go."

She invited Soli to accompany her, but Lalo had followed Soli to the entryway and the solemn talk upset him all over again. He hung on her skirt, whining. She decided it was best not to leave him. She would wait here for Meche.

Tía Pancha patted Soli's arm. "Don't worry, my dear," she said. "Your sister seems a very independent and resourceful girl. She's probably just gone for a walk to clear her head."

Soli wanted to believe her, but she wasn't sure. What if Meche applied her resourcefulness to trying to get back to Baalam Kab?

Hours passed and Meche did not return. It was almost six. The sun was about to set.

Soli got Lalo ready for bed. It was early, but he was tired out. They both were. Sitting on the bed, she tried to explain that Texas was a place, but Lalo shushed her and put his warm little hand over her mouth. He whispered to her, reminding her that saying the word "alux" aloud was bad luck. It could call them to you, and you never knew what those Mayan sprites would do. They might be helpful, but they could be very wicked if you upset them, and they were ever so touchy.

"I didn't say "alux," silly," Soli said.

The little boy's hand clapped over her mouth again.

"Shh!" he said, eyes wide.

In the absence of real information, Lalo had gotten it into his head that Texas was the given name of an alux, and he whispered this information to Soli. He no longer needed to know about Texas. What he wanted to know was why Mamalú would get mixed up with an alux, or was it that Texas was a particularly kind one?

"Lalo," Soli said, "aluxob do not exist, any more than goblins or fairies do."

"They do, Soli! Meche said so."

"I've told you before not to believe Meche's Mayan nonsense."

"It's not nonsense. I saw one. He was smaller than me, and dressed in white clothes like the workers. I saw him and then I got sick with fever."

"Lalo, you did not!"

"I think we should stay away from Texas Alux," he whispered.

She sighed and thought, I couldn't agree more.

Meche made a beeline from the house—the direction didn't matter as long as it was away. She walked down one street after another, not stopping or slowing until she found herself on an empty stretch of beach.

Picking up a rock, she hurled it into the waves. She took in a gulp of salt air, and another, and then her tears gushed forth, hot and angry.

She felt so helpless.

She plunked herself down on the ground, barely noticing the damp rocks beneath her. As her crying ebbed, her stony perch became more uncomfortable, but she did not move. She looked to the horizon.

"Mami?" she said aloud, surprising herself. Not so much because she seldom thought of her mother, but because she suddenly sensed her—intense, flashing remembrances of scent and touch.

Was she here somehow? Her mother, Blanca Estela Cruz. Blanca: white. And Estela: the wake of a boat or the tail of a comet. Beautiful, luminous, fleeting.

Meche had few memories of her. She'd just turned nine when Blanca Estela died, but her mother had been ill off and on before that

—present sometimes, other times confined to bed. She remembered that once she had sneaked into her mother's room and climbed into bed with her. Her mother had held her close until Susana de los Ángeles discovered her.

"Your mother must rest!" Susana de los Ángeles had scolded.

Meche knew that her mother had grown up in Campeche City. Now she wondered where in the city she'd lived? And how had she met her father?

She didn't know. Did Soli?

Was that why the city attracted Meche so? A bond transmitted in the womb? Maybe her mother had sat at twilight on this same beach, on this very spot.

The tide was receding—pulling away from her, gradually and steadily, like everything and everyone in her life—slowly, oh so slowly. Of course her father had disappeared all of a sudden. But his fondness for her, that had been waning for some time before.

She felt as if a glass float were lodged in her chest. The rocks beneath her seemed colder and more unyielding. She stood up and brushed off the back of her skirt and went closer to the water, let it lap at her boots. The sun was drifting ever closer to the horizon—Jaguar approaching the Otherworld for his nightly struggle with death. Her heart sank with foreboding for her own future.

Her face felt flush and puffy from crying, the skin taut with dried tears. She reached down and splashed water on it. The sea water felt thicker than well water and gritty with sand.

Spent, she turned and walked until she saw the San Román church tower. When she reached the park by the church, the street lamps were lit, and loud voices poured from the bar on the far side. Steering clear of that side of the street, she stumbled her way back to the house.

She didn't have a key and was loathe to knock. She thought about turning around, but she was weary, hungry and cold from the damp beach. Besides, where would she go?

She knocked.

Almost immediately Soli threw open the door—she must have been listening for her. She grabbed Meche roughly by the arm and pulled her into the unlit parlor.

She hugged Meche tight, and Meche let her, but then pulled away as usual.

"You scared me!" Soli said.

"I'm what scared you? What about our crazy stepmother?"

"She's just doing what she thinks is best."

"Going to fucking Texas, that doesn't scare you?"

"Meche! Your language!"

"Now you're upset with my language? Christ, Soli! Aren't there more important things to be upset about?"

Meche plopped on the yellow silk couch. She felt her damp skirt and slip against her skin and thought, if Soli knew she was getting the sofa wet, she'd rebuke her.

"But, Meche," Soli said, dropping next to her, "aren't you scared about the Revolution? Not even a little bit?"

Meche shrugged. "We can't leave just because there's a war."

"Just?" Soli slid out of her slippers and tucked her feet next to her on the sofa.

"Leaving is cowardly. It would be deserting," Meche said.

"Well, we can't fight."

"Why not?"

"Meche!"

"Do you think Father would approve of us leaving?"

"He'd want us to be safe, don't you think?"

"We were taught how to shoot, Soli."

"To protect ourselves."

Meche lifted her palms to the sky as if to say, there you go—you proved my point.

"From wild animals, from Indian attack," Soli said, "not to fight in a revolution! Anyway, it isn't our decision to make."

"But it's our life, and that Lulu's crazy. Nobody else thinks it's a good idea."

"Nonetheless, she is our guardian."

"I want to scream!"

Soli reached out and touched Meche's knee.

"Meche, I was so scared tonight when I didn't know where you'd gone. Anything could have happened to you, and I imagined each horrible fate. We've already lost Mamá and Papá. I don't know what I would do if I lost you."

"What about losing Baalam Kab?"

"We still have each other. You, me and Lalo."

"Lalo! A lot of help he is."

"Meche, I'm serious."

Meche grumbled, "I know you are."

"Please, please promise me you won't run away again."

Even in the dim parlor, in only the scant light from the lamp by the front door, Meche saw that Soli's face looked stricken. She saw in it, too, a glimmer of their mother's face.

"I won't run away," Meche said.

Soli jumped up and pulled Meche off the sofa. She embraced her and cried. Meche had no tears left.

"Dios mío, Meche," Soli whispered. "Fucking Texas!"

Meche slapped Soli on the back of the head. "María Soledad, you shock me. What language!"

Soli giggled. Then they were both giggling.

The front door opened and Ruby came in. Meche glimpsed her in the entryway light—felt her presence shift the atmosphere of the house into something more stable, more comfortable—then watched as she walked past the parlor, pretending she hadn't seen them.

That night Ruby woke with a start—she heard a deep-voiced roar that vibrated in her spine, raising the hairs on the back of her neck. Then grunts. Growls. Growls like barks. Jaguar sounds? She was awake, she was sure of it—and heard the impossible. Baalam stalking its prey, creeping down the streets of the city, draping itself in a tree in the plaza, paws dangling, guarding a haunch of meat.

Her heart pounded. Was she going mad?

From her cot, she became aware of Aunt Pancha's snores and Lulu's murmurs, their noises edging out the jaguar sound as it faded, until the two women were all she could hear. She must have been dreaming, but she was fully awake now. She lifted on one elbow and made out the dark contours of their bodies in the bed—Sierra Pancha, Sierra Lulu. The air in the room was thick with humidity, breath, the scents of night sweat and lotions. She lay back and stared up into the blackness. God knew why Lulu had gotten this bee in her bonnet about Texas, but there it was —her sister could be surprisingly stubborn.

Ruby couldn't help but wonder, what would happen if Lulu left a second time. These past eight months without her, Ruby had been scrambling to keep the business afloat. And although, so far, Lulu hadn't been of any help since she'd come home, Ruby had still hoped to get her back in the studio.

Ruby wanted, needed, two things: to make art and to make a living. If Fotografía Eckart failed, then what? It was hardly a propitious time to be moving about the country in search of work. And would a larger studio in some other city even hire a lady photographer? She did have the house—it wasn't large, but if worse came to worst, she supposed she could take in a boarder or two. It's how other women got by on their own. But put up with strangers to barely scrape by? No thank you. Or, go live with Aunt Pancha in her rented room in Mexico City? God forbid.

She would just have to keep the business limping along. There was no other choice.

Why couldn't Lulu simply stay put and resume her work at the studio?

Because, she argued with herself, Lulu had always hated working in the studio, and now she considered herself above it. And yet, Ruby grudgingly allowed, perhaps she was being unfair to Lulu. After all, Ruby had never lost a husband. She'd never been shot at. Was it so farfetched that Lulu's decision was rooted in fear? Or even that her decision might be the right one?

There was no doubt that the Revolution loomed. Aunt Pancha spun these fanciful post-war utopian visions, but Ruby didn't buy them. Meanwhile there was the war, and war meant soldiers, and any band of soldiers was a threat. Would they enter the city? Would there be bombs? Looting? Raping?

But the war wasn't here. Not yet.

And after all, Campeche was small potatoes—a backwater burg far from Mexico City, far from the principal port of Vera Cruz, far even from the city nearest them, Mérida. The fighting might bypass them entirely. Wasn't it better to wait and see?

It was not Ruby's way to indulge in mental wanderings like this—looking ahead. Anticipating anything beyond the length of time it took to develop a photographic plate was not her strong suit.

Studying the shades of darkness above her, she listened for jaguars and heard only female snoring.

Ruby couldn't remember the last time she'd been to the docks. A fishy smell mingled in the salt air with the odors of hair pomade, creosote, sweat, overripe fruit and fried food. After saying goodbye to Lulu and the three kids at the gangplank, Ruby and Tía Pancha were jostled by the crowd and pushed further and further back from the edge of the pier. Such a press of people—gringos, negros, gachupines, mestizos, indios: passengers clutching carpetbags, baskets and valises; shipping agents rushing to and fro; porters lugging impossibly large trunks on their backs; food vendors of every age hawking their offerings; businessmen in three-piece suits, crew members in uniforms, humble women in sandals, their heads covered in shawls, their wealthier counterparts with pointy-toed shoes, broad-brimmed hats, and parasols to protect them from the sun. The shouts of sailors and the strident calls of seagulls added to the hubbub as ragtag boys chased one another and stray dogs sniffed about. Ruby and Tía Pancha locked arms to avoid being separated and strained to see Lulu and the kids at the upper railing of the steamboat.

It was a small steamship of two levels, its style reminiscent of the old paddle wheelers Ruby remembered from childhood. Lulu hated boats, and she'd stepped onto the gangplank with an air of martyrdom and contained panic. Well, Ruby thought, it served her right for deserting her. Again.

Don Mauricio had made the travel arrangements. First stop—Vera Cruz, Mexico's biggest port, where they would transfer to a larger ship that would take them to New Orleans. Don Mauricio had professional connections in that city who would see to it that Lulu and the children were met at the ship and helped transfer to a boat for Galveston, where one of the Texan cousins would meet them and travel with them by train to San Antonio.

Ruby had refused to discuss the route or the destination. Now she brought to mind her father's map of the country—how the coast of Campeche Bay cradled the Gulf of Mexico, how it formed the inner curve of the cornucopia that was Mexico. She wondered if the boat to Vera Cruz would take them straight across the large body of water or if it would hug the coast. Tía Pancha would know—she made the trip every time she visited—but Ruby did not ask.

Looking up, she saw three pelicans flying overhead, brown wings against the blue sky, white necks cocked, long bills parallel to the ground. Ugly, ungainly, and yet aloft.

Ruby still couldn't believe it—how Lulu had made such a momentous decision, and then clung to it without waver. And how quickly Aunt Pancha had acquiesced to the hare-brained scheme. The only other time she'd seen Lulu show such resolve was in her decision to marry Ernesto, and look how that had turned out. Clearly, Lulu was indulging in some fantasy, casting herself in the role of one of the heroines in the novels she was addicted to—love stories with adventures and rosy endings. Anytime Ruby raised a doubt, or tried to, Lulu quashed any discussion.

"Ay, hermana! Don't be such a killjoy," she'd say.

Up on the deck she could see Soli by Lulu's side, solicitous as always —the true martyr, Ruby thought. She didn't see Meche, but there was Lalo, appropriately wearing his white sailor suit. Soli held him by the hand, tethering him as the little boy leapt about.

The steamboat whistle blew and Lalo pulled his hand from Soli's and covered his ears, all joy dissolved. Ruby saw Soli lean over, get the little boy's attention and point out Ruby and Tía Pancha on the dock. Then Lalo lit up all over again. He was waving, his mouth wide open, shouting—the kid certainly had a pair of lungs on him. Soli clapped a hand over his mouth.

Then Soli raised a gloved hand to wave to them once again, but it froze and hung in the air. Even from this distance, Ruby saw her face fall. She was gripping the railing and shouting to them, but Ruby couldn't make it out.

"Look there," Aunt Pancha said. "I wonder what's wrong."

Ruby felt a hand slip into hers. She recoiled but the hand gripped hers hard. She turned to find Meche next to her, her defiant eyes searching Ruby's face.

Ruby looked at her, uncomprehending, as at something familiar but unrecognizable because it was out of place.

"I'm not going to any stinking United States!"

Ruby looked from the girl's determined face to Tía Pancha, who gave a surprised snort of a laugh.

"I'm an Hernández Cruz," Meche said, a bit of a quaver in her voice, "and Hernández Cruzes don't run away."

"Meche!" Soli called out.

Now she understood what Lalo was shouting about. She gripped Lulu's arm, and pointed.

"What a wicked girl," Lulu said, shaking her head.

She looked irritated, exasperated, but to Soli she really seemed no more concerned than if she'd misplaced her parasol. Clearly she wasn't going to be of much help.

Soli foisted Lalo onto Lulu and rushed for the stairway down to the first level and the gangplank. At the sight of Soli running away from him, Lalo started screeching and thrashing. He broke free from Lulu's grasp and threw himself into the mass of legs and skirts in pursuit of Soli. As he latched onto her, Soli thought bitterly that Lulu hadn't tried very hard to restrain him. Soli grabbed his hand and tried dragging him after her through the crowd, but he wasn't having it.

"I don't want to get off!" he screamed.

She picked him up to carry him.

"I want to stay!"

He struggled and wriggled so, she couldn't keep her balance, not and go down the stairs. His face turned red and his howls rose above the commotion on both the deck and the dock. Then Lulu was next to them. She knelt down and Lalo hugged her neck. Soli dashed down the stairs, but the gangplank had already been raised and the crewman securing it would not listen to her. She gripped the railing and stared in disbelief at Meche on the pier.

An ocean was opening up between them.

"Meche!" she screamed.

Meche looked up at the boat in a very general way, avoiding Soli's gaze, but then their eyes locked on each other. It was, for a moment, as if no distance separated them. Soli's vision was blurred by tears and she wiped at her eyes. The gesture broke the link between them. The figure of Meche on the dock grew smaller and smaller. Soli was sobbing. It felt like her lungs were being sucked from her body.

This was all Tía Ruby's doing! She'd mesmerized Meche. She'd stolen her sister from her. Soli hated them. Meche. Aunt Ruby. She hated them both.

As the steamboat pulled away from the dock, Meche felt herself alone in a cold and silent void, as if all noise and movement around her had frozen. She watched transfixed as Soli's anguished face shrank to a pinpoint. Felt the invisible thread between them stretch, fray, and snap.

She shivered. What had she done?

She'd been lonely the last few years—her mother but a faint memory, her father's conduct toward her ever frostier, and she and Soli always at odds. Always. But that loneliness was but a shadow of the absolute aloneness she felt now. She fought the urge to run along the dock after the ship. She crossed her arms and held tight—she'd made the right decision. She had.

"Oh, my," Aunt Pancha said drily, eyebrows arched.

Ruby stared at her aunt a moment and then back at the steamship slipping away. She turned to Meche, speechless.

"I can stay with you, can't I, Aunt Ruby?" the girl said. "I'll help you at the studio. I'll pay my way."

Ruby ignored her and addressed Tía Pancha—Tía always had an opinion, and for the first time, Ruby wanted to know what it was. "Now what do we do?"

In the Plaza de Independencia, Pancha sat with Meche on a bench in the scant shade of a tree. The plaza, enclosed by an iron fence, occupied an entire city block. The cathedral loomed on one side, its two white towers gleaming in the sunlight. Colonnaded stores, government buildings, a hotel and bank edged the others. A streetcar line ran down one of the broad bordering streets. There were street vendors and beggars. People bustled and jostled as they got on and off the street cars, went in and out of buildings, made their way along the tunnel-like arcades or cut across the plaza, while others strolled the walkways that radiated from the central fountain.

Pancha was content observing all this, entertaining past memories of the plaza, but also on the alert for ideas to write about. She was aware that the girl next to her was restless, her legs bouncing. Earlier on the dock, for a moment, Lulu's stepdaughter had looked a bit pale, a bit shaky, like the motherless child she was. But that had passed. The girl was resilient, she thought. You had to give her that.

"Can't we just go to the studio?" Meche said.

"Your Aunt Ruby wants us to wait here," Pancha said.

"Why?"

"You know why. She's trying to wire the boat."

"I'm not going to stinking Texas."

"And if that doesn't work, she'll have a telegram waiting for them in Vera Cruz."

Meche's chin jutted forward. "You can't make me go," she said.

Pancha considered the girl and snapped open her fan, flapping it below her chin.

"I don't know whether to spank you or salute you," Pancha said.

Meche leaned back and looked sideways at the older woman.

"I can't stand that Lulu."

"I'll have you remember that that Lulu is my great-niece, whom I happen to love."

"She wants to sell the rancho. She has no right. It's my home."

Pancha nodded in understanding.

"I could run it, you know. I know Baalam Kab like the back of my hand. I'd be a better foreman any day than that no-good Escalante."

"Admirable, I'm sure, but there's your age to consider, and then there's the Revolution. What happens to your rancho may well be out of your control, or Lulu's."

"She doesn't like me," Meche pouted.

Pancha snorted, "Can you blame her?"

Meche glared at her.

"You know, child, if I had to choose to live with either Lulu or Ruby, and I love them both, mind you… Well, I think you may have chosen to follow the wrong sister."

"I'm not going to stinking Texas."

Pancha sighed. Maybe Ruby and this girl deserved each other.

"Won't you miss Soli?" Pancha asked, curious.

Meche took a deep breath. "No," she said, but her voice wavered. "I'm tired of her breathing down my neck."

"What if you don't get on with your aunt Ruby?"

"I will."

"That's it? That's your contingency plan?"

Meche scowled at her.

Ruby strode towards them. Standing in front of them, she raised her hand to cup the crown of her head. It was a mannerism Pancha recognized as her father's and knew that her mother ("A lady does not touch her face or hair in public!") had done her best to beat it out of her.

"That's done," she said. "We'll have to wait to hear when they'll come back for her."

"But Aunt Ruby, I want to stay here with you. Please!"

Ruby looked past the girl and addressed her great-aunt, "I suppose the logical thing would be for me to take her to Vera Cruz, but I can't take the time. Tía, maybe you could…?"

"Sorry, my dear, not possible. You see in Vera Cruz…"

Ruby raised her hands, palms toward Pancha. "I don't want to know."

"Please, Tía Ruby, I want to stay with you."

Ruby finally turned her dark eyes on the girl.

"Why?" she said, totally bewildered.

"That's what I asked her," Pancha said. She was struggling to decide if this situation was amusing, or if she should feel alarmed, or sorry, for one or the other, or both.

Ruby glowered at her aunt. "I have to get back to the studio. Would you make sure this child gets to our house and stays there?"

"Let me go with you. You can't…" Meche started to protest, but she stopped abruptly when Ruby's dark eyes bore into her.

1 9 1 0 ...

"**E**duardo Ernesto, where are you going?" Soli said. "You haven't excused yourself."

Ernesto heard his daughter scolding Lalo on his table manners but did not aid her with his own gruff rebuke. His mind was elsewhere, in Campeche City to be precise.

"I dropped my napkin," Lalo pouted.

The family was finishing the last course of the afternoon meal. Ernesto sat at the head of the table. The chair opposite was Blanca Estela's. Almost four years since his wife had passed and they still left her place empty. No china or goblet or silverware, just the stark white of the tablecloth. And that only because early on he'd snapped at Susana de los Ángeles, "For Christ's sake, woman, stop laying a place setting for the señora."

"I'll tell Señorita Soli, Don Ernesto," she'd replied.

She hadn't said it to escape blame, he knew. Susana de los Ángeles was reminding him that Soli and Meche were grieving, too, and that Soli, not quite thirteen, was stepping into Blanca Estela's shoes as best she could.

After that there were no more plates, no array of forks and spoons as if Blanca Estela were about to come through the door, just her absence at the opposite end of the table. Lately, that void had begun to strike him as morbid and unwholesome.

Lalo deposited his wadded napkin on the table, and Meche, who sat next to Lalo, held his extra cushion in place as he climbed back onto his chair.

A moment later Soli said, "Lalo, take your hands out of your lap. A gentleman leaves his hands on the table where they can be seen."

Meche rolled her eyes, "Soli, for Pete's sake…"

A sharp knocking on the front door interrupted Meche and jerked Ernesto's attention to the here and now.

The dining room was situated towards the back of the house between the interior patio and the kitchen, but the startling rapping at the front door was so loud and forceful that Ernesto and the children all swiveled to look in that direction. Baalam Kab, set well back from any road, did not occasion random visitors. It was miles to the nearest rancho or hacienda. Soli leapt to her feet and Susana de los Ángeles rushed out of the kitchen.

Before sitting down, Ernesto had removed his gun and holster. Blanca Estela, may she rest in peace, had trained him not to wear it at the table or hang it on the back of his chair. Instead, it rested in a drawer kept empty for that purpose in the sideboard behind him. He projected a calm manner, but he was aware that his daughter Meche didn't miss a thing. She saw him glance back at the sideboard, saw him deciding not to remove the Colt revolver from its drawer.

Ernesto motioned Soli to sit down.

"Susana, whoever that is, tell them we are at table," he said.

Ernesto resolutely picked up his fork and addressed his plate, but Lalo squirmed in his seat, and the girls, alert, exchanged glances. Soon they all heard the easy, low tones of men's voices, which soothed their alarm, but not their curiosity.

Susana de los Ángeles returned. "Señor Manuel Solís Jurado and companions, sir. They apologize for interrupting, but they've come all the way from Dzibálchen and beg you receive them.

Upon hearing the visitor's name, Ernesto smiled at his children and rose, saying, "Well that is a good ride.

"Susana, bring refreshments to the parlor."

The three men each wore a suit with a stiff collar and held a felt hat in his hand, their boots dusty from the road. Solís Jurado smiled broadly and shook Ernesto's hand. Both men were of average height and weight, although Solís Jurado was much more slightly built and at least ten years younger than Ernesto's fifty-one. His curly hair had won him the nickname of Crespo. He introduced Ernesto to the other two, who greeted him solemnly.

"Manuel, you and your friends are most welcome."

"And who are these princesses?" Solís Jurado said.

Ernesto turned to find his children behind him. Why had Soli not kept them in the dining room? He'd thought it obvious that they were not to tag after him.

Lalo came out from behind Soli's skirt and stamped his foot. "I'm not a princess!"

"So I see," Solis Jurado said. "And you are…?

"A prince!" Lalo asserted.

Solis chuckled. "Your highness," he said with a nod of his head and tousled the little boy's hair.

Ernesto introduced the children, hiding the tinge of embarrassment he felt, but not his irritation.

"Ernesto," Solís Jurado said, "we have something of import to discuss with you."

Ernesto nodded. "Soli, take your brother and sister into the patio."

Soli, uncomfortable around people she did not know, was clearly not unhappy to do this. But Lalo cried at having to leave. Ernesto didn't remember the girls whimpering all the time when they were little like this one did, but then their mother had been around to deal with such things. Still, no one wanted a crybaby for a son.

Soli hushed Lalo and swooped him up.

"Come along, Meche," she said.

Meche, who hated being dismissed, had her jaw set but she curtsied to the men before she left. And Ernesto raised an eyebrow, taken aback by her good manners.

Ernesto and Manuel settled into their chairs and the other two men sat stiffly on the horsehair sofa. The thickset one unbuttoned his straining suit jacket.

Once outside the parlor, Meche could be heard announcing, "I'll help Susana de los Ángeles with the refreshments."

"No," Soli said, "you play with Lalo."

"Why are you always so bossy?" Meche complained.

"Shh!"

Ernesto straightened in his seat, jutted out his chin, and pretended not to hear. Other people's children seemed so well-behaved. It was damn inconvenient being a widower. If only he were younger and a more fitting suitor for a young lady.

"So, gentlemen, why have you come all this way? I hope there is no trouble."

One of the three, a thin, reedy man with a voice to match, introduced as José del Carmen Gómez Peralta, huffed an ironic laugh.

Ernesto took offense at the man's manner and glared at him. Turning back to Solís Jurado, he said, "This has the look of a delegation."

Susana de los Ángeles and Soli, dutifully, entered with trays of coffee.

"And so it is," said the third man, one Leal Silva. With meaty hands, he took one of the cups from the housekeeper's tray and served himself several lumps of sugar from Soli's.

Ernesto saw her go from pale to pink, and her tray shook. It occurred to him that she needed to get out and meet more people. But then he did not like the expression on the man's face when he thanked Soli. Isolation had its advantages.

When Susana de los Ángeles and Soli withdrew, Ernesto added a shot of brandy to his cup and passed the decanter. He addressed Solís Jurado. "You know full well, I'm not sympathetic to your cause."

"It's not a cause, Ernesto, it's a principle: 'No to Reelection.'" He raised his hand to silence any protest from Ernesto. "And it makes good sense, good business sense."

Gómez Peralta sneered at that comment. "No, Crespo. It's what's right and just." Then he addressed Ernesto, "It's the 20th century, man. Come September, we'll be celebrating the 100th anniversary of Independence. By God, let's make sure it's a true celebration and not a farce."

"Elections are scheduled for July," Ernesto countered.

The man leaned back against the sofa and groaned with impatience. "Do you really think Díaz will ever allow free, open elections?"

"Ernesto," Solís Jurado said, calling Ernesto's attention back to him, "we're here to ask you to join the Club de Simpatizantes de Francisco Madero."

"But, Manuel, you're more than sympathizers, aren't you?" Ernesto said.

Gómez Peralta stood and paced.

Solís Jurado spread his hands. "If the elections proceed fairly and legally, and Madero is elected and inaugurated, then we are sympathizers."

"And if you don't get your way, then what?"

"We fight," the beefy man on the sofa said.

Ernesto looked angrily at Solís Jurado, who raised his shoulders and cocked his head, as if Leal Silva's statement were a small thing, a natural thing.

Ernesto lowered his voice, speaking only to Solís Jurado, "I cannot thank you for bringing sedition into my house."

Gómez Peralta stopped his pacing, interrupting before Ernesto could ask them to leave. "Good God, man! It's simple: no re-election! Díaz has been in power since 1876. That's 34 years. Thirty-four years!"

"I don't need you to give me a lesson in history or arithmetic."

"Of course not, Ernesto," Solís Jurado said soothingly. "We're here precisely because you are an intelligent man with a stake in Campeche's future, both for your rancho here and for those children playing in the patio."

Leal Silva, still seated, gesticulated with his fist. "It's our country, and Madero wants us Mexicans to reap the benefits of its riches. Díaz promotes progress, but the profits of this so-called progress get tied with a ribbon and given to the gringos, the Brits, the gachupines, anyone but us."

"What about all this talk of land reform?" Ernesto said. "At least Díaz is a known quantity."

"It's common sense, Ernesto," Solís Jurado said. "How many peasants have lost their land under Díaz? Hundreds of thousands? Maybe more? Their misery must be alleviated, or we'll end up slaughtered in our beds.

The government says the Caste War here on the Peninsula has been over for close to a decade, but we know that's not entirely true. You lived through that war. Do you want another, another that would span the whole nation?"

Ernesto gave him a skeptical look.

"Land reform is only fair and just!" said Gómez Peralta.

"And what is your profession, sir?" Ernesto said. "I believe I recognize the name. A lawyer, aren't you?"

"Yes."

"Then it's not your land and livelihood that's at stake."

"Ernesto," Solís Jurado said. "I would understand your concern if you had one of the big haciendas. But you don't even have peons, do you? Nor do I imagine there's anyone to make claims against your land."

"If they start confiscating land, it will be the hacendados who'll have the power to steer the reformers away from their properties. My farm will be easy pickings."

"Madero would not allow that. He's incorruptible!" the lawyer said. "Tell him, Crespo."

"Manuel, who is this... innocent you've brought with you?"

The man took offense, and Solís Jurado stood to calm him.

"I sincerely hope the election proceeds fairly and lawfully," Ernesto said, "whoever is elected. But forming half-cocked revolutionary groups beforehand will not contribute to a peaceful election."

"I trust that when the election goes badly, as we both know it will, you will not oppose us," Solís Jurado said.

"Badly?" Ernesto said.

Solis Jurado clapped a hand on Ernesto's shoulder. "Who's playing the innocent now?"

"Lulu, I don't want to tag after you and Ernesto," Ruby said.

"And I don't really want you to," Lulu said lightly.

They were in their bedroom, Ruby leaning against the door frame and Lulu in front of the mirror pinning and re-pinning her hair, trying to get the fashionable amount of poof below her topknot, but the fineness of her hair kept foiling her attempts. She looked at her reflection and bit her lip. A little asymmetry was fetching, but she just looked lopsided.

"Then for Pete's sake, just go on your own," Ruby said.

"I can't do that! How would it look?"

Why was Ruby distracting her? She gave up on her hair and opened the little round tin of rouge.

"Who cares?" Ruby said.

"Ernesto, for one."

Ruby groaned.

The truth was, Lulu cared too. The last thing she wanted was to give Ernesto the idea that she was anything but proper.

"He's not exactly a young man," Ruby said.

"What does that have to do with anything?"

Lulu picked up the little pad inside the tin. She needed to apply the rouge as lightly as possible. She mustn't look painted.

"It means he's not the kind of man who invites gossip."

"Maybe not. But what about me?"

Lulu met Ruby's gaze in the mirror and saw her make a show of biting her tongue, sticking it out between her teeth, and smiling.

"What are you doing?"

"It's just I don't know how interesting your virtue is to anyone at this late date. You are twenty-eight."

"And you're mean. You're always mean to me."

Lulu felt a tightness in her chest that threatened to leap into her head. She simply could not get a headache now. With Ernesto due to return to his farm in two days, there was so little time.

"Wait." Lulu turned to look at Ruby directly. "You're not serious about not going with us, are you?"

Ruby gave her a tight-lipped smile.

"You can't just not go, Ruby! You can't do that to me!"

"You didn't even ask me. You just assumed."

Lulu sputtered. "Of course I assumed. You're my sister!"

"Oh, Lulu, just go for your walk with Ernesto and leave me out of it."

Ruby turned on her heel and left.

Lulu screeched after her, "You're ruining everything! I hate you!"

When Ernesto arrived at the house, Lulu told him Ruby might not be available to accompany them. She made light of her sister's capriciousness, smiling apologetically, pouting just a bit, prettily. But, in truth, she was afraid; so much depended on what Ernesto did in the next moment. Without a companion, he might cancel their date, and she might not see him again before he left the city. Months could pass before he returned, if he returned. But if he didn't cancel, she would have to steel herself to be the one to refuse to go out, because if she stepped out with him unaccompanied, he would think less of her. Worse yet, if he encouraged her to accompany him unchaperoned, then she would know he was not serious about her as a prospective wife. She snapped open her fan to avert her eyes and hide her lower lip, which was quivering.

When she glanced back, she was tickled pink to see that Ernesto looked quite distressed. He insisted on paying his respects to Ruby, and Ruby grudgingly presented herself in the parlor.

After a few moments of chitchat, which Ruby suffered through with little grace, Ernesto invited Ruby with great warmth to accompany them.

Behind Ernesto's back, Lulu was making funny faces and pleading gestures. She saw Ruby's mouth twitch.

"Señorita Ruby," Ernesto went on, "please reconsider. I was very much looking forward to taking you and your sister to the ice cream parlor near the beach. Please honor us with your company."

Lulu rushed to Ruby's side and grasped her arm as if in encouragement, but she was actually pinching her.

"Ouch!"

"Please, Ruby, dear. Do come. You know how fond you are of ice cream sodas."

Ruby scowled at Lulu, but acquiesced.

After leaving the ice cream parlor, Ernesto strolled the malecón with Lulu's hand perched on his arm. Ruby, with a desultory air, walked alongside them.

To Lulu it all felt perfect. She and Ernesto looked very refined, and if Ruby looked a tad shabby in comparison, a bit odd, a bit out of sorts, well, that made it all the more obvious that Lulu was being chaperoned.

But as usual, Ruby was difficult. Despite the time of day and the social occasion, she'd insisted on bringing her new folding camera. They'd argued over the thing when Ruby bought it. Since it was of no use whatsoever in the business of the studio, Lulu had deemed it an unjustifiable expense, no more than a whim, a whim now hanging around Ruby's neck. Her sister looked absurd dragging the contraption around, and worse, she kept lagging behind, so that Lulu worried that people would think she was promenading alone with a man at sunset. She was also concerned that Ernesto would be similarly uneasy. Ruby was putting their whole courtship at risk.

At least Lulu hoped this was a courtship. Ernesto was a fine man. She thought him handsome, proper, honorable, and although he'd made it clear to her that he was not wealthy, he did own land, and the rancho, by all accounts, was a going concern. If she and Ernesto married, it would no longer be of any concern to her whether or not Ruby wasted hard-earned money. Once she married, ledger books and waiting on tiresome customers would be a thing of the past.

The blue sky had become dusky and the sun threw beads of pink across the waves. The breeze tugged at the broad brim of Lulu's hat, but she had it tied beneath her chin with a scarf, as women did when riding in automobiles. Ernesto's hand gripped the brim of his homburg for the same reason. Lulu appreciated his decorum, that he did not take his hat off, did not let the wind blow his hair about.

Lulu tightened her hold on his arm as if otherwise the wind might blow her off her feet. The delicious breeze, and the warmth coming through Ernesto's sleeve and passing into her gloved hand, made her feel as if the pink swath of light lying across the water were caressing her deep inside.

To amuse him, Lulu told Ernesto how, seeing that they lived on Mexico's eastern coast, her father had never gotten used to the sun setting in the ocean, and he insisted the girls study the map of the coast with him, pointing out again and again how the mendacious curve of land created such an effect.

"'I will not have you two believing that the sun sets in the east!'

"'Leave them alone,' my mother would say. 'The sun sets where it sets, ya.'

"I agreed with my mother," Lulu confided, "but not Ruby. It gave Ruby the idea that Campeche was magic," she said, and laughed as charmingly as she could. She thought Ernesto was the type of man who would appreciate her being down-to-earth, while also being attracted to her lightheartedness.

Lulu glanced back. Ruby was staring out to sea, probably longing to capture that glittering pink light, when all she had was that silly box that froze everything in black and white. Lulu, thankfully, was unfettered by such mechanical limitations. She was here, with Ernesto by her side. She was seeing the sun descending, feeling the breeze rippling her skirt.

Ernesto had stopped, as others stopped along the length of the sea wall, all there to enjoy the sunset. But while the others watched the horizon, Ernesto gazed into Lulu's eyes, his hand on his hat brim, and again she felt the pink light bubble within her.

The sun touched the water, and people exclaimed and applauded. Ernesto glanced about him, and assuring himself that all eyes were on the sunset, he leaned in to kiss her.

A smile played at Ruby's lips as she watched the setting sun. Her mother used to point out to sea and say, "Imagine, girls, Cuba is out there, just out of sight. That's where your father took me on our honeymoon."

"How can Cuba be to the west, woman?" her father would sputter. "Don't confuse them. It's over there, and he pointed inland."

"Who's being foolish now, an island in the middle of land?"

That's why Ruby smiled—at the sun, at the tricks vision and perspective can play, at her improbable Campeche.

She glanced at Lulu and Ernesto and saw their kiss. Some chaperone she was. Some hypocrites they were, dragging her along. The expression on Ernesto's face was new to her, and the openness of the expression on Lulu's was familiar more from childhood than recent years—they were both so unguarded it took her breath away. She felt heat in her face and a hollow in her chest.

This man, this stranger, was he really going to carry Lulu off and change everything? Would Lulu really live on his rancho out in the bush? If that happened, Lulu, of course, would ask her to come with her to the farm, but Ruby did not consider that an option. Be the old-maid sister, that is to say, free housekeeper and nanny for life? At the mercy of Ernesto's beneficence? No. Never.

She would be fine on her own, thank you very much. On the whole she would prefer it. ...Although Lulu had always been there—on the other side of the bed, across the dining room table, in the next room at the studio. Always.

Ernesto and Lulu turned away from the darkening ocean, and Ruby joined them, locking arms with Lulu—Lulu's other arm was entwined with Ernesto's. He asked them if they knew the Mayan legend about the setting sun, that it was the jaguar sun god sinking into the inframundo to battle his way through the night. Lulu feigned shock and crossed herself, and Ernesto smiled, charmed, and lifted her gloved hand. He bent his head to kiss it, and for a moment the masculine scents of his toiletries cut through the salty breeze to reach Ruby's nose—a small-scale assault, to be sure, and yet it proclaimed: I offer more than you. I am greater than your sordid studio and your squalid little life with your sister. It said: I am here to stay.

Ernesto tenderly replaced Lulu's hand on his arm and covered it with his own hand. Ruby felt a flash of fear, and of hatred. She could not wait to be away from them.

Ernesto skewered one of the lengthwise slices of fried banana on his plate with his fork. They were gold and brown and glistening with oil. He cut off a bite-size piece.

"I thought when one was smitten, one lost one's appetite," Mauricio De la Cruz said, gesturing to the enormous breakfast in front of Ernesto.

"Nonsense," Ernesto beamed. "Happiness stimulates the palate."

The two men sat across from each other at a café facing the plaza. De la Cruz sipped coffee and picked at a plate of fruit.

Ernesto pointed his fork at the lawyer's light repast and said, "What's your problem?"

De la Cruz leaned back in his chair and hooked his thumbs in the armholes of his vest.

"Not a thing," he said. "You see before you a contented married man. I breakfasted earlier with Hermelinda, but gladly accepted your invitation."

"Good man." Ernesto grinned and applied his fork to fried eggs.

"Well, I didn't want to miss a chance to see you before you headed back to your rancho tomorrow."

For some time now Ernesto had trusted the young man with his business affairs, an association that was vital with Baalam Kab, located as it was, far from Campeche City and its government offices, banks and markets. But over the past eighteen months, as his visits to the city had become more frequent and of longer duration, Ernesto had grown to relish their conversations. It could be damn lonely in the countryside.

In fact, despite his pose of bonhomie on this fine morning, the prospect of returning home gave Ernesto a sinking feeling. Business was his pretext for coming to Campeche City, but it was María Luisa who was the reason. María Luisa, his sunny Lulu with her sky-blue eyes. He still felt awash with pleasure from their evening together. The magnificent sunset, her sweet hand resting on his arm…

He pushed the memory aside and stabbed a piece of ham.

"Besides," he said, "courtship is demanding, One must keep one's strength up."

As soon as he'd said it, he regretted it. His desire had announced itself, in spite of himself, and in front of De la Cruz.

De la Cruz sat to attention and slapped the table, "Aha!" he said. "So you admit you are courting the Señorita Eckart Reyes."

"No, no." Ernesto said, shaking his head. "A slip of the tongue."

The younger man said nothing. He merely watched Ernesto with raised eyebrows. The bustle of the café continued around them, but Ernesto grimaced into the sudden silence between them. Was he using some courtroom tactic on him?

"The thing is," Ernesto said finally, "I've nothing to offer the señorita. As you know, I'm not a wealthy man. I live a simple, rustic life. And on top of that I have three children. Not to mention, I'm old enough to be María Luisa's father."

With those last words, all buoyancy drained from him, he felt every one of his 51 years and saw the bleak course of his future. His real life was not here, where he rose late, ate sumptuous seafood meals, and played at being a boy sweet on a girl. It was back at his farm, where he was a stern father who rose before the sun, studied ledgers, directed the planting, the cultivation, the harvesting, and made sure his foreman kept the workers in line.

"Ay, Mauricio. She's a lovely thing, and I enjoy her company, but it's a friendship. Purely platonic."

Ernesto felt heat in his face and a quickening in his heart. Did De la Cruz notice that he'd stumbled over the last word? He did intend his association with María Luisa to be chaste, but the night before on the malecón, he'd kissed her. He was ashamed of it now. He'd let himself be carried away.

"All quite proper," Ernesto insisted, to convince himself as much as De la Cruz. "Chaperones and that sort of thing."

Mauricio stared him down. "But," he said, "you've been seeing her every day, have you not?"

"Yes, counselor. What is your point?"

"Just that from where I sit, it looks like a courtship. I imagine it looks that way to Miss Eckart, too. After all, it has all the markings, save for the proposal."

"Are you speaking to me as my friend or my lawyer?"

"The two are not incompatible."

Ernesto put down his fork. María Luisa made him feel both very young and very old, but mostly very young. The sensations he'd felt the night before when they'd kissed came back to him. For that moment they had been as one, and nothing else mattered. It was intoxicating. But that was last night.

He heaved a sigh of sadness. "I know, I should stop seeing her. That's what you're saying, isn't it? I should stop pestering her, go back to my farm and stay there."

"I'm saying nothing of the kind. But if your age, finances, domicile and family situation are all that's holding you back..."

Ernesto barked a laugh and pushed his plate away.

"Forgive me, Ernesto." Mauricio raised his hands, palms out in appeasement. "But the señorita, despite all her virtues, is not a seventeen-year-old girl whose father is sifting through a pile of marriage offers."

Ernesto scowled at him.

"What I'm saying is, don't presume to make this decision for her. Let her decide your merits and your suitability as a husband."

A newsboy entered and wove between the tables with newspapers under his arm. Ernesto, glad of the distraction, hailed him and bought a paper. He tried to steer the conversation to the headline.

"Look at that." He tapped a story with his finger. "The Nicaraguan army is losing ground to the U.S.-backed rebels. Well, that's one advantage to our president being so buddy-buddy with Taft, keeps the gringos at bay."

Mauricio made a noncommittal nod, "Ernesto, think about what I said."

Ernesto feigned interest in the newspaper.

Mauricio insisted. "Propose. You should be married."

Ernesto made his own noncommittal nod.

"Tell you what, this evening after you take your leave from Señorita Eckart, how about we go out with some ladies I know for an improper, chaperone-free night?"

"And then up early to start a two-day ride home? You may have noticed, I'm not a young man anymore."

"Nonsense. It will give you something to think about on the long ride back to the rancho."

Ernesto gave him a doleful look.

"Fine," De la Cruz said, giving in, "but don't leave me in suspense about the señorita. Come to the house, no matter the hour. I want to hear your news.

"There will be no news."

"We'll toast to your future happiness."

"There will be no… There will be no news."

"Fine. Then we can discuss world affairs over a brandy or two, enough talk to hold us till your next visit."

The invitation was appealing. At home Ernesto had no like-minded equal with whom to discuss the many issues of the day. The visit from Crespo Solis and his cohorts came to mind, bringing a bitter taste to his mouth. Opposition to Porfirio Díaz was clearly brewing, coalescing as never before. Like the onset of a cow's birth pangs, he thought: the restlessness, the increased lowing and pissing and shitting. He was pleased with the analogy. How long and severely would the contractions go on? Would the cow survive the labor? And would the resulting calf be healthy, stillborn, or maybe monstrous?

When Ernesto and Mauricio parted outside the restaurant, Ernesto still had not told him that María Luisa's sister had sent word to his hotel, summoning him for a private word at the studio at 10:00 AM precisely. In the end he'd decided not to mention it because it struck him as ungentlemanly to gossip about María Luisa's eccentric sister in a public place.

Now he wondered anew what she wanted. Something about Lulu, of course. Unless it was money. He hoped she wasn't going to ask him for a loan!

He really didn't know what to make of the lady and her unseemly love affair with chemicals and exploding powders. He was curious what Mauricio would have to say. Well, if need be, he could discuss it with Mauricio that night.

Ruby looked at her father's pocket watch. It was 10:10. She felt a tightness in her chest. Would Lulu's beau come in time? Would he come at all?

She'd picked a time when Lulu would be out of the studio. At 10 AM, Lulu would be at the bank—she liked to be first in line when it opened. Then to keep her away longer, Ruby invented other errands: the purchase of chemicals for developing at the druggist's and a grease pencil at the stationery store. When she mentioned that she'd heard that Galerías San Rafael had gotten in new shipments from Europe, she saw Lulu's eyes light up.

"Maybe, I'll take a look. You don't mind, do you? There's nothing scheduled until noon."

Ruby heard the front door open and shut in the next room, and her face scrunched up in distaste. This would be easier if she felt some affinity, any at all, for the man, but he was a stuffed shirt who had no use for professional women.

She heard him clear his throat. Ruby took a deep breath and strode into the reception, her hand extended.

He'd set his hat on the counter, and was smoothing his hand over his hair. It was grey at the temples and slightly wavy.

"Señor Hernández, thank you for coming."

He gestured to her long leather apron. "You look like a cobbler." His smile was quick and twisted.

She guessed this was his idea of humor and ignored the comment.

"Follow me," she said.

She ducked back through the dark-green velvet curtain that separated the reception from the studio. When Ruby turned and saw that he'd not followed, she marched back to the front.

He gestured to the two chairs against the wall. "Shall we sit here?"

"It's more private in the studio."

She didn't want word of this meeting making its way back to Lulu. Besides, she would feel more confident on her own turf.

"Heavens! Don't look so miserable," she said. "I don't bite. And I have no interest in poaching my sis's beau, if that's what you're concerned about."

The look on his face was almost comical.

"I wouldn't say beau," he stammered. He glanced at the curtained door. "I don't want to compromise you."

"Well, this is a place of business—no chaperone on the horizon."

"Perhaps we could go out, for a cup of coffee."

She laughed. "That would definitely set the gossips talking, and I can't leave the studio unattended. Please, just come in here."

She pulled back the curtain and this time waited for him to enter. He made a great show of reluctance. Once inside, she stepped past him to the dais. She sat in one of two chairs in front of a red damask drapery and motioned to him to sit in the other.

"I'll get to the point. My sister and I have no relatives in the offing, male or otherwise. So under the circumstances, I've appointed myself to ask: just what are your intentions towards my sister?"

If he'd looked uncomfortable before, now he hung his head, abashed.

"Look," she continued, "I don't care about your age or any of that other rot which seems to be worrying you, or so you would have Lulu believe." A thought struck her. "Wait, you're not already married, are you?"

"I would never…" he sputtered, offended. "I would never deceive your sister. I am a widower, as María Luisa must have told you."

Ruby waved his explanation aside. "As I said, I don't care about any of it, and neither does Lulu, so would you just ask her to marry you and get it over with?"

His face flushed. Was he embarrassed? Angry? She couldn't tell. Maybe he didn't actually love Lulu.

"Understand," she said. "I'm not trying to marry her off. It's certainly not in my best interest for her to go live on that rancho of yours, leaving me alone to run the business. But this not knowing if or when, well, it's driving me mad, and Lulu too, for that matter. I told her that she should just propose to you, but she looked at me in just about the same way as you are looking at me now."

"Lulu seems to love you. I won't stand in her way. And if you're worried about taking me on as a dependent…"

More sputtering, "If María Luisa and I were ever to marry, you would of course have a home with us."

"I assure you, I would not."

"But what would you do?"

"Carry on here, of course. I'm quite suited to stand on my own. Lulu, however, is not. Look, Ernesto, if I may call you by your given name, patience may be a virtue, but it's not mine. I think you love Lulu, so just get on with it, will you, or leave us alone? That's all I have to say."

She stood and he quickly got to his feet.

"If you tell Lulu about this conversation, all bets are off. I shall have to kill you," she said.

Then seeing the anxious expression on his face—he seemed to be taking her literally—she laughed. This man was so dour, she found herself laughing more than she ever normally would, just to create some kind of balance.

"Seriously, Ernesto, Lulu would be furious with me if she knew. She might even turn you down in some misguided attempt to save face. There would be a lot of tears all around, and that is precisely what I'm trying to avoid."

Susana de los Ángeles and Señorita Soli worked alongside each other in the kitchen preparing the afternoon meal. Susana remembered when the señorita was very little —the child hanging on her leg as she plucked a turkey or a pheasant. Susana de los Ángeles would give little Soli a tail feather to play with to distract her. And how she always placed a ball of masa in Soli's chubby little hands for her to play at patting it into a tortilla, until one day, they were making the tortillas for the table side by side, the girl only nine or ten. Señorita Soli gave the orders now, and Susana de los Ángeles took it in stride. She was proud of her young mistress. She and the señorita's mother had taught her well.

In truth, Susana de los Ángeles would not have liked it if she'd been put in charge of the household when Doña Blanca Estela had passed. She would have resented working alone—the family ringing little bells at her when they wanted something. This way was companionable—she and the señorita worked well together.

Everything prepared for the meal, Señorita Soli carried the pitcher of agua de papaya into the dining room and took her place next to her father, leaving Susana de los Ángeles to ready the serving dishes and put on the finishing touches. As Susana de los Ángeles brought in the first course, Meche was making the rounds with the pitcher, filling the glasses in order of age: first her father's, Soli's, then her own glass—Meche, at thirteen, was two years younger than Soli—and finally little four-year-old Lalo's. Susana de los Ángeles placed the tureen of pumpkin soup made with venison broth in front of Soli, and Soli served the soup in the same order as Meche had poured the agua fresca.

"Susanita, the radishes," Soli said.

"Ay, sí, señorita."

Several months back, there had been that very long week when Señorita Soli was in bed with a fever, and Meche had insisted on presiding over the table in her sister's place. Meche did not have the training or the temperament for it. She'd snapped orders at Susana de los Ángeles, who grumbled about having changed Meche's diapers and glowered as she came in and out of the dining room. It put Don Ernesto in a foul mood and Señorito Lalo, always sensitive, whined through every course of every meal. They'd all breathed a sigh of relief when Señorita Soli was back on her feet, except for Meche, who'd sulked at her family's ingratitude.

Susana de los Ángeles put aside the unpleasant memory and circled the table collecting empty soup plates.

"I'm returning to Campeche tomorrow," Don Ernesto announced.

Señorita Soli and Meche exchanged looks. Meche's face brightened with rising spirits—her father's absence would not be a burden—and Soli's face darkened with disappointment.

"Papá, must you go already?" Señorita Soli said.

Susana de los Ángeles noted that he no longer complained when he had to make the trip to the capital. In fact in the past year it seemed like he spent more time there than at home. And when at home, he seemed ever more restless. Señorita Soli was aware of the change, too, and it worried her.

"Susana de los Ángeles, do you think Papá is going to Campeche to see doctors?" Señorita Soli had asked her.

"No, niña," she'd answered. "Your father is healthy as a horse, a real stallion. Don't you worry."

When Susana de los Ángeles reached for Lalo's bowl now, he banged his spoon in it, making a loud clanging noise and splattering soup. A speck of it splashed into his eye and the little boy howled.

"Eduardo Ernesto!" his father exclaimed. "If you cannot behave properly, leave the table."

"I hate her!" Lalo cried.

Susana de los Ángeles' ears pricked up. She saw dark blood rise in his father's face.

"And who, exactly, do you hate?" Don Ernesto demanded.

"Campeche. I hate her."

The father hid a smile. "Susana de los Ángeles…"

"Mande, señor," she said.

"Remove the child from the table. This is no place for malcriados."

Malcriado: a brat, that is, a child poorly-raised. She saw Señorita Soli flush, feeling it as an insult more to herself than to Lalo. Lalo cried and protested.

Soli stood. "I'll take him, Susana. Please serve the next course."

Señorita Soli lifted the little boy out of his chair.

"I don't wanna!" Lalo yelled, as she hustled him out of the room and through the kitchen.

"Don't just stand there, Susana. Bring the rice," Don Ernesto grumbled ill-humoredly.

Meche got up, intending to take Señorita Soli's place serving. Susana de los Ángeles groaned inwardly.

"Sit down, Meche," Don Ernesto ordered. "Susana de los Ángeles can serve. If you'd be so kind, Susana."

"Of course, señor," she said, tossing a satisfied look at Meche, who looked away.

With Señorita Soli out of the room, the tension between father and this his other daughter increased. Don Ernesto asked her to pass the lime. And the tortillas. He took a radish.

"Have a radish, hija. They're good for the lungs," he said, reaching over his shoulder and thumping his back.

"Papá, may I go with you?" Meche said.

"To Campeche? Of course not."

"No, this afternoon, around the rancho."

"Why would you do that?"

"I think I should know more about managing the farm. Soli runs the house, and I could…"

"Hija, that's not work for a señorita."

He was throwing her a bone, Susana de los Ángeles thought, promoting her from little girl to young lady, but Meche's face hardened.

"Soli's got her work, it's true," he said, "but you, you're…"

Her father did not finish his sentence, because Señorita Soli returned to the table. Susana wondered what description he would have ended with. The pretty one? The clever one? She was certainly the stubborn one! Meche looked like a pot of burnt beans.

"We're ready for the main course," Soli told Susana de los Ángeles. "And then will you make a plate for Señorito Lalo. He's with Juan in the back patio."

"Now, this is better, nice and quiet," her father said.

"It's just that Lalo misses you, Papá," Soli said. "We all do. Must you leave again so soon?"

"Sit down, hija," Don Ernesto said. "I want to talk to you and your sister."

Susana de los Ángeles set the platter of roast venison in front of Soli, and stood by as Soli placed a slice of meat on her father's plate.

"It's time to tell the two of you," he said, "the reason for my frequent trips to Campeche."

The color drained from Señorita Soli's face—she was imagining illness, gambling, bankruptcy. She was very young to worry so much.

"After this next trip, things are going to change."

Señorita Soli slid a slice of meat onto a plate for Meche.

"Because this time when I'm in the capital, I'm getting married."

Meche's mouth dropped open. And Soli drew in a sharp breath.

"Of course, after a brief honeymoon I'll be bringing my bride back here to live. You'll meet her then."

Susana de los Ángeles masked her face and withdrew to the kitchen. There she let her eyes grow round and made the sign of the cross. Out of Don Ernesto's line of sight, the door ajar, she could see Señorita Soli and Meche stare at each other in shock.

"Married?" Señorita Soli whispered.

"And you're telling us now?" Meche said. "We don't get to meet her until it's all over?"

"Who I marry is my business, little girl, not yours."

"I think if I'm going to have a stepmother, it's very much my business!" Meche spat back. "We don't even know her name!"

"Lower your voice this instant! You may leave the table. I will not be grilled by my own children!"

Meche threw down her napkin and flounced out of the room.

Don Ernesto turned to Señorita Soli. Her face was bathed in hurt, which only seemed to irritate him.

"Both of you," he snapped.

Señorita Soli fought back tears. It was not unusual for Meche and her father to butt heads, but never Soli, and she hadn't said a word.

How dare he cause her grief, Susana de los Ángeles thought.

Her father softened. "Nena, sit down." He reached out and placed his hand on hers. "M'ija, you've worked so hard, taking on the household, being a little mother to the others. This marriage will allow you to be carefree and enjoy yourself. Lulu, that is, María Luisa is going to plan a big quinceañera party for you."

"But I turned 15 months and months ago."

"I know that, but it's never too late to celebrate, is it?"

"Lulu, María Luisa. What am I to call her?"

"Well, we can't very well have you calling her Señora de Hernández, can we?"

"Please don't ask me to call her 'mother', Papá, I just can't."

"How about simply madrastra—stepmother—or madrastra Luisa."

"That's a bit of a mouthful for little Lalo." A tear escaped her lashes.

"Hija, there's no need to cry. María Luisa's a fine girl, great fun. You'll see, it will be best for everyone."

Susana de los Ángeles turned her back to the dining room and rolled her eyes.

*R*uby, kneeling on the bed, reached down to line up her slippers on the tile floor, and Lulu thought she looked like a little girl in her white cotton nightgown and her thick black hair in a braid down her back. But Ruby was not a child. It was her time of month, with the sweetish smell that accompanied it. Such, Lulu thought with a twitch of her nose, were the intimacies of sharing a bedroom with a sister. Ah well, soon she would be sharing a bedroom with Ernesto instead.

Oh dear, she thought with a jolt, soon she would be sharing a bedroom with Ernesto! What intimacies would that entail, other than the obvious?

For the sake of her nerves, she'd done her best to push musings of the wedding night out of her mind. She'd also avoided reflecting on all the nights that would follow. She'd certainly not given thought to the man sounds and smells that she would be subjected to. Nor to (how mortifying!) the embarrassing emanations of her own person that might be revealed to Ernesto!

She shook her head. She could not think of that now, or she would never get to sleep, and tomorrow she would have a headache, and Ernesto would see her looking pinched and with bags under her eyes.

She observed Ruby cross herself before muttering a brief prayer to the Guardian Angel. It was a child's prayer. Another of Ruby's quirks. Lulu smiled benignly, apparently at her sister's piety, but she was actually recalling that distant time: life before Ruby.

When Lulu was a very small child, the bedtime hour had been a sweet time. A single candle on the nightstand held Lulu and Mamá in its glow as Lulu recited the Guardian Angel Prayer: Lulu on her knees by the bed, the palms of her hands pressed together, the tips of her fingers tickling her chin; and Mamá sitting on her bed, listening with complete and loving attention.

Then Ruby came along.

That was annoying enough, but then Ruby learned to climb out of her crib. And suddenly Lulu had a bedmate. After that, as Lulu recited her nightly prayer, Ruby would be there squirming and bouncing, chiming in a word here and there. Mamá scolded her, but to no effect. Then, after the prayer when it was time for Mamá to tuck them in, Ruby would rebel against sleep and refuse to settle down. More reprimands. Mamá's voice became shrill, and there were often tears, sometimes Ruby's, sometimes Lulu's.

Now, finally, their paths were to diverge, and while one moment Lulu looked forward to her freedom from Ruby and the studio, the next she felt tenderly toward her little sister and awash in nostalgia.

"Ruby, do you remember me teaching you the Guardian Angel prayer?"

Ruby looked at her blankly.

"You remember," Lulu said. "I drilled you in secret so that we could surprise Mamá."

They had indeed surprised Mamá, who'd showered Lulu with smiles and crooned, "What a good little girl you are!"

Ruby shook her head.

"You must remember," Lulu insisted.

Ruby shrugged. "I must have been really little."

Having been interrupted, Ruby crossed herself again, shut her eyes, and began to mutter:

> *Angel of God,*
> *my guardian dear,*
> *do not forsake me,*
> *stay ever near,*
> *until in joy*

my soul you carry
to be with the Saints,
Jesus and Mary.

Ruby said amen and did not cross herself. She never did at the end of the prayer, which annoyed Lulu. It was like leaving a button undone or a shoelace untied.

Ruby climbed under the covers. She turned on her side facing away from Lulu, as was her habit, and Lulu leaned on one elbow to blow out the candle. Laying on her back, she cricked her neck to look up at the large crucifix of dark-brown wood. During the day it loomed on the white, plaster wall over their bed, but she could still discern its shape in the dark room.

Praying to guardian angels at Ruby's age, Lulu reflected, was babyish and unseemly. Any normal person would have long ago moved on to praying the Rosary. She herself had when she was ten or eleven. But she supposed Ruby couldn't be bothered: the five decades with their repetitive prayers for each bead. That added up to fifty prayers right there, plus the various others. But like so many things about Ruby, Lulu didn't really know.

She whispered in the dark, "Ruby, why don't you say the Rosary?"

"Why don't you?" Ruby said.

"I do. Sometimes."

"Well, I say my angel prayer every night."

"As if I didn't know that," Lulu grumbled. "But why?" Now that her life with Ruby was coming to a close, it seemed important to know this small thing.

Ruby turned to face Lulu, but Lulu could not make out her expression.

"I guess because it would seem odd not to."

"That's a strange reason to pray."

"Is it? For luck, then," Ruby said.

"But that's just superstition."

"You know what Papá would have said about that."

Lulu could hear the smile in her voice.

They were whispering in bed together as when they were children. The whispering was purely out of habit. The only other person in the house, María Asunción, couldn't hear them from her cot off the kitchen. Habit was the same reason they still shared a bed.

A few months after their father died, Lulu announced that she wanted his larger room, and Ruby helped her clean it out. Even though their mother had died a number of years before, everything was still as she'd left it: tonics and rosary on the night table, creams and hair pins and jewelry box on the vanity, dresses in the wardrobe. Their father had not touched a thing.

Once installed in her new bedroom, Lulu claimed it was a luxury to stretch out in bed with no one kicking her in the night, and it was so much cooler without Ruby's furnace of a body heating the bedding.

After several sleepless nights, Lulu climbed into bed with Ruby without explanation. Ruby did not protest. Maybe she hadn't liked sleeping alone either.

Now, after a moment, Ruby whispered back, "What about you, Lulu? Why do you pray?"

"…It's what one does, isn't it."

"But why do you?"

"…I guess to remind God I'm here. …And it makes me feel close to Mamá."

They lay silent again.

"Well," Ruby goaded, "I'm sure Ernesto will be happy that his wife says the Rosary."

Lulu noted the nasty edge in her voice.

"I can see it now. You'll be there on your knees in front of a little statue of the Madonna, and he'll be counting the beads too, getting more and more excited. By the time you say amen after the last prayer, he'll be ready to lower the mosquito net and other things as well."

"Ruby! Stop it! You're terrible. Don't you think I'm nervous enough?"

"Are you?" Ruby sounded surprised, as if the thought had not occurred to her.

"Of course I am."

"Ha! Is your face red? I bet your face is red."

"Ruby!"

"Red as a tomato," she teased.

"You're just jealous."

Ruby snorted. "Of your betrothed? Hardly!

Lulu did not believe her. How could Ruby not envy her?

"Holy wedlock? You can keep it," Ruby added.

Lulu knew that Mamá and Papá (trapped in their iron-jawed union, as Ruby termed it) had soured her sister on marriage. "Not even gnawing off a limb would have freed them," Ruby would say, disgusted. But Lulu had never been put off. She'd always dreamed of a happily-ever-after marriage, light and easy-going, and she expected her marriage with Ernesto to be filled with banter and laughter. Still…

"Do you think Mamá and Papá would approve of Ernesto?" Lulu wondered aloud.

She felt Ruby shrug.

"Well, since they never agreed on anything," Ruby said, "it's a safe bet that one or the other would have opposed him."

Lulu moaned.

"What does it matter?" Ruby said.

"Can't you ever say anything nice, something comforting for once?"

"I did. I said it didn't matter."

Lulu sighed in the way she knew irritated Ruby. Then she made a quick, silent plea to the spirits of Mamá and Papá, that if they didn't approve, to please keep their signs to themselves.

Lulu and Ruby lay side by side, separated by the dark, the silence and the threshold of their separate futures. She listened to Ruby's breath thickening, and recalled Ernesto's proposal.

"My dear María Luisa," he'd said. "I know I am not any young girl's ideal beau, and that marriage to me entails duties that you might find burdensome. But if you do me the honor of marrying me, I pledge that I will endeavor to make your responsibilities as light as possible. And although Baalam Kab is no grand hacienda, it is a profitable operation. I can promise you you will be comfortable."

She smiled at the memory and felt warm inside. He had to know he was saving her from spinsterhood and a tedious life in the photography studio, and yet he was too gallant to ever acknowledge such a thing, and she was touched. The truth was that she loved him, him and the expansive life that lay ahead.

Ruby, not asleep after all, startled her by whispering, "So, you actually are nervous?" The edge in her voice was gone.

"Of course I am."

"You know," Ruby yawned, "there may be advantages to marrying an older man." Her voice had taken on an annoying analytic tone.

"Please, Ruby, don't tease."

"I'm not. I'm speculating."

Lulu asked her not to.

Ruby ignored her and explained that an older man like Ernesto would be apt to take things slowly.

"He's not old," Lulu pronounced. "And I'm sure what you mean is that he will be considerate and understanding."

"Well, less driven, anyway. A man like that might ease his bride into her 'conjugal duties,' as Mamá would term it. I mean since his appetite will be dampened by age…"

"He's not old!"

"He might wait weeks, months, even."

Lulu blanched. She had her reservations, but months? Was Ruby, again, delighting in tormenting her?

"Or conversely," Ruby continued, "he might just force the issue and get the suspense over with."

Despite the dark, Lulu covered her eyes with her hand. She would not let Ruby make her cry.

Ruby fell silent, perhaps deciding to take pity on her.

After a bit, Lulu's breathing became more regular, without any hitches when she inhaled. She was finally feeling drowsy.

"They say it hurts," Ruby whispered.

"What?" Lulu said alarmed.

"You know, the tearing of the maidenhead."

"Oh, Ruby! Don't!" Lulu covered her face with both hands and started to sniffle.

"What? I'm sure it will be fine. Eventually."

"Ave María Purísima! Give me strength!"

They were silent for awhile.

"It will be fine," Ruby whispered.

"Really?" The knot in Lulu's chest loosened, and she lowered her hands.

"Maybe even agreeable."

Lulu smiled, knowing Ruby could not see it and make fun of her.

"Maybe," Ruby poked her in the ribs, "…thrilling."

Lulu could imagine Ruby's thick black eyebrows jiggling. The sisters giggled like schoolgirls.

"Ruby, to tell you a secret, just the thought of, well, presenting myself to Ernesto, with my hair down, in my nightgown…" She felt the heat from her blushing and was glad of the darkness.

Ruby interrupted. "Myself," she said, "I'd forget the nightgown."

"Ruby!"

"What? I think it would be nice to lie naked in someone's arms. To sleep all smooth and cool."

"Ruby, really!"

"Maybe that's what I'll do when you're gone. Throw out all my nightgowns."

"Don't you dare. What if there's a fire?"

"I can't see you wearing that on a farm." Ruby said.

"Of course not," Lulu said, turning this way and that in front of the mirror. "It's a traveling suit."

Apart from her confirmation dress, it was the nicest outfit she'd ever owned. When she'd brought it home, wrapped in tissue in a large box, she'd planned to keep it out of Ruby's sight. But today she just had to try it on again, and even Ruby must have found it fetching because she reached out to feel the sleeve, rubbing the fine cotton-and-silk material between her thumb and fingers.

It might not be the most practical item in her wardrobe, but it was so lovely, so stylish! Her one splurge. When Doña Olimpia had shown her the fashion plate of the suit with its long swallow-tailed jacket, Lulu had oohed over the design, and then when the dressmaker showed her the dusty-rose fabric, she was sold.

"Ay, señorita," Doña Olimpia had said, "You will look so smart in this, and with your fair skin and hair, you will look a confection."

"I adore the Chinese frog fasteners! And the cord braid on the sleeves. Can you really match the color exactly to the fabric, as it is in the picture?"

"I'll do my best."

Lulu pictured herself wearing the suit when she alighted from the train in Mexico City, and Ernesto beaming with pride as she leaned on his steadying arm. And she would be wearing it when she arrived at the rancho and met her stepchildren. First impressions were so important.

"Oh, Doña Olimpia, my sister will kill me, but I absolutely must have this suit."

Ruby, who before had always left Lulu to worry about their finances, was suddenly questioning every purchase. For the most part, Lulu was being frugal and, as always, cutting corners wherever she could. Doña Olimpia was refurbishing her white tea gown for the marriage ceremony. It would have lace on the bodice, elbow-length sleeves and a silk flower at the waist. And it was Ruby, not she, who insisted she buy a new corset cover and a nightgown, a nice one. Other than that, Lulu would be making do with the two dark skirts and three soft-hued shirtwaists that she wore to work, and a reasonably new lilac-colored dress that bloused over the bosom. Still, her trousseau, modest as it was, had to be paid for.

They decided to go through their parents' things and look for items to sell. Special keepsakes were off the table, Ruby keeping their father's gold cufflinks and pocket watch, and Lulu, their mother's ivory-beaded rosary and crystal drop earrings.

"Well, what's left?" Ruby said.

Lulu laid out a large silver comb and long black lace mantilla on the bed, along with several rings and a couple of necklaces.

"Do you think these are worth anything?" Lulu asked, hoping Ruby would say no, and they could put them away again.

Ruby held up the mantilla, then refolded it and laid it on her lap. She smoothed it with her hand.

"We should keep this," she said, to Lulu's surprise.

Lulu picked up the comb that went with it, and set it on Ruby's lap.

They extended their search through the house: a silver paper knife, a German-Spanish dictionary, a crystal candy bowl, a pair of bronze and red-marble candlesticks. Lulu didn't want to part with any of it. Too bad they'd didn't have their grandparents' small upright piano anymore. Lulu wouldn't mind selling it. For her it merely represented hours of tedious practice. But after Papá died, they'd needed the money, and it had brought in a tidy sum, all spent now.

In the parlor, Ruby lifted the lid of the mahogany humidor and sighed. There were still cigars inside and the sweet smell of tobacco wafted into the room. As if taken by the shoulders, she turned and faced the large painting over the yellow sofa, and put her hand on her head.

"I've always hated that painting," she said. "Worthless, I'm sure, but maybe the gilt frame..."

Their father had always mocked the painting as absurd: a Bible scene in which the people were dressed like French courtiers. But Lulu liked the painting. At least she thought it belonged on the wall where it had always been.

"Well, we could sell a piece or two of furniture, if you prefer," Ruby said.

Was Ruby going to completely dismantle their home?

"Once I see Ernesto's house, there may be something I want to send for. Besides, you can't just get rid of the furniture."

"I don't see why not."

"This is our home."

"Lulu, you'll have a new home."

"I'm sure some of the smaller items will bring in enough money," Lulu said. "After all, I'm not even getting an evening gown." She'd refrained from ordering one from Doña Olimpia, though she'd been sorely tempted.

"An evening gown! What would you do with something like that on a rancho?" Ruby scoffed

"Quit saying that!"

"But you are going to live on a farm, Lulu. Dirt, cornfields, pigs…"

Lulu's nerves got to her and she rushed from the room. Ruby had again succeeded in provoking her, and she threw herself on the bed. Her sister seemed to think she hadn't given any thought to what life on a rancho would be like, but she had. She just didn't want to dwell on it. Besides, first there was the wedding and the trip to the capital.

Ruby followed after a bit. She leaned against the doorjamb and said, "Just ask Ernesto if you're going to concerts or balls or whatever in Mexico City. And if you are…"

Lulu perked up and lifted her head.

"…we still can't afford it."

Lulu whimpered, and Ruby sighed. She sat next to Lulu on the bed and stroked her shoulder, or maybe she was caressing the luscious pink fabric of the new travel suit.

"Just ask him. Then we can consider."

"I can't ask him that!"

"Fine," Ruby returned to the doorway. "then if he takes you to the opera, he'll have to buy you a dress there."

Lulu brightened. "Mexico City is sure to have department stores! They say you can just walk in and buy a gown that's ready-made.

Do you think such a dress could possibly fit, and look nice, too?"

Ruby left the confined space of the darkroom and hung her leather apron on a peg by the door. She rolled her shoulders and stretched her back as she sauntered out to the front desk to check on the next sitting. Parting the curtains covering the doorway to the reception area, Ruby was hit with the scents of her sister's eau de toilette and Ernesto's cologne. The commingled odors set her teeth on edge, and she was faced with the repulsive sight of Ernesto nuzzling Lulu's neck. Right there in the reception area!

Ruby was fed up with the both of them. Ernesto's betrothal to her sister had only exacerbated the man's imperious and self-satisfied manner. And since his return, Lulu—her head in the clouds and increasingly remiss in her work—was giving Ruby a glimpse of what she would be up against running the studio on her own.

The night before, Ruby had startled awake in the middle of the night with a cold pang of fear. How *was* she going to manage at the studio on her own? What exactly did Lulu do? She was vague whenever Ruby asked her for details. She knew there were the books, the appointments, the photography supplies. She'd lain awake listening to Lulu snore, worrying about each—an unfocused frog-hopping amongst unfamiliar details: bank accounts, glass plates, appointment books, billing... The tasks were all new to her, as was worrying about them—worrying was Lulu's job.

As she waited for sleep to overtake her, fretting gave way to anger— her thoughts never used to be jumbled like this!

Damn Lulu! Damn Ernesto! Damn them both!

First thing in the morning, Lulu had again babbled excitedly about the preparations for the marriage. And as usual, she was annoyingly coy and, to Ruby's mind, unduly skittish about the impending wedding night.

Ruby, rubbed raw, had exploded.

"What about the rest of your life?"

Up till then, she'd mostly held her peace and marveled: did Lulu

really harbor no doubts about Ernesto, about being married to him—
"till death do you part"—or about living on a rancho out in the middle
of nowhere and taking on stepchildren she'd never met? Did she have no
second thoughts about leaving everything and everyone she knew
behind, no regrets about leaving Ruby? Because Ruby did. When she'd
nudged Ernesto to propose, she'd been reacting to the situation at the
time, the uncertainty of it and Lulu's unhappiness. Clearly, she hadn't
thought it through.

Lulu saw Ruby come through the curtains and she pushed Ernesto
away coquettishly. Ernesto cleared his throat and nodded to Ruby. His
muttered greeting was drowned out by Lulu squealing with what Ruby
could see was feigned delight.

"Look, Ruby," Lulu said, waving some papers at her. "Steamship
passages from Vera Cruz! Ernesto has just surprised me with them."

"Oh?"

"Yes, isn't it exciting? There's a change of plan. We are to go to New
Orleans for our honeymoon trip!"

Ernesto stood by, looking pleased with himself and with Lulu.

Ruby smirked at the image of Lulu on the ocean, of Lulu in the
United States!

"Lulu, have you forgotten that you're terrified of boats and get seasick
just looking at the ocean?"

Ernesto's face fell, and he at once looked every year of his age.

"Oh, Ernesto, dearest," Lulu patted his arm. "Don't listen to her.
This is different. Like you said, it's a modern steamship, not like a boat
at all."

"And how do you think you're going to get from here to Vera
Cruz?" Ruby snapped. They both knew that small steamboats were the
only option.

Ruby herself never gave much thought to travel—she found peace in
the confines of her routines, routines which sustained her work. But now
she imagined herself wandering the streets of that famed city, taking
pictures—different streets, different kinds of faces—and walking into a

Ernesto's kids? Lulu seemed untroubled, but in the wee hours it was something Ruby stewed over—the fact of their existence.

Before disappearing behind the green curtain, Ruby muttered, "You don't even have the gumption to have your own children."

Ruby, trailing Doña Anastasia and the bride, arrived at the civil registry office a few minutes past eleven—Ruby, a brooding shadow to the other two, with their surprisingly girlish high spirits. They swept inside in a swirl of chatter, their fans aflutter and their heels clicking on the checkerboard of oxblood- and bone-colored tiles. The men inside turned to look at them with stern faces. Lulu and Doña Anastasia, chastened, assumed a more decorous demeanor. As for Ruby, already subdued, the registry's oppressive air of officialdom made her skin crawl.

Ernesto was there waiting, conversing with the justice of the peace while keeping a keen eye on the door. He rushed forward to claim his bride, and led her and her companions over to the official. The light fabric of Lulu's and Ruby's narrow-skirted dresses whispered between them, while the long taffeta skirts of Doña Anastasia's old-fashioned dress swept the floor with a loud rustle that grated on Ruby's nerves. Licenciado De la Cruz and his law clerk had yet to arrive.

The justice of the peace, who had just been berating his clerk, turned and smiled benevolently at the bride and her retinue. He was not much taller than Ruby, and while dapper in a three-piece suit, his physique in profile formed the shape of a capital "D". Following introductions, he pronounced the weather unpleasant—spring being the hot season between the dry winter and the wet summer. Doña Anastasia flicked open her fan and agreed that the heat was dreadful. Ernesto pointed out that on the rancho it was a tense time waiting for the rains to begin. The other two men feigned interest in the planting season, and then fell silent.

Ruby and the widow—both small and wiry—attentively flanked Lulu, who was taller and well-padded—she'd had a matronly figure since she was fourteen. The three turned away from the men—it was unseemly for the bride to have to wait.

Ernesto, frowning, pulled out his pocket watch every other minute, and several times checked himself when he started to pace.

Ruby knew that if the witnesses didn't show up, they could simply enlist random strangers in the building, but she fantasized something quite different—a big row with Lulu blowing up at Ernesto, Ernesto throwing his arms up in the air and storming out, Lulu in tears, the marriage plans terminated forever—life returning to normal.

But the missing witnesses appeared. There was a general exhalation of relief, except for Ruby, who took a sharp intake of breath.

Ernesto made the introductions, and the two latecomers greeted each person in turn. These rituals always tried Ruby's forbearance. She groaned—inwardly she thought, but since Lulu gave her a sharp nudge, perhaps out loud.

The eight of them filed into an interior office that was cramped and airless. Sweat made the linen bodice of Ruby's dress stick to her skin.

"Why not hold the ceremony in the patio where one can breathe?" Ruby complained to no one in particular.

The registry clerk, a stringy, rumpled man, took it upon himself to answer, "Because, señorita, this is a serious civil contract, not a picnic."

Ernesto nodded his approval, and Lulu, of course, blushed.

The justice of the peace cleared his throat, called them to order and began to hold forth on the importance of the separation of church and state as promulgated by President Benito Juárez in the Reform Laws, and the establishment of the institution of civil marriage, July 23, 1859.

"Which," he lectured, "is the legal union of one man and one woman who, in order to perpetuate the species and help each other bear life's burdens, are united in an indissoluble bond, to be terminated only by the death of one of the spouses. It is a legal and valid civil contract entered into before this civil authority."

Ruby's stomach felt scraped hollow.

"Today," he enunciated somberly, "April 17, 1910, in virtue of the rights conferred upon me by the Civil Code, and in accordance with the Constitution, we will proceed with the celebration of the civil marriage between Ernesto Ezequiel Hernández Hernández and María Luisa Eckart Reyes."

Ruby observed Lulu. Beneath her broad-brimmed straw hat—refurbished for the occasion with white net—Lulu looked stoney-faced, and paler than ever. With all that white—tea gown, long gloves, stockings and shoes—she looked like a pillowy white column, like stacked scoops of coconut ice cream. Next to her, Ernesto stretched his neck discreetly as if his collar were too tight, and it did look particularly tall and stiff.

"At the request of the two parties gathered here," the justice of the peace continued, "the marriage application having been processed and no legal obstacle existing to impede this marriage, we read articles number…"

He droned on and on, code this, and whereas that—bureaucratic gibberish that in no way could coincide with Lulu's, no doubt, romantic vision of her wedding. Of course there would still be a church ceremony, which although having no legal standing would be the one that would count in Ernesto's social circle. In theirs as well, Ruby supposed. Unfortunately for Lulu, the church service would have to wait. Ernesto's wish to hold it after they were settled at the rancho, perhaps at the chapel at Hacienda Chun Ek with the local priest officiating and his children, neighbors and local dignitaries attending, outweighed his compunction about the impropriety of their traveling as man and wife with only a civil certificate. Lulu was not happy about the delay, but she'd agreed. After all, what Ernesto described sounded much more grand to her than a wedding held here in Campeche with just Ruby and a handful of acquaintances.

The speechifying tone of the justice of the peace seemed to change to something more personal, and Ruby turned her attention back to him.

"In virtue of these principles and in accordance with the Civil Code, I ask you, Don Ernesto, do you freely and voluntarily, without coercion, consent to contract marriage, and to do so with María Luisa?

"I do." His voice was husky with emotion.

"Doña María Luisa, do you freely and voluntarily, without being coerced, consent to contract marriage with Don Ernesto?"

"I do," she said, in not much more than a whisper—with head bowed, her hat hiding her eyes from both Ernesto and the justice of the peace. No doubt Lulu intended her manner to project maidenly modesty.

"In virtue of the affirmative answer of both, manifested freely amongst those present at this civil ceremony and according to their wishes, I declare on behalf of the Law and Society that Ernesto Ezequiel Hernández Hernández and María Luisa Eckart Reyes are united in matrimony…"

Doña Anastasia sniffed loudly.

"With all rights and privileges granted and all obligations imposed by law.

"I also declare that marriage is the only moral means for the foundation of the family, the continuation of the human species and the correction of the failings of the individual, who…"

Ruby felt like she was suffocating. She glanced at Doña Anastasia, who smiled at her from beneath the lace handkerchief she held to her cheek. The widow linked her free arm through Ruby's and gave it a squeeze. *She's thinking of Mamá*, Ruby realized—the widow often commented on Ruby's resemblance to her mother—*and, of course, she's sorrowful that her lost friend isn't here to see her daughter's wedding.*

"Man," the justice of the peace was saying, "whose principal qualities are courage and strength, must give and shall always give the wife protection, sustenance, and guidance, treating her always as the most delicate, most sensitive, and finest part of himself, and with the magnanimity and generous benevolence that the strong owes the weak, above all when the weak devotes herself to him, and when Society has entrusted her to him."

Ruby felt hemmed in, and Doña Anastasia pulling down on her arm as she held on to it made her feel off balance.

"Woman, whose principal qualities are self-denial, beauty,

compassion, insight and tenderness, must give and shall always give the husband obedience, solace, comfort, and counsel, treating him always with the veneration owed to the person who supports and defends us, and with the delicacy of she who…"

Ruby rolled her eyes. What would Aunt Pancha have to say about this drivel?

Now the little man was blathering on about being good examples to their children.

How odd, Ruby thought—just like that, Lulu had children. Lulu, a mother! The whole enterprise was madness!

Finally the justice of the peace stopped talking and closed the book he'd been reading from.

"Now man and wife will come to the table and sign the registry. The witnesses will also approach and add their signatures."

Ruby felt like there was a pit opening in her chest now, as well as in her stomach. The room felt very close, and her skin, clammy.

Licenciado De la Cruz clapped Ernesto on the back, otherwise, the stifling solemnity of the ceremony continued unabated. Ruby followed Doña Anastasia in signing her name and particulars in the bulky, leather-bound ledger, as well as on the marriage certificate. Don Mauricio pressed forward for his turn. Ruby jostled people to get to the back of the room—she needed air.

But apparently they weren't done yet. The justice of the peace was speaking again, this time to the couple.

"You may now, if you so wish, seal this union symbolically with a kiss."

Lulu looked up at Ernesto, and he bent under the brim of her hat to kiss her.

A chill ran through Ruby. She'd seen them kiss before—that time on the malecón, with a cool breeze off the water. But that was a stolen kiss. This was so… so public.

Only then did Lulu and Ernesto smile at each other, and turning—clinging to each other as if to life itself—they bestowed their smiles on their witnesses. The legal solemnity of the ceremony broke apart, and congratulations flowed over the couple.

Ruby's lungs burned. There was no air left in the room. Panicky and teary-eyed, she pushed out of the office. She found no relief on the street. The sun blazed fierce and high in the sky, and breathing felt as if she were drawing hot, soupy air in through a straw. She scrambled away from the registry building, vision bleary, head swimming.

Ever since Ernesto had proposed, Lulu had been dreading the appearance of unwanted omens, queasy with fear that something would prevent their marriage, that at the last moment living happily ever after would slip from her reach forever. So when Ernesto kissed her, there in front of everyone in the registry office, and no church bells rang in warning, no earthquake shook the building, no marauding pirates swooped in waving their cutlasses as in the tales that had frightened her as a child, Lulu's heart soared. She knew it looked immodest, but she couldn't stop smiling.

Of course there was Ruby tearing out of the registry office as if pursued by demons!

Doña Anastasia asked the young law clerk to see if Señorita Ruby needed any assistance, but he returned, saying she was nowhere to be seen.

"Not to worry, Auntie" Lulu reassured her, miffed at Ruby for drawing attention away from her and Ernesto. "She's to take our wedding picture at the studio before we continue on to your house for our wedding luncheon. It's her wedding present to us, and you know she won't miss the chance to take a photograph."

"All right, my dear. Don Mauricio is going to escort me home so that I can check on the preparations. We'll wait for you there." She took both Lulu's hands in hers, and pulled a bit so that Lulu bent toward her. She kissed her on the cheek. "Your dear mother would be so proud of you today, and I am so very happy for you."

Lulu thought to herself, oh, me too! Me too!

The studio was empty when Lulu and Ernesto arrived. Lulu unpinned her hat and carefully lifted it from her head. She laid it on the counter next to Ernesto's homburg.

Ernesto looked at his watch.

"Should we be worried?" he asked.

Lulu set her chin high. "No, mi amor. She'll be here."

She had better, Lulu thought, because if Ruby didn't show up, she would never forgive her.

Ernesto pulled Lulu to him with a sharp tug, something he'd never done before, and he secured her against him with his other arm tightly around her waist. Lulu felt both alarmed and thrilled. She almost protested, but they were married now! His kiss was something new, too. It made her feel strange, something like a swoon. She did pull away then.

"Ay, mi amor." She patted her hair. "The photograph. My hair."

He smiled at her. "You look charming."

At that moment, Ruby stormed in, charging directly into the studio without a word to the couple or a glance in their direction.

Ernesto started to protest, but Lulu raised her hand and shook her head. Ruby was Ruby. They followed her into the studio, and Ruby then deigned to look at them, giving them a curt nod.

She sat Ernesto in the high-backed chair on the dais. She directed Lulu to stand at his side and placed her hand on his shoulder.

"Ernesto, rest your hands on your knees," Ruby directed. "Now, lift your chin. Not so much."

Ernesto was not used to taking orders, even minor ones like these, from anyone, much less a woman. Lulu saw that Ruby, intent on her work, did not notice him bristle. Or perhaps she just didn't care. It dawned on Lulu that this was one of the reasons they'd been struggling with the studio: gentlemen didn't like being at Ruby's mercy.

Lulu's thoughts turned wistful. This was to be her wedding photo, but there would be no church wedding today.

Before Ernesto had requested they postpone the religious ceremony,

Ruby had suggested they get married at the church near their house. Ruby loved San Román with its carved altar of dark mahogany and its black Christ on a silver cross. Lulu did not. She found it dark and dreary, inside and out. She would have chosen the grandeur and airiness of the Cathedral with its crystal chandeliers and the lovely statue of the Immaculate Conception. Or maybe, because it had been her mother's favorite, the Temple of the Sweet Name of Jesus—very small, like a little jewel box.

Ruby came out from under the cloth. She was frowning.

"What's wrong?" Lulu asked.

"It's too staid."

Lulu glanced at Ernesto. Yes, his right eyebrow had raised.

"But Ruby, everybody's wedding photograph is posed like this."

Ernesto shifted in his chair. Ruby put a new holder with its glass plate into the camera.

"We can do better. Ernesto, stand up. Push that chair out of the way. That's it. Now face each other. Take each others hands. Fine, but Ernesto, don't scowl so."

"Ruby," Lulu complained. "you know I don't like my profile."

A side view would show her wobbly chin and emphasize her ample bosom.

Dutifully, Ruby came and turned Lulu more towards the camera.

After the luncheon at Doña Anastasia's house, the widow took Ruby aside to again express her concerns, both practical and moral, about Ruby living alone. Ruby fended her off as best she could and made for the door without saying goodbye to the bride and groom.

Once outside, with the celebrants all safely contained behind the walls of the widow's house, Ruby slumped a moment in relief and fatigue before making her way through the narrow streets towards the family home, like a riderless horse heading single-mindedly for its stable.

Ruby knew Lulu loved their house. She seemed to relax into it the moment she crossed the threshold, as if slipping into a cozy shawl and soft slippers. For Ruby it felt more like a hair shirt, like boots that pinched and rubbed her heels raw. And yet all through lunch the image of the house had intruded on Ruby's thoughts—the house and her sister, tied together in her mind, inseparable. And it was only then that it struck her that her sister's absence was going to have some import beyond the studio. She just couldn't fathom yet what it would be. Now as she walked, rather than think about Lulu, she went over the physical details of the house's exterior—the pinkish-orange color, the stone arch framing the substantial mahogany door, the three stone arches over the windows facing the street, and the varnished wooden shutters.

Her mother, María Petrona Reyes Tun, had grown up in the house and had always despised it, situated as it was—outside the walls that had once enclosed the city. In the seventeenth century, when the walls were new, the gates were locked at 6:00 PM—only Europeans and criollos were permitted to remain inside. And so a mostly mestizo neighborhood of boat captains, shipwrights, sailmakers, sailors and fishermen grew up outside the southwest wall: San Román. Although her mother's maternal name, Tun, signaled Mayan ancestry, what she bragged about was her paternal grandfather who had been a ship captain from Spain.

Petrona had always dreamed of leaving San Román behind and living within the city walls, and when she married her German husband, she assumed her dream would come true. But Ruby's father declared the ambience within the walls claustrophobic. A different kind of man would have humored his wife's social-climbing aspirations, but not Paul Eckart. To his wife's dismay, he leased a house in San Román in the same block as her parents, and when his father-in-law died, he bought the house from his widowed mother-in-law, who afterwards lived with them. Petrona's older brother was not around to approve or complain—he'd set off years before for the gold rush in Tierra del Fuego, Chile, never to be heard from again.

And now there was the familiar facade—Ruby had arrived at the house. From now on she would be alone in it—no mother, no father, no

Lulu. Just adobe and plaster. She wondered, what, if anything, made it her home.

Lulu went to the window and looked down at the plaza. She felt very strange being alone in the elegant hotel room, and she wished Ruby were here to admire it. Ernesto usually stayed at a simple businessman's hotel when he was in the city, but for their wedding night (their boat for Vera Cruz would leave the next morning), he'd booked this room at the grand Hotel Cuauhtémoc. After saying their goodbyes to Doña Anastasia, De la Cruz had brought them to the hotel in his carriage. Now he and Ernesto were smoking cigars in the lobby to give Lulu some time to freshen up.

What did that mean exactly?

It meant, silly, she told herself, that the moment of truth was at hand. And she didn't know what to expect. Worse, she did not know what Ernesto expected of her, but then she recalled how he had kissed her in the studio when they were waiting for Ruby.

The room was warm despite the ceiling fan, and her slip and other underthings stuck to her skin. Should she take a bath? Was there time? What if he came back before she was presentable.

She sat down at the dressing table and peeled off her long white gloves. She removed her broad hat, laying the hatpins on the dressing table, and the hat on the bed. She looked at it there and blushed. She moved it to the top of the highboy dresser. Deciding not to risk a bath, she washed her face and neck and sat at the dressing table to tidy her hair. Electing to be bold, or as bold as she could bring herself to be, she took down her hair and brushed it. She looked at her reflection and flushed. Too brazen. She put her hair into two braids.

She ran a bath after all, and opened her trunk. Her pink traveling suit lay on top. Because Doña Olimpia could not get a good color match on the braid, she'd fashioned cloth roses instead: large ones for the jacket buttons in front, and small ones dangling from the cuffs and from the hem in back. She couldn't wait to wear it for Ernesto.

She held up the new nightgown, but put it aside. If she wore a nightgown in the middle of the afternoon, what would he think? Instead, as a compromise, she took her pale-yellow cotton wrapper from the trunk. She locked herself inside the bathroom and undressed. All this white skin of hers suddenly seemed too much, too pale. She felt like an albino whale.

She bathed quickly and put on the dressing gown over her chemise and bloomers, leaving off her corset, petticoat and stockings. She lay on the bed. She'd pinned her braids up to keep her hair dry in the bath, and now the pins hurt, so she got up and let the braids down, Then she lay down again, arranging herself. Maybe she should sit in one of the armchairs. And what, stare at the door, waiting? No, she returned to the dressing table. She could pretend to be tidying her hair.

All the while Lulu could not get Ruby out of her head. She kept seeing herself as a series of posed photographs. New bride looking at herself in the mirror. New bride arranged on the nuptial bed. New, but older, groom in the hotel doorway.

Ruby leaned against the stone doorframe, as exhausted as if she'd spent the day lugging stone. Her hand unsteady, she fumbled with the key. María Asunción was not there to let her in—Ruby and Lulu had given her the afternoon and evening off in celebration of Lulu's marriage. She was visiting her sister's family and would not return until the next day.

Once inside, Ruby closed the heavy door and leaned against it, felt the cool wood against her back.

The house was eerily lacking in human sounds. This made her smile —for one thing, she'd had enough of people for one day, and for another, she would not have to face María Asunción's questions about the wedding, at least not until tomorrow—but when she threw the bolt, her smile faded.

She wandered into the tiny courtyard and spent a moment listening to the call of a mourning dove. Then she drifted from room to room. In each she stood and listened to the silence. For better or worse, she was utterly alone. It felt so much stranger than she'd imagined.

She collapsed on her side of the bed—she would rest for a moment. But when she opened her eyes again, it was deep dusk. In minutes it would be completely dark. She lit a lantern and wandered into the kitchen—she'd barely eaten at the luncheon. She poured a glass of tamarind water from the covered earthen jug on the counter, grabbed a banana, scavenged a dried-out roll left over from breakfast, and sat at the kitchen table. Her feet were hot and sore. She thought, there's nothing to keep me from pulling off my shoes. I could sit here stark naked for all anyone would care or know.

She nibbled at the banana and did not stir from her chair.

Lulu turned from the vanity mirror as Ernesto hung his hat on the brass coat stand.

"May I," he said, indicating his jacket.

Lulu nodded, and giggled.

He looked relieved. "There's my jolly girl. You've been so solemn since we left Doña Anastasia's, I was afraid you'd repented marrying me."

He sat on the edge of the bed and beckoned to her with a tilt of his head. Feeling ever so awkward, she rose and went to him. He took her hand, kissed it and placed it on his chest. He stood and took one of her braids in his hand and kissed the tassel of hair below the tie of pale yellow ribbon. Then he gathered her up in his arms. She had read that term in novels, "gathered her up in his arms." Once when Lulu had read Ruby a passage with that phrase, Ruby had declared it silly. "She's a woman, not a sheaf of cornstalks."

But what did Ruby know? Here, Lulu was the heroine of her own story, and she felt just that: gathered, brought together in her essence.

Ernesto staggered a step and laid her on the bed. Sitting next to her, he leaned over and kissed her as he had earlier at the studio. The swooning feeling swept through her and she thought it lovely. He asked her to help remove his collar, and with shaking hands she reached up and undid the collar studs and handed them to him. With a happy sigh, he rubbed his bare neck and set the studs and collar on the night table.

He lay on his side alongside her and kissed her longer than she thought possible.

Heavens, would she faint from lack of breath? Would his mustache pressed against her face leave a scraped mark so that all would know? She heard Ruby's voice in her ear. "What do you imagine people will think you've done in a hotel room on your wedding day?"

Lulu was disconcerted by the weight of Ernesto's hand on her body, and by where he was touching her. Some of it felt good. Some of it, not. It all felt peculiar. She wanted it to stop. She wanted it to not stop. She knew she was blushing terribly. She must be as red as a watermelon.

The touching turned to fumbling with clothes.

The fumbling turned to discomfort.

She'd never been so close for so long to anyone in her life. It was embarrassing and hot and absurd. If she asked him to stop, would he? Would she really get accustomed to this? The marriage manual Aunt Pancha had sent her (she could not bring herself to read past the introduction) assured her that she would grow to enjoy it. For now, she just wanted it over.

He was on top of her. The weight of him. She felt her limbs grow more and more tense. Her hands balled into fists. Her jaw clenched. She was trying not to cry.

Abruptly, Ernesto stopped. He let out a sharp breath. Was it over? Lulu's eyes were closed, but she felt his gaze on her, and felt and smelled the heat of his body. She squeezed her eyes tighter shut, too ashamed to look at him. Then, with his palm on her cheek and his other hand squeezing her bottom, very businesslike, he stuck his thing in her.

The pain was sharp, very sharp, and she gasped. He gasped. And then it was over.

Ernesto had fallen asleep, a bare arm over Lulu's bosom. This was yet another surprise. She was used to sharing a bed, but with Ruby, and they never touched. Although Ernesto's arm was heavy, and hot, she decided that she liked lying close to him.

It was growing dark. She slid out from underneath his arm and tiptoed into the bathroom. The hotel had electric lights! She turned one on and cleaned herself. She felt raw down there.

Maybe the mystical union of souls would come later, with (as Tía Pancha's manual implied) practice, which made her recall her piano teacher making her play endless scales. She shook her head at the disconcerting thought.

She leaned forward and examined her face in the mirror. No mustache burns showed, but her face looked puffy and pink, and her plaited hair, frizzed and tousled. She washed her face in cool water. Coming out of the bathroom, she left the door ajar for the light, and moving as quietly as she could, re-dressed in her tea gown. She sat at the dressing table and brushed out her hair. Quickly pinning her topknot in place, achieving a far less perfect poof than she would have liked, she saw that her face had become its usual pale color of "milk without peaches," as Ruby called her complexion.

Lulu realized that the soft snoring at her back had stopped, and she saw in the mirror that Ernesto was watching her. Keeping her eyes on his, she smiled at him. She feared it was a bit forced, but he grinned back.

"You're all dressed. Going somewhere?" he said.

She hoped so. She wanted to take a turn around the plaza as a married lady on the arm of her husband. The new Señora María Luisa Eckart Reyes de Hernández for all the world to see. And she wished to go to evening mass and ask God's blessing and forbearance about postponing the religious ceremony, and to light a candle and ask the Virgin for protection on their sea trip.

"Let me guess," Ernesto said. "Seeing that your crazy sister rushed from Doña Anastasia's house like a bat from a cave, you want to go check on her and say goodbye properly."

Actually, Lulu didn't want to do that. But it was sweet of Ernesto to suggest it, and so she nodded.

She looked away as he pulled on his loose, one-piece undergarment. He drew near and put his arms around her. In the mirror she saw the bare skin of his arms dark against her white dress and his darkly tanned face cheek to cheek with her pale one. He still looked clean-shaven, but she could feel whiskers against her face.

"But, mi amor, maybe some ice cream first?" she said.

"Lululululu," he murmured in her ear as he squeezed her. "You sound like my children. What have I gotten myself into?"

Descending the broad marble steps to the hotel lobby, her gloved hands possessing her husband's arm, Lulu felt absolutely queenly. What did it matter: the boat trip, the rancho in the middle of nowhere, the new stepchildren, or the insufferableness of Ruby? She put it all out of her mind, like turning the page of one of the studio ledgers. It was the one good thing about account books: you could always turn to a new page, or better yet, slam the book cover shut.

Many people were out enjoying the evening air. After a stately walk about the plaza, lit by the gas streetlamps, she asked that they go by the Sweet Name of Jesus Temple, because of all the churches in the city, it had been her mother's favorite. When they arrived at the narrow little church with its stark, yellow, buttressed walls, Ernesto said, "Dear one, you're not going to drag me to mass on our wedding night, are you?"

In fact that had indeed been her plan. Lulu couldn't think of a more appropriate thing for husband and wife to do on this day than kneel side by side for all to see, but she smiled and said, "Of course not, mi amor."

"I'll stay out here and have a smoke then."

Disappointed, she pouted a little. But he did not then offer to accompany her, so she did not have the chance to demur, and for him to then insist, and for her in turn to smile at him gratefully. Somehow this wife business felt a bit like being Ruby's sister; seldom getting her way. Except with Ruby she would have complained and nagged. With Ernesto, she felt she had to put on a good face, to not disappoint him.

He kissed her cheek, "You look lovely, dear one."

Well, there was that, she thought. Ruby was not one for compliments, and Lulu so loved a good compliment.

At the doorway, she looked back and scanned the small area in front of the church. It was enclosed with fencing of black wrought-iron spears between white stone stanchions, and there she saw Ernesto (her husband!) lean against one of the pillars and pull out a pouch of tobacco to roll a cigarette. She gave up on the idea of mass. She entered the church but made her prayers brief. She wanted to get back to Ernesto.

When she came out, there seemed a commotion in the street with people standing about, talking and pointing. She craned her neck looking for Ernesto. He was outside the enclosure on the street corner, talking with several men she did not think he knew. Shouting could be heard from down the street, from the direction they were all looking. She made her way to Ernesto and took his arm. He turned to her startled.

"What's happening, mi amor?" she asked.

"A political meeting of maderistas. Seems the authorities have decided to break it up," Ernesto said, and turned to lead her firmly away in the opposite direction.

A gun shot cracked. It was not a common sound in the city, but what else could the explosive blast be?

She and others cried out.

"Santa María Purísima! What's happening?"

It was as if the commotion were a dust devil rolling towards them along the narrow street. There were shouts and the loud footfall of men running. Ernesto and Lulu both turned to see a slender man in a suit tearing past them. His derby flew off. His hair was very curly.

"Solís!?" Ernesto exclaimed.

The man turned and saw Ernesto. Slipping as he pivoted, he grabbed Ernesto and held on, panting, as if Ernesto had saved him from falling from a great height. Ernesto kept him upright.

"Ernesto!" the man exclaimed.

"Solis Jurado! You, here?"

"Farmacia Ayala. Please Ernesto, which way? I've got to get there."

"But Manuel…"

Another man raced by. "Solís, this way," he shouted as he passed. More men came running behind him.

Manuel, his hand now on Ernesto's shoulder, turned away to tear after them, but Ernesto caught his arm and pulled him back.

Manuel, alarmed, shouted, "Man, let go! Are you turning me in?"

"No. Crespo, Come this way," he said, and he started to pull the man east down the cross street. "Lulu, do you have your key to the studio?"

The question took Lulu aback. Did Ernesto intend to take this revolutionary into her family's photography studio?

"But I must meet up with the others," the stranger protested.

"Don't be foolish, man, this is no time for your damned meetings." Ernesto tried to move him away from the corner, but they were jostled by another knot of men running past. This time with police in close pursuit. Bystanders shouted from the sidewalk. Through it all Lulu clung to Ernesto's arm.

A snarling policeman grabbed hold of Ernesto as another officer, eyes wide with fear, took hold of Manuel.

Lulu shrieked, "Let go of him! He's my husband. Let go!"

The policeman grinned at her. "I don't know you from Adam, but I got me a revolutionary here."

"Don't be idiotic. We just got married!"

Manuel took advantage of the distraction and jerked away. He pulled a small derringer from his pocket and shouted maderista slogans, "True Democracy! No Re-election!"

Another policeman chasing down the street, his revolver drawn, saw Manuel and the gun in his hand. The officer stopped abruptly, sliding a bit as he fired.

The sound seemed to explode inside Lulu's head. Her hands flew up to her ears.

Manuel, wounded in the upper leg, staggered. Ernesto instinctively lurched towards him to steady him. In doing so, he inadvertently freed himself from the officer's grasp. He appeared to be escaping. The policeman who'd fired his gun, his footing and aim surer now, reacted and shot again, Ernesto in his sights.

Again, the explosion was tremendous and Lulu squeezed her eyes shut.

When she opened them, she saw that Ernesto had pulled up short before reaching Manuel, as if he'd come to his senses about helping the man. But then he twisted in an odd way and his eyes met Lulu's. He collapsed near a streetlamp, his eyes drawing hers down to where he landed on the paving stones.

Suddenly the street was empty. The politicos had passed on, pursued by the police, and the bystanders had scattered when the shots were fired. Now a few men returned, and along with the two policemen, they formed a ring around Ernesto, with Lulu on the outside.

"No!" Lulu screamed.

She pushed her way into the circle and dropped down next to Ernesto. There was blood on the pavement. She took his hand and searched the faces of the men looking down at her.

"Don't you understand?" Her voice wavered between fierceness and pleading, "We got married today!"

She lifted Ernesto's head into her lap. The movement made him cry out.

"I'm sorry, mi amor," she said. "I'm so sorry."

Ernesto shook his head, almost imperceptibly. He squeezed her hand and tried to speak. She leaned her head close to hear his words.

"Mi rancho," he implored, his voice thin.

His forehead glistened with sweat in the light of the streetlamp, and his eyes with tears. One escaped and ran down the side of his face. Lulu wiped it away. His hand relaxed its grip, but his eyes stayed on hers. His next breath was slow in coming.

"…Take me home."

"Of course, mi amor, of course."

Her chest hurt waiting for his next breath.

"My children…"

The words were so faint she could hardly make them out.

She nodded again and again.

His eyes held hers another moment.

Then she watched as the life in his gaze ebbed to nothingness.

Nothingness.

Lulu felt cold and clammy, wrapped in silence. And yet there was moaning, "No, no, no!" The noise seemed to be coming from her.

Her vision was blurred. She rubbed at her eyes, and found her hand wet with tears.

A man leaned over and closed Ernesto's eyes. Two others were trying to lift Lulu to her feet. What were they doing?

"No! Let go of me," she protested. "You think he's… You're wrong. He can't be. We got married today," she reasoned. "Don't you see? He can't be!"

Still they pulled at her.

"Let me be," she screamed at them. "You'll see. He'll open his eyes, if you just let us be."

They lifted her to her feet and held her upright. Her dress was smeared with brown dirt and her white gloves were stained with red.

Someone bumped into her, hard. It was that man, Manuel, the one who'd caused all the trouble. That stupid little gun still in his hand. He was wrestling with several policemen. Some men surrounded her; and others, him. Everyone pushing and shoving. She felt as if she were in a game of tug-of-war.

"No re-election!" the man was shouting. "Viva Madero!"

"Shut up!" Lulu screamed. "You stupid, evil little man!"

A policeman held the man's wrist away from himself as a bystander tried to wrest the gun from his hand. She felt a particularly sharp shove. An explosive sound hurt her ears and there was more yelling. The man who'd been holding her up let go of her as he ducked for cover. She fell, landing rather unladylike on her bottom, and found herself on the ground next to Ernesto. She'd lost sight of him in the tussle. She reached for him, but feeling a stab of pain, she pulled back. Her hand went to her midriff, and she noticed that the large white silk rose at her waist was hanging by a thread. That's when she saw what looked like a red rosebud on the bodice of her dress. She stared at it as it bloomed into a full-blown hibiscus flower.

And then it was dark. All these people leaning over her. They must be blocking the streetlamps. So dark.

Lulu awoke in her bed at home, which seemed only natural, but her head felt full of cotton. Morning light streamed through half-open shutters, and she could see Ruby's familiar form sitting in a chair next to the bed. An odd thing for her to do. Lulu shifted slightly, intending to stretch, but her stiff muscles groaned, and a sharp tearing sensation below her shoulder made her cry out and brought tears to her eyes.

Ruby came to attention. "Shh, hermana," she cooed to her, "Stay still. You're fine."

Lulu wasn't home after all. She could see that now. There were other beds around her with people in them.

Confused, she looked at Ruby. "Where…?"

"Hospital Civil Manuel Campos."

"Don't be silly. Why would I be at a hospital?"

Speaking exhausted her, and she let her eyes droop. As she fell back asleep, she saw Ruby's thick black eyebrows, like two centipedes bowing to each other, and almost knocking heads.

Ruby had sat by Lulu's bed throughout the night and into the morning, seldom taking her eyes from Lulu's wan face. Her fair skin had lost all color and looked waxen. Ruby feared she was foreseeing her sister's corpse.

The doctor came by, nodded to Ruby and made a cursory examination, barely rousing Lulu from her sleep. He smiled at Ruby, bowed slightly and turned to the patient in the next bed.

Ruby grabbed his arm. "Doctor!"

"Señorita?" he said, removing her hand from his sleeve.

Ruby lowered her voice. "My sister… She's going to die, isn't she?"

"Not from that gunshot wound."

"Please, doctor. Speak frankly."

"I assure you that I am being quite candid with you. I'm not known for my tact."

"But she looks, she...."

"Like death warmed over? Yes, I agree. Anesthesia was used during the operation. It takes the patient to the door of death, but not through it. The operation went well, but the body has suffered a shock, and she's lost blood. Of course her natural coloring is also quite pale."

"Yes, but not grey."

"I'm sorry you're not pleased with her looks, but I'm a doctor, not a cosmetologist."

Ruby wanted to believe him, believe that Lulu would recover, but she could not. Someone touched her arm, said her name, was speaking to her. She looked up to see a familiar face, familiar but out of place. A face from the Civil Registry. From the wedding luncheon. Ernesto's lawyer friend, Mauricio De la Cruz.

"How is the señora?" he said quietly.

"Who?" she said, not without irritation.

He looked at her oddly, "Señora Lulu, your sister."

Ruby lay her hand on top of her head. "Of course. I'm sorry. The doctor says she'll be fine. But look at her, Licenciado."

"It's the shock, señorita, that's all." He nodded toward the man in the white medical smock across the ward. "If Dr. Luzzato says she'll be fine, she will be."

"You think so? Truly?"

"The good doctor does not know the meaning of sugarcoating. He's a pessimist by nature, a characteristic he cultivates as a virtue."

Ruby searched the lawyer's face for signs of mendacity. She looked back at Lulu lying under a starchy white sheet.

"Señorita Ruby, you look in need of refreshment. Allow me to escort you to a café."

She shook her head.

"Surely, you..."

"No. I don't want to leave her."

He nodded. "Of course. I know that you are a strong-minded lady…"

She glared at him.

"And devoted to your sister."

She realized that he was trying to be kind, and that this was a difficult time for him as well.

"Forgive me, Licenciado." She touched his arm. "My condolences. You've lost a friend."

"And you a brother-in-law."

She shrugged. "Of several hours."

"That is, in part, why I've come. There are matters that must be dealt with."

"Surely they can wait."

"There is the question of the body."

"Oh."

"I will handle everything, if you so direct me, on your sister's behalf."

"Yes, Licenciado, please. I would be so grateful, and Lulu, too, I'm sure."

He nodded, took her hand and kissed it.

Ruby felt Lulu watching her as she bustled about their bedroom getting dressed, but she did not meet her eyes. It was good to have Lulu safely out of the hospital and convalescing at home, but she was unsure how to behave around her.

"You're not going to the studio this early are you?" Lulu complained.

"I must, my dear."

"Maybe if you put a cot for me in the darkroom, I might see you once in a while."

"Don't exaggerate. Besides, you have María Asunción to keep you company."

Lulu took a furtive glance about her. "María Asunción is not company! She's driving me crazy with her chatter, morbid chatter at that."

"How can one chatter morbidly?"

"It's her special talent. Her family and acquaintances seem exceptionally prone to freak accidents, from which they inevitably die. I've heard about every one of her relatives, and now she's started on friends and distant relatives of neighbors."

Ruby kissed her cheek. "I'll try to be back for lunch."

Lulu made a face at her.

Ruby arrived at the studio with the intention of working on the plates of the christening photograph of the Caña Suárez baby. She'd taken them weeks before the wedding, and the customer was getting impatient—not to mention that the income would be most welcome. Unlocking the door, she wondered what she should do about the plates she'd taken of Lulu and Ernesto. Should she develop them? File them? Break them?

Before heading to the darkroom, she forced herself to sit at Lulu's desk. She glared at the pile of papers that had accumulated in little more than a week. She attempted to sort them but gave up. She blinked at the ledger without comprehension. She rifled through the accounts payable and found the address of the supply company in Mérida where Lulu had set up an account. She wrote out an order, and called it good. But she must get to a pharmacy soon—she was almost out of silver nitrate.

That afternoon, arriving home for lunch, neighbors stopped her at her door and asked after Lulu. As Ruby thanked them for their good wishes, she reflected that it was pleasant knowing she would find Lulu waiting in their bedroom—and that Lulu would be glad to see her. Afflicted as Lulu was these days by alternating bouts of weeping and boredom, Ruby provided her a welcome distraction, even though every time she opened her mouth, she seemed to say the wrong thing.

Now she gathered her thoughts before striding into the bedroom. She kissed Lulu on the cheek—her face no longer grey, but not yet pink.

"The Zavalas asked after you," she said cheerily from the washstand.

Lulu groaned. Ruby, eyes wide with fear, wheeled to face her.

"Oh, I'm fine," Lulu said with a wave of her hand. "It's just embarrassing to have everyone know."

"What do you mean?"

"Ladies don't get gunshot wounds, do they." Her chin wobbled. "And certainly not on their wedding day."

She burst into tears and Ruby put her arms around her.

"Oh, Ruby, for the rest of my life, people will whisper behind my back, 'There goes Lulu, shot in the street like a dog.'"

"Oh, Lulu. They won't."

"And I've lost Ernesto. I can't believe I've lost him!"

Ruby thought, you still have me—we'll return to our life before Ernesto, and all will be fine again. But she bit her tongue.

"It's not fair! I will forever be the one-day widow, till the day I die. And I hate black," she sobbed. "I hate it."

Lulu felt the railway car jolt into movement, and as it inched away from the station, she thought of her father, who'd been a great enthusiast for the establishment of railroads. She recalled how he would exclaim, his r's all guttural, "Prrrogrrress! New errra! Prrrosperrrity!"

When Lulu was eleven, he'd taken her and little Ruby to the inauguration ceremony for this very railway line, the first in the state, from Campeche City to Hecelchakán, 70 kilometers to the northeast. But Lulu did not feel nostalgic about her childhood, or excited to be on the train (well, she was a bit excited). Mostly she was sad. Ernesto should be by her side. Not, she shuddered, in a box in the baggage car. Ernesto's overseer, Eusebio Escalante, was to meet her at the end of the line in Hecelchakán, as arranged for by Licenciado De la Cruz. The rest of the trip to Baalam Kab would be by wagon on dirt roads and tracks. Even though the rains hadn't started yet, it would take several days.

The carriage rocked terribly, making her stomach queasy. What would she have done on a boat? Spend her honeymoon vomiting? Her heart constricted. Her honeymoon! Would these random knives of memory never cease?

The train was unpleasant in every way: loud, smokey, smelly, and the windows so dirty she could only make out the vaguest of images outside.

Even so, the first ten kilometers she felt righteous and brave.

Ruby had been flabbergasted when Lulu told her she was taking Ernesto's body back to his rancho and taking charge of his children.

"You don't have to do that," Ruby had said. "No one will expect you to."

"But I want to," Lulu said. "I want to get away from here. Don't you see? Here, they're already calling me the virgin widow. I can't bear it. Besides, it was Ernesto's last wish, and I intend to honor it."

"But a farm? And what are you going to do with a gaggle of kids?"

"Carry on," Lulu said, sticking out her chin.

Ruby had looked at her, incredulous, and Lulu lifted her chin higher, but looked away.

"And what about me?" Ruby blurted.

"You?"

"Yes, me." Her hand cradled the crown of her head. "I need help at the studio," she admitted. "I'm already making a mess of things."

That had given Lulu satisfaction. Ruby finally understood that it was she, Lulu, and her dogsbodying, who kept the business afloat.

"You can hire someone. A bookkeeper, at least."

"With what?" Ruby shot back.

"Well, you won't have my expenses. That will help. And I'll try to send money, if I can, til you sort things out."

This had made her feel very expansive, very much the lady of charity, but Ruby had not responded with gratitude.

During the first hour on the train, she held close the gratifying memory of Ruby's reaction to her announcement: astonishment and her all but begging Lulu to stay. But now, at kilometer 11, she was no longer so sure of herself. She felt the coldness in her face as it turned pale. Lately, instead of the sudden heat of her blushes that had plagued her since childhood, she was now afflicted with this opposite sensation, as if her heart were sucking all the blood back into it, pulling it in to puddle and chill. Her hands trembled.

"Madam," the lady seated across from her said, "Are you unwell?"

Lulu shook her head no, although her shoulder ached terribly from the lurching of the train. She adjusted her shawl, which she wore draped to hide her black sling. She did not mind the attentions of strangers. In fact she welcomed their solicitude and pity, as long as they did not know the circumstances of her widowhood.

The lady was accompanied by a man, presumably her husband, and she held a child on her lap. The child kept staring at Lulu.

The man glanced at her, and Lulu smiled. She wasn't flirting, not really.

The child tugged at his mother's arm. "What's wrong with that lady?"

"Hush," her mother said.

"But, Mama, why's she that color?"

"She's in black because she's in mourning. She's lost someone."

"No, why is her face that color?"

"How old is the child," Lulu ventured, less as a pleasantry than as a way to change the subject. Then she heard herself say, "You know, I have children of my own."

Having tried out the phrase, she rather liked it. Then she felt a panic. What if the woman asked about them? To avoid more conversation, she raised her black-gloved hand to her eyes and lowered her head.

"Mamá!" The little boy insisted.

"Shh. Let the lady rest."

The train continued rumbling down the track. The air in the coach was sooty, and the wooden slat benches seemed to grow harder and harder. They were crossing a broad plain with low hills on the horizon. Her heart sank. They were moving farther and farther away from civilization. And closer and closer to those children. What had she been thinking?

De la Cruz had visited the day before with her train ticket. He'd reviewed the arrangements he'd made and reassured her, "Señora Lulu, the foreman, Escalante, is capable and he will run Baalam Kab for you. But a word of advice: you must at least make the pretense of overseeing his work."

He also explained that Ernesto had told him that the man, not content with being the foreman, wanted to be mayordomo, but Ernesto had filled that role himself. He was his own farm manager.

"Under the circumstances, you might allow him the title," De la Cruz suggested, "but you must establish yourself as the señora del rancho from the moment you step from the train."

"Oh my. You alarm me, sir. I wouldn't know how to do that."

"No need to be concerned, Señora Lulu. I'm sure you'll do splendidly."

But he had looked worried. She would have discussed it with Ruby, but Ruby had already said something similar about the children.

"You'll have to take charge, Lulu, if you're to do them any good. Remember, kids are like any animal, don't let them smell your fear."

"Ruby, really! What do you know about children? Or animals? And who said I was afraid? I'm sure they're perfectly charming children."

Lulu just wanted someone to love her. Ernesto's children, they would have to love her. They had no one else. Besides, she was young and fun-loving. They would get along famously. Wouldn't they? This Eusebio Escalante person would manage the ranch. There was a housekeeper to manage the house. She and the children would have fun together. She wouldn't be strict.

And best of all, she'd never have to keep books or take care of customers again. She thought of her mother, who'd opposed opening the photography studio and been dead set against Lulu's working there. Well, now Lulu would finally be the lady her mother had intended her to be.

Alerted by the dogs' barking, Soli tore off her apron, and she and Susana de los Ángeles rushed to the front of the house. Meche and Lalo came up behind them, and all strained to see the wagon pass under the wooden sign hanging from the iron arch: Rancho Baalam Kab. Before the wagon could travel the long, straight track to arrive at the house, Meche hightailed it in the opposite direction.

"Meche!" Soli shouted.

Soli wanted, and needed, Meche by her side when they met their father's new wife, but there went Meche, rounding the back of the house without even looking back.

The wagon proceeded slowly.

Little Lalo pulled on Soli's hand. "Play hide and seek with me, Soli."

"Not now, mi amor. See here comes the wagon with Papá. Papá and your new stepmother."

Lalo jumped up and down in excitement. Part of Soli wanted to jump up and down, too. She'd missed her father and couldn't wait to see him. Still, a part of her sorely wished she could follow Meche, wished she could hide from the changes coming.

Soli grew bewildered as the wagon drew closer. She did not see her father, and she might have concluded it was some unexpected visitor, except there was no doubt that that was their wagon and horses, and it was clearly Don Eusebio holding the reins. But there was just one other person in the wagon: a woman. And dressed in black, she didn't look like a bride. Soli felt cold shoot through her veins. Susana de los Ángeles came up to her and laid her hand on Soli's arm.

"Niña…"

"Take Lalo inside, will you?" Soli whispered.

Susana de los Ángeles, who'd been making a cake to welcome the newlyweds, lured the little boy inside by promising him a taste of the icing.

Soli felt very still, almost frozen, as she waited for the wagon to pull up. She used the time to study the woman who must be María Luisa and to look for some clue that would reveal an outcome other than the one she feared.

She studiously kept her eyes from straying to the back of the wagon.

Before the woman's eyes settled on Soli, Soli saw her scan the facade of the house. Its exterior had been built for security, not beauty, and Soli saw a look of disappointment cross the woman's face. Soli also noticed that the woman's arm was in a sling.

Don Eusebio stopped the wagon and nodded to Soli, then leaned towards María Luisa and muttered something. The pale woman turned even whiter. "What?!" she said, looking at Don Eusebio with dismay.

"It wasn't my place, ma'am," he said.

He helped her down, and despite the heat, she tugged a shawl over the sling.

She and Soli faced each other in silence, each waiting for the other to speak first. Then the woman turned all fluttery and cooing.

"Are you María Soledad?"

Soli nodded, and the woman gave her a one-arm embrace.

"Oh my poor darling."

Soli searched the face of this woman, this stranger. "And Papá?" she managed to croak.

Soli shut herself in her bedroom. It was almost dark when Meche slipped into the room and furtively closed the door behind her.

"Ha! You've been crying!" Meche said. "So, she's as bad as I said she'd be."

"Oh, Meche, don't," Soli said.

"Don't what?"

Soli jumped up from the bed and, bursting into tears, hugged Meche. Meche pushed her away and held her at arm's length.

"Soli, what's going on? You're scaring me."

Soli, shook her head and took Meche's hands in hers.

"It's Papá," she said. "He's dead!"

"What do you mean, dead?" Meche's voice was icy.

"Some kind of political disturbance in the city. He was shot."

"Shot?! By whom? Why?"

Soli shook her head again.

"But Soli, that makes no sense. You know Father didn't get involved in politics."

"Apparently when he and his new wife came out of a church after mass, they inadvertently got between some maderistas and the police. It was a mistake."

"A mistake!"

Soli nodded yes, and began to cry again. She tried to embrace Meche, but Meche escaped her.

Soli recalled the first week or so after their mother died, when she and Meche were never out of each other's arms. But then in the months that followed, how many times had Soli pushed her sister away because she couldn't muster the strength to comfort her? There was Lalo to tend to, the work of the house to do and her own grief threatening to overwhelm her. But not at first. Now Soli felt like she'd been trampled by a horse. She ached all over and yearned to be held.

Meche took several steps away and crossed her arms about herself. She turned away, blinking back tears. When she turned towards her sister again, she seemed more angry than sad. She paced like a caged animal, her face fierce.

Soli, desolate, dropped onto the bed. At least Meche hadn't bolted yet. Soli blew her nose and dried her eyes, and watched. The pacing seemed to calm Meche. Her stride slackened.

Soli called to her and patted the bed.

Meche sat. The sisters faced each other, each with one leg cocked.

Soli reached for her hand, and Meche did not pull away. In fact her grip was strong, almost painful. They sat in silence, each running the maze of their thoughts.

Meche spoke first. "If they were together, how come Papá got shot and she didn't? If someone got shot, it should have been her!"

"She did get shot, but she's recovering."

"Well, bully for her."

"Meche, it's her loss too.

Meche harrumphed.

"You know, she really doesn't seem so bad."

Meche rose from the bed. She paced a few more times and then faced Soli, hands on hips.

"How soon can we send her packing?"

"Meche!"

"Well?"

"We can't."

"Why not? She's nothing to us. We don't need her. You can keep running the house and take care of Lalo, like always, and I can run the farm."

"Don't be an idiot. They'd never allow that."

"Who's they?"

"They. The powers that be. The grownups. It will never happen."

"Why not?"

"You're just a girl, Meche."

"But if she's not here…"

"Don't you understand? Without her, we'd… Meche, she may be the only thing between us and an orphanage. She may be the only way we can stay together."

"But we don't need her!"

"Papá's dead, Meche."

Meche pouted. She looked more angry than sad.

Soli stood and gave her a hug. Meche stood rigid in her arms.

"I'm going to go help Susana de los Ángeles with dinner. You'd better be at that table, Meche. And you better be nice to Lulu."

"Lulu?"

"That's what she wants us to call her."

Meche groaned and rolled her eyes.

"And so you know, Papá's coffin is in the parlor. It's sealed. He's to be buried in the chapel yard.

Susana de los Ángeles served dinner, and Soli wondered if her own eyes looked as red as hers.

"Susana," Lulu said, "please put something on Señorita Meche's plate. Meche, my dear, I know you're sad, we all are, but you must eat something."

"It's not our custom," Meche said.

Lulu looked at her quizzically.

When Meche did not explain herself, Susana de los Ángeles said, "Señora, the señorita means that the Maya fast during mourning."

"But she's not an Indian. Meche, you're not an Indian."

"No, stepmother," Soli interjected, "but my sister has a special affinity with our workers and for…"

"Oh, Soli, please," Lulu interrupted. "Do call me Lulu."

Soli looked down at her plate.

"I know this is not how things were supposed to be," Lulu cajoled, "but we all loved your papa, and now, because of him, we have each other. We can be great friends. After all, I'm not so much older than you."

"Aren't you, like, 40?" Meche said.

Lulu turned pink. "I'm 23," she said.

Meche raised her eyebrows dramatically.

Soli remembered her father saying that his bride-to-be was indeed young, a dozen years older than Soli, and Soli was almost 16, but she said nothing and kept her eyebrows at an even keel.

Little Lalo, like a colt, ever sensitive to the currents about him, whimpered and squirmed.

"Must he fidget like that?" Lulu asked Soli. "Lalo, I know you're sad, but must you fidget like that?"

"Yes, he must, " Meche said, jumping up. "Come on, Lalito. Let's eat in the kitchen."

"I don't want to."

Meche grabbed him under the arms and dragged him off as he kicked and screamed. One kick connected with the table and the china rattled.

"Oh my heavens!" Lulu exclaimed.

Soli directed a look at Susana de los Ángeles, who picked up Lalo's plate and followed Meche into the kitchen.

"Your Susana is a very good cook," Lulu simpered. "Quite a pleasant surprise way out here. I wasn't sure what to expect."

Susana de los Ángeles, having returned with a message, said, "I am just Señorita Soli's helper. She is the real cook, señora."

"Really?"

"She's exaggerating," Soli said, eyes down.

"Well, I wouldn't know how to begin to put together an excellent meal like this, or a bad one, for that matter."

"Señora," Susana de los Ángeles said, "the workers have begun gathering in the back patio for the vigil."

Soli watched as Lulu peeked out the kitchen door at the small candle-lit gathering.

"They're so quiet," Lulu said with a shudder.

Then she drew herself up. She touched her face with her black-edged handkerchief and held it there. Soli hung back, embracing Lalo, who stood wide-eyed, his little arms flung around her legs.

Meche abruptly laid claim to Lulu and pulled her through the door. Taking it as her due, and ignoring Don Eusebio, Meche introduced each worker, starting with Pedro Mu and his family.

Then Don Eusebio motioned to Pedro, and they and several men entered through the kitchen, stopping to pay their respects to Soli. Susana de los Ángeles showed them into the parlor, and the men carried the coffin back through the kitchen and out to the patio. The metal-lined, mahogany-and-brass coffin was particularly heavy, and despite being accustomed to considerable burdens, the men strained under its weight. They positioned it on a table they'd set up with trestles, taking care to align it east to west. Within minutes the table was covered with flowers, pitchers, candles and bread.

With Lalo still clinging to her, Soli went and stood in the doorway. The sight of her father's coffin, the patio filled with familiar faces, each illuminated by the candle or lantern they carried, their offerings on the table, the smoke and scent of copal incense thick in the air, all of it brought home her loss. The finality of it.

Soli, shaking with sobs, saw her sister in the patio, her face as stricken as her own. Their eyes met, and abandoning Lulu, Meche rushed to Soli. The girls embraced and wept together. Wary, Lulu stood in a circle of emptiness as the mourners in the patio began to pray and wail. Their lament rose, swallowing up Lulu's stunned silence and the sisters' mournful crying.

Lulu heard voices in the kitchen: Susana's, sounding stern, and a man's. She felt a pang of alarm. There were so many alarming things here, so many trying situations. Her nerves were quite frazzled.

Susana, emerging from the kitchen, was saying quite firmly, "I will announce you." She came to Lulu and said, "Señora, Don Eusebio wishes to see you."

Lulu looked at her blankly. Of course she remembered who Don Eusebio was. What she was wondering was if she could turn him away. And if not, where did one receive one's overseer? The parlor didn't seem appropriate.

Susana must have read her mind because she added, "In Don Ernesto's office."

Lulu nodded, distracted because looking over Susana's shoulder at the framed mirror on the wall, she saw her father's eyes looking back at her from her reflection. Only his eyes had been a shocking sapphire, while hers were some paler, indeterminate color. She suddenly missed her sister, who had their mother's dark brown eyes. Looking into Ruby's eyes was both a comfort and a hurt, for while they looked like her mother's, they did not shine with love for her, at least not with a mother's love for her favorite.

She wiped away a tear. She had to face the foreman and she didn't feel she had the strength.

Meche exhausted her with that insolent stare of hers, looking down on her from the high dudgeon of her 13 years. She was just a child, but all the same it made Lulu wither inside. She knew she shouldn't let herself be intimidated by the girl, but Meche was so confident, so strong-willed. So arrogant! Why did she hate Lulu so? As for the other two, Lalo was a handful, Lord knows, but an affectionate little fellow, when he wasn't throwing a fit. And Soli, well she was a little martyr, wasn't she? All competent and respectful. At least she seemed able to handle the other two. And she hadn't relinquished her duties running the household, which was fine with Lulu. But the rancho! Soli, so helpful in other ways, seemed to know next to nothing about its operation.

Don Eusebio followed Lulu into the office, a cramped cubbyhole at the front of the house, taken up almost entirely by a leather-topped mahogany desk. His boots were lusterless, and dark against the woven palm floor mat. He held his straw cowboy hat in one hand (not so insolent as to keep his hat on, nor so deferent as to hold it in front of him in both hands). He was no laborer, but neither was he a gentleman, and she felt uneasy. His gaze was too frank. She remembered Licenciado De la Cruz giving her advice on this subject. What was it? Something about establishing her authority. But how was she supposed to do that?

After a hesitation, she sat in Ernesto's chair and swiveled to face the overseer standing near the doorway. Should she be imperious with Don Eusebio and leave him standing? While she debated, he sat without invitation in the one straight-backed chair next to the desk. Should she rebuke him? He was already talking, explaining that Don Ernesto used to meet with him formally in this office once a week, and would also be in communication out on the rancho in between times.

"You mean he would give the orders to you here, but he was also outside directing the work?"

"Not exactly, señora, but I would keep him posted on how the work was progressing."

This overseer, Lulu wanted to trust him. She needed to trust him, but now he was explaining that he wanted more money, that he was acting as farm manager, not just as a foreman, and he wanted the title and better pay.

"The boss used to say that he didn't need a manager," Don Eusebio said. "He said he was a farmer, not some hacendado lolling in a mansion in Mérida. But since he started courting you, señora, I've been running things, and that's a fact. He spent a lot more time in the city than he did here. The rancho may not be large, but there's a lot to do. Just look at these books."

He stood and leaned over her to reach the accounting books on the desk. He smelled of horses, wood smoke and sour sweat. He hefted the bound books to the corner of the desk nearest him and, still standing over her, explained briefly the use of each one.

"These are my notations in them, and have been for more than a year now. The person keeps the books, well, anyone will tell you, that's the farm manager."

It wasn't that he was disrespectful, exactly, maybe just impatient, but she felt hectored, hemmed in.

"There's a lot of work to do," he continued, "work that can't be put off. There are things that have to be done before the rains and things to do during the rains, some on the full moon, some on the new, some before the dew dries, some at sunset. If not, you don't have a crop. No crop, you got nothing to sell, and then you can't pay the workers or the bills that need paying."

"Don Eusebio, I've done the books for my father's photo studio…"

"Ma'am, with all due respect, a rancho is a big complicated operation, not some store-front business."

"I'm aware of that, but I do know the concept of income and

expenses, overhead, taxes. I'm not..." Her voice was going to break, and she wondered if that might give her an advantage with this man. Or would it put her at a disadvantage?

"Pardon me, mi señora, I spoke out of turn. It's just that most ladies have not had your experience," He said with a nod.

Why did she feel insulted?

"I need some time to consider what you've said, Don Eusebio. Now if you'd be so good as to excuse me." She lifted her right hand, and then not sure if she should shake his hand, instead raised her fingers to her forehead.

He snapped his head in a bow and headed for the back of the house, where she heard the murmur of his voice in the kitchen and the laughter of Susana and Lalo.

She spent some time trying to decipher the ledgers. She didn't know what any of the abbreviations referred to. Dare she ask Soli, or even Meche, to help her? Defeated and discouraged, she put the books aside. Would she never be free of stodgy old columns of numbers? She wished there were a sympathetic ear to listen to her. With a sigh that shook her body, she took out several sheets of paper. She would write Ruby. But she must attempt to put a good face on things. She didn't want Ruby to say she'd told her so.

Several weeks later, she received Ruby's scrawled reply.

> *Lulu, dear sister,*
>
> *I'm sorry to hear that you are having frequent headaches. How is your shoulder? Is it troubling you? Are you still having nightmares? Is there someone there to wake you when you do?*
>
> *I don't like the sound of your overseer, but he's right of course, a farm manager is what you need. "Is he trustworthy?" That is an excellent question, and I am heartened that you are being cautious. Are there perhaps acquaintances of Ernesto's who could advise you on this*

question? Perhaps one of the hacendados you mentioned who visited to offer condolences? In this Escalante's favor, I suppose, is that it's unlikely that Ernesto would have kept the man on for so many years if he were not to be trusted, nor would he have left him in charge while he was here with us in the city.

I'll have you know that despite my impatience with politics, my worry about you in this time of unrest has me reading the newspaper assiduously! Do you get any news there? I know you don't want to hear anything about Madero, but you should know that support for his candidacy is growing stronger every day. Everyone says he will become president, but Aunt Pancha is convinced otherwise. She says that Díaz is dead set on securing a seventh term, and will keep Madero from taking office one way or another. She expects Madero will soon find himself in jail, and that that will incite a revolution. And she is, of course, convinced that it will succeed. You know what I think about Tía Pancha's hare-brained ideas, so I asked Licenciado De la Cruz if she might be right. He pooh-poohed me, and assured me that that would never happen. Still, I hope you will consider selling the rancho—right away!—before the election this summer. I'm sure the profit from the sale could be invested to support you and the children here in the city. Does that not seem the best option?

As for the children, better you than me! Reading between the lines, it sounds like you find Soli starchy, Meche a terror and the little boy a spoiled brat. That seems more than enough to deal with without the rancho as well.

As for me, the business and I are staying afloat, but just. I would like to make postcards—it's the coming thing. I need to look into how much money it will take to get started. More immediately, it is clear that I will need to hire someone to take care of the front, the money, order supplies and do errands. The advertisement will read: "Wanted: one Lulu, sister and business partner extraordinaire." Think I'll have any takers?

Take care of yourself, my dear.
Love,
Ruby

Tears filled Lulu's eyes when she read this, for Ruby was not given to displays of fondness.

She went to her room, the room that would have been hers and Ernesto's. Her clothes were still in her trunk because Ernesto's hung in the wardrobe, which she kept closed in order to preserve his scent.

She lay on the bed, closed her eyes and remembered her wedding day. She'd felt so proud and happy, walking with her hand on Ernesto's arm, how in front of the church they'd looked into each other's eyes. The love in his had made her stomach do flip-flops, as did the memory of it now. Then the commotion, the running and yelling. No! She needed the memory to stop with his eyes looking tenderly into hers and her insides turning somersaults.

The pain in her head was becoming a vise, and she cried anew. What was left for her? What?

1 9 0 9...

January 23, 1909

Another overcast day here in the capital, and reflective of my mood.

Note:

> *Jan. 10, coal mine explosion in Zeigler, Illinois, US. Fatalities: 26.*
> *Jan. 12, Switchback, West Virginia, US. Fatalities: 105.*
> *(Same mine last month: 51)*
> *Jan. 14, Ajka, Hungary. Fatalities: 55.*

Last night I could not lure my thoughts away from these disasters, nor lull my indignation to sleep. Then when exhaustion finally won out, what did I dream about? A jaguar of all things! It must have been my unconscious mind dredging up that Mayan myth (and linking it to the miners): the jaguar sun going underground every night, fighting for his life and losing. I awoke in a panic.

Today, in the light of day (grey though it may be), it's white and black that's niggling at the back of my mind. Why? Because the Brits have planted their flag at the south pole! Imagine that rag of cloth flapping in all that whiteness. What to think? The advancement of scientific knowledge? Imperialism at its most absurd?

White and black. Endless icy day versus the black coal pits, miners burning to death, suffocating in the heat of relentless darkness, endless night. White and black. Thus, asleep or awake, my brain stirs and spins ideas and images. I am impatient for it all to coalesce into something I can use in my column.

Note:

Feb. 27, 1908, not even a year ago, our own Santa Rosita Mine in Coahuila: 200 miners dead.

Coal mining is truly an industry from hell, evil and reckless, swallowing the lives of men and boys. The fact that the Santa Rosita is the only mine in the country <u>not</u> run by foreigners, that Compañía Carbonífera de Sabinas is our only wholly Mexican-owned mining company, is testimony that the callousness of capital recognizes no national sentiment or loyalty.

On a happier note, I received a letter from Lulu, bringing with it some Campeche sunshine, of course without even a postscript from Ruby.

It may seem strange to an onlooker that of the two girls, Lulu is my favorite. (I'm not a mother, only an aunt, and a great-aunt at that, so I am allowed favorites.) Lulu acts the fool, all fluff and frills, but there's something in her that calls to me, and I seem to prompt an equally inexplicable fondness in her. Rational as I strive to be, these are the mysteries of blood.

As for Ruby, she may seem the level-headed one, the one with her feet on the ground, and indeed she herself would tell you the same lie, but I think the world has always been a slippery place for her, misty and mutable. She's never been able to get a hold on anything. That is until she discovered the camera. What a neat trick it does, framing bite-size pieces of life, defining them and holding them forever still. Oh, she'll talk about her fascination with the technology and the challenges of art, but as crowds and colors and odors swirl dizzyingly about her, she clings to that box as a child to her mother's skirt at market.

Thus I ask myself, how do I see the world? Certainly not like rosy Lulu with rows of figures that always add up (her father knew what he was about, making her the studio's bookkeeper). I am, perhaps, like Ruby, only words do for me what the camera does for her. Although unlike her, my vision is broad. I perceive the universal, if unpleasant, laws governing life:

the facts of predator and prey, of reproduction and natural selection. That evolution is a reality is the world's saving grace. We can <u>evolve</u>, we can make things better. I think there's an article in that.

Anyway, when I respond to Lulu's letter, I can take satisfaction in knowing that whatever I say will, in equal parts, warm Lulu's heart and irritate our Ruby.

"There she goes again," Lulu will say with a fond smile (Lulu finds my "politicking" amusing). Ruby, I suspect, will say the same, "there she goes again," only with a grimace. Lulu, oblivious to the substance of what I've said, and Ruby, feeling I'm haranguing her in particular. And she's right. She lives her life as she likes, for which I applaud her, but she refuses to understand that her independence is a hard-earned legacy from individuals who have gone before. Individuals, I dare say, like myself.

February 15, 1909

It's a critical time. (Granted, in this new century of ours, the situation always seems dire.) Now, however, our printing press has been confiscated, poor Ramírez is in jail, and the rest of the members of the committee are in hiding. Now that I am seventy, I find the prospect of imprisonment and its hardships more daunting, so I'm off tomorrow, incognito. I will take the train to Vera Cruz and then a steamer to Campeche. Thus, far from the fray, I can continue the work.

The heat of Campeche and the sea breeze will be a welcome change, and it will be good to see my girls again.

Pancha's two nieces met her at the dock: Lulu, radiant and tittering with hugs and kisses, and Ruby hanging back after a peck on the cheek.

"About to arrest you again, were they?" Ruby said, taking Pancha's bag and portable writing desk. "Are you compromising us with your presence, Tía?"

"I wouldn't think so, my dear. I'm a troublesome old woman, but not worth the manpower to track me down."

"Are you all right, Auntie?" Lulu fussed.

"I'm fine, dear." Pancha said, patting Lulu's cheek. "My, you are aglow!"

"She has a beau," Ruby said with a curl of the lip.

Lulu blushed and swallowed a grin. "Please be happy for me, Tía. You know I'm not cut out to be a feminist or a suffragist, anarchaiquist, or whatever. And I don't want to be stuck in the studio the rest of my life. You know I've always hated it."

"But you're rather good at the work, aren't you?"

Lulu waved the comment away as if it were a criticism. She slipped her arm into her aunt's.

"When you meet Ernesto, you must promise me to be on your best behavior." She lowered her voice conspiratorially, "He doesn't approve of women in public life."

Pancha raised her eyebrows and Ruby grinned.

"I can't wait for the two of you to meet," Ruby said.

Lulu squeezed her aunt's arm. "Oh, yes. I do so want you to meet him!"

"Well, where is this prince charming?"

"You just missed him," Lulu pouted. "He left for his hacienda last week."

"Ay no, Lulita! Not an hacendado. Please not that!" Pancha said.

Ruby laughed. "She's exaggerating. According to the man himself, it's nothing grand at all. Just a rancho. Maybe a peon or two," she added maliciously.

"A peon or two too many! Lulu you can't!"

"But, Tía, he's a wonderful man!"

"Don't forget the children, Lulu," Ruby added.

"Children?" Pancha said.

"He has three," Ruby said.

"Three children! Ay no, Lulu!"

Later when Ruby and Pancha were alone, Pancha asked her about Lulu's romance.

"Ruby, are they serious?"

"I expect so, Tía. He hasn't proposed or anything, but he comes to Campeche pretty regularly. I wonder that he can afford it. I hear agriculture prices are very low these days."

"What do you think of him?"

Ruby shrugged. "He's an old stick in the mud. But he does seem quite fond of Lulu."

"But what about you? If she marries him and goes off to live in the campo, what will happen to you and the business?"

Ruby bristled. "I'll be on my own. Like you."

Pancha thought that it wasn't the same at all. When she was teaching she'd been surrounded by students and colleagues, and she could count on a salary, meagre though it was. And now she had the support of the committee and their newspaper.

"But, my dear," Pancha said, "Can you run the business on your own?"

"I'll have to, won't I?" she said with bravado, but Pancha saw a flash of uncertainty.

"Maybe I could come help for awhile."

Ruby did not disguise her alarm. "No thank you, Tía. You'd probably scare away all our customers and get me shut down by the police. Likely thrown in jail, to boot."

Several days later Pancha was observing her nieces and pondering the possibility of Lulu marrying.

"I've drafted an advertisement," Lulu announced to Ruby. She read:

> *Fotografía Eckart, known throughout the city for its quality photography, now offers its services to amateur photographers of all ilks.*

"I don't think 'ilks' is the word you want," Pancha said.
Lulu nodded and scribbled on the paper.

> *…offers its services to the amateur photographers of Campeche. You can entrust your film to us. We will develop it with the same care and expertise that we apply to our studio photography.*

"What a clever idea," Pancha said.
"Let me see." Ruby took the sheet of paper. The palms and fingers of her hands were stained with dark splotches from the silver nitrate she used in the darkroom and there were burn scars from an accident with the flashlamp.
Lulu wrinkled her nose. "Couldn't you wear gloves to hide those hands?"
Ruby ignored her. "Is that how you spell 'amateur'?"
"It's how everyone spells 'amateur'."
"And 'expertise'?"
"Ruby! Please. You can't even spell 'burro'."
"Alright. But can we afford an ad like this?"
"We've talked about this. If we run it for one month, the developing of ten rolls will cover the cost, and at the same time it serves as an advertisement for our studio photographs."
"Ten rolls!"

"That includes the cost of paper and chemicals. And remember, you photographers are like opium-eaters. Once we get a customer to bring their film in for developing, it will be steady income."

"And a waste of my time on the dreck of dilettantes!"

"Ruby, be practical! Think of the income."

"Fine," she grumbled. "When will it start?"

"I'll take it over to the newspaper now. Tía, want to come?"

Ruby placed her hand on Lulu's arm. "Would you wait until the next appointment gets here?"

"The Carvajals?" Lulu said. She checked the time and nodded reluctantly. "Fine, I'll greet them and get them situated, although you could do it yourself."

Ruby waggled her fingers in the air. "With these disgraceful hands?"

"I'll have to put it on account, you know, the advertisement," Lulu said as Ruby drifted backwards towards the curtained door of the studio.

"I know you'll take care of it."

Lulu sighed. "Certainly! Don't mind me. You just go back to playing the grand artiste."

Ruby smiled and slipped through the curtain.

Pancha decided that the sisters were not as ill-matched as they seemed. How, she wondered, were they going to function apart?

It was before dawn when Meche stole outside. She wasn't running away—she was heading for Pedro Mu's house.

She often escaped the house for the fields, although not usually this early. And she particularly liked trailing after Pedro. His manner was calm, but not somber, and she liked the curve of his nose and his alert, dark-brown eyes. She knew he only tolerated her because he saw no way to get rid of her, but there was much she wanted to learn from him. She wished he was her older brother or an uncle, and not one of the sharecroppers—her father allocated a portion of land to him to farm in exchange for a percentage of the crop and his working for him on Mondays. Pedro worked other days, too, for wages, but not today, and she was eager to catch him before he left for his field.

Today he would be getting it ready to burn in preparation for next month's planting of the corn. She was especially curious about the planting—the measuring and laying out of the field with its prayers and rituals—but today was important, too. She wanted to follow the process start to finish.

That morning the air was already thick with smoke, as it had been all week—fields were being burned throughout the region. With a canteen slung around her neck, she followed Pedro and his male relatives out to the field, a good half-hour walk. She wore a broad-rimmed straw hat, lace-up boots—ankle-high and pointy-toed—and a drop-waist dress. Being twelve years old, she was, thankfully, too young for that whalebone nonsense, but she wished she could wear a huipil like the women in Pedro's family. The light cotton hung loose from the shoulders, with no waistline at all, or hipline, those annoying sweat-makers.

When they reached the milpa, the men set to slashing the dried out cornstalks with their machetes. They made brush piles, and Meche, ignoring Pedro's protests and worried looks, helped carry stalks and branches to the piles. Pedro raked debris away from several trees that he wanted to save for their shade, and the men dug a fire line around the field to control the blaze.

It was not yet five in the morning, and Soli and Lalo were asleep; their father, once again in Campeche City. But Meche was wide awake, excited about the day's work ahead. A month had passed since she'd helped clear the field, and today Pedro and the others would lay it out. She crept from the house and then rushed to the track between the cluster of workers' huts and the swidden field.

Pedro's face turned stern when he saw her, and he tried to send her home.

"This is man's work, laying out the milpa."

"Please, Pedro. I'll stay at a distance and just watch. I promise."

"But señorita, you are female."

"Yes, but I am just a child, as everyone is so fond of telling me."

He strode off, trying to ignore her.

She called after him. "You go ahead. Don't give me a second thought. If I get bit by a snake, I'm sure my father won't blame you."

Pedro stopped, hung his head, not in shame but in anger. That gave her pause—it was not an emotion he often showed—but she did not back down.

His brother-in-law came out to meet him on the path. Unlike Pedro, Santiago was talkative, with quick, jerky movements.

"What's wrong?" he asked in Mayan. "Are we not ready to measure the milpa? I have the sak'hu."

Meche caught up with them, eyes shining—she'd heard of the sacred drink.

"Really? Can I see?" she said.

Santiago frowned. "Señorita," he said, and doffed his hat.

"The señorita insists on watching us lay out the field." Pedro said.

Santiago gave him a worried look, but smiled when he turned to Meche. "But, little señorita,…" he said.

"Don't waste your breath," Pedro said.

The two men regarded each other gravely. They were probably thinking that to remove her one of them would have to throw her over his shoulder, and that would never do. Besides, although each was more than strong enough, she'd be an awkward bundle, especially if she struggled—neither of them was more than a couple inches taller than Meche. Then there was the time lost, the scene of returning her to the house, waking the whole household…

"Maybe your abuela would accompany her," Pedro suggested, "to forestall any problems and…" he lowered his voice, "keep the Santos Padres of the Winds appeased."

Santiago looked doubtful, but he returned home to ask.

"If *Chiich* María Inés consents to chaperone, you may come along," Pedro said, "but you must stay by her side and do what she says. Remember, it is unseemly to chatter in the fields. This is sacred business, measuring the field, and one must be respectful. We do this our way, the way that works, the way it's always been done."

Pedro looked down at his sandals, his brow was furrowed and the hand holding his machete tapped against his thigh. After several moments he said, "Please, Señorita Meche. Reconsider. We measure the milpa and make the required sacrifices. There's nothing to see, but it's serious. And it's private."

In response, Meche dug in, hands on hips. At that moment Santiago returned. "Mi abuela wants to meet this upstart—her word, little señorita, not mine. Please, follow that path. It's the third house. You'll find my chiich sitting under the tamarind tree."

Meche stuck out her chin and squinted at them. "Is this a trick to get rid of me?"

"No, little señorita, my grandmother says she is willing. Perhaps. She must meet you first."

Pedro and Santiago waited for her to start down the path before continuing on towards the field. Although the sun hadn't yet risen, it was easy to follow the track of white earth.

When left to their own devices, the Maya started working before dawn, so that by the time the sun reached its zenith, they had already put in a good day's work and would head home. They thought it crazy how late the whites got up, wasting the freshest part of the day and then working through the heat of the afternoon. So when Meche arrived at the houses—oval huts whose walls were formed of upright sticks and topped with thatched roofs—the women were busy sweeping the dirt floor of their houses and washing clothing, because after lunch everyone would bathe and put on fresh clothes.

In the milky pre-dawn light, Meche saw an old woman sitting on a bench under a tamarind, its broad branches profuse with fern-like leaves. The white of her huipil glowed—the embroidered flowers that still looked black would bloom red and yellow when the sun rose. As Meche got closer, she started making out details—the woman was tiny, as shriveled as an old potato, her white hair bound up in a knot, a shawl about her shoulders. She was sipping from an earthenware cup held between her hands—atole, judging from the sweetish, earthy smell that wafted from it.

"Good morning, Chiich. I'm María Mercedes Hernández Cruz." Meche curtsied. "I'm pleased to meet you."

Doña Maria Inés did not look up from her cup.

"May we go to the new field, Abuela. I need to see how they do the measuring," she said in Mayan. "Now, please?"

Doña María Inés sighed. "Child, the Gods value respect and patience. Such rushing would displease them."

Meche noticed that the old lady said Gods. Most Mayans were careful to say God, singular, around white people.

"Ma' taali' teni'," Meche apologized.

"…And it's a long walk for an old woman."

It was Meche who sighed this time. She felt in her pockets, but she already knew she had no coins.

The old lady glared at her. "That's not what I meant."

Then what? Meche wondered what her sister would do. Soli seemed to have no trouble ingratiating herself with grown-ups.

"Sit here, until I finish my atole," the old woman said as if reading her thoughts. "If you can do that without prattling, I will consider taking you."

Meche made as if she were Soli. "Of course, Grandmother," she said and sat with her ankles crossed, her hands folded in her lap and her thoughts squirreling about in her head.

In the end, Meche never got to see the measuring of the field. Doña María Inés needed to do this, then that, then the other, all excruciatingly slowly. Several times, angry and disappointed to the point of tears, Meche almost flounced off, but each time the old women enticed her with a tidbit of knowledge, speaking to her in a quiet voice and short repetitive sentences. In the end Meche found that spending time with Doña María Inés was an unexpected balm—the old woman radiated a warm calm whose tendrils drew Meche in, caressed her and held her gently. She found she could not be truly angry with her—well, a bit irritated, yes.

Before she left, Meche said, "Chiich, would you at least take me to the milpa when they plant?"

Doña María Inés shrugged. "I have good days and bad days. We'll see."

When Meche got home, Soli was already ladling out the soup for the first course of the midday meal. She plopped in her chair.

Soli looked at Meche askance. "Where were you?"

"I wanted to watch Pedro Mu measure one of the swidden fields."

"Meche!" Soli said, scandalized.

"I need to understand how the farm works."

"What's to understand? The sharecroppers pay our family its due.

Beyond that, whatever goes on in those fields is none of your business."

"That's fine for you to say, you've got the house!"

"What do you mean? It's our house!"

"But you run it." Meche said, thinking the job tedious and boring and that Soli was welcome to it. "And I want to run the farm."

There, she'd said it aloud, and it felt good.

Soli shook her head in disbelief. "Father would never let you."

"He will when I know as much, no, when I know more than he does. And I will."

"When the time comes, running Baalam Kab will fall to Lalo."

"Lalo!" Meche scoffed.

"He won't always be a little boy. And you, you shouldn't be traipsing about with the workers!"

Meche frowned. "The truth is Pedro wouldn't let me go with him."

"Thank goodness for that."

"I ended up spending the day with his brother-in-law's grandmother."

"Oh?"

It was clear that Soli was undecided as to whether that was an improvement or not.

"Yes, all very proper," Meche said. "Annoyingly so. Look, Soli, the abuela is very old, and I'd like to do something nice for her."

"Are you asking my advice?"

"Yes. I don't know why it is, but you're nice, and I'm not."

Soli started to contradict her, but stopped and said, "Well, you could ask Susana de los Ángeles to make up a basket from the pantry, say some jam, some bread. You can leave it to Susana de los Ángeles."

Meche frowned. She wasn't on the best of terms with Susana de los Ángeles. Besides, Meche wasn't sure what she would say to such a request —Susana de los Ángeles kept herself somewhat apart from the Maya. She was Campechan born and bred, but descended from one of the Aztec families that had come to Campeche with the Spanish conquistadors. In fact her last name was Azteca. No huipil for her—she wore a full skirt and two braids down her back tied together at the ends with red yarn.

"Well," Soli said, reading Meche's mind. "Ask her to do it, and I'll check it over."

Soli was sound asleep when Lalo padded into her and Meche's room. At Soli's side of the bed, he whispered her name and patted her cheek. When Soli opened her eyes, he was peering into her face from inches away. She stifled a groan. Lalo often climbed into bed with them, but he squirmed and kicked so, it was hard to sleep with him.

"Ay, Lalo! Go around and climb in with Meche," she whispered, slipping back into sleep.

"Meche's not here."

"Of course she is," she muttered.

"She's not!" he said, snuggling up to her back from Meche's side of the bed.

Soli jolted awake. The room was dark, and she got up and opened the shutters. The sky appeared pearly with the palest of light just before dawn, and she saw that Meche's side of the bed was indeed empty and that on Soli's side, Lalo had already fallen asleep, baby snores coming out of his open mouth.

Soli's stomach flip-flopped. Pushing down panic, she put on her slippers and dressing gown. Where could Meche be?

When she reached the dining room, she could hear Susana de los Ángeles already moving about in the kitchen. Soli saw her look of surprise when she entered.

"Good morning," Soli said. "Have you seen Meche?"

"At this hour? No, niña."

Soli went back to her room and got dressed, an infuriatingly slow process now that she wore a corset, blouses with a myriad of small buttons, and boots that required a button hook. She must, she thought, look composed, be careful not to raise a general alarm. Or was that what she should do? No, she must not be seen as hysterical. She brushed out her hair and tied the strands above her ears at the back of her head with a ribbon. The light was slightly brighter now and she saw Meche's white nightgown against the white sheets. She stared at it a moment, feeling hollow. Her fearless, headstrong sister! Lord knew what she might be up to. Soli reined in images of Meche being carried off by a jaguar, bitten by a snake, falling into a well.

"She's fine," Soli said aloud, a tremor in her voice, and thought, she's not stupid, just incredibly thoughtless.

Soli would have to ask for Don Eusebio's help. When their father was away, the foreman slept in a hammock on the gallery of the back service patio, so he would be easy to locate. But she found him in the kitchen with a cup of coffee, flirting with Susana de los Ángeles.

When told of the situation, he strode into the yard and shouted out names and orders. Juan, one of the peons, set to saddling Don Eusebio's horse. Juan's two boys, who had just delivered firewood and water to Susana de los Ángeles for the day's cooking, ran home to ask if anyone had seen the young señorita. Before long, Don Eusebio had learned of Meche's whereabouts and was riding out to the Mus' milpa to bring her back.

Pedro was lifting the cup of sak'hu to the five directions when he saw the dust that announced a rider in the distance—only the patrón and the foreman rode horses. Santiago lifted his hand to his eyes, but Pedro persisted with the prayer—calling on the Santo Padre of the East Wind, the Santo Padre of the West Wind, of the North, the South—the milpa was their truest church and he refused to be distracted. It would be a lack of respect that the four Lords of the Winds would not forgive.

Meche saw the dust too. She had wrangled her way into watching the planting, but she and Chiich María Inés stood at such a distance that Pedro was a small figure, and Meche could not hear his words. She'd been warned about disrespectful noise, and she hoped the rider, no doubt Don Eusebio, would not arrive too quickly or in too foul a mood. She did not want to be blamed if something went wrong and the spirits took offense. The aluxob might then guide the rains past Pedro's field, put a snake in his path or make his machete slip. Even if she didn't believe, and she hadn't made up her mind yet whether she did or not, Pedro's and

Chiich's reverence was infectious. Besides, fifteen percent of the crop belonged to her family—it was in her best interest for it to do well.

Don Eusebio pulled to a halt in front of Meche, an old mare in tow.

"Your horse, señorita. You are needed at the house. Now!"

Her instinct was to rebel, but seeing Doña María Inés's stony face, she mounted without protest. She felt sick. She prodded the horse and rode away from Don Eusebio, her cheeks burning. She fumed all the way home, and stormed into the kitchen.

"María Mercedes!" Soli began to scold.

Meche passed her without a glance or a word.

The next days were long for everyone—Meche refused to talk to Soli, and little Lalo, always a sponge for emotion, was whiney and combative by turns. On the third morning Meche went to the kitchen with a basket and set to pulling items from the pantry shelves.

"Do you have Señorita Soli's permission to take these things?" Susana de los Ángeles challenged.

"I don't need permission—it's my house."

Susana de los Ángeles took a jar of preserves from her. "Not that one," she said.

Soli came in, and Susana de los Ángeles turned to her, "Ay, Señorita Soli, la Meche is taking all these things to that old witch."

"It's the least we can do after ruining the planting ceremony," Meche said.

Soli looked like she was about to protest, but under Meche's glare, she bit her lip.

After a moment Soli said, "I'll go with you."

"No. You won't!"

As Meche walked along the path to the cluster of houses where she would find Doña María Inés, the women and children disappeared from sight—she caught only glimpses, flashes of white as someone ducked into one or another of the oval huts.

Only Doña María Inés remained, sitting on her bench under the tamarind tree as usual. So maybe, Meche thought, she didn't blame Meche for what happened at the milpa. Or, maybe she just couldn't move fast enough to vanish.

"Hello, Grandmother," Meche called.

The old woman ignored her, and Meche's heart sank.

"I'm sorry about Don Eusebio, Chiich."

Silence.

Just when Meche could bear the old woman's rebuff no longer, and her mouth filled with angry, hateful words, jostling to be let loose, Doña María Inés shook her head sadly and looked up at her.

Her gaze was stinging.

"It is a dangerous time for our family."

Meche's pride cracked. Abashed, she stared at the ground.

"I am sorry, truly, if Don Eusebio, if I, we, ruined the sak'hu ceremony," she stammered.

Doña María Inés nodded—in agreement, not in pardon. "It is feared that the offering was not accepted," she said.

Meche lifted her basket. "I brought some things. Maybe... Maybe you can use some of it for a new offering."

Silence.

"The time is dangerous," Doña María Inés repeated, and looked away.

Meche's stomach was one knot; her heart, another. Her instinct was to run away. But the thought of Pedro angry at her forever, of the grandmother shunning her forever... It was too terrible. There must be something she could do.

"Isabel," the old woman called out, and Santiago's wife peaked out of the doorway of one of the houses. "I want to go inside," *Chiich* said to her, even though Meche was standing right there and could have helped her up.

Meche headed home, her vision blurred by tears. The old woman's rejection hurt more than she ever could have imagined. When she arrived at the house, it occurred to her that what was needed for an offering wasn't jam or piloncillo sugar, but báalche. Well, she didn't have any of the bark and honey drink, but surely something else alcoholic would be the next best thing. She went straight to the cupboard in her father's office, and snatching a bottle of rum, ran back to Chiich. This time she surprised several of the women in their yards.

"Look, Grandmother. Surely the gods will accept this. Surely they know this is all my fault and won't let anything happen to Pedro or Santiago, or the crop."

The old lady accepted the bottle and gave a little nod. "I have been remembering," she said. "It's what old people do best, remembering."

The way she settled herself on her bench, Meche knew she was about to tell a story.

"When I was a girl, people still told this story. People talked of the thing that had happened a long time before. It was hundreds of years earlier. Hundreds. A peon on an hacienda had a child. A daughter he had. He worried about this daughter. The hacendado, he noticed her too much. The hacendado saw the girl. She was watched. The hacendado lived in a big house. He ordered the peon to send his daughter to work in the big house. The father heard the hacendado. He told the mother. The mother heard the news. They worried about the girl. The mother and the father. Worry ate at them. They stalled. They played for time. They said she was ill. Sick and feverish.

"The peon did a ceremony. He asked for protection for his daughter, his child. He pled to the One True God and Our Mother Mary. He begged St. Joseph. He asked the chac-ob, the helping spirits, the spirits who protect us at night. He asked God and Mary. The saints were asked. The chac-ob were pled to.

"But the father was distraught. He was in a real state. Worried. Unhappy. So he lost his place in the prayers. The prayers were ruined, spoiled. The ceremony was a mess. The one True God and Mother Mary were not pleased. He offended them. He displeased the chac-ob. The chac-ob were offended. The special beings, they refused his offerings. The father knew the prayers had failed. He'd muddled them good. He knew they'd turned out bad because that night his daughter fell sick with a fever. A real fever. Deathly ill. She was nudging death. Death was nudging her.

"The father went to the h-men, the holy man, and begged for his help. 'Help me,' he begged. But it was a Wednesday. Wednesday was the day, and on Wednesday the h-men cannot communicate with the Santos Padres of the Winds and the chac-ob. Only on Tuesday and Friday. Those are the days. Thus is it written in the old calendars. The father feared his daughter would not survive until Friday. Friday was a long time away. He was distressed. His wife was distressed.

"The man went to a mound, a hillock. He walked to it. The man, the father walked. It was said to once have been a temple, a sacred place. A holy temple. He began to set up an altar. He aligned it to the directions as was fitting. With care the altar was being made. An old man with a long beard came along. An old geezer, ancient. He came to the altar. The father saw the old old man. The old man addressed the father. He asked him something. He asked what he was doing. The father did not want to be disrespectful. But he had a ceremony to do. He wanted to do everything right and correct, proper, in order to save his daughter. He did not want his child to die.

"'I'm sorry, old man, but I cannot talk now,' he said. 'I must perform this ceremony perfectly. My prayers must be exactly right. Now is not the time to talk. Forgive me.'

"The old man stood aside. He waited, and the father finished the altar. He recited the prayers. He did the ceremony. Prayers were said. He begged the One True God and Mother Mary and all the spirit beings to accept his humble offering. The offering was heartfelt. As the ceremony progressed, the father felt more and more calm, more serene. He offered báalche to the four directions and to the vertical axis, He knew the offering was accepted because he felt lighter. The father felt at peace. After a respectful time, the father looked up and saw the old man.

"'Father,' he said, 'please have some of this báalche. The Gods have taken its essence. The offering was accepted. Please drink.'

"The old man asked why he was asking for protection. The father told him. The old man heard.

"The old man took the gourd. The liquor was downed in one gulp. He drank all of it. He drank it fast. And then he belched. It was a huge belch he let out. A roar of a belch was heard. Then the old man pulled out a huge cigar. He lit it with a bolt of lightening. Zas! The cigar was lit and smoke rose from the tobacco. That's when the man understood. The man knew. This was one of the four Lords of the Winds, one of the Santos Padres of the Winds. The man was astonished. He felt awe. So much awe, he fell into a faint. He dropped to the ground.

"When he awoke, it was night. The Lord of the Wind was gone. He was alone. The Lord of the Wind had left. Fearful, the man made his way home in the dark, but the alux were with him. They protected him. He was watched over. He heard a jaguar cry, but it was moving away from him. The jaguar took no interest in him. The sound, the cry became distant. He was safe from the jaguar. The moon came out. The moon was bright and it came out. He could see the track home. When he got to his house, his daughter was sitting up. She was not dying. She was well."

Doña María Inés had come to the end of the story, and she now spoke to Meche in her everyday voice. "So, hija, while the gods insist on respect and correctness, they understand and judge the heart of the supplicant. This I have remembered. We will make another offering."

With that she sent Meche off with her blessing, as if she were her own grandchild, and Meche felt a lightness that stayed with her until she crossed the threshold of her house.

The old woman's daughter brought her some star-apple water. "That girl should stick to her father's house and leave us be."

"She feels herself alone, so she comes to us. She's an in-between spirit."

"Why did you tell her the story like that? 'Hundreds of years ago!'"

"Age gives weight to a story."

The thing was, as her daughter knew, Doña María Inés, herself, was the girl in the story. In her father's faint, he'd had a dream. And the very night of her recovery, they stole away, making their way south and east. In a village there, they met a young man who agreed to lead them into the jungle to one of the illegal pueblos kept hidden from the whites and mestizos. But on the trip, she'd fallen in love with their guide. Within a year María Inés was a young bride living with him in the village where they met, while her parents remained invisible in a jungle pueblo.

Soli wondered if she been hard on Meche because Papá was absent? Or was Meche just more out of control with him gone? Either way, Soli was lonely: she missed their father, away again in Campeche City, and every time she reached out to Meche, Meche backed away. It was as if she and her sister stood on the opposite sides of a smoldering cornfield, the smoke stinging Soli's eyes. She had Susana de los Ángeles for company, but she missed the camaraderie of a sister.

True, Meche had started talking to her again, but it seemed to be only to harangue her about their bedroom. Apparently the issue was that it faced west, which, Meche claimed, was the direction of night creatures and creepy-crawlies and death.

"But east, Soli, east is the direction of all good things, good things to eat, of life, don't you see? And Lalo's room is east-facing."

Meche's insistent voice bore into Soli. She was tired and worried. The incidents with Meche and the Mus were upsetting, their father should have been back by now, and on top of everything else, Don Eusebio, the overseer, was on her mind.

"Soli, you're not listening to me!"

"Of course I am."

"Then say something."

"Fine. I think it's a bunch of claptrap."

Meche, hands on hips, glared at her. "I don't care if you believe it or not."

"Good, because I don't."

"You can't keep me from moving into Lalo's room!" Meche said.

Lalo slept in a nursery off their parents' bedroom on the opposite side of the patio. That Meche gave credence to this nonsense about the directions was exasperating. That she didn't seem concerned about leaving Soli behind in the nasty west hurt her feelings. And if it were all a pretense to get out of sharing a room with her? That, too, would wound her deeply.

"But the room is too small!" Soli said. "You would barely fit in his little bed. I'd have to bring Lalo to sleep in here, and you know how he kicks and sprawls. I'm not going to do that, not to cater to some silly superstition you've got into your head."

"It's not superstition, and it's not silly. And it's not your decision!"

"Fine. When Papá gets back from Campeche City, pester him about it," she said, thinking, *see where that gets you.*

Susana de los Ángeles was in the kitchen with Señorita Soli, wrapping tamales in banana leaves, when Don Eusebio came to the open door. Soli had her back to him, but Susana de los Ángeles saw him pause and hungrily appraise the freshness of the girl's 15 years—her trim figure in a sand-colored skirt and white blouse, the large white apron bow at her waist, her dark-brown hair, a pink ribbon in it, hanging down her back.

She resembled her mother more everyday. Don Eusebio had commented on it to Susana de los Ángeles. She was aware that he'd had a huge crush on Doña Blanca Estela, back when he was a young man, all cow-eyed and tongue-tied around the boss's wife.

Señorita Soli turned to see him. He made his eyes soft and adoring, but she and Susana de los Ángeles had seen the other look. Soli's face reddened.

"Señorita Soli," he said, with a slight bow.

"Would you mind finishing, Susana de los Ángeles?" Soli said, a bit flustered. "I'd better check on Lalito."

Señorita Meche had just come to the doorway from the dining room, and Señorita Soli almost walked into her.

La Meche glowered at Don Eusebio and stuck her tongue out at him. She turned and followed Soli.

What was he thinking, Susana wondered. He had to know that the boss would never allow him to court his daughter. But if the girl fell in love with him, that could be a different story. Things might happen. Was that his game? The girl was at a vulnerable age, with no young men of her own age and class about. And Don Ernesto was away much more than was wise. Leaving the fox guarding the henhouse! Susana would have to keep her eyes peeled. Maybe she should broach the subject with Soli. Maybe with Don Ernesto.

Eusebio had a woman, Mirza Francisca. Everyone knew about her, including the boss, but Eusebio had recently sent her and the kids packing. Not far—one ranchería over. Out of sight, but close enough to ride over to see her when so moved.

Susana did not like the way he was gazing after Soli.

"Hey!" she said.

He turned to her, slowly.

"She's not a sack of beans, you know."

He smiled at her. "How about a cup of coffee, guapa?"

She slammed an earthenware mug down, and when he reached for her, she slapped at his hand, without a glimmer of a smile.

Meche caught up with Soli in the interior patio.

"Soli!"

Soli, miserable, turned to her. "Not now, Meche."

"I don't like the way Don Eusebio looks at you."

Soli was shaking. "I don't either."

Meche felt a rush of protectiveness towards her sister. It was unsettling to see her unnerved like this. She placed her hands on Soli's arms, as if to steady her.

"Are you going to tell Father?"

"How can I? Papá relies on him. And now that he's away so often, we have to rely on him too."

"Then I'll tell him."

"No, Meche, please don't. Don Eusebio's never done anything. He's never even said anything."

Meche squeezed Soli's arms, and Soli rested her forehead against Meche's.

"Well, he'd better not," Meche said. "That's all I have to say."

1 9 0 4...

Mexico City | Pancha's Diary

Saturday, *November 26, 1904*
Mexico City, D.F.

The day may be mild, but my mood is cold and damp. I can't bear the thought of being in this city for yet another presidential inauguration: all the bunting and folderol, all the false hoopla. We all knew what the outcome of the election would be, and yet I am as depressed as if I'd had hope. Twenty-seven years now that reactionary son of a bitch has been in power, 27 and counting. It's as tedious as it is infuriating,.

I'm sure there are men who actually do vote for Díaz, for what they calculate they can get from his corrupt rule, or perhaps from fear of an alternative to his so-called "Order and Progress." Zúñiga y Miranda, that perennial candidate, claims, again, that he won the election, that the election was, once again, a fraud. I don't know if that stick of a man won or lost, but who can believe he received zero votes? Zero! Presumably he, at least, voted for himself. In addition to everything else, Díaz insults our intelligence. He banks on our credulity and on our timidity.

So, in order to avoid another black December 1st, I've decided to decamp to Campeche and stay for the holidays. At least there will be sun there, and family, as well as the ocean, the tang of salt in the air and my favorite fruits and seafood. I'm working on an article about the travesty of another Díaz term; in lieu of democracy, institutions and ideas, he's turning our nation's citizens into a passel of fawners at best, and prostitutes at worst. If I can finish tomorrow, I'll turn it in first thing Monday and make my escape.

...

Monday, November 28, 1904
Vera Cruz, Vera Cruz

I am spending the night with Mirta's sister, Jacinta, who does not approve of her little sister having gone off to the capital to work in a factory. Mercifully, Jacinta is unaware of Mirta's labor activities, so I am keeping mum, playing the part of a simple retired teacher, for Mirta does not want her to worry any more than she already does.

I am bunking with the children, who have been put on blankets on the floor. Jacinta's husband works on the docks, and hasn't gotten home yet. Tomorrow I take a steamer to Campeche.

Earlier today, as the train left the altiplano behind (winding through lush green hills, the air growing thicker and warmer as we descended) my spirits lifted and my thoughts turned toward what awaits me in Campeche. It's been almost a year since poor María Petrona died, and I am curious how my great-nieces and their father are doing without her iron grip on the family.

...

Monday, December 6, 1904
Campeche, Campeche

This visit has been instructive. One doesn't really understand the underpinnings of a marriage until one of the spouses is gone. Having been here a week now, I would revise what I termed my niece's "iron grip," to her "steadying hand." I see now that Paul's adventurous, restless spirit (which carried him all the way from northern Germany to Texas, and then from Texas here to the south of Mexico, that impelled him to desert his studies at a seminary to become a surveyor, and then abandon that trade to take up photography) was ultimately in search of a tether, and that tether, chafing as it was at times, was Petrona. I shall never know what she gained from him in exchange, apart from two daughters. Of course, she was thirty when they married. I despise the term old maid, but in this case it is perhaps apt. I expect, also, that she valued the social status of marrying a European, eager, too, to overwhelm, or at least dilute, the Tun line of the family with the introduction of a Teutonic bloodline. Such is the insidious poison of our colonial caste system. Although abolished when we gained independence, it persists in the national psyche. It is like a colony of termites eating its way through our society, riddling it with holes, undermining any progress we manage to achieve. And yet I can, and do, envision the day it is finally eradicated.

As for Paul and daughters, I am content to see that they are carrying on reasonably well. Although Paul looks less than hardy these days, a bit grey. Mourning or bad health? He and Ruby are united in all things photographic. It's Lulu who is a bit on the outs. She is glad to have me here to talk to about her mother, whom she misses terribly; the others prefer not to speak of her.

Although Petrona hated the photography studio, now, in her absence, it is serving as an important focal point for holding the family together. I've never been an advocate for, or devotee to, the construct of family (with its inherent subjugation of women, and of children, too), but in this case I am glad they have each other. And yet, how the girls squabble! I thought they would grow out of it. And under the circumstances, losing their mother, I expected some solidarity, some sisterly loving kindness. Their bickering quite wears on me. If only I could make them see that there are true enemies out there, and life-and-death obstacles to overcome, the struggle for liberty that needs be fought!

Blanca Estela stroked her belly absent-mindedly as she observed her daughters with a soft gaze and fond regard. Standing in the dining room doorway, she could see Soli, age ten, at the little table in the corner of the interior patio, head bent, pencil in hand, her attention switching back and forth between her notebook and textbook, while Meche, two years younger, sat on the edge of the small fountain, swinging her legs and trailing her fingers in the water, her pencil tucked over her ear.

Father Patricio used to trek out to the rancho every couple weeks to instruct the girls for a few hours. Blanca Estela would then help them with their studies until his next visit. Sometimes he spent the night, although he usually timed things to take advantage of the comforts and attractions of nearby Hacienda Chun Ek, whose owner, like himself, was a devotee of chess.

The girls could now read the catechism book, recite the answers to the questions, write simple notes of thanks or condolence, and, since Father Patricio was relatively enlightened, add and subtract three-digit numbers. And so, earlier that year the priest had declared the girls' education complete. Blanca Estela adamantly disagreed with him. Her own education had been scanty at best, and she wanted better for her daughters. Father Patricio rejected her entreaties, adding that he was getting too old to be traipsing about the campo. But he did help her persuade Ernesto that it was his Christian duty to employ a tutor to teach the catechism to the children of the rancho's workers and, since their mother was so insistent, he might also tutor the little Señoritas Hernández. Ernesto grudgingly acquiesced.

Father Patricio found a tutor for them, but the isolation of Baalam Kab did not suit the young man. He might have cut a fine figure in town, but in the campo he was morose and skittish to the extreme. It did not help any that Meche loved regaling him with gruesome stories about death in the countryside: machetes, snakes, jaguars and even Xtabay, the beautiful forest spirit with flowing black hair who seduced men and led them to their death.

Blanca Estela did not reprimand Meche for this. What kind of man needed protection from an eight-year-old girl?

After several months, when they literally saw the back of him as he and Don Eusebio drove away in the wagon, Ernesto said, "Good riddance," and the little girls ran inside giggling, where they held hands and jumped up and down. Blanca Estela felt lighter, too. She'd found the tutor to be a dampening spirit in the house. But then, to her dismay, Ernesto balked at finding a replacement. He said it was all fine and well for a big hacienda like Chun Ek to back a school for the children of their many peons, but he was not made of money. Baalam Kab was just a simple rancho with a handful of workers. And as for the girls, he declared that what they needed was practical training. He envisioned them marrying rancheros or even hacendados in the region, and what they needed to know was not European history or Latin, but practical skills essential for housekeeping on a remote agricultural concern: cooking and food preservation, sewing and mending, medicaments and the treatment of fevers and injuries, as well as how to oversee workers and do household bookkeeping.

Blanca Estela could not get him to budge. At least for now, in the tutor's wake, she had the textbooks he'd brought for the girls, and she'd observed how he'd organized their studies.

After Soli and Meche went to bed, she would study their books to keep ahead of them.

Watching the girls now, she didn't know which one worried her more, her little pig-headed Meche or Soli. Soli was such a good little girl. Would she learn to stand up for herself? What if she arrived at a certain age and rebelled, with disastrous consequences? What if she just never learned to have fun?

Blanca Estela roused herself. "Girls, come with me," she said.

Meche jumped up, and Soli rushed to finish the sentence she was writing.

That evening Blanca Estela lay in bed next to Ernesto. He brushed a stray hair back from her ear and then rested his hand on the mound of her stomach.

"Mi cielo," he said, "do you think it's such a good idea for you to teach our daughters to shoot?"

"Well, I did ask you to do it."

"But they're just little girls, young and innocent."

"You thought it was important to teach me when I came to live here. I was pretty young, and totally innocent." She poked him with her elbow.

"But when you came here, my brave little bride, the War of the Castes was still raging."

"You know my father tried to forbid me from coming here until the war was over."

"I'm glad you didn't listen to him. It was agony being apart from you."

"I felt the same.

"Ernesto, about the girls: the fighting may be over around here, but the war hasn't ended, not really. Not in Yucatán. It's only been, what, three years ago that General Bravo succeeded in occupying Chan Santa Cruz, and he's still there, isn't he? What if the government withdraws the army? What if unrest returns here? What I'm saying is one never knows what's coming. Consider the girls learning about guns part of their 'practical' education."

He ignored the intonation she put on "practical."

"I leave our daughters' education in your beautiful and capable hands."

"If this baby is a boy, I wonder if you will be so lackadaisical about his education."

"There's nothing lackadaisical about you, mi cielo. I know you will do an excellent job of educating all our children. Still…"

"What?"

"The idea of a gun in little Meche's hands is a bit frightening."

Blanca Estela laughed. "You should see her. She is so serious, so intent. And most keen to impress you. She keeps asking when we can show you."

"And Soli?"

"Oh, she hates it. The gun is heavy, the oil is messy, the smell of gunpowder is stinky. And the noise! She can't stand the noise. Meche pretends to adore it all, but that's just to annoy her big sister. But Soli applies herself. She's actually the better shot."

"Poor little Soli. I feel we're corrupting her."

"Oh no. Meche talks a big game, but I'd hate to be the snake that ventured into Soli's patio or the fox that came after her chickens."

1 8 9 4 ...

Hey were supposed to call her "Tía" Anastasia, but she wasn't their aunt, only their mother's friend, and Ruby did not want to go to her house—it was boring. She had to dress up and be on her best behavior, which was never good enough. Lulu, almost five years older, was excited about the visit. Of course she would be—Tía Anastasia was always making over her, "She's becoming such a young lady!" While the best Ruby got, and from her mother, was, "Well, she is only seven."

When they were ushered into the parlor, Ruby froze, transfixed. On the floor lay something new—a jaguar rug! She gawked at the animal's spots—all different shapes, some like blossoms, some like letter Cs, some circles and squares, some outlined in black, some with black dots in the center, all on a tawny background—nothing like the polkadots painted on her little toy jaguar, the one she'd had since before she could remember. It was like gazing at clouds and seeing hidden shapes there, only these drew her in. It made her a bit dizzy.

Her mother nudged her forward. Her touch broke the spell, and Ruby saw the animal in its entirety. The ugly shape of its splayed body. The terrifying head—the mouth open and snarling, the fangs threatening, the glassy eyes staring at her. Of course she understood the thing was dead, and that was terrible, too. Horror and fascination tumbled together— thoughts that slithered out of reach and feelings she had no names for.

She loved her toy jaguar. In her play it ran through jungles and lounged in trees. It was big and sleek, strong and beautiful. Her jaguar, this jaguar, all jaguars. Ruby started to shake—swallowed whole by a terror apart from words and beyond reason—and then she was wailing.

Her mother dragged her from the room. When Ruby finally quieted and her mother tried to take her back into the parlor, she screamed bloody murder.

The visit was cut short.

On the way home their mother marched ahead—Lulu skipping to keep up, and Ruby lagging farther and farther behind. Finally her mother turned and scolded. Face pinched, she waited, and when Ruby caught up, she grabbed her roughly by the arm. Once home, she turned Ruby over her knee and spanked her with her bedroom slipper. Tía Anastasia had gone to so much trouble to plan a lovely afternoon. Whack. They had all so looked forward to it. Whack. And Ruby had ruined it. Whack. She had embarrassed her mother. Whack. She had embarrassed her sister. Whack. And, most of all, she had embarrassed herself. Whack. She should be ashamed.

"But the jaguar," Ruby sniffled.

"It's a rug, for heaven's sake! A rug!"

Ruby sniffled louder.

"Don't you dare start up again!" her mother warned, and sent her to her room without dinner.

Ruby wanted to run to her father, bury her face in his chest, hear the tick of his pocket watch under her ear and smell the odor of tobacco and starch and cologne. But he was out of town on a surveying job. He was almost always out of town.

That night, once they had their nightgowns on, Lulu tormented Ruby by describing the yummy dinner she'd missed. Ruby stomped her foot and covered her ears, so Lulu took up Ruby's little wooden jaguar and chased her around the bedroom with it until their mother came in to see what the ruckus was.

"Carmen Rubina, be quiet this instant!" her mother snapped. "And María Luisa, you know better than to get your sister wound up at bedtime."

Their mother listened to their prayers, tucked them in, made the sign of the cross on their foreheads, and turned out the lamp.

Ruby's stomach growled, but, exhausted, she began to drift into sleep.

Lulu gave Ruby's braid a yank, and whispered in her ear, "I'm going to ask for a jaguar rug for our bedroom. I'm going to ask Mamá first thing tomorrow."

"No!"

"I am. I'm going to beg and beg until she gives it to me. And since I'm her favorite, she will."

"No!"

"I'm going to put it right there by your side of the bed. So that when you step on it in your bare feet, you'll feel its fur."

"No!" Ruby shouted, and kicked her hard.

Lulu yelped, and then howled, "Mamá!"

1 8 9 3 ...

Sr. *Ernesto Ezequiel Hernández Hernández*
Rancho Baalam Kab
Hopelchén, Campeche

March 17, 1893

My dearest Blanca Estela,

We are in the midst of harvesting the corn, and all the while my thoughts and desires are with you and our future marriage.

Your latest letter, the one dated March 1st, was very businesslike indeed. I understand that you do not trust the confidentiality of the mail between here and the capital, and so I will construe your questions and the plans you wrote of as professions of love, and am content because it means that you have not changed your mind.

How resourceful of you to consult your doctor and secure a book on first aid. The workers here go to a local healer, called a h'men. I believe he uses some herbal remedies, but it's mostly a bunch of mumbo jumbo. You need not worry about your youth or inexperience; your ministrations will be most welcome. The list of medicines, chemicals and supplies your doctor drew up looks excellent. I am including a list of some items that we use in treating the animals. With those additions, we can use your list as a comprehensive inventory for the rancho's medicine cabinet.

Of course I agree to you bringing the girl with you. It is an excellent idea. Bringing someone you can train to suit you will be a great help to you, especially once we start our family. And we'll have lots of children, just as you wish. I anticipate many sons, with a couple daughters thrown in for good measure. But you say this girl, Susana de los Ángeles, is only nine years old. Mightn't you look for someone a bit older who can be of more immediate help and also provide you with some company? I know you make light of my worries on that score, but it concerns me that you will be lonely here, that you will miss the city and be unhappy. For my part, I will be delighted to have you all to myself.

You once mentioned some uneasiness of living so far from the sea. I pray that the immense stretches of land and open horizons here in the interior will take its place in your heart, that you will grow to love Baalam Kab as I do. And if you do miss the sea, we will visit the apiary so that the hum of the hives may caress you like the whispers of the waves, and hopefully thus assuage your longing. The bees are amazing creatures, docile and brave all at once, one of the many wonders here at Baalam Kab of which I am eager for you to know.

In the past you expressed concern that I come to marriage after many years of solitude. Be assured, mi cielo. I enter this marriage without a single doubt or misgiving. I know exactly what I want: you, me and our children thriving here at Baalam Kab. It can be a challenging life out here, but it is an adventure, our adventure. My beautiful Blanca Estela, I cannot express the joy you bring me. You are the love of my life.

Before I retire this evening, I will go out into the patio. The Milky Way fills the night sky here. Wait till you see. It's luminous, overwhelming; it draws the earth in. I've spent hours marveling at it of late, for you haunt me, and thinking of us together, as man and wife, keeps me awake. I have the rings under my eyes to prove it. If only you were here with me now.

You will remember that the name of the rancho means Jaguar Bee, or as we say in Spanish, queen bee. You are my jaguar bee, Blanca Estela, I will care for you and give my life if need be to protect you, my queen, mi alma, mi cielo.

With all my love and devotion,
your Ernesto

Lulu pushed Ruby.

And, Ruby, though only six, kept her feet and pushed back, harder. Lulu fell on her behind and started shrieking.

"Mami! Ruby pushed me!"

Their father strolled into the small interior patio. "Then you'd better get up, hadn't you?"

Lulu shrieked, and her mother rushed in. She swept by her husband and, leaning down, helped the older of her two daughters to her feet. She comforted and cooed and brushed off the back of Lulu's skirt.

Their father caught Ruby's eye, gave a little jerk of his head, and Ruby ran off, a half second before her mother turned to scold her.

"Where did that little Indian go?" she said.

She took out a handkerchief and wiped Lulu's tears.

"She tried to kill me!" Lulu said and started to blubber again.

Her father snorted. "If she'd tried to kill you, she would have succeeded. Your sister's not one to do anything by halves."

The hint of pride in her father's voice stung Lulu.

She supposed that, at least sometimes, she, too, was a bit proud of Ruby. Ruby had their mother's beautiful dark-brown eyes and hair, and she was surprisingly strong for a little kid. But mostly, Lulu was baffled by her sister. For one thing, she always noticed things that Lulu didn't, got all absorbed in them, too. And unlike Lulu, she never got bored. Never!

Her mother, outraged by what her husband had said, spun round to face him and let fly a rapid stream of invective, almost knocking Lulu off her feet. Her father's expression told Lulu that he wasn't even trying to understand. Lulu didn't catch all the words either, but the meaning was clear enough: Lulu may have got his coloring, but Ruby, his barbarian character.

Lulu felt a momentary surge of pride to have caused this argument, but then her stomach churned, as usual, and she threw up. Her mother called for María Asunción to come clean it up, but to first take Lulu to her room to get changed.

"Sí, señora," the maid said, but once she'd pulled Lulu into the corridor, out of sight of the patio, she put a finger to her lips and they both listened, with Lulu able to peek a bit.

"Liebling," her father said in the overly patient voice that so irritated her mother, "you know it's Lulu who always starts these tiffs."

"Tiff? You call this a tiff? Young ladies do not push each other into the dirt."

"What dirt? The tile is spotless. And they're not young ladies, they're little kids." His voice sharpened, "Kids push each other."

"Maybe in Germany, but not in San Francisco de Campeche. Here we are civilized Christians."

He sighed. "If I were you, Petrona, I'd be more concerned that Lulu is such a cry baby."

"A young lady is supposed to be sensitive."

"The child needs to learn to stand on her own without her mama's help. Especially since, I'll lay you odds, she had it coming."

"Lay odds! Where do you think you are? This is a decent home, not some cantina."

"The point is you go running every time she whimpers."

"That's because I'm a good mother."

"And what about Ruby? I don't see you pampering her."

"Ah, I'm too soft on Lulu and too tough on Ruby. I can't do anything right!"

"I did not say that. I just wish you'd be kinder to our Ruby."

"Now I'm unkind. And why aren't you kinder to Lulu?"

"Can't we talk, without you getting your knickers in a knot?"

"Madre María Santísima!"

"Or without you calling on a deity or two?"

"There is only one deity, you heathen, and it is not María, who, as you very well know, is the mother of God."

"That so?"

"I can't believe I must be on guard for the souls of my children, my poor innocent babes, here in my own house with their own father." She crossed herself.

He slapped the paper he was carrying against his leg; she flinched, stifled a cry, and rushed from the room. He ran his hand through his hair and muttered some oaths in German.

María Asunción pulled Lulu into her room.

"See what you have caused?" she said to Lulu.

"Ruby started it!"

María Asunción said nothing.

"She did! Why doesn't anyone ever believe me?"

Lulu's mouth tasted horrible from throwing up. She swished water in it and spit into the bowl on the washstand.

"Someday you will discover what a great gift a sister is."

Lulu squinted at María Asunción. "Some gift!" Her eyes landed on her babydoll lying on the bed. "I'd rather have a new doll," she declared. "A grown-up one with real hair and a frilly, pink dress."

"Ruby," María Asunción called, "you can come out now."

Ruby opened the door of the wardrobe where she'd taken refuge. María Asunción shook her head.

María Asunción spun Lulu around and unbuttoned her dress and pulled it over her head.

"Ooh, stinky," Ruby said, pinching her nose.

María Asunción wadded the dress up and placed it under her arm. "While you're in there, grab Lulu a fresh dress." She turned to go.

"Who's going to do it up in back?" Lulu whined.

"Ask your sister," María Asunción said as she left the room.

Ruby hopped to the bed on one foot, holding a dress out in front of her.

"You shouldn't get sick just because Mami and Papi are fighting," she said.

"Who said they're fighting?" Lulu pouted.

"Well, they are, aren't they?"

"I didn't mean to make them fight," Lulu said, feeling miserable.

"You didn't. You're not that important. They fight all by themselves." Lulu started to protest.

"I'm not that important either," Ruby said.

"I hate it when they fight."

Ruby shrugged.

"Papi likes you better. He thinks I'm a crybaby," Lulu said.

"You are a crybaby. But Mami likes you best. She never wrinkles her nose at you and calls you a little Indian."

"But Papi calls you mein Indianerlin."

"That's different. He says it with his soft voice. And his nose doesn't wrinkle."

"Would you rather have Mami like you than Papi?" Lulu said, shrugging on the clean dress.

"No."

Lulu was much taller than Ruby, so Ruby stood on the bed to button her dress.

"I think some parents like all their children," Ruby said.

"It's our fault they don't," Lulu said.

"Don't be a ninny. It's just the way it is."

"Sorry I pushed you," Lulu said grudgingly.

"Sorry you got sick."

"Though I'd still rather have a lady doll in a pink dress."

"I don't know why. Dolls are boring. I'd rather have you."

Epilogue

...1 9 7 6

Grandma Soli was nestled with her memories in her forest-green Naugahyde recliner. With thick glasses on her nose, she pored over the photo album in her lap with a magnifying glass. She found herself yanked back to the present in all its immediacy when her granddaughter Debra, red-faced and fists clenched, flounced her 13 years into the living room. She did a one-eighty and screamed down the hallway, "I hate you!"

"You can't. You're not allowed," came a voice from the other room. "I'm your sister."

"I don't care. I'll hate you forever!" she shrieked and burst into tears.

The old woman sighed. She put the book and glass on the table next to her and opened her arms. Debra flung herself into the chair. They both fit; the girl was not fully grown yet and Grandma Soli, although once considered tall for her generation, had been shriveling for decades. Debra pushed hard to pop the footrest up (raising the emotional drawbridge) before sobbing on her grandmother's breast.

Soli petted the back of Debra's head, and when the little-sister offender took up a position in the doorway with her feet apart, chest out, ready to continue the fracas, Soli waved her away. When the girl hesitated, Soli gave her a wink, and the girl, with a big roll of her eyes, plodded away down the hall.

Soli's youngest daughter—her pragmatic, ironic, dependable Marilyn, whom she adored—was the mother of these girls. "For my sins," Marilyn would say out of earshot of her children.

Of her many grandchildren, it was this one, Debra, sobbing on her breast, who reminded Soli most of Meche. Debra's eyes were hazel rather than brown, but just as fierce. And the way she would stand was pure Meche: chin out, hands on waist with thumbs forward and fingers down. Also like Meche, when pressed, she would disappear, much to her mother's consternation.

And these bursts of emotion!

All this, viewed from her vantage point now, as an old woman, seemed not only familiar, but natural. She tried to reassure Marilyn of that, but Marilyn, being the mother, fretted all the same. As Soli herself, she remembered with pain, had brooded and worried about Meche at this age. Each outburst, each little escape had scared the living daylights out of her, and rightly so as it turned out. But Marilyn was not Soli. Marilyn would not fail with Meche. She corrected herself: not Meche, Debra.

Her eyes flitted over the black-and-white photographs on the wall. She smoothed Debra's hair behind her ear and compared it to the closeup picture of the woman's ear with the little gold hoop, which she knew was Meche's. Identical. She smiled and felt sad all at once.

What was it that Meche believed, or said she did, something about having several souls? Or was it that we could lose pieces of our soul? Maybe she'd been onto something there, because at this time in Soli's life, her dead were legion, and it felt like each had taken a piece of her with them. But of her many losses, the one that niggled and nagged at her was Meche.

Earlier that day, Soli had pulled the antique pink and grey hatbox from her closet and set it on her bed. She'd taken off her navy-blue tennis shoes and put her feet up, rubbing her nylon-clad feet on the white chenille. She felt both the slipperiness and the resistance between the two materials. The hatbox smelled slightly musty on the outside, but lifting the lid released the medicinal tang of the lavender sachet inside. She'd untied the ribbon around one of the bundles of letters and selected a letter at random.

The handwriting was cramped and she turned on a bedside lamp to see better. The letter was dated 1919, and in it she told her sister about baby Jack, her first-born, some six months old. There was an erasure that went right through the paper.

Her mind was on that letter now as she waited for Debra's sobbing to subside. She could feel the girl's tears where they'd soaked through her blouse.

Soli said, "Mi'jita, know what purgatorio is?"

Soli's accent, which had faded with the years, had recently been reasserting itself. After spending her entire adult life speaking English, it was as if Spanish were an animal coming out of hibernation and reclaiming its territory. The younger granddaughter had trouble understanding her, but Debra didn't seem to.

"Purgatory," Soli corrected herself.

"Oh, yes," Debra said. "Where saved souls go for purification before they can enter heaven. Sister Agnes says they suffer torments, but not the torments of hell."

Soli smiled. Her own religious education was far scantier than her grandchildren's.

"Ah!" Soli said. "Know what I think purgatorio is?"

"What?"

"Living with a sister," she said.

Soli felt the contraction of the girl's smile against her chest.

"And know what hell is, mi'jita?"

"What?"

"Living without her."

The End

Acknowledgements

A great deal of research went into this novel. In particular, I would like to thank Lic. Francisco Javier Rivas Cetina, who generously sent me his thesis, *Relaciones sociales y productivas en las haciendas de Campeche del siglo XIX*. I am also grateful to Enrique Rocher for his insights on the history and archeology of Campeche. Any cultural and historical errors are entirely my own. The only historical discrepancy I knowingly made was to give Campeche City a newspaper in the first decades of the 20th century. The city has a long history of literary magazines, but the only newspaper I found for this period was an official bulletin put out by the government. Also, the malecón as I described it in 1910, probably came into being with improvements and expansions in 1914 and in the 30's. In 1910, it was likely more a place of work and commerce than of recreation.

I've studied with many wonderful teachers over the years. In particular, I would like to thank my extraordinary high school writing and literature teachers in Centralia, WA: Jean Bluhm and Noreen Higgins (d. 2017). I am also especially indebted to my professor of Latin American literature, Nancy Lester of Central Washington University. Although I may fall short, I still strive to meet their high standards.

Thank you to Nancy Zaffaro and Karen Lewis for slogging through the first draft. The shape and depth of subsequent drafts is greatly due to their comments. Thanks to Susannah White, who has been endlessly supportive. And to her, Maggie Brown and Brian Jelgerhuis for being first readers. Thank you, Sandy Carter and Marilyn Katcher, for editing and proofreading. And always and forever, Brian Jelgerhuis for his boundless support and encouragement and for designing the print book and creating the cover.

I had planned from day one to dedicate this book to my sister, Susan. She died unexpectedly in 2020, shortly before I finished writing the almost-final draft of this novel. For the record, she and I did not suffer any of the tensions or issues of the sisters in this book. I am bereft—sad that she will not read this, sad for the loss of everything she will not do, and for the time we will not spend together.

About the Author

Leslie Hayertz was born in Washington State. She earned a BA ed. at Central Washington University, and an MA in Spanish at Middlebury College. She is the author of *Down to the Soul*, a novel; *You Can't Pick Your Ghosts*, short stories for children; and *The Subwhative?: A Step-by-Step Workbook and Guide to the Subjunctive in Spanish.* She teaches Spanish in the Portland Metro Area of Oregon.